The Lost Throne

ISBN: 978-1-61899-067-9 (Paperback)
ISBN: 978-1-61899-068-6 (eBook)

BY

SAMANTHA GILLESPIE

To Haeleigh,

Readers like you are the ink with which writers' pens flow.

1

Meredith

My sword slashes through the wintry air and connects with my target's chest.

"Ow."

With the crook of my elbow, I wipe the gathering dampness off my brow. "Sorry."

Lief seizes the opportunity to smack my shoulder with a blow of his own. The wooden sword thwacks against the dozens of crisscrossing crystal beads wrapped around the sleeve of my dress.

"'Tis death to drop your guard, my lady."

"A sword to the chest is also death."

A flash of dimples and white teeth. "Not if you're wearing armor, it isn't."

"Then I suggest you wear some next time."

We both know that wearing heavy armor while we're still training with wooden swords would be ridiculous. Besides, I can only fasten so much metal plating over a dress. As it is, I find it hard enough to train with this mess of skirts tangling around my legs.

It was Ethan who—at my request—took on the task of improving my nonexistent weaponry skills. But as a prince of a mighty kingdom, spare time is a luxury, one he can't always grant me. Not the type to wait around, I set out to train on my own, drawing from the knowledge he'd shared in his few lessons. It was that or wallow in unbearable memories. I was a pathetic spectacle, but the bashing and whacking allowed me to channel my anger and chip away at the solid rock of pain lodged in my chest. It was on one of those lone training days that Lief, the questionably young member of the guard I had met at the military outpost on my way to Alder City, watched me pummel a hay-stuffed sack and felt obliged to offer his help. I was a bit leery of a fourteen-year-old's tutelage at first, but he soon disavowed me of my prejudice. What he lacks in strength and size he makes up for with keen wits and quick feet.

"Are we done for the day?"

Now that he asks, I'm suddenly aware of how sore my arms are. I consider putting up the swords, but one glance at the sun tells me it's too early. If I go back inside the castle now, I will likely end up at some social gathering. The last time I made that error, I was ushered in to watch a gossipy group of women play cards. They barely even pretended to be interested in the game while blathering on about marriage prospects and some feast. Every now and then, I caught curious glances in my direction, accompanied by whispers. Rumors of my unladylike activities are apparently great conversation starters. Lorette, my new lady-in-waiting, likes to remind me of this—every day, it feels like—as though it will convince me to change my ways and become a proper lady. And whether it's proper or not, I care more about my chances in a fight now than I do my reputation. But even so, people at court in Alder regard me with an air of neutrality, neither unkind nor unfriendly.

"Let's train a while longer," I say.

Obliging as always, Lief drops his casual stance and readies his sword.

I charge, thinking of the one thing that spurs me to train harder. The reason why I get up every morning.

Elijah.

Just the thought of him makes my blood boil.

He found us, that night in the forest. He was there to kill me—to finish what he'd started at the summer ball. Connor and Holt had protected me from him and his men, and he killed them for it.

Ethan wanted revenge as much as I did. He would have led Alder's great army to Theros's doorstep, but lacking his father's consent, he had to resort to his own devices. I wanted nothing more than to hunt down Elijah, to chase him like he pursued me, and make him pay. But this, too, the king denied us—he couldn't justify risking his only heir. So Ethan had to send mercenaries to find him and bring him to us. And all these months, we've been waiting.

Lief's sword thumps against mine in midair. Deadlocked, we fight for dominance.

"You are too easy to find," calls an approaching voice.

Ethan strides briskly from under the archways of the stone walkway that confines the small, deserted courtyard. The prince carries himself like a king, tall and proud, and the black coat that drapes over his shoulders, amply lined with gray fur, accentuates the effect. He seems unhurried and relaxed, but I know better than to think he's come just to visit.

Lief greets Ethan with a respectful bow. I would respond in kind if Ethan hadn't asked me to refrain. He wants us to get to know each other as equals, unburdened by the prejudice of titles and society.

He smiles. "My father is requesting an audience in his private office."

I raise my eyebrows. "With me?"

"With both of us."

I follow Ethan through the drafty corridors, relishing the warmth from the torches and candelabras that light our path. The flames flicker with a subtle breeze that wafts through the narrow window slits, casting dancing shadows on our faces. I steal a fleeting look at Ethan; his golden-brown hair is deceivingly blond in this light.

"Do you know why he sent for us?" I ask. Ethan meets with his father on a daily basis, but this is a first for me.

He gives a slight shake of his head. "I imagine it's something to do with . . ." He pauses.

"Our union?" I venture.

Five months should be sufficient time for two people to get to know each other, but that has not been the case. Just as with training, leisure activities allowing us to spend time alone together have been rare. I see him every day at supper, but those evening hours are shared with the king and queen and the rest of the court, all of them vying to converse with him while I indulge in the comfort of wine. It doesn't help that I try to avoid him whenever the opportunity arises. A side of me dreads getting to know him—dreads opening up and finding there's nothing left for me to give.

We do have one thing in common though: we are both miserable and furious. My first week in the castle, I roamed the grounds like a floundering ghost. Bending a corner, I spied Ethan whacking mindlessly at a log hanging from a rope. It swung and twirled with every hit. His expression was wreathed in a mix of rage and grief that resonated with my own wretchedness. As I watched him, all I could think was how much I wanted to be the one with the sword.

I watched until he tired, dropped his sword, and walked away. When he was gone, I reached for it. The intricate workmanship on its golden pommel and hilt was impressive. It was too bad the blade was ruined, bent and dulled. I traced the slash marks on the wood, which was still swaying slightly, and wanted desperately to add my own. I wanted to inflict pain upon it, hoping that would ease mine. But my feeble, untrained arms struggled with the sword and only managed a few nicks. I eventually gave up and threw the sword, leaving it to the sloppy patterns of frustration on the damp dirt beneath my feet. If I'd had any doubts about training before, they were certainly gone after that.

The Ethan who smiles at me now seems like a completely different person from the broken prince I saw that day. His chestnut, doe-eyed glance lingers on me with a glint of curiosity.

"Does it make you unhappy?" he asks.

"No," I answer truthfully. The thought of marrying him had made me unhappy for so many years. Now it makes no difference to me whether I marry him or not. It's clear the idea makes both of us uncomfortable, and I find that oddly reassuring. Probably guessing my thoughts, Ethan offers an encouraging, lopsided grin.

"Any news of your men?"

His grin fades as he breaks my stare. "No," he says, sighing through his nose.

I swallow my own disappointment.

We walk into the king's private office to the sound of a weighty and . . . familiar voice. The discussion yields abruptly. The king and one other figure huddle around the slab of wood that must have once been a magnificent tree. Now it has been reduced to a hefty table, where a detailed map of the Eastern Continent is on display.

My gaze falls on the guest.

I gawk and go still, my feet grounded to the floor by invisible chains. I hear the voice of the king . . . but he sounds far away. The sight of Connor's aunt yanks at the stitches of my wounds.

But why is she here? Jessamine wouldn't abandon her farm

without good reason.

Her weathered face crinkles with joy when she sees me.

King Perceval addresses Ethan and me. "Mistress Grieves brings news of the Borderlands," he says, and his stare falls on me. "Given your past involvement, I thought you might want to hear it." I blink as an odd feeling expands in my chest. This is the most consideration I've ever received from a king.

Perceval inclines his head to Jessamine. "Please."

Jessamine tells us of a large group who arrived in the Borderlands pulling dozens of loaded carts and wagons. "It seems they . . . delivered them to the Borderlords."

The king's eyes narrow with suspicion. "A shipment? Do you have any knowledge of the contents?"

"We didn't at first. But then they began to build, and we made our own conclusions." As she says this, Jessamine shoots a wary look my way, conveying her concern wordlessly.

If a third party is meddling with the Borderlords, it can only mean bad news. Until recently, the Borderlords had been allowed free reign of the Borderlands, profiting from the fees they collected from the farmers in exchange for protection from thieves and pillagers. But during my brief stay there last summer, we learned the Borderlords had grown greedy, extorting farmers for sums they could not afford to pay without jeopardizing their harvests. When I informed Ethan of the situation, a troop of soldiers was swiftly dispatched to set things back in order. I can only imagine the Borderlords were not pleased.

The king leans forward on the table. "Build, you say?"

"I believe it is some sort of fortress," Jessamine says with a nod.

Perceval taps a finger on the map. "Can you elaborate on the origin of the shipper?"

Jessamine shakes her head absently. "Their garments were plain, common enough for any traveler."

The king shares an ominous look with Ethan before pushing himself away from the table. Carried into his own thoughts, he seems to forget about the rest of us for a moment, leaving us in expectant silence. Could Theros be behind this? It doesn't seem very farfetched, considering he sent Elijah to infiltrate Father's court to kill me and stop the alliance. And though Elijah failed, he succeeded in murdering a part of me.

My eyes stray to Jessamine, who turns at the weight of my stare. She questions me with a small smile, her eyes wondering.

She doesn't know.

I assumed she'd been told months ago, when the king's men were sent to deal with the Borderlords. But here she is, apparently ignorant. That's why she's here, I realize. He didn't return like he said he would.

Ethan clears his throat, prompting Perceval to find his voice again.

"I thank you for the information, Mistress Grieves. We'll send another troop to look into it immediately."

With a nod of dismissal, Jessamine steps over to me. Her

hands are quick to clasp mine as she looks at me in earnest.

I manage a weak smile. The fated question, however, does not come from her.

"Where's Connor?"

The demanding voice comes from a shadowed corner. I spot the redheaded girl, her arms crossed, leaning against a wall of bookshelves.

Krea.

Unlike Jessamine, her manner is direct and businesslike; she's withholding her more amiable side for the one person she is here to see. Before, the affections of Connor's childhood friend would have sparked feelings of jealousy, but all I sense within me now is pity.

"H—he . . . ," I begin, but the knot in my throat chokes me. I look up helplessly at Jessamine, whose eager smile is beginning to fade.

"I believe there is no gentle way to put this." Ethan speaks for me, sensing my struggle. He pauses, looking ill at ease. "Connor is no longer with us," he finally says.

Jessamine releases her hold on my hands, the trace of her warmth in my palms growing cold within seconds.

The king, from across the table, adds, "Connor gave his life honorably to ensure the safe arrival of Princess Meredith."

Jessamine is so still I start to wonder if she even heard anything.

"I'm so sorry," I blurt out.

In a flash, Krea barrels down on me. Her knuckles flash before my eyes as they connect with my jaw. I feel my head jerk sideways with the force of the blow, my teeth clamping hard against my tongue. The warm, metallic taste of blood fills my mouth.

Ethan rushes to my side, gripping my shoulders to steady me.

"Madam, contain yourself," he shouts at Krea.

I clutch a hand to my throbbing jaw. "It's all right, Ethan."

The king's voice rings low. "Your ways may not be as ours, but take heed, girl, for I will not tolerate violence in my court."

Krea ignores them both. She glowers at me.

Knuckles white at her sides, Jessamine asks, "Why was I not informed?"

Perceval bows his head regretfully. "For that, I owe you an apology, madam. I was under the impression my commander had delivered the news."

Ethan tries to comfort her. "If you need a moment—"

"No." She draws a sharp breath and straightens, eying Ethan with the same determination I saw in her the night she refused to give up on her farm after the Borderlords burned her harvest to the ground.

"Take me to his grave."

Ethan does a good job of hiding his anger, but the twitch in his jaw gives him away. "It's empty . . . the one who killed him burned his body, along with the bodies of others. We had no way of identifying his remains."

Jessamine squeezes her eyes shut. When she opens them again, they are glassy and cold. "We must go now." She motions at Krea with a look over her shoulder.

"Then we bid you a safe journey, madam. My condolences. Connor was a beloved member of my court, and we mourn his absence."

Jessamine nods at the king. I watch her, feeling the pain hidden beneath her composed face.

She pulls me into a tight embrace, her arms strong and firm around me. My closely guarded heart thumps against the fragile barricade I fought so hard to build, and it takes everything in me to keep myself together.

"He did what he had to do," she whispers in my ear. Her words are candid, and yet they only bring me pain. I know it isn't my fault, but I am still responsible, however indirectly. The gleam of accusation in Krea's eyes affirms it.

"Maker's blessing," Jessamine says when she pulls away.

I gather my breath before I dare speak.

"Maker's blessing . . . Jessamine, I . . ." I'm not sure if I mean to console her or myself, but the words become a tangled mess in my throat. In the end, I speak the only phrase my tongue is willing to enunciate. "Be careful."

I watch them go, my chest tingling with dread. Something is brewing in the Borderlands. If Connor were here, he would fear for his aunt's safety . . . and I can't help but feel the same way.

2

Connor

I am a young boy—five, maybe older. I dash through the corridors of a warm house. My house. A golden-furred puppy bounces in my arms. He's heavy. I can scarcely hold him.

"Mother!"

"In here, darling," says a muffled voice from the parlor.

I sprint into the room. The window behind Mother casts a brilliant light on the flowing, butterscotch hair that drapes down her back.

"What did I say about running—"

Her blue-eyed gaze drifts to the small animal in my arms.

"Please let me keep him," I say.

She sets down her knitting on the settee and kneels beside me, the azure skirts folding around her as she does. She reaches for the dog, inspecting it. The puppy licks her chin, and she laughs, pulling away from its tongue. "Where did you find this poor little creature?"

"Sir Rodrik said I could have him."

Mother's brow furrows. "That's very kind of him."

"He'll take offense if I give him back."

I know what you're doing, her eyes say, with a considering smile on her lips. She cups my cheek with her hand. "You are too clever for your own good. Just like your father."

I want to smile, but I wait for her answer.

Mother sets the dog down on the slate floor. His tail wags mindlessly as he sniffs his way around the room.

"Well . . . what shall we call him?" Mother asks.

"Connor?"

I blink.

A plump orange waits to be plucked from its branch. I glance down the ladder at Raven. She squints up at me, one hand at her temple, blocking the glare, a bucketful of oranges dangling from the other. She's unusually tall for a girl, but you wouldn't know it from up here.

"The sun is angry today," she says, reminding me of the humid, blistering heat. "We should rest a bit."

I swipe my rolled sleeve across my forehead and pluck the bright orange before me, dumping it in the bucket hanging from a crook on the ladder. It's full enough to make a trip back.

Sun's always angry, I think as I climb down.

After weeks of orange picking, my body is familiar with the task. I've embraced the routine of early mornings and long days. Only the heat wears on me. Most nights, I nod off to sleep the second I slump in bed. Then I wake up and do it all over again. But the harvest will end soon, and with it, so will my diversion.

Caked with dirt and sweat, I walk with Raven through the rows of trees laden with oranges. The heat of the sun radiates from the dry soil. Raven and her father live outside the village of Fhalbo, sharing the valley with a handful of neighbors settled in shacks fenced by backwoods and split ranges of forested dome mountains.

"You were distracted up there." Raven gestures behind us with a tilt of her head. "Other memories come back?"

I nod, blue eyes flashing in my thoughts. It's not the first time I see my mother. Reliving memories of someone I don't recognize . . . it makes me restless.

"Nothing useful," I say. Glimpses of childhood memories aren't much to go on. My soft accent and fair skin make me an outlander. A *Northerner*, they say. They also say the North is a broad expanse of land.

"And the girl? Have you seen her again?" Raven asks.

There's that.

I wouldn't call those images memories. They feel more like dreams than anything else.

I shake my head. It's a relief not to see her. It unsettles me more than I care to admit. She calls to me, asks for my help. And Maker's hell! I want to help her; I just don't know how. I've memorized everything about her: the golden hair, the button nose, the bare tenderness in her amber eyes, and the hopeful curve of her small lips.

I *know* her.

But her name slips my tongue.

Raven's bright-green eyes glint, conspicuous against her olive complexion. “Be patient. The mind needs time t’ mend wounds. It will come back t’ you, I’m sure o’ it.”

She has the tongue of a healer, offering encouragement and advice on a daily basis. I listened to that voice through a month of bed rest. There was little else to do with a set of fractured ribs. I had one leg in the grave when her father found me, tossed unconscious on the side of a road. He had been drawn to me by the vultures circling above. Other people must have passed me by, but Asher hauled my battered body onto his cart and brought me to his cottage.

Being bedridden for so long left me restless. It shed light on my dark state of mind, which I found exhausting most days; my barren thoughts had nowhere to go.

Raven’s full skirt brushes the tufts of grass on the trampled path, marked by our daily to and fro. Sunlight glistens on her cheeks, and she keeps her ink-black hair in twisted braids atop her head, allowing the nape of her neck to breathe. The orange grove is her pride and joy. You wouldn’t think she’d be fit for hard labor with such a spindly frame, but this has been her routine for years, and she goes it alone, harvesting the fruit that Asher takes to the market each dawn. She was eager to teach me the ropes, and I was grateful for the diversion.

As we near the house, my attention drifts to the road. Three men on horseback, covered in military leathers and red capes; the latter wave in the wind like a warning. The men flank a wagon steered by a pair clad in green tunics. The wagon’s contents, I can't discern. Two bodies drag from the back of the wagon, their ankles tied together with rope.

I take a step in the men's direction, but a hand clasps my elbow.

"Don't," Raven warns in a low voice, her hardened stare fixed on the wagon.

"Who are they?"

"Collectors. They come every month. Those two they've got there"—she points with a jut of her chin—"they were short on payment."

My eyes shift back to the dragging bodies. On closer inspection, I register wormlike jerks.

They're alive.

A muscle in my jaw flexes. I consider untying those ropes and setting the pair free. But I am ill equipped to tangle with armed soldiers; the wooden bucket in my hand won't do much damage.

"Your king stands for this cruelty?"

Eyes flat, her voice curdles as she says, "My king is dead. The Usurper rules now. He's the one who ordered the collections."

"The Usurper?"

Raven's mouth curls, her attention still on the wagon. "It's what we all call him behind closed doors. Before he claimed the South, he was the king o' Talos. Word in the market is he calls himself emperor now."

The bodies move with the bumps of the road now.

3

Meredith

The king dismisses me after Jessamine's departure, eager to discuss matters with Ethan and the council. Under different circumstances, this might have disappointed me. But today is different, and I'm no less eager to leave. My feet make haste to my room and its promise of solitude. I cage myself away from prying eyes, propping my back against the sturdy door, letting the weight of my body press it closed, and slide down to the cold, tiled stone floor, feeling the snap of the string that holds me together. I squeeze my eyelids shut, but the tears come anyway, blurring my sight and spilling down my cheeks.

I had things under control.

Seeing Jessamine reopened the wound, bringing back all the buried memories. A renewed vow for vengeance comes with them, rushing at me like a tidal wave.

I don't know how long I sit there.

Eventually, I tire of feeling sorry for myself and drag my body off the floor, drifting to the wine bottle on the desk to pour myself a cup. I take a big gulp, swish the cup a few times, then tip my head back and empty it. I fill the cup once more and bring it back to my thirsty lips. As I savor the velvety, earthy flavor of the wine, my eyes wander to the oak chest pressed to the corner beside the desk. I stare at it, feeling my muscles go still. It sits under a fine layer of dust, purposely forgotten. Like everything else, I had locked it away, thinking I would never open it again.

Just this once . . .

I drain the half-filled cup in my hand and set it down. The drawer's knob is cold within my palm as I pull it open. A single metal key rests in the otherwise empty box, waiting to be used. I stare at it for a long, dreadful moment, debating. I pick it up. I turn it in the chest's lock, feeling its click as though it came from within my ribcage. Gritty specks of dust cling to my fingers as I open it. I peer with bated breath at its contents. The sight of his things gives rise to a strange mix of heartache and solace. With slightly trembling hands, I reach for the folded jerkin, and as I clutch it between my hands, pressing it to my chest, panic swells in me at the absence of his scent. I hold the cold leather fabric to my nose. Nothing. Not a lingering trace.

A sob dislodges from my throat.

It feels as though I've lost a piece of him. I don't have much left to hold on to in the first place. I fold the jerkin back into the chest and pick up the bow. I let my fingers slide over the smoothly crafted wood, and my thoughts fetch the memory of his calloused hands on mine, guiding my grip, his breath at my neck. I want to turn around see him there, to bask in him and remember every line of his face. How long will it be until I can no longer remember what he looks like?

The echo of his woodsmoke voice springs from my thoughts: *Do you trust me?*

I was quick to say yes then, blinded by my feelings, which I had yet to understand. But it hadn't been just that. He *had* earned my trust. Completely and wholeheartedly. Could I really have been so wrong about him? Was there not a smidgen of truth in what he claimed to feel for me? I tell myself to forget about it, that it doesn't matter anymore if it was real or not, but it's no use.

A knock at the door brings me back to the present. I startle at the sound of it, fumbling with the bow, my hands suddenly slippery. By the second knock, I've managed to lock the chest and return to my empty cup. After the third knock, I clear my throat and call out. The door opens with a questioning squeak, and Lorette's delicate face edges into view. Her eyes trail to the cup in my hand, and the lines of disapproval crease her forehead. "My lady," she greets me with the usual curtsy. "You're in sober spirits, I hope?"

"That depends on what you wish me sober for," I halfheartedly jest.

Knowing Lorette, I can only guess she is here to lure me to away from my solitude.

Her sharp gray eyes widen a fraction, and she lets out an uncomfortable cough. "Her Majesty requests your presence in her chambers."

"Sober it is."

The queen is busy with two of her ladies when Lorette and I step into the sitting room. When I enter, a large gilded mirror on the wall at my right vies for my attention. It reflects the vast room, crowded with tables and chairs, richly upholstered sofas and embroidered throw pillows. There is nothing plain or bare in sight. The tea tables around the queen are neatly cluttered with an assortment of trinkets, scented candles, decanters, and bowls of fruit. The leaded glass windows on the wall behind her are diamond shaped. I trace a familiar honeyed fragrance to a pair of vases filled with the butter-yellow petals of winter sweet flowers, the same shrub that perfumes the castle's courtyard and garden, the wonderful scent so pungent even a stuffed nose will pick up on it.

Queen Edith's wine-red gown twirls elegantly as she pivots in our direction. She offers a warm smile. As usual, the queen keeps her gray-streaked fawn-colored hair parted at the middle and tied back in an impeccable braided bun. But as delicate as her softly aged features are, the fine lines of her face emphasize a fierceness that inspires and intimidates all at once.

Lorette and I acknowledge her with a unified, "Your Majesty."

The queen's brows rise a little when she takes a good look at me.

"Good heavens, that cheek looks dreadful."

Instinctively, I cup a hand to the numb side of my face. Edith doesn't ask the question, but her eyes do.

"There was an incident with a girl that arrived from the Borderlands this morning," I say.

Edith makes a sound in her throat. "Yes, the king mentioned their arrival." She waltzes to the middle of her sitting room, where sofas surround a round walnut table of finely carved legs that end with caryatids, and motions for Lorette and I to join her. But Lorette remains standing, head bowed, hands primly clasped in front of her. Does she miss waiting on the queen? I wonder. After attending someone like her, assisting me must feel like a demotion. "And this girl, she did that to you?" Edith asks as she takes a seat, a frown wrinkling her porcelain features.

Though the queen doesn't know Krea, it feels wrong to let her think ill of her simply for my sake. "She was a close friend of Connor's," I explain, resting stiffly on the sofa across from her; it's less comfortable than it looks. "She blames me for his death."

The queen's ladies flock to bring us tea, setting a polished silver tray on the table between us.

"We all mourn Connor's death, of course, but that does not give any of us the right to commit transgressions against others. Ladies especially should take great care not to act on impulse."

Act on impulse. That's exactly what I would do if I saw Elijah. The scenario has played in my head over and over.

"Life is different in the Borderlands," I say in Krea's defense, remembering Connor's words. "Their ways are not ours."

"Indeed. The king would rather not have to deal with them at all, but the wheat imports from the Borderlands are a lifeline we cannot do without. Their granaries easily feed a third of our kingdom."

"A third?" I ask in awe. Stonefall relies on Borderland wheat even more than that, but I'd figured a kingdom as large as Alder would be less dependent.

Edith nods. "Alder's northern lands are covered in snow year-round, which makes them unsuitable for crops, if not uninhabitable. You may not be aware of it yet, but you'll soon learn our summers are shorter here than they are in Stonefall, limiting the harvests. And no ship can sail the Frozen Sea, so we have no ports to open trade with." The queen leans forward. "How does Stonefall's trade fare these days?"

I've watched the queen at supper every night, listened to her conversations. A nimble counterpart to her husband and son, she carries herself with finesse, and her words are always polite, but her exchanges with courtiers address politics and matters of economy, things I never dreamed a queen would know. Things that—thanks to my father—I'm distressingly ignorant of. And this is no different. I'm awed at her seemingly bottomless sea of knowledge, and embarrassed at the shallow puddle that is mine. I briefly wonder how she came to be queen. Did King Perceval choose her because of her intellect or her beauty? Perhaps it was the combination of the two that did him in. I don't claim to possess much of either. But uninformed as I am, I've always craved knowledge in its written form. It occurs to me then that I haven't so much as set foot in the castle's library. Like the grove and the music room, the library back home had been one of my favorite areas of the palace. I would get lost in books, in that sense of escapism only they can provide.

"Forgive me, Your Majesty, but I'm poorly versed in matters of trade," I sheepishly admit. I can't imagine she called me here to speak of crops and trade relations, nor for a frivolous chat over tea. Perhaps she means to express her disapproval of my extracurricular activities. Father would have a stroke if he knew I spend my mornings learning how to wield a sword. But Queen Edith isn't my father, and I don't dare presume her thoughts. My eyes stray to Lorette, who stands at my side like a demure shadow. Her hushed demeanor gives nothing away. "I hope that's not the reason you've called me here . . ."

The queen dismisses my notion with a wave of her hand. "No, no. Nothing of the sort." She pauses, assessing me. "Though I appreciate your frankness. Most subjects never dare admit their shortcomings to their queen."

I try not to wince at her words. "My father believes ladies need only be schooled in the arts."

"Noble ladies, yes. But a crown princess should understand the inner workings of her kingdom if she is to be queen." Another frown curls Edith's mouth. "It troubles me your father did not raise you as such."

My eyes fall to my lap, where I rest my clammy palms.

When I give no response, the queen's voice grows quiet, her tone gentler. "I wished to speak with you about your birthday. My son tells me it's only days away?"

My birthday. It's next week. Celebrating has been the last thing on my mind.

Ethan remembered.

He'd asked me once, during a brief and awkward conversation about the marriage contract, which states I must marry once I turn eighteen.

The queen's eyes continue to study me as she takes a prim sip of her tea.

I squirm in my seat. "Yes, Your Majesty."

Edith sets down her tea cup next to a bowl that's overflowing with green grapes and gently clasps her hands together. "Then I will make arrangements to honor your birthday at the feast. We have yet to formally introduce you to the court, so it shall be a fitting announcement."

"The feast?" I ask, dreading the sound of it.

"Yes," she answers. "Wintertide. I assume you were informed?"

Lorette shifts on her feet, scowling at me out the corner of her eye. Had she mentioned the feast before? I don't mean to tune out her prattling, but it takes much effort on my part not to ignore her constant gossiping.

"Lorette did speak with me about it," I say quickly, unsure if I'm lying or not. "But I forgot all about it. I've had a lot on my mind as of late."

The queen lifts her chin. "I imagine you have. This must be a whole new world for you. But it's a good thing you've come to us now, well enough before the wedding, and acquainted yourself with my son. I trust you two are getting along?" Though her tone is agreeable, there is a defensive glint in her eyes. If I were to guess, I would say the queen cares for Ethan above all others. No matter what her mood may be, it always warms in his presence. In a way, it makes me envious of Ethan, receptive to that particular void in my life.

"Ethan has been most gracious, Your Majesty."

"He also tells me you like to spend your time training with swords."

Lorette lets out a cough. I steal a glance in her direction and notice her cheeks look as red as mine feel.

"I—yes, I do . . . Your Majesty," I stammer.

"A brazen choice of entertainment for a lady." Her dark-brown eyes absorb me in the bat of an eyelash. "Your skin is unbecomingly dark for it, all that time under the sun."

Detached as I am from courtly life, I am not ignorant of its standards. A pale complexion is the comely ideal for ladies. Just as fine fabrics and luxurious possessions do, it displays a high status in society, as the wealthy do not toil under the sun in manual labor. My toes curl within my boots as I grope for words, unsure of how to respond, hating the shame that heats my cheeks. Is it so wrong for a girl to want to be able to protect herself?

The sofa suddenly feels very much like a cage, and my eyes dart to the closed doors. The queen goes on. "Were another girl in your shoes, she'd be shunned and excommunicated from court. But fortunately for you, you're a princess." A pause. "And our future queen. So if my son has no qualms, I don't foresee any real harm to come of this"—she glances at my bruised cheek—"aside from bodily injuries and gossip. Although I would encourage you strive to keep those to a minimum. A favorable public opinion is paramount for a prosperous rule."

I let out a soft breath. Though I wasn't after the queen's approval, it's a relief to have it just the same.

Lorette remains stiff as board, but I can tell she, too, is relieved. Perhaps she'll be less opposed to my training from now on. Not that it makes any difference, but it would be nice to have her support.

"Thank you, Your Majesty."

"The king and I will set a date for the wedding soon." The queen reaches for her tea, her fingers practiced on the silver cup's stem, and I remember I haven't touched mine. Filled to the brim, the herb-infused water nearly spills as I bring the cup to my lips, tasting a well-balanced mix of lavender, chamomile, and cinnamon. "Will your family be joining us?" Edith asks when I set the cup down.

I blink at her, pretending as though her question doesn't sting. Of the three people I would invite to my wedding, only one of them is family. But I doubt my horrid aunt would let Charles come all this way without an invitation for the rest of her family.

I sigh inwardly. "I don't believe so, Your Majesty."

"It is an odiously long journey," the queen notes, assuming logistics are the hindrance.

"The queen has traveled to Stonefall?" I ask, curious.

She gives me a small smile. "Many moons ago, when you were but a bump in your mother's womb."

My voice is just above a whisper. "You . . . met my mother?"

Edith nods. "She was a kind woman. Quite beautiful, too." She considers me a moment. The hard lines on her face soften and her expression grows thoughtful. "A pity you never knew her. Most girls who lack a mother's love and tutelage in their infancy grow up to lack character, but you seem to have grown strong in spite of it. "

"I owe it to my chambermaid," I say, thinking of Anabella. She raised me like a daughter, loved me as though I was her own flesh and blood . . .

I miss her so much.

The queen presses a hand to her chest. "Your chambermaid?" she asks, as though she heard wrong.

But a guard opens the doors before I can say another word.

"Your Majesty, forgive the intrusion. I have orders from the king to escort the princess to his council meeting."

I stare at the guard. Me? Summoned to a council meeting?

Ethan and his father were readying to discuss Jessamine's news with the council when I left the king's study, and now they wish to include me in that very meeting? Could it be I might know something they do not? Or perhaps the king would like to hear my opinion? It's as far-fetched a notion as there ever was one.

The queen's voice draws my attention from the guard. "Very well," she says placidly, oblivious to the drumming of excitement in my chest, "I've kept you long enough."

4

Connor

I welcome the quiet of the late afternoon, basking in the clammy breeze that cools my skin, watching the blurred silhouette of the collector party recede in the distance. I stood at Raven's side the entire time, as a crinkled-skin man stepped down from the wagon to count Raven's silver. I couldn't see the couple tied at the back, but I could hear their groans of pain.

"Will they kill them?" I asked Raven when I was sure our conversation was no longer audible.

"They'll drag them back t' the village. If they're still alive then, they're free t' go." I watched her closely as she said this, peering through the layers of cold detachment masking her lithe features. She hides her misery well.

Footsteps patter behind me. I glance over my shoulder at Asher. The one-eyed man settles on the ground next to me, which kicks up a cloud of dirt. "Mutton and cabbage tonight," he mutters. I nod, placing the familiar salty scent that wafts in the air behind us. Asher hikes one of his gray brows. "What a long day, aye?"

"Has anyone risen against this Usurper?" I ask, still fixated on what Raven said earlier. The closed look in Asher's eyes is unreadable, which is strange, given his approachable nature.

"No one has, lad. Theros reaped the southern kingdoms unopposed." His expression sharpens. "I hear part of the North is his now, too."

"Is he that powerful?"

"Aye. Sunder never stood a chance. The Usurper has amassed quite an army." He looks south, toward the market. "The redcloaks you see here are only a fraction of their force, like roaches crawling out of the wall. And their numbers keep growing. Without battles, there are no losses to be suffered; Theros grows his power with all the resources he plunders."

"These kings he overthrows simply give him what he wants?" I ask.

"It's not as simple as that. Theros invades from the inside. He's like a parasite." Asher's gravelly voice drips with repulsion. "Members of Sunder's court were his spies for years, setting his plans in motion, preparing for the Takeover. They turned the lords against King Seram, which wasn't hard to do. He was a young king, crowned after his father's untimely death, and he wasn't prepared for the role." The scowl on Asher's face sobers to a frown, contemplative. "There was a dreadful drought not long after he became king, and the people blamed him for it, thought it was a sign from the Gods that he ought to be removed from the throne." He chuckles to himself joylessly. "Theros exploited our weaknesses, and we played right into his game." As I take all this in, he looks up from his mud-crusted fingers. "His name mean anything to you?"

I shake my head. "Should it?"

"Lest you hail from a different world, I reckon it should."

"I hardly remember my own name," I remind him.

Asher's eyes crinkle at the edges. "Ah, don't worry yourself, lad," he says. "Perhaps deep down you don't want to remember . . . some memories are best left forgotten."

Says the man with his thoughts intact. "Our memories make us who we are."

Undeterred, he claps my shoulder and smiles. "So make new ones." A shrug. "Live for your future, lad, not your past." His hand still on my shoulder, he nudges encouragement. "Take it from someone who's a stranger in his old memories."

I study his blood-flecked brown eye, dulled with age, and wonder how long it's been since he last saw through both eyes. "What happened to you?" I ask.

Asher chuckles under his breath. "Was wondering when you'd ask . . . I was a thief for most of my life. A good one too. But we all get caught eventually, one way or another." His finger traces lazy circles on the dirt. "The lord I stole from thought branding one eye would help me see the error of my ways." His head shakes in amusement at the irony.

"And did it?"

He lowers his chin, ashamed perhaps, and sighs. "Aye, I wish I had. The bounty was too fat, and I was too greedy. It took something far worse to change my course." Asher looks away. I wait for him to say more, but he doesn't.

"Your accent isn't the same as Raven's," I say after a bit of silence. "Why is that?"

Asher blinks at me. Normalcy returns to his timeworn face, erasing the shadows that plagued him moments ago as though they were never there. "You're quite the observer, aren't you?" He squints up at the sun's fading brightness. "I was born in the northern lands. Grew up there. But after I lost my eye, I never stayed too long in one place. I became what you'd call a wanderer, plundering where I went. Raven was a wee orphan when I found her selling wildflowers in the market." A wistful smile glances over his mouth. "I took her under my care, and she changed me for the better. For the first time in all of my life, I made an honorable living."

It never occurred to me that Raven isn't his daughter. Then again, she looks nothing like him. "Why haven't you left?" I ask.

He looks out at the rows of orange trees ahead. "I considered it. I came to the conclusion that it doesn't matter where I live, as long as Raven is at my side. She's my home. But the grove, it's Raven's home. She helped me plant it, and she grew up with those trees. It would kill her to leave it behind. As long as the fruit continues to sell, well, here we are." His one eye meets my gaze. "And now we have you. You might not believe it, but the Gods placed you in our path when they did so that you could have a future." Asher shakes his head as if remembering. "Gods, you were a gruesome sight when I found ya. Clearly not the winner of that fight, eh? But it *was* a fight, lad. You had the bruised knuckles to show for it . . . I've been wondering if that's what you need to help you shake a few memories loose?"

I give him a look. "A fight?"

"No, no," he says, flashing a set of dull, imperfect teeth. "Come with me, lad."

I follow him into the cottage, past the steaming kitchen where Raven is too busy cooking to notice us, and into his bedroom at the end of the homely corridor. He peels back the worn rug by his straw bed to uncover a trapdoor. His fingers fumble with the latch, seeming to struggle, but he tugs it free a second later, revealing a hole. Then he dips his arms in, procuring a muslin sack. Once the sack lies flat on the wooden boards, some of the objects spew out, glinting with the light flooding through the window.

Weapons.

"Well, have at it, lad. Pick your poison." I kneel on one knee, my hands rifling through the small cluster of weapons: A couple of swords, several daggers, and a spear. My hands trace the sharpness of one of the blades. Sounding pleased, Asher mutters, "I had a feeling you'd approve."

"Why hide these?" I ask, eyes glued to the steel.

"The Usurper prohibits their purchase. Only his soldiers have the right to weapons."

"A defenseless people," I whisper.

"Or so he thinks," Asher says with a sly smile and a wink. "Oh. Here." He reaches once more into the hole, and what he pulls out steals my full attention. I stare at the bow and quiver, riveted despite the crude design and the poor choice of wood. Asher lets out a low whistle. "Now there's a reaction. 'Tis a shame I don't have any arrows."

Instinct answers for me. "I can make them." In my mind, I'm already scraping and sanding wood, chipping stone, burning charcoal and resin . . . How is it that I know by heart a craft I have no memory of?

Asher's brow rises. "So what does that make you, lad? A fletcher? No, you don't have the look of a merchant." He considers a moment, trained on the shoddy bow in my hands. "Something tells me you're a marksman."

I spend the rest of the afternoon collecting saplings, resin, and bird feathers, and chopping small olive trees from the backwoods. By the time I return to the cottage, it's well past evenfall. I pile the chopped wood into a pyre outside, cover it in dry leaves, and plaster a mud mound over it, leaving a hole at the top to light and smoke it, and several more at the mound's base to let air in. Before long, bright angry flames gush from the opening at the top.

"What is that for?" Raven asks when she comes out to offer me a cup of hot tea. The smoke is so overpowering that I can only smell the mint and nutty herbs when I lift the cup to my lips.

"Charcoal," I tell her.

She yawns and bids me goodnight not long after that.

When the fire is visible through the mound's bottom holes, I grab more mud and cover them, plugging the smoke hole at the top as well, sealing it closed. Then, while the charred pyre cools, I start another fire and use the heat of the flames to make the sapling pliable. My mud-dried hands mold the shaft, straightening the waves.

Accuracy is a function of straightness. The phrase is like a tattoo, imprinted in my thoughts. But where did it come from?

Using the sharp end of a rock, I scrape the shaft a little and sand it smooth over stone until I'm happy with the feel of it. Asher watches from the porch, slurping his tea every few seconds. I think it's his third cup. Mine sits mostly full, probably cold by now. I'd drink it, but I don't want to stop; I'm itching to finish.

One hour and four finished shafts later, I remove the mud from the pyre. The branches have charred perfectly.

"Raven could use some of those coals," Asher says as he comes close to inspect. "Gods know we could do without all that smoke in the kitchen."

"I only need a little. Raven can keep the rest."

I mix the charcoal with resin and melt it over a fire until it becomes an adhesive goo to bind the arrowheads into the notches. Then, once the adhesive dries, I wrap bark fibers to further secure the arrowhead and seal it with another douse round of charcoal goo. I test the arrowhead with my thumb and index finger, making sure it doesn't budge, and, at last, I glue on a pair of black feathers to make the fletching.

All this work for one arrow. It's exhausting, and yet, time couldn't move faster.

"Aren't ya the handy little lad?" Asher laughs. "I should've shown you that bow weeks ago."

For the next two hours, my charcoal-dusted fingers work tirelessly to finish, melting adhesive, securing the arrowheads with bark, and burning feathers into shape.

By the time I'm done, my eyes burn from smoke and fatigue, and Asher has long since gone to bed. I let out a breath and look at my work. Four arrows. It isn't much. I'd love a quiver's worth, but four will have to do, else I'll be making arrows through dawn. My knapping isn't my best—the arrowheads could be sharper—but the shafts, at least, are straight. Tired as I am, I would love to test them now, but without good light I'll make a lousy shooter.

I swallow my eagerness and put out the fire.

Sixteen hours later, I'm trudging out of the grove with the day's harvest. At the cottage, I set aside one of the taller baskets, removing two bushels of oranges to make room for the bow and arrows.

With the heavy basket in my hands, I leave the cottage, waving to Raven's emerging silhouette from the grove, and cross through the open, sunny field, past the neighbor's small cabbage farm, toward the backwoods. I return to the area where I chopped wood, pushing through the branches and into the clearing. In doing so, I manage to scare off a black bird that squawks and disappears into the brush, where other birds chirp and coo.

I'd felt strangely at home when I was here last night, as I do now.

I fetch an armful of oranges, one for each arrow, and balance them atop the sturdier-looking branches on some spindly trees nearby. Then I walk back and observe my targets. At a distance, their vivid color makes them easy to spot. A kind of second nature guides my hands around the bow, and I'm comforted by the feel of the arrow's shaft as I grip it between my sunbaked fingers.

Steady and swift, I draw the bow with practiced control, testing the tension of the string at full draw on my fingers. The string presses lightly into my chin as I aim at an orange nestled thirty paces away. I release the arrow. The feel of the release is intrinsic to my muscles. I watch the arrow bore into its target in a split second, casting the skewered fruit out of sight and into the small bushes below.

Snap.

I swivel to my left at the sound, my free hand fetching for another arrow. Leaves rustle. I aim. "Come out."

Twigs and branches rattle, and a scraggly haired boy pokes out from the bush.

I relax my grip, cautiously lowering the bow. He's young. Not very tall. Seven? Maybe eight. The angles of his face are sharp with malnutrition.

A hesitant smile. "You're good," the boy mutters.

My gaze sweeps the woods again. "Are you alone?"

He nods.

"How long were you hiding in there?"

"Not long." His throat bobs. "I saw ya coming, and my mama says I should always hide from strangers."

"She's right," I tell him.

The boy stumbles out of the bush, clutching a dry twig. A frayed, flat-looking satchel hangs across his chest. "I'm Pip."

I say nothing, and Pip steps closer, looking up at me inquisitively. There are holes in his shirt, the seams of his sleeveless tunic frayed at the shoulders. "What's your name?" his mousy voice asks.

"Connor."

The boy flashes a toothy grin. "Now you're not a stranger."

I throw a glance around the backwoods. "What are you doing out here?"

"I came t' play, same as you . . ." He waves the twig like a sword. "I've never seen you here before. Do you live 'round here?"

I drop to a knee and level with him. "Where are your parents?"

"It's just me and my mama. She lets me come here t' play once we're home from the market, says it's safe from the redcloaks." The boy's eyes trail to my bow. "Did you steal that from 'em?"

"No."

"Oh." Is that disappointment I hear in his voice?

Pip's curious gaze falls on the basket. He bites his lower lip, staring at the oranges with hungry eyes.

I take one and offer it to him. He snatches the orange from my open palm. It can't be often that food is given freely to him. I watch him rip the skin of the fruit with ravenous fingers and bite into the flesh, juice dripping down his dirty chin. A few bites in, he stops, dropping the half-eaten fruit in his worn satchel.

"Aren't you hungry?" I ask, knowing he is.

"I want t' share with my mama; it'll make her smile."

And here I'd designated the oranges for target practice. Giving them away shouldn't be an issue, except the fruit is a direct link to Asher and Raven's grove. If the kid mentions to the wrong person that a stranger with a bow gave them to him . . .

Against my better judgment, I fetch the three oranges I didn't get to shoot and pick another two from the basket.

"You can have these," I say, and set them on the thin bed of dried leaves between us.

Pip's black eyes widen as a grin fills his gaunt face. He dives to his knees to collect the oranges. I walk back the way I came as he folds them into his tunic, hoping this small act of kindness won't come back to bite me.

5

Meredith

A roomful of bearded men stare me down. I recognize most of the council: a retinue of twelve elders who advise the king. I see those faces in passing on a daily basis, always flocking around the monarch like shadows. They look uniformly surprised at my entrance, and it quickly dawns on me that my attendance was not openly discussed among them.

The council's master, Grand Councilor Rowan, appears to be the most displeased.

Soft light percolates from a set of honeycombed windows that overlook a courtyard one level below, lighting the long table where the councilmen convene. From one end, the king motions to the empty seat that crowds the space next to Ethan.

Behind them, the captain of the guard, Captain Offa, stands tall and rigid in steel armor, ready to protect the king at a moment's notice.

Uncomfortable with the dozen hard looks on me as I approach, I direct my attention to the large tapestry that dresses the wall above the captain.

Is this what it's like for Ethan? Running from obligation to obligation until the day is gone?

I take the empty chair at Ethan's side and, to my relief, the council's attention shifts back to the king.

"I requested Princess Meredith's attendance today so that she may help bring light to our discussion," he tells the councilmen, who come alive with whispers, shaking heads, and a jumble of nods.

"Sire, are you sure this is wise?" the grand councilor asks, the warning in his tone strongly suggesting I'm some sort of security risk. It's all I can do not to glare at the man. His features strike me as oddly familiar, as though I've met him before . . . but maybe it isn't his features at all, and just his expression. That sneer he gives me, as if I am his enemy, reminds me of Elijah.

"Rowan, if I needed your opinion, I would have asked for it. Let us get on with it." The king's mighty stare turns to me. "Are you aware of any association your father may have with the Borderlords?"

The question takes me by surprise, not only because it's not what I was expecting, but because the thought never crossed my mind. Alliance law decrees the Borderlands are to be excluded from sovereignty to encourage solidarity and the economic prosperity of free trade, but the king clearly isn't referring to the import of Stonefall's wheat.

At least you're not entirely ignorant.

"No, Your Majesty."

Rowan's scoff echoes from the other end of the table. "Did we really expect her to say otherwise?"

I blink, feeling my stomach tighten. "Are you calling me a liar, sir?" I dare ask the councilor.

"Well, aren't you?" Though he speaks calmly enough, the words are laced with spite. "We have no reason to trust you. You are the princess of Stonefall," he says matter-of-factly, as though that explains everything.

Ethan is suddenly on his feet, his chair screeching behind him on the stone.

"Is this what you brought her here for?" he barks in outrage at the king. "To be interrogated like some criminal?"

Perceval's lips press into a hard line. "Calm down, my son," he chides. "Rowan has our kingdom's best interest at heart." The king's admonishing glare falls on his councilor. "Though he ought to remember that, Stonefall or no, the princess may one day be his queen." Displeased as he looks, Rowan lowers his gaze.

I would have enjoyed the small victory, were it not for the king's choice of words.

Not *will. May.*

Ethan sits, meeting my eye as he does and mouthing an apology.

"We are not accusing King Edgard of anything. We are simply considering all the possibilities," the king explains.

"And given your father's reputation," Rowan remarks, "it is incumbent of us to confirm his innocence."

I remember Ethan's vague words the day we met. He mentioned our fathers' differences in policy and said they were the root of our kingdoms' discord, promising to tell me all about it. And perhaps he would have, had I not been so adamant about training. "Your Majesty, I am not privy to my father's dealings; I'm quite ignorant of his transgressions."

"Your father is a very desperate—" Rowan begins self-righteously, but another councilor cuts him short.

"Remember your manners. This is the princess's father you speak of," protests the older councilor, one I've seen often at Ethan's side during functions and dinners. Next to the hardened stares and unforgiving postures of his fellow councilmen, he looks rather gentle.

"Take your propriety elsewhere, Milus. It has no place in this council," Rowan counters, leaning to rest his elbows on the table. "I will not gloss over truths only to spare the lady's feelings."

"What truths?" I demand.

Rowan's voice leers. "In spite of my king's objections, your father has sold, and continues to sell, slaves to the southern kingdoms."

"Slaves?" I echo, baffled. It's been over two hundred years since the end of the slavery era in the northern kingdoms, paving the way for the rise of merchants and artisans, and free peasants who collect wages for their labor. I never once heard anything about slaves. Had I been so blind not to notice? But it makes no sense. Wouldn't the servants have known about it? Surely Holt or Beth would have mentioned it. "I don't understand."

"What's not to understand? He picks up street rats, beggars, serfs sold by their own masters, and sells them to the highest bidder," Rowan answers with a dismissive shrug.

"Why?" I ask, horrified.

"Because he's drowned your kingdom in debt," Ethan explains in a quiet, sympathetic voice, like he can see how much it pains me to hear it.

Just when I thought I couldn't think any less of my father . . .

"It seems, then, that his slaves are in demand, no?" The one called Milus asks. "One has to wonder where all these poor souls are being sold off to."

"The dealings of the southern kingdoms are of no interest to us," another councilman comments.

With an uncomfortable swallow, I ask, "Say my father is involved with the Borderlords, what happens then?"

"That depends," the king answers, hands steepled on the table, giving me a look that makes me want to turn away. "If King Edgard has broken any of the alliance laws, I will forfeit the contract. And I will send you home."

The stars glimmer above me, vibrant and defiant in the moonless night. Leaning over the balcony outside my bedroom, I gaze at the small dots of flickering light that populate the slumbering city of Alder. The iron weight of my eyelids tells me it's late. Even so, I can't sleep. The throbbing ache between my brows doesn't help, either. My mind is awake with thoughts of the council meeting, thoughts of my father and his possible entanglement with the

Borderlords.

I can't go home. Not now. Not ever.

I can't allow Connor and Holt's sacrifice to be for nothing.

Don't embarrass me.

I scoff at Father's last words. He dared lecture me over my lack of grace and choice of friends while he dragged Stonefall to the ground. The irony is laughable.

Mighty King Edgard, I think bitterly.

The old Meredith trembled at the thought of standing up to Father. Though I sneer at my forgotten weakness, I can't help but wonder if my newfound grit would instantly dissolve under the weight of his scrutiny.

I'd like to think myself indifferent to him, just as he is to me, but resentment rumbles in my chest. I don't have to dig deep to comprehend it. I hate him. I hate knowing that I am his daughter, his flesh and blood.

Stonefall deserves better.

I deserve better.

And I'll be cursed if I'm going to let him drag me down with him.

Thinking of home, my mind strays to Anabella. What is she doing now that I'm gone? Was she assigned a new post in the palace? I can't rule out the possibility that Father may have sent her packing to the streets.

Or worse.

But I can't think like that. I'll go mad if I do. I promised her and Beth that I would send for them. And it eats at me that I haven't. Their presence would do me so much good. And yet, I can't bring myself to ask Ethan. Not until—

There is a knock at my door, so soft I question my ears. It's not exactly visiting hours. I glance over my shoulder and into my dim room. Of all the candles that I lit when I got out of bed, only one remains, burning its wick like a champion.

A second knock. I pick up the candle and approach the door. I hug my sleeveless velvet overcoat to conceal the chemise underneath and open the door, surprised to find myself looking at Ethan, hands clasped behind him, fully dressed, brocade jacket and all as though it's midday.

He offers a tight-lipped smile. "I know it's late, I . . . saw the light under your door . . . I was hoping you'd be—I didn't wake you, did I?"

"I couldn't sleep."

"Nor I."

My eyes glance around briefly. "Is there something you need?"

He coughs, embarrassed. "I have a surprise for you." His arms unfold, revealing an object he'd been hiding. The reflection of the torch's flame dances on the shiny steel.

A longsword.

Stripes of gold mark the dark cast metal of the hilt, and at the guard, a two-headed eagle on checkered red and white.

"Stonefall's crest," I gasp, tracing the small metal reminder of home with my thumb.

"Is it to your liking?"

"It's beautiful," I say in awe, my voice soft with gratitude.

I peel my eyes away after a moment and look up to find Ethan's face beaming at me. "It was supposed to be a birthday gift, but after what happened at the council meeting . . ." He rubs at the back of his neck, looking uncomfortable. I smile inwardly, amused to see the confident prince out of his element for once. In the end, he simply says, "Happy birthday."

The corner of my mouth nudges my lips, threatening to break into a full grin. "Thank you."

"I would suggest you hold off on training with it for now, though. I'd like to keep Lief in one piece," he says, eyes lit with a twinkle of mischief.

"Ha ha, very funny."

When the mirth on Ethan's face starts to fade, he adds, "I'm sorry I'm not around more often."

I shrug off the unnecessary apology. "You are the crown prince. You have obligations."

"You make it sound so tedious," he chuckles. "But you would be surprised."

"Really?" I ask, doubtful.

"Princely duties can be fun sometimes." He regards me a moment, his kind chestnut eyes contemplative, and I can't help but wonder after his thoughts. "I'm playing tennis with the vis-count tomorrow at noon. You should come."

Then he steps closer, creating an intimacy between us, and my walls shoot up like claws, but to my relief, Ethan is only after my hand. As regal and cordial as ever, his soft lips briefly brush my knuckles, eyes locked with mine, and as my heart invisibly drums with trepidation, he bids me good night.

6

Connor

"Any idea how you earned yourself that scar?" Asher asks early the next morning as he pulls Beast from his bridle. I was surprised when he requested I accompany him to the village. He's managed well on his own all this time, and of the two of them, Raven needs the help more than he does.

I trace the raised mark on my face with my thumb. There is no telling how long it's been there. "No."

"Ah, well…was hoping for a good story there," he mutters, fingering his white beard with his free hand. The nonchalance of his answer disagrees with the tone in his voice, making me frown. There must be something else on his mind, something that's troubling him. I gather our trip to town might be it.

Dawn breaks over the road that cuts through the flat-floored valley, turning the black sky a deep amber. A cartful of oranges turns on rickety wheels behind us.

"What about you?" I glance at the black patch over his eye. "Any good stories to share?"

"Quite a few, I reckon. None worth repeating, though."

"Does Raven know about these stories?"

"Why, you think you'll hear them from her instead?" He

chuckles. "No, lad. She does not care to know, and I'm happy to keep it that way."

The village is an hour's trek from the cottage. A cluster of thatched roofs appears in the distance, and soon enough, the sharp stench of manure invades the open country air, growing stronger as we near the pastures within the village. Encroached on by a patchwork of grassy fields, the main road opens to the market, where all the other farmhouse roads converge. A well marks the center of the square. Traders gather around it, seeking their next sale within the shuffling crowd by shouting their bargains. Beyond the well stands a scaffold, propped like an omen, its four nooses waiting in eerie stillness for their next victims. Commoners in brown dresses and trousers chatter in a chaos of sorts, pushing carts and herding chickens.

I trace their sidelong glances to the silhouettes of red capes and white tabards armored with chain mail and leather breastplates. Pairs and groups of soldiers guard the village conspicuously.

"You're not setting up in the square?" I ask when Asher doesn't stop Beast, but before he can answer, a piercing wail cuts through the village.

Two soldiers drag a woman by the arms. She fights their hold with a violence bordering on madness.

"I want my son," she bellows, thrashing her head around. Dried blood covers the left side of her temple. "Give me my son!"

The onlooking villagers watch for only a moment before returning to their activities. Asher moves on as well, pulling Beast forward. "We are making deliveries today," he prompts with eerie calm when I don't follow.

"Why did they take her son?"

"No one knows. But he's not the first to be taken, and I doubt he'll be the last."

Not a single pair of eyes dares another glance at the wailing woman as the soldiers shove her into an empty cage. It's unbelievable.

"Best to steer clear of trouble, lad," Asher mutters. "Won't do you no good to play the hero."

It feels wrong to look the other way, but I have enough good sense to know that Asher's right. There's nothing to be done for the woman.

We come to the blacksmith's shop. Asher hauls a sack of oranges on his shoulder. "Don't ask questions," he whispers as he walks past me and pushes the solid wood door open. I follow him inside, where the heat seems to double. A fire blazes and pops in the forge behind the scowling blacksmith, who sets down his hammer as we walk in. "He's safe," Asher says to the blacksmith's questioning look.

The blacksmith picks a blackened rag off the table and wipes his hands. He's as gray haired as Asher, though not yet past his prime.

"Flynn," he says in cold greeting to me.

I introduce myself as well. "Connor."

"Where do you want these?" Asher asks after he turns the lock on the door, cocking his head at the sack on his shoulder.

"Give 'em here."

Flynn steps to a large metal bucket on a table lined with dangling hammers of multiple shapes and sizes, and carefully empties the sack atop it. Then he moves over to another table, covered by a neatly arrayed set of short swords. He drops three of them in the sack. I watch Flynn smuggle the weapons, and I don't wonder why but rather for whom. Asher has no need for them.

Flynn begins to cover the mouth of the sack with oranges but Asher stops him.

"Wait, let the lad look at the bow."

"What for?" Flynn asks, scowling again.

"He's good with it."

Flynn taps a finger against the table, considering.

"All right," he mutters. "Help me move that, would ya?" His gaze points me to the wrought iron anvil he was hammering only moments ago. We grasp either side of the table on which it sits and walk it aside. Flynn then kneels by the gaping square left uncovered beneath it.

He pulls out a stunning longbow of reddish-brown bark and intricate engravings…with a full matching quiver.

"It belonged t' someone we lost recently," Flynn says as he offers it to me.

I admire the weapon in silent appreciation. I test the spring; the load seems evenly distributed. The weight of the stave is perfect, tough and springy, with immaculate tapering. It's hard not to gawk.

I steal a glance at Asher, who watches me rather intently. Is this why he brought me here?

"I would like you to have it," Asher tells me, and his eyes drift to Flynn, who crosses his arms and stares back at Asher, communicating something in his hard gaze, suggesting there is more to the bow than his sentimentality.

But after a terse moment, Flynn sighs. "I'm trusting you on this, Asher."

"I'll take good care of it," I assure Flynn, unsure of how else to thank him for such a fine weapon.

"Put it t' good use, lad, that's all that matters."

Asher takes the bow and quiver and hides them beneath the oranges with the rest of the smuggled swords. He's about done adjusting and filling the sack with fruit when the shop's door rattles in its hinges, followed by a series of impatient knocks. We all freeze.

"Open up, blacksmith!"

Flynn shares a warning glance with Asher before he crosses the shop. Then, as Asher drops the last of the oranges in the sack and twists its mouth closed, the lock clicks and Flynn opens the door.

A soldier storms in, shoving Flynn out of his way. "Why was your door locked, blacksmith?" The red-faced soldier narrows his brown eyes at Asher and me, surprised to find us here. "And who are you?"

I stand cautiously still.

"I'm buying a bushel o' oranges from 'em," Flynn politely replies.

The soldier turns his suspicious gaze on the sack, his red cape shifting like a shadow. "You didn't answer my first question," he mutters, his suspicion growing by the second. But Flynn is quick to respond.

"The lock needs some work." He plays with the metal as if to show him. "It locks when you close the door too forcefully."

Either he was prepared for the question, or he is quick on his feet.

The soldier strides over to Asher, who dips his chin and averts his eyes from the redcloak, same as the villagers outside. "Show me," he demands.

Unease crawls through my skin as Asher untwists the burlap.

From across the shop, I can't see what the soldier sees, but it must be only oranges, because the man clicks his tongue in disappointment. But then he turns to Flynn and asks, "What do you need all this fruit for?"

Flynn is stripped of his quick wit and scrambles for an answer. Behind the soldier, Asher stands upright once more, eyes pinned on the soldier's back.

"T' make an offering t' the church is all," he stammers after too many seconds. "They feed the orphans."

This seems to distract the redcloak. "What orphans?" he

gloats, smiling. "We've taken them all. Haven't you been paying attention, blacksmith?"

Flynn swallows hard and lowers his eyes to his boots. "My work keeps me busy," he says in a quiet voice.

"*We* keep you busy," the soldier corrects him.

Eyes still lowered, Flynn asks, "Have you come with another order?"

"The commander wants another shipment ready in a fortnight," says the soldier.

Flynn looks up and nods, hands clasped at his chest. "It'll be done." He's managed to steer the soldier toward the door. He's about to make his exit, but something crosses his mind. "Don't think you'll be needing all these," he says, whipping back to the oranges. His hand dives into the sack to steal a handful . . .

"Smugglers!" he hisses, and draws out his sword.

7

Meredith

I tilt my head for a better view, but it's no use. The crowd is as dense as a haystack, packed into the viewing gallery that wraps around three sides of the tennis court. Amid the excited gasps of the gambling spectators and the resounding bounce of the ball, all I get are glimpses of Ethan and the blur of his racket through the netted window.

We are on one of the upper levels of the castle, which explains the cold air that even the bountiful sunlight that bathes the tennis court can't squelch. I try to peek at the open sky, but I'm too far back. The sloping roof of the gallery blocks my sight.

Coming here was a mistake.

I've never played tennis, or seen anyone play before, so naturally, I was curious. But the mass of tightly packed courtiers feels suffocating, and though Ethan asked me to come watch him play, I doubt he'll notice my absence until the match is over. *Perhaps not even then,* I think, glancing at the swarm of spectators around me, puzzled by the disappointment deflating my chest. It's not like I'd come hoping to spend some time with Ethan . . . had I? No. He simply wanted me to see the fun side of being a prince, and I guess, out on the tennis court, it must be, but within a gallery full to the gills and with a limited view, there is no room for enjoyment.

Deciding a walk through the gardens is in order, I do my best to wiggle around toward the exit, tugging the hem of my skirts out from under people's shoes. As soon as I'm free of the gallery, however, I'm hounded by a pair of curtsying brunettes.

"*Princess*," the tall one gushes over my quiet groan, "I don't believe we've met. I'm Lady Katrina Heron of Endor Manor." She pivots toward her blushing companion. "And this is my sister, Rose." The two ladies-in-waiting at their backs remain unintroduced. If Lorette had her way, she, too, would be trailing my every step.

I bow my head in a curt greeting. "It's a pleasure to meet you both," I say, and try to get away. "Excuse me—"

Lady Katrina steps into my path, thwarting my feeble attempt to flee. "We were on our way to the library for a greet-and-tea with some of the ladies who've just arrived at court," she gushes in one breath. "It would be a great honor if you joined us."

I stare at the pair, wishing they hadn't asked. I have no interest in tea—I'd rather pluck weeds or peel potatoes—but if I'm to take the queen's advice on favorable public opinion, I can't deny them; the alliance is delicate, and I'm the only one here who will fight for it.

While Rose gazes down to her feet and bites her lip, Katrina eyes me eagerly, face beaming. "Tea it is," I mutter, at which Katrina claps her hands together and lets out a muted shrill of excitement.

On the way to the library, Rose remains tight-lipped while her sister jabbers away. Katrina is lively and cheerful, and her words flow like a river's rapids. The family semblance is evident in their similarly shaped almond eyes and dainty noses. And the hair. The only real physical difference seems to be their height. I listen to Katrina, struggling to keep up. From what I catch, I learn that their family arrived at Alder court two days ago, in attendance for the upcoming feast.

"We've been begging our father to bring us to court ever since we heard the news of your arrival," she says with a grin. The more she speaks, the more guilty I feel for having wanted to shake them off, realizing I misjudged them by association; Stone-fall court taught me that courtiers were nothing but self-important wasps ready to sting, so I learned to steer clear of them. Old habits are like shadows.

Assistants in tow, we parade toward the first level, climbing down spiral stairways, crossing courtyards, and bending corners through stony corridors. "We would love to hear about your training," Katrina says when she's done gushing about her family. Surprise must show on my face, as she is quick to rectify. "It is true, isn't it? You train with swords?" It sounds more like a statement than a question.

Rose blushes a deeper red, averse to eye contact.

I consider denying it. A simple no would suffice. But the thought of getting caught in a lie sours my stomach. "I do," I cautiously admit after a moment's hesitation.

Katrina grins with an air of triumph as we arrive at the library. "My, how adventurous of you, my lady," she says without a drop of judgment, mitigating my unease. Perhaps the idea of a swordswoman isn't as scandalous as I thought.

The pair of soaring arched doors at the library's entrance stands open. Katrina and Rose stroll inside, but I pause, slack-jawed, peering at the wonder inside. I don't think I've ever seen a library this big. It's built like an atrium, easily twice the size of the Feast Hall. The ceiling—at least four stories high—is split in its center by a long strip of latticed glass, flooding half the vast room with sunlight. Rows of giant carved-limestone bookshelves line the opening in the ceiling on each side of the library, connecting the roof to the blue-and-gray diamond slate flooring. Wooden ladders are scattered across the space, ready to escort the scholars to the higher shelves in the room. To my right, on top of a desk covered in stacks of books, a large book with yellowed pages lies open on a pedestal.

There's so much to look at. I'm still drifting toward the pedestal when something else catches my eye. A map. Framed in gold leaf and hung above a mantle, the carefully drawn lines trace the Eastern Continent. Alder, encased by inked mountain ridges, is easily a quarter of the continent. My eyes mull over Stonefall. I've always known it's small, but seeing it on paper next to Alder makes it look so insignificant, like a flea on a giant. It's a wonder Alder didn't try for an alliance with Valar, the other nearest neighbor kingdom in the region. It appears to be five times the size of Stonefall, and, if I were to guess, they probably have a better king sitting on the throne. I suppose I should thank the Borderlands and their precious wheat. To the south, the name *Talos* pens the lay of the land like a weed, rooted on the southern coast. I pity the kingdoms of Sunder and Masphey. With Talos at their borders, they were likely the first lands to fall to his rule. The Blue Abyss spans all across the south, dividing the continents. Just how long did it take the Mad King to cross it, all those years ago?

Excited chatter brings me out of my daze, reminding me why I'm here. Reluctantly, I peel my eyes away from the map, taking my desire to continue reading it with me, and steer to the left side of the room, where six pretty and unfamiliar faces converse by a round oaken table set with pewter teacups and a pot. Their ladies-in-waiting sit patiently on a row of chairs at the wall behind them, hands folded in their laps, watchful of their mistresses' needs.

Rose and Katrina have already claimed their seats.

"Princess Meredith," someone mutters in surprise, and chairs scratch against the tile as the ladies rise to curtsy.

"Rose and I ran into her outside the tennis court," Katrina brags. "Naturally, we extended an invitation."

The ladies return to their seats and nod, commending Katrina, as though she's just admitted to feeding the poor . . .

Except for one.

A stately girl in a pale-yellow dress pins a condescending eyebrow on Katrina. Long and smooth ebony hair drapes over her arms as she crosses them over her chest, but Katrina seems oblivious, and whatever it is the girl objects to, she doesn't voice it.

One of the ladies—a freckle-faced girl with red curls who reminds me of Krea—offers me the seat next to her. It's hard to relax on the sturdy chair: the seat is quite unforgiving, and the carved resting rail digs into the back of my neck, forcing me to sit upright. Even when the conversation picks up, I still feel their wayward glances. A smiling lady-in-waiting appears at my side to fill a cup for me. I thank her as she leaves and sip the hot water, the vessel warming my fingers, filling my mouth with traces of barley and honey; I can't remember the last time I sat at a table like this, surrounded by ladies and tea.

I keep half an ear on their gossip while my eyes stray back to the shelves. Why hadn't I come here sooner? Is it that I can't justify wasting time getting lost in books, or is it a fear of finding my thoughts can no longer disappear into the pages? I shudder to think it's the latter.

At some point, Katrina brings up her love of dancing, and the conversation sways toward hobbies and pastimes, many of them shared by more than one lady. Knitting, painting, music, dancing—all the interests, it's understood, a lady ought to enjoy. Gambling, I note, is the closest thing to rebellious, mentioned at the table by the stoic girl in yellow. The ladies seem to be slightly frightened of her. None dare hold her strong gaze, and those on either side of her maintain an obviously calculated distance. The topic finally makes its way to me.

The entire table stares. Some of the ladies lean in, expectant. I steal a glance at Katrina, who smiles reassuringly. Beside her, Rose looks away. Lorette's fussing rings in my head, cautioning me. I go with my gut and play it safe. "Pianoforte, and horseback riding," I say. A half-truth, as I still enjoy riding, but it's been a long time since I've touched the keys of a piano.

"Is that all?" Krea's doppelganger asks, and I realize they're all waiting to hear me say it, to admit or dispel the rumors. My palms are moist with sweat around the cup. I'm not sure what to expect. Though Katrina and Rose took it well, that doesn't mean the others will, too. But it's too late to lie.

I inhale courage and say, "I don't train with a sword for my leisure."

My words are met with silence.

Glances dart around the table, as if they don't know how to respond. And that's when I notice the sly curve on Katrina's lips. She leans back in her chair, at ease, and her lips twitch when she finds me staring.

She meant for this to happen, I realize with a sinking heart, dashing any hopes I had of gaining the ladies' approval. Katrina played me for a fool. Now I understand Rose's discomfort. I should have known better. I should have been more careful about who I trust. How can I expect to win the favor of a people when I can't even charm a handful of girls over tea?

The girl in the yellow dress breaks the silence. "What an admirable sacrifice, my lady."

All eyes around the table shift to her. But unlike me, this doesn't seem to faze her.

"You could be playing music and riding horses, and yet you choose duty over pleasure and train instead. I can't imagine a more deserving subject to be our next queen."

"*Duty*?" Katrina scoffs. "What duty?"

Several pairs of eyes widen, incredulous of Katrina's brazen tongue.

"All great kings ride into battle, do they not?" the girl in yellow asks. "Shouldn't queens be prepared to do the same in the absence of their kings?"

Silence again. But this time, a series of stiff, shy nods spread through the table. The smugness in Katrina's expression vanishes, the curve of her lips flattening into a sour, thin line.

The girl in yellow rises, towering over the table with her statuesque figure. "You'll excuse me, but my tea has bittered." In a sleek stride, she makes her way around the table to my chair. "My lady, I am in dire need of air and intellectual conversation. Would you do me the honor of your company?"

"Lady Heloise Cresten," the girl says to me when we exit the library.

Feeling both grateful and suspicious, I say, "You saved me back there. Why?"

She takes my arm and loops it through hers as we fall in step through the corridor. Though I'm surprised by her familiarity, I welcome her boldness. It's a nice change from the everyday stuffy decorum.

"I don't need any favors, if that's what you're wondering."

"It did cross my mind," I admit.

"You are to be queen. It *should* cross your mind, especially after today . . . I knew Katrina was up to no good when she brought you in."

I hate the disappointment I feel. At least the courtiers I knew back home never tricked me into thinking they liked me. Ironic that I've now come to appreciate their honesty. "Is everyone else at court as crafty she is?"

"You give her too much credit," Heloise says, flashing a magnetic smile. "I don't blame you for thinking the worst of her—I don't think highly of her myself—but deceiving you like that, it was tasteless of her."

"But why would she do that?"

We round a corner, our steps echoing against the walls. "Rose and Katrina are the marquess's daughters," she tells me, as though that's supposed to make sense to me. "Rose is the king's choice to be the prince's bride in the event the alliance with Stonefall is annulled." Her words come off casually, like she doesn't believe that will ever happen.

"Which makes me Rose's only obstacle to the throne," I mutter in understanding. Heloise nods as we come up the same flight of stairs I walked down with the pair of sisters. In spite of myself, curiosity begs me to ask, "How did the king choose her?"

"She's well-liked at court. Even in town people hold an agreeable opinion of her; Rose is blessed with a gentle soul and happy manners." *A favorable public opinion,* I think dejectedly. Things are starting to look worse and worse by the minute. "The rulers of Alder have always valued the people above all else," she goes on, guiding me along. "As queen, Rose would easily earn the love of her subjects. I myself prefer a woman with some backbone to sit on our throne, but I suppose if she was to marry Ethan, it'd be he who would have to make the tough decisions. And Rose would be there to comfort him."

I can't help but compare myself. Am I capable of earning the love of a people?

"Rose also happens to be infatuated with Ethan," she adds, "And Katrina, zealous tigress that she is, takes it upon herself to fight her sister's battles."

At that, I soften a little. I don't approve of Katrina's methods, but I could respect her love for her sister.

"You are quite the mystery to everyone," Heloise quips.

I shake my head. "Believe me, there's nothing mysterious about me."

"This is only my second day at court, and I've heard your name in conversation a great deal." Her voice takes an air of exaggerated gravity. "'The elusive Stonefall princess, who may or may not hide a sword under her skirts, delivered to the castle at the behest and sacrifice of the respected—'"

My feet stop. The memory scours my calloused heart. Is this

what he's been reduced to? A frivolous piece of gossip? "I don't want to hear."

Heloise eyes me curiously a moment. "Not a fan of gossip, are you? All right, then. We shan't speak of it," she says with a shrug and resumes our walk.

"Where are we going?"

"I told my brother I would meet him after the tennis match. It should be over soon."

"Is he up there making bets?" I ask, thinking of her earlier admission.

Mirth glints in her eye. "Marcus is a terrible gambler. His talents are best suited for physical endeavors, so he's upstairs putting them to good use playing against His Highness."

The viscount, I remember Ethan telling me. If she's his sister, that makes her a count's daughter.

"Forgive me if I'm blunt, but why do I get the feeling the ladies are afraid of you?" I ask.

She laughs, the sound soft and charming. Graceful. Just like all her other traits, it seems.

"You noticed, did you?" We climb to the fourth level and cross through the courtyards toward the distant echo of a tennis ball slamming against walls. "My sharp tongue has earned me a reputation at court."

And then, as we cut through a pebbled courtyard, she ushers me into a connecting corridor under an L-shaped flight of stairs, shooting glances right and left. Curious, I peer back into the courtyard. It's still empty, nothing but a tall, twisting yew tree spruced in its middle. In the corridor, only the windows and sunlight and the burning torches keep us company, but Heloise lowers her voice just the same. "Pray tell, what kind of swords do you train with?"

I stand straighter, thinking I heard wrong. And for a second, I consider if her friendliness stems from some ulterior motive.

"Only practice swords, perfectly safe," I say reluctantly. "The guard I train with says I'm not ready for the real thing."

A crease wrinkles Heloise's brow, but when she speaks, she surprises me yet again. "That's no fun." Her catlike eyes light up. "You should visit our chateau in the spring. We have a proper training yard and plenty of steel to practice with."

Baffled, I step back and feel the cool wall behind me. Is she really offering her home for such sport? Won't her family have a say? Or are they as candid and rebellious as she? But she smiles like it's nothing, chipping away at my apprehension.

"I have four brothers who would love to spar with you," she goes on, her lips turning devilish. And then she stoops to whisper, "Or you could train with me. Though, I should warn you, I have the meanest swing of all."

8

Connor

"On your knees, you filthy swine!" The soldier points his sword, the sharp, clean metal seeking blood. *It's only one man.* There's three of us. Sword or no, we can take him down.

Asher and Flynn inch to their knees, cautious and quiet. They both send urgent looks my way, demanding I follow along. Pulse thrashing, I crouch down, mirroring their surrender.

"That's where you rats belong." The soldier paces before us, a smirk on his leering face. "I'm surprised, blacksmith. Didn't think you had the guts to break the law. Things have been dull around here, so I can't say I'm disappointed." He chuckles. "Wait until the commander hears of this; he'll make a good show out of you."

"Breaking the laws of a false king is no crime," Flynn dares, his voice calm and collected.

"Save your gall for the noose!" the redcloak snarls. "And as for you," he says, turning to Asher and me, "if you answer all my questions, I will end your miserable lives with a swift and merciful death. Refuse, and I will pry the answers out limb by limb." He pauses to examine us and seems to take our silence as agreement. "Where were you planning to take those weapons?"

"Bandits made a deal with us," Asher answers, eyes on the

floor. "They offered to pay good silver for 'em. We need it for the collections—"

The soldier kicks Asher on his side. "I didn't ask for your excuses, you goat!" he yells to his face.

I survey the distance to the soldier. If I can get to him before he swings his sword—

Asher spits in the soldier's eye.

The soldier grabs Asher by the collar and hauls him up to his feet in a split second. "Insolent fool," he seethes, nostrils flaring. Asher bluffs frailty, limping as the soldier lugs him around to one of the worktables and runs an angry arm across the cluttered surface, shoving an array of tools and scraps to the ground in a cacophony of clattering metal. He forces Asher's hand on the now empty table and lifts his sword.

My body goes taut, ready to spring.

The soldier drives the blade through the back of Asher's hand. Asher stifles a scream, groaning instead as his head droops over the table by his bleeding hand, which is now pinned to the wood by the sword.

The soldier stands over Asher's shaking frame with bold arrogance, savoring the moment.

I'm deliberating on which sharp object to dart for when Asher snaps out of his suffering and jams something into the redcloak's eye. The soldier tumbles backward, hands flailing at his face. He's screaming now, trying to pry the embedded object when Flynn rises and closes in on the wailing soldier in one swift motion, driving it deeper into his skull.

Silence.

He drops like a fly to the floor, and for a moment, we simply stare at the dead soldier. Though he came alone, he was sent here on a task, and when his superiors realize he's missing, someone else will come asking questions.

Grunting, Asher yanks the sword out of his hand and drops it, taking a moment longer to recover, his body bent over the stained table.

"Shouldn't you lock the door?" I ask Flynn. If other soldiers heard that scream, they'd be charging in by now.

Asher answers for him. "Not yet."

He approaches the dead soldier and plucks the two-pronged iron fork out of his eye. Asher dumps the fork in the forge, exchanging it for the poker, its sharp end glowing with heat, and presses it to the raw mass that used to be the soldier's eye. The flesh hisses on contact with the heated metal, cauterizing the wound in seconds. "We need another sack to hide the body."

"He won't fit," I say, surprised that I have to point it out, but in reply, Asher lifts the soldier's right arm and bends it farther than he should . . . until the elbow joint snaps.

"We'll make him fit."

Watching him continue to break the soldier into a mangle of skin and bones springs more than one question in my head, but now is not the time to ask them. So I glide to the door, where Flynn remains on guard. "I'll get it," I say, and he opens the door just enough for me to pass, nodding me on.

Outside, the village carries on, oblivious to my roving gaze. No one appears to have heard the soldier's short-lived screams. Or perhaps those that did walked on, just as they did when they heard the woman in the square. I approach the cart while combing the area for soldiers. A pair of them loiter under the shade of another shop several paces away, their slouched stances and crossed arms hinting at boredom. Hopefully negligence, too.

I take one of the three bulging sacks and tread back as swiftly as I can without drawing attention to myself. "It's me," I say at the door when I knock. It opens a quarter of the way, and I squeeze through. This time, Flynn locks it after me, pushing the metal lever in place with a loud clank.

Asher is well on his way to fully dissembling the soldier.

The body, a myriad of oddly bent lumps, is looking more and more like a puppet than a corpse.

As Flynn returns to the smuggled weapons, I empty the sack, overfilling the bucket with oranges. A few stragglers roll away across the floorboards and disappear under worktables.

"Hold it open," Asher says when I approach, and as I do, he begins stuffing the soldier in, head first, twisting the flaccid limbs around the torso to fit him through the sack's mouth, mushing him in the rest of the way through the pair of unnaturally folded legs. When he's done, he wipes his brow with the sleeve of his tunic and lets out a tired breath. "They might come looking for him," he says to Flynn. "You should head for the camp."

Flynn's eyes are hooded as he picks up a clean rag from his worktable and hands it to Asher, who uses it to stanch his wound. "Aye," he says gravely, "but you and I both know I can't. I'd have t' leave Margie behind. I can't do that, Asher. She won't survive without me."

"She can stay with us. We'll look after her," Asher offers, but Flynn shakes his head.

"Then all o' you would be in danger. And I can't risk 'em redcloaks following my trail back t' the camp."

"What's it to be then? Let them catch you?"

"I can lie my way out o' suspicion," Flynn answers. "Make 'em look for blame elsewhere."

Asher stares at his friend for a long time, his lips pressed thin. "And if you can't?"

"Then I'll take my secrets t' the grave," Flynn tells him flatly.

9

Meredith

Lief finds me in the courtyard the next morning, sparring with myself over the winter-damaged turf. It's easier like this, without snow to sink into and wet my boots.

"You're early, my lady," Lief says as he trots across the path to join me, training sword in hand, his short curls still wet from his morning bath.

I can't help the grin on my face. In spite of myself, I'm giddy with excitement. Being able to relate to another girl at court is new to me, a breath of fresh air to fill my stagnant lungs.

"What's this?" Lief asks, smiling back.

"Do you know Lady Cresten—the count's daughter?"

"I only know a handful of courtiers by name, my lady."

"Well, you'll know her soon enough," I say, grinning again. "She should be here any moment."

Lief blinks at me. "*Here*? She's coming here?"

I give him a look, one brow lifted. "Yes, Lief, what other kind of *here* is there?"

She had insisted on watching me train, claiming she was deprived of the sport herself, being away from where she could practice freely. I could hardly say no. Nor did I want to. I still can't believe I met another female with an appreciation for swords, and one of noble birth no less, with more refinement and elegance than I could ever hope to master. Fitting in at court is not a skill I've ever possessed—quite the conundrum for a princess. I always believed it to be impossible, that there was nothing I could do about it, because I'll always be, well, me. But Heloise, too, is different, and yet she works the ropes of society like fine strings around her finger, inspiring fear and respect from her peers. I envy her that.

"Is it wise, my lady?" Surprise colors Lief's face. "Ladies have a penchant for gossip."

"I'm aware. But Heloise isn't like them. I wouldn't have agreed if I thought she was a snoop."

I want to tell Lief about her, how she's trained to wield a sword, knowing I can trust him not to repeat it even in his sleep, but it's not my secret to tell.

Lief's readies his timber sword. "As you wish, my lady."

I raise my harmless weapon in response, and we fall into the motions of circling, parrying, jabbing, evading, our swords thunking and smacking as we trample the brown dead grass, and though I'm focused, my thoughts still manage to wander. Meeting Heloise underlines the obvious: I don't have friends in Alder. If it wasn't for Lief's constant presence, I'd be all alone.

"How come you've never spoken of your family?" I ask Lief as our swords whack, feeling guilty. All these months, and I've never once asked him anything about himself. Has my misery soured me so that I can't be bothered to care about the only person in this castle who spends time with me out of his own free will? I free my wooden blade from his and lunge forward, but Lief sidesteps away with those nimble feet of his, and I stumble into the boulder behind him.

"You've never asked, my lady."

I round on him, taking a large step to get in his line of attack, and at the last moment, I adjust my stance and strike his side.

"I'm asking now," I pant, wheeling around to face him.

We swing at each other, once, twice, thrice. A thwack ripples down to the hilt and through my gloves with each parry. On the fourth, I err in my swing, overreaching, and miss his sword by an inch, my arm batting at the empty air as Lief jabs me in the inside of my shoulder.

"I'm the bastard son of a painter," Lief says simply. We circle each other. "My father's wife wouldn't let him keep me," he says between swipes, "so he offered me to the guard when I was five." Lief counterthrusts into my attack, slapping my outstretched arm at the elbow.

I jump back. "He gave you up to be trained as a guard?"

"A servant," he corrects. "My job was to clean their weapons and armor, and in return they kept me clothed and fed."

It's hard to fathom the skilled boy before me, the youngest guard in the king's employ, scrubbing blades for bread. "Is it customary for the guard to train its servants?"

"No, I trained myself. Alder is too peaceful." He ducks away from my blow. "There isn't enough crime to keep guards on their feet, so the outposts hold first-blood tournaments each month. I watched them studiously. Most everything I know, I learned from those tournaments. When I was strong enough to lift a sword, I made myself train each night with their weapons while they slept."

I stop, my arms falling at my sides as a small smile tugs on my lips. I've all but dropped my sword to the grass, wanting to hear the rest of his remarkable story, my guilt doubling at not having asked before.

"*This* is your trainer?"

Heloise walks up, wearing a sleek emerald gown of silk and chiffon that hugs her bust and waist, accentuating her lithe frame.

"My lady." Lief bows despite the jab.

"He's stronger than he looks," I say, wiping stray locks of hair away from my sweaty face.

"Deceivingly disarming," Heloise murmurs, appraising Lief, and I hold back a smile at his flushed cheeks. "Think you can best me in a sword fight?" she asks him, lips pursed.

So much for reticence.

It takes Lief a second to react. "You . . . you're trained?" he stutters, briefly glancing my way.

"A consequence of growing up in a household full of boys and with a father that dotes on my swordsmanship," Heloise coos. "I trust you'll keep my secret as well as you keep hers." She points her perfectly squared chin at me.

Lief nods, and I offer my wooden sword to Heloise. "Have a turn," I offer, more than curious about her ability.

She flicks a glance at the sword as though it's a dead rat. "If that were steel, I'd be tempted to say yes. But alas, my mother forbids me to play with swords outside the walls of the chateau." She sighs. "It's her golden rule. As long as I don't break it, I don't lose my privileges."

"Or your reputation," I muse.

But she shrugs at that. "Not all of us can afford to be reckless. Now Lief, if you don't mind, I'd like to oversee my future queen's training."

Lief's brows rise quizzically at Heloise's back as she retreats to the stone bench near the arched walkway.

I let out a soft laugh. "I told you she was different."

Turning to me, Lief shakes his head and readies his stance. "She thinks I'm a boob," he scoffs quietly.

He's right to feel offended, as he is quite the opposite.

"Don't show off."

Lief returns my smile, and his expression is nothing short of innocent. "Never."

Deceivingly disarming indeed.

In the days that follow, Heloise's presence becomes somewhat of an elixir, spreading life and warmth through my barren heart. Most days, when she's not occupied by the social engagements her mother plans for her, she shows up unannounced, content to watch us train from the bench in stoic silence.

"My mother is desperate to find me a suitor," she tells me one day as we stroll arm in arm through the gardens. "Regrettably, she has her work cut out for her."

I laugh. "I find that hard to believe."

Her full lips curve in amusement. "Looks will only get you so far; my mother has yet to introduce me to a boy whose attraction to me runs deeper than his intimidation."

Unlike me, Heloise loves being at court. While I prefer to avoid the gossip, she soaks it up like a sponge. Extravagant entertainment, she calls it. In the span of a single week, she's dragged me to more games and hunts than I've attended in the past five months, and I can't tell what surprises those in attendance more, that I bother to show up, or that I'm Heloise's companion. I meet her strapping brothers: Marcus, the charming, ambitious athlete—a favorite among the ladies, Heloise tells me; Humphrey, the reckless prodigal son with a mischievous and teasing smile identical to his sister's; Arthur, the pragmatic businessman; and Tristan, the youngest, who is too shy for conversation and seems to prefer brooding in his brothers' shadows. I think I like him the best. As different as they all are, they seem to get along well, never too far from one another, as if tied by some invisible, brotherly string. And oh, how they dote on their sister. Their affection for her is as transparent as water. Even the reclusive Tristan can't help but smile when she draws near; it's no wonder Heloise is so bold and fearless. Anyone who crosses her would have to answer to her band of brothers.

For once, time passes like a welcome breeze, and I look forward to getting out of bed each morning, to partake in whatever it is Heloise might have in store. A whole week abundant with sun and shared laughs and wine comes and goes, and before I know it, it's Wintertide.

With Lorette in step behind us, Heloise and I walk through the open doors into the firelit Feast Hall. The enormous, majestic room is so packed with courtiers that I can't even see the tables. It's hard to see anything besides the decorations on the walls, plastered with painstakingly detailed tapestries of winter in various splendid shades of blue. At the far end of the hall, a pair of illustrious blue-and-gold banners sprawls down the length of the great stained-glass windows that serve as a backdrop for the dais. In all my evenings at supper, I've never seen this hall so crammed with people. Every lord and lady in the kingdom is here tonight, hailing from provinces near and far, and the vast hall is hardly large enough to fit them all. Above, the gallery is filled with musicians who fiddle their pipes and strings, their festive music spilling down below.

As my gaze scans the crowd, my heart hitches at the sight of a stitched golden lion on a familiar navy-blue jacket. Connor wore that same uniform the night of the ball. The memory comes alive like a black-and-white painting suddenly blooming with color. The light of the chandeliers illuminates the extravagant fixtures of the hall, and I can almost feel the fabric of that fated blue dress, before the stain of blood ruined it. I see those enigmatic dark eyes, scolding me over a cup of wine I shouldn't drink. His words echo in my ear, and I want to drown in the sound of them, in that voice. I'd give anything to hear it just one more time. The soldier in my sights turns, his face that of a stranger, just as I expected, and yet I can't escape the crushing disappointment it brings.

I snatch a goblet from a passing servant's platter and bring it to my lips, tilting my head back. The long-sleeved lilac bodice of my gown might survive a stain or two, but the white skirt below the belted golden ribbon at my waist would prove most unforgiving. As I wipe the corner of my lips, I catch Lorette's disapproving scowl. She looks as plain and prudish as any other day, clad in her favorite dull-gray dress, her dark hair neatly hidden away in the same plain low bun she always wears. I might have pitied her for not being able to wear anything else tonight, almost invisible with all the bright colors around her, but the pride in her eyes and posture is hard to miss. She values her station. It's no wonder she frets so around me. I mustn't make her job easy.

"Starting without me, are you?" Heloise asks, fetching a goblet for herself.

And to Lorette's never-ending mortification, we fill our cups, as we have in the days prior, leaving the comfort of the entrance and delving deep into the swarm of courtiers buzzing around the long rows of trestle tables. Pairs of eyes peer at us as we pass, some more inconspicuously than others, unsure of what to make of the pair of us. I recognize people as one might recognize faces in a painting. They're familiar strangers, people I might have exchanged a cordial word or two with before. But the wine makes it easy to smile at them, and my smile widens when they politely return the gesture, encouraging me onward through the hall to my dutiful place near the dais.

But there is one name in the crowd I do remember.

Even now, at such a festive occasion, his eyes remain cold and unforgiving. Grand Councilor Rowan mingles with his retinue of councilmen, and when we push through the crowd nearby I catch snippets of conversation that sound unsurprisingly political. Thankfully, none of them mention Stonefall or my father.

After what seems like an eternity, we reach the foot of the dais, where servants work to set a roasted turkey and a steaming pig over a platter of decorative greens atop the royal table. Fourteen tall chairs strapped in leather border the grand piece of carved chestnut wood. Generous servings of breads, cheeses, and pumpkins, and heaping bowls of bright, colorful citrus fruit fill the length of the table.

Not a minute later, the trumpet fanfare echoes through the hall, followed by the herald's announcement of the king and queen, and the crown prince. The crowd impossibly parts in two, crammed to each side of the hall as the trumpets continue to blare, and the king and queen come into view, looking every bit like a walking masterpiece of eye-catching fabrics and jewels. Queen Edith dazzles in tones of amber and gold, and unlike her many other beautiful gowns, this one is accentuated with a full-length golden cape that flows with each of her steps, lined with a ruffled gray collar that reaches to the nape of her neck. King Perceval is attired in like colors, embodying the very image of a powerful monarch. I can't help but think of Father, who dressed as opulently, only he never needed a festive occasion to do so. The pair offers gracious smiles to their subjects as they pass. Ethan tags a few paces behind his parents, looking rather majestic himself in a long black jacket brocaded with silver. His hair is parted to the side at an angle, keeping his long bangs away from his well-defined face.

The royal entourage of three walks up the dais and turns to the crowd, silencing the trumpets.

"Lords and ladies of Alder." King Perceval spreads his arms wide. "Once more, we come together to celebrate winter," he begins, speaking with emphatic pauses, his voice booming through the Feast Hall. "Tonight, we honor our ancestors. We honor their legacy. We honor the future they have laid out for us. And as always, we honor you, the people of Alder. All of you present tonight, and all those celebrating in the streets of our cities and our towns at this very moment, you are the soul of this kingdom, and it's an honor to serve as your king."

Ethan's smile for his father is wide and proud. Queen Edith stands with her chin held high, gleaming at the gathered court as it roars in enthusiasm, their applause steadfast for several seconds, a unified echo booming in my ears, and when it finally tapers off, the king pivots to his right, an outstretched arm in my direction. "On this special evening, I would also like to formally present our guest of honor: Princess Meredith of Stonefall."

Hundreds of eyes are on me. My cheeks flush, and I hear a soft chuckle from Heloise, but Perceval holds up his goblet and calls for a toast in honor of my birthday. An army of cups follows, raised to the ceiling, lowered a second later and emptied at the king's invitation.

Before silence ensues, he encourages his guests to enjoy the food and drink, and the words work like magic. People come alive around their neighbors, leaving all thoughts of my awkward introduction forgotten at the bottom of their goblets. Bards, jugglers, and puppeteers cycle through the tables, the echo of their music and voices begin to fill the air with celebration. Across the hall, on a setup stage, a small group of thespians start their play, enacting what looks like a battle, pivoting and striking with play swords in rehearsed fashion. I chuckle to myself, wondering if that's what Heloise thinks of when she watches Lief and me spar.

Heloise's eyes flare when she turns to me. "I can't believe you didn't tell me it's your birthday," she chides.

"Actually, it was a few days ago."

She scoffs. "That's even worse. How ever should I punish you?"

"I hear she hates dancing," Ethan says in greeting to Heloise when he joins us, seeming pleasantly surprised to see her in my company.

Heloise curtsies like it's a dance, slow and elegant. "Your Highness."

"Lady Cresten. How does your family do?"

"They are well, thank you."

"And your father, does he still hunt?"

"Quite often, much to my mother's chagrin; the countess is very fond of animals."

"So I've heard," Ethan replies with a knowing smile. Then he leans in to me and says, "Has Lady Cresten mentioned her father is the best hunter this court has ever seen?"

I shoot Heloise a sly glance. "She has not."

"You spend too much time with Marcus, Your Highness. He's the one who gloats."

Ethan laughs, nodding. "That he does. How does your brother fare? I haven't seen him since the match."

"He is yet licking his wounds." Heloise's smirk peeks out from behind her goblet as she takes a sip. "He's not accustomed to losing."

"I wouldn't be opposed to a rematch," Ethan offers, pragmatic.

"Oh, I'll be happy to tease him with that," she says, curtsying good-bye to join her family. "Don't get into any trouble without me," she murmurs under her breath to me before she goes on her way, disappearing into the crowd in search of her brothers.

Ethan rubs his thumb at the side of his temple, eyes bright with mirth as he turns to me.

"What?" I ask.

"It shouldn't surprise me that you're the only lady at court at ease in Heloise's company. Had I known you would get along so well, I'd have introduced you months ago."

"What shouldn't surprise you is that she's the only lady at court who's at ease in *my* company—besides Lorette, of course," I say with a glance at my perpetually silent lady-in-waiting, who keeps her head piously lowered in Ethan's presence.

"Nonsense! The ladies don't fear you. They simply don't"—he eyes the crowd and shrugs—"understand you."

I frown, following Ethan's gaze, observing the array of smiles and gestures of friendly conversation throughout the hall, and find Rose looking in our direction. Noting my attention, she darts her eyes back to the ladies around her. It takes me a minute to recall her surname.

"Lady Heron," I say, unsure of how to broach the subject without prying too much. "Heloise tells me she is next in line to wed you."

"Rose," he says, nodding, but his face remains blank. "She's a sweet girl. Have you met her?"

Sweet and beautiful, I think. "Briefly." I return my gaze back to the lady in question, but she's gone. "I found her very agreeable."

Her sister, on the other hand . . .

"She is," Ethan agrees, but offers nothing else, leaving me to wonder if it's because he has nothing more to say, or because he'd rather keep his thoughts to himself.

While scanning the crowd, I'm drawn to the play again. The theatrical battle seems to be reaching its end, except there's no apparent victor. It dawns on me then that the few plays I've seen at Alder court have all been comedies, lighthearted entertainment meant to draw laughs.

"Interesting choice for a play," I mutter.

"Not just any play." Ethan takes a small sip of wine. "It's the Battle of the Storm, the reason we celebrate winter."

"Oh." I meet Ethan's stare, intrigued. I know so little of Alder's people and its history. Yet another reason to return to the library. "I'd love to hear about it."

Ethan's eyes light up, seeming happy to oblige. "The Elders—our ancestors—ruled this realm for centuries. Back then, before the kingdom was forged, they called it Aldergard, after the first Elder. The old scrolls tell of many who came and tried to take the land from them. Some battles were lost, but the Elders reclaimed those lands, and over the centuries, as the population grew, the territory expanded. The Elders believed they were pioneers, discovering the uninhabitable lands of the North and learning how to survive the perpetual cold. But eventually, the Elders ventured into the mountains and stumbled on Lucari territory."

"Lucari?" The word feels out of place on my tongue.

"Savages," he explains. "Some refer to them as wolf people. They live in a system of caves that tunnel the White Mountains."

"Is that who your ancestors defeated in the Battle of the

Storm?" I ask, watching the spectators clap at the thespians on the makeshift stage.

"The Elders fought the Lucari, but they did not defeat them."

I look up at him. "Alder celebrates a lost battle?"

"Not exactly. The scrolls speak of a massive, blinding blizzard, the likes of which Alder had never seen. No man could have survived that without strong shelter and a large fire. It forced an end to what would have been a massacre; the Lucari had the higher ground, and they outnumbered the Elders. Had the battle come to pass, we likely wouldn't be here enjoying this wine," he says, sipping from his goblet.

"The storm saved your people," I mutter in understanding.

"The Maker was on our side," he says with a nod, reverence gleaming in his eyes.

"Did the Elders ever fight the Lucari again?"

Ethan shrugs. "If they did, there is no record of it. From what we learned of the old scrolls in the library, the Elders never returned to the mountains, and there is no mention of the Lucari after the Battle of the Storm. Scroll scholars interpret the aftermath of the battle as something of a truce, where both sides remained on the defensive, waiting for the day the other would attack, but that day never came. With time, the Lucari became lore. Some used to believe the Lucari were nothing more than a folk legend, an old tale that children tell to scare one another."

I give him a blank look. "*Used to*?"

Ethan angles his head close to mine, and I can smell the tart sweetness of clementines and the bold oak aroma of the wine on his lips. "The Lucari surfaced again about a hundred years ago."

Queen Edith appears at Ethan's side then, and I release the curious breath caught in my chest.

"Ethan, the food is getting cold. Why don't the two of you continue this over dinner?" she says, all smiles and tenderness, gesturing a palm to the empty seats at the royal table; Ethan really does soften her sharp edges. The music and entertainment continue down the aisles between the joined trestle tables, but most of the lords and ladies are already enjoying the food.

I ask Ethan to finish the story. His smile is discreet, pleased at my interest. "A small group of elk hunters lost their way in the snow," he begins as a servant pushes my chair in. "Thick clouds covered the sky that day. There was nothing to give them a sense of direction. All they could see was the vastness of the snow. If they left it to chance, they risked going farther into the Snowlands and running out of food, or finding themselves in a freezing storm without shelter. Their only choice was to go up the mountain."

A bard makes his way to our table, singing poetic verses to the tune of his lute, and I have to lean into Ethan's shoulder so that he can hear me. "So what happened?" I ask.

Ethan glances at the food on his plate and pauses. "I should warn you. This part of the story is not one to share over dinner." He makes a face. "It's a bit . . . gruesome."

I might have hesitated if I was hungry. "I can handle it."

"One of the hunters got separated from the group, and Lucari ambushed them," Ethan continues. "He hid behind a rock and watched the whole thing. Some of the details are probably embellished, but the story goes that the Lucari hung the hunters by their ankles and slit their throats to collect their blood, and then cut off their limbs"—his voice lowers an octave—"and *ate* them."

I feel my face blanch as my lips pull back in revulsion. "Cannibals?"

Ethan gulps his wine as if trying to swallow away the unpleasant topic of conversation. "The old scrolls mention this behavior, and it's likely why the Lucari were reduced to folklore over the years. It makes them sound like monsters. And perhaps they are, but we've recently learned they don't do it for sport. It's more a"—he extrapolates with his hands—"matter of survival than anything else."

Somehow, that doesn't make me feel any better.

"Learned how?" I ask.

"Captain Westwend was their captive for a year. He—"

"Connor?" I blurt out despite myself, dropping my fork on the plate. Spoken out loud, his name feels odd in my tongue. Like the name of someone I knew from another lifetime.

"His father, the former captain of the King's Guard," Ethan corrects me, blind to the brief slip of my heart. "He was scouting the Snowlands on a hunt for a traitor when he and his men were attacked by Lucari."

"How old was Connor when this happened?"

Ethan presses his lips in thought for a second before replying.

"I was twelve years old at the time, so that would make him thirteen or fourteen. His mother had passed years before, and he was all alone in his family's estate, so my father sent for him to live with us here . . ." His thoughts lure him away for a moment, glossed in nostalgia. "Connor and I were good friends from childhood, but it was during those months that we became brothers," he says quietly, and the fond, bittersweet smile that tugs at his lips makes my throat go tight.

I try not to think about how lonely Connor must have felt after his father's disappearance, probably thinking he'd lost him, too.

"Did the Lucari give the captain back his freedom?"

"He escaped. The tribe that held the captain prisoner was attacked by another Lucari tribe. Amid all the commotion, his cage was broken, and he was able to break free. He was skin and bones and on his way to the Maker when a merchant found him collapsed on a road east of the city, nothing but a ghost of the mighty captain; Connor hardly recognized him."

I clear my throat. "What about his men?"

Ethan starts cutting into the turkey leg on his plate. "All dead. Captain Westwend came to understand the Lucari kept him alive so they could study him. The leader of that tribe was curious about him. Of us. He said the Lucari would attempt to communicate with him, teach him their tongue..." He gestures pointedly at the pile on my plate. "You haven't touched your food."

The stewed squash has gone cold, but I force a forkful into

my mouth and chew it anyway. When Ethan doesn't continue right away, I ask in a quiet voice, "So the Lucari ate human flesh out of necessity?" I realize my terrible timing as Ethan stops to look at me midchew, but after an awkward pause, he forces his food down and nods.

"The captain observed the Lucari way of life as ruthless. Food is scarce in the White Mountains; it makes survival difficult, so they eat all manner of flesh. Animal or human. Anyone who is an outsider to a tribe is considered fair game. Lucari, or Alderian, or snow leopard—it makes no difference to them."

I feel disgusted and fascinated all at once. "But Alder has the largest army in the world at its disposal. You could defeat them if you wanted to, couldn't you?"

"Lucari continue to have the higher ground, and they know those mountains well. They could easily kill a large number of us before we scaled up the terrain. Not to mention, we don't know what kind of numbers to expect, or how many tribes there are. The Lucari have lived up there for centuries, just as we have lived down here. There could be thousands of them for all we know. But they don't seem to have an interest in our lands. Aside from the ambush of Captain Westwend and his men, which was likely a trespass on his part, they have not given us reason to attack."

I look down at my plate. The roasted turkey leg stares back at me, daring me to bite its flesh. Do humans taste any different? I fight back a gag. *Animal flesh, Meredith. It's animal flesh.* I wonder if this why Heloise's mother doesn't eat meat.

I feel eyes on me. Resentful eyes.

"Does Councilor Rowan always look so cross?" I ask Ethan, cutting the squash into smaller pieces just to give myself something to do.

I figure Ethan must have eyed Rowan, because when I glance up again, his glare is elsewhere.

"He has for years, since the disappearance of his son," Ethan whispers, leaning slightly toward me. "It was a long time ago, so it's no excuse, but I doubt Rowan ever recovered. He's grown more bitter through the years." Ethan's lips press into an emphatic thin line as he looks back in Rowan's direction. "I suppose time can't mend all wounds."

"I'm sorry to hear it." Despite my dislike of the man, I can't help but pity him. I've fallen through the shattered hole of a dark past myself, one I haven't quite managed to get out of. "No one knows what became of his son?"

"There was no trace of him. He was declared dead on the first anniversary of his disappearance, and a small ceremony was held in the gardens."

He says something else, but his words are drowned by the blare of the trumpets, announcing that it's time for the first dance, signaling to those who are interested to make way to the center of the hall.

"Ethan, darling, you should ask our guest of honor for a dance," the queen primly suggests from across the table, setting off alarm bells in my head.

"Of course, Mother," Ethan replies, rising from his chair as I remain frozen in mine. When he meets my eye, I try the most dreadful expression I can muster. To no avail. He takes my hand in his and pulls me to my feet.

"I can't dance!" I whisper angrily.

He ignores me. "Five months ago, you didn't know how to fight either," he says over his shoulder.

"That's different," I hiss, not knowing what else to say.

I can hear the laughter in his voice. "Is it? You can tell me all about it while we dance."

The harps and cellos start to play, and I feel anxiety rise to my throat. "*Ethan!*" I whisper again, pulling uselessly to free my hand of his gentle yet firm grip.

"Just follow my lead," I hear him say over the music. I have to say something, else I embarrass him—and myself—only the words to express just what a disaster I am as a dance partner fail me. "I've got you," he whispers, grinning like a child who's been given candy, and wraps an arm around the small of my back. "Step onto my feet."

I stare at him. "What?"

His eyes point me down. "Go on, step on me."

Well, *that* I can do. Gingerly, I place one foot atop his, and then the other, holding on to his shoulders for balance, and like a ripple through water, he sways us around the other couples, moving to the music with effortless elegance.

He gives me a crooked smile, pleased with himself.

"See? It's not so bad, is it?"

So far. "There's still plenty of time for things to go awry."

He lifts a sly brow. "You hint at sabotage?"

"Sabotage comes naturally to my feet," I warn him, and a smirk breaks across his face.

"I think I like this side of you," he says, his eyes appraising me.

"What side is that? Clumsy and afraid?"

He pauses, his expression turning to something that wants to pierce through me, but he doesn't get to answer.

Seemingly out of nowhere, Councilor Milus appears at Ethan's side to whisper something in his ear.

Whatever the councilor says to him, it sobers Ethan. He whips back to face me, and in one breath he says, "Come with me."

"What—" I try to ask, but he's on the move, chasing Milus through the crowded hall with fevered steps. I stay on Ethan's heels as he and Milus wind through the gaps in the crowd, skirting around dancing couples who flow to the music, the happy rhythm at odds with the uneasiness that creeps up my arms. By chance, I glimpse Heloise on the dance floor, lush with wine, smiling up at the young man who holds her hand, her bright scarlet gown distinct among the pastels around her. In my distraction, I bump elbows with a woman. She gives me a look, but I can't bother with apologies. Ethan and Milus move so fast I can barely keep up, and I'm falling behind. I press my feet to catch up, ignoring the unbridled gasps and murmurs that follow me as I carve my own path through the crowd.

To my relief, they wait for me in the candlelit passage outside the Feast Hall, where the music and conversations dwindle to echoes in the background.

Ethan clutches his hands like he can't be still. The look on his face prickles my scalp.

My voice is a thin, wary whisper. "What is it?"

"The mercenaries have returned from Talos . . . he's here."

10

Connor

With the added weight of the weapons and a dead body, Beast's pace is slower than usual. I'm anxious to put some distance between us and the village, but our leisurely gait blends with the flow of the square. The dead redcloak stuffed in our cart basked in the thrill of uncovering a crime, and these other soldiers are probably no different. Still, for soldiers keeping watch, they're inattentive, their eyes lazy and unfocused, yawning and slouching, or laughing at the expense of villagers; the plight of the people is their entertainment. I see now how fortunate Asher is to live outside the village, a fact he's no doubt well aware of. I'd assumed he'd tasked Raven with the grove because he himself was too old, but after everything I've seen today, I think that's the furthest thing from the truth.

"There are no bandits, are there?" I ask as soon as the village blurs behind us.

"I'd be a fool to make a deal with their kind," Asher says, scratching the white scruff at his jaw.

"So who are the weapons for?" I ask, unsure if he'll feed me another lie.

Asher squints at the farms and fields that speck the valley.

He's looked troubled since we left Flynn's shop. "They call themselves the Brotherhood."

"Who are they?" I prod when he doesn't continue.

He waves his wounded hand in front of him, a red blotch now stained on both sides of the rag wrapped around it. "The resistance, rebels, outlaws . . . take your pick. They banded together after the Takeover, and now they are the only hope we have left. The Usurper thought he could crush our spirits. He thought the more atrocities his soldiers committed against us, the less likely we'd be to rise against him. Aye, he was wrong. He just doesn't know it yet. And there's nothing better than a fooled enemy," he says with a pointed finger.

"So you're a part of this organization?"

He doesn't answer straightaway. "I shouldn't be telling you any of this. The only reason our operation has worked thus far is because we've managed to keep it a secret. Not just from the enemy, but from our own. The Brotherhood's leader doesn't like taking unnecessary risks."

"And yet you bring me along to help you carry out one of their tasks," I say, and Asher falls silent. Am I the only exception to his oath of secrecy? I wonder. "Does Raven know?"

"No. And I intend to keep it that way," he warns me.

I shrug. "It's not my secret to tell. But what happens when this leader finds out you've told me?"

"You mean, *if* he finds out?" He pulls on Beast's bridle to yank him off a tuft of grass on the side of the road. "I'm not sure I want to know the answer to that."

We bury the mangled soldier near a bush miles away from the grove. By the time we return to the cottage, the sun is making its descent behind the mountains. Raven is pacing by the front door when we arrive, hands perched on her waist. Her head snaps in our direction as we come within sight, and she runs to meets us at the shed, where I help Asher unhook the cart from Beast's straps.

"What took ya so long?" she asks, arms folded at her chest.

"Didn't mean to worry you, my sweet girl," Asher says in a honeyed voice. She fixes on the cart, and a deep crease spreads across her temple.

"You hardly sold anything," she tells him.

"We'll make do."

"Why's your hand bleeding?" she frets, noticing the bandaged hand. She tries to reach for it, but Asher pulls away. He settles Beast and locks him in the shed, making no move for the burlap sack of weapons buried in the cart. He dusts his hands on his trousers before he rests them on Raven's shoulders. "It was an accident," he says dismissively before walking off toward the candlelit cottage.

Raven turns her frown to me. "Did something happen?"

It irks me to keep things from her when she's been nothing but open with me, but I have to respect Asher's wishes.

"There was a woman in the square screaming for her missing son," I say, and she assimilates the news with no trace of surprise, the strained lines on her face showing only a muted rage.

She lets out a defeated breath. "Things seem to be getting worse by the day." Her distant gaze sharpens on me. "I was really worried when you two didn't come home."

"I wouldn't worry too much," I reassure her, remembering the way Asher snapped the dead soldier's limbs.

Back in the confines of the cottage, the smell of peas and burned bread clings to the walls. Raven rushes to the hearth, removing the bread from the fire and dropping it on the table. "I hope you don't mind a bit of char on your loaves," she mutters.

Asher takes a loaf and bites off a blackened corner. "A little burned flavor never—"

A racket at the front door, silencing the kitchen, save for the sound of simmering soup and the pop of the fire.

Asher slips the one knife on the table inside his sleeve. Raven remains in the kitchen, shooting nervous glances my way while Asher snakes to the door, burned loaf still in his grip. I take Raven's hand and slink back through the corridor, placing us out of view behind the turn, just a step from Asher's room, ready to sprint for his weapon stash if need be.

Another series of angry knocks shakes the door, ringing through the cottage like warning bells. Asher reaches for the handle, and my body goes still, my eyes homed in on the slit of space that widens as he pulls the door open.

The bloody face of a woman screams at Asher. "They took him! They took him!"

Asher takes her in and shuts the door. The woman's face is

grotesquely disfigured with bulging, bruised skin. Her right eye is swollen shut, the other is red with tears. Her lips are split open and bleeding, her shift and bodice torn, ripped around her middle, exposing an indecent amount of skin.

Raven makes a beeline for the woman. She attempts to guide her away, but the woman won't budge, shaking Raven's cautious hands off her shoulders.

"They took him!" she wails again, her voice breaking with sobs.

"Where did they take him?" Asher asks.

"T' the cages—they're going t' hang him in the morning!"

Asher lifts a hand to his eyes, giving himself a moment. But the woman won't have that.

"You have t' help him," she pleads through her bloody, trembling lips.

"I'll do what I can." He turns to Raven. "Get Margie cleaned up."

Margie reluctantly agrees to be led down the corridor but stops short at the sight of me. She crosses her arms across her half-exposed chest, suddenly self-aware. Once they disappear into the bath, I approach a sullen-looking Asher. He asked Margie no questions, so I make the only assumption I can.

"Is it Flynn?"

His lips tighten. "Aye." He nods down the corridor. "That's his wife in there." Then he slams a fist into the wooden wall behind him. "The fool! I told him to leave. Margie will suffer even more now."

"What's the plan then?"

Asher laughs bitterly. "There is no plan . . . we can't help him."

I lower my voice so that only he can hear. "What about the Brotherhood?"

He shakes his head, and a grimace curves his lips. "His fate is in the hands of the Gods now."

"Then why give his wife false hope?" I ask; the woman will be crushed when she learns the truth.

His eyes turn to slits. "Didn't you see the poor lass?" he whispers in anger. "She's falling apart! Would you have the heart to look at that face, after *Gods* know what she just went through to get here, and tell her there's nothing to be done?"

"Yes," I say automatically.

Asher rounds on me. "I suppose it's easier to be cruel when you don't have skin in the game," he sneers.

As much as his defensiveness irks me, I can't fault him for it; his friend is about to hang.

11

Meredith

I walk at Ethan's side through the dim corridor of the castle prison, ignoring the shifting shadows behind the bars we pass. The prison's warden leads us through the darkness by the glow of torchlight. The lack of smell surprises me. It's musty and cold—typical for a dungeon—but the human stench is hardly noticeable.

While on a tour of the castle shortly after I arrived, Lorette told me King Perceval had this prison built for a certain breed of criminals: traitors to the crown, enemies of the state. From spies to conspirators, they all get locked up in here. Other criminals, from thieves to murderers, get thrown into the city prison. It's too cold a climate to have loophole windows in the cells, so these prisoners live their days without even a glimpse of sunlight or the occasional caress of the wind or the calming song of birds. They have only dampness and torchlight and the jangle of metal. I can almost feel the misery seeping from the walls. Traitors though they may be, it's hard not to pity their coughs and whispered moans, sentenced to live the rest of their days in this place.

My breath hitches as we press deeper into the prison, down flights of rough-cut stone steps and a labyrinth of corners. I begin to feel oddly out of control with a barrage of emotions coursing through me. I don't know what to expect, only that it can't be anything good.

We stop on the lowest level where there is only one cell. A well-lighted one. Torches burn hot and bright at each corner, driving away the cold. Two guards block my view of the prisoner. One turns to open the iron gate, and the other steps out of the way. The prisoner comes into full view then. Chains hanging from the ceiling bind each of his arms, keeping him on his feet. His head droops, as though unconscious, covered in a curtain of unkempt strawberry-blond locks.

That's all it takes for my body to tense, for rage to stampede through my veins, pulsing and pounding hatred with each heartbeat.

As if sensing me, the prisoner raises his head and looks straight at me. His nose is bloody, his right eye swollen shut, but he peers at me with his left, the gleam cutting me like a dagger. Seconds crawl, freezing me in time. He smirks, slowly and deliberately, revealing bloodstained teeth.

I feel robbed that someone else has already begun what I intend to finish.

Elijah's voice comes like a punch to the stomach. "Hello, Princess."

My shaking limbs scream at me to lunge, to tear him apart with my bare hands, to make him feel all the pain he caused.

I don't know how I keep myself grounded to the stone below my heels.

"Is this he?" Ethan asks.

I nod as Elijah eyes me appraisingly.

"Rage suits you."

I squeeze my eyes closed for a second, trying and failing to clamp down on the loathing that thrashes inside me. I see Holt's eyes as they glaze over, facing death under the moon's gaze, Elijah's dagger sticking out from his chest. Holt was *my friend.* The one who could always make me laugh no matter the situation. The friend who shared my childhood, despite the starkly different lives we lived, and made my world all the better for it. But now he's gone, burned like a pest in a forest without proper burial, and I'll never see him again.

And Connor . . .

A painful swallow makes its way down my throat, and I stop my train of thought, refusing to remember the rest.

"You killed them," I whisper, seething.

"Them?" he asks. "I've killed many, Your Highness. You'll have to be more specific than that."

He's playing with me, but I'm unable to contain myself. "My friends," I hiss.

"Oh. Right. Is that why I'm here?" Elijah grins. "Guilty as charged. Do you miss them? I could arrange a meeting, if you like."

His flippancy enrages Ethan, who marches past me and swings a fist at Elijah's face. Elijah spits blood and smiles in spite of it.

"You're going to let Prince Charming do all the work for you?" he taunts.

In quick succession, Ethan lands a punch on Elijah's left eye, then another in his gut. Elijah's arms pull uselessly against the shackles, his body unable to curl over the pain. Once he recovers his breath, he levels an amused, knowing eye on me. "He doesn't know, does he?"

My lips part of their own accord as I stare at Elijah, which only gives him more satisfaction.

In all my rage and misery, I failed to remember.

He'd seen us.

Connor and I had been seconds away from a kiss when he barged in that night in the forest. Connor tried to reassure me; he wanted me to know that he'd fight for us even though the odds were against us . . .

Or perhaps that's what he wanted me to believe.

"Know what?" Ethan asks.

"Ah, but it doesn't matter now, does it?" Elijah says, winking with his swelling left eye.

If I clench my jaw any tighter, I might crack a tooth. I've had enough of his mocking face and his laughing smiles: his death is long overdue. Blinded with hatred, I go for Ethan's scabbard, yanking his sword free.

But Ethan is on me before I can wield the blade.

"Meredith, don't." His voice is an order, but his eyes beseech me.

"He deserves to die," I hiss, eyes pinned on Elijah, cold and determined. Isn't this why he sits in the lowest level of this prison?

Ethan pries the sword from my unwilling fingers. "What he deserves is to suffer," he whispers, vehement, as though uttering a creed.

"You know, come to think of it, he didn't die that night," Elijah quips from behind us.

I feel my heart skip a beat, my brain grasping at threads of memory.

The bodies were burned beyond recognition. Is that why he did it? To tease me later? I assumed Elijah was covering his tracks, leaving no discernible evidence of Talos's presence. The guards said as much.

I don't dare hope, and still, I find myself whispering, "He's alive?"

"You should see the looks on your faces." Elijah chuckles. Then, cruelly, he adds, "I almost wish he were alive. Imagine the kind of leverage I would have over the two of you! Truly, though, I had every intention of keeping him alive. But alas, patience is not a virtue of mine."

"What did you do to him?" Ethan growls.

Unruffled, Elijah tells us: "I was bringing him home with me to Talos. He did such a fine job of protecting the princess, and I thought: *Why waste his talents? Why not make him one of my personal guards?* All I needed was a little"—he deliberates, twisting his lips for the right word—"persuasion. It wasn't a bad plan, and it worked for a time, but I was ill equipped for the long trek." He shrugs. "What can I say? Even the most perfect of men can't anticipate everything."

The nonchalance in his words makes bile rise in my throat. I want to stick a knife in his gut and twist it to his last breath.

"Connor would never serve you," Ethan scoffs in disgust.

"Oh, but he did." Elijah's smile widens with each word, his split lip cracking and bleeding. "And it gives me so *much* satisfaction knowing he spent his last days serving me."

Before I know what I'm doing, my clenched fist slams into his bloodied face, knuckles to cheekbone, shooting satisfying pain up my arm.

Elijah laughs that mocking, *awful* laugh. Delirious with hate, my hands are at his throat, squeezing so hard it hurts. Even when Elijah's laugh is cut short, he smirks at me, flashing a set of bloodied teeth.

Suddenly, Ethan's hands are on my arms, staunchly and forcefully pulling me away from Elijah. Away from my vengeance. From *justice*. He drags me in all my wrath up the steps and through corridors and out into the cold, away from the ears of the prison guards, where the wintry night air blows by, draping us with its numbing bite. But I don't feel it. I feel as though I'm boiling inside.

Ethan finally lets me go, and I glare up at him, nostrils flared. *"Why?"*

Beneath the anger, the question is but a plea. How can he rob me of this, when it's all I've thought of for months?

"I loved Connor like a brother; you think I don't want to split Elijah apart?" Ethan's shaking, and not from the cold. "Don't you see? This is what he's after. It's clear he wants to get under our skin—and it's working." He breathes hard, and his eyes flash with a feral glint. "I want to rip out his entrails and stuff them down his own throat!"

"I'll do it for you." *Gladly.*

I take a step toward the prison, but so does Ethan, blocking the entrance. Not that he needs to. He could simply order the guards to deny me. Though his face is unreadable, I see the wildness that overwhelmed him seconds ago fade.

"Death would be a kindness," he says in soft bitterness. "We can't let him off so easily . . . not after everything he's done."

Elijah *should* suffer, I silently agree. But how he dies doesn't matter to me. Slow or swift, painful or merciful, I don't care. The Maker will see to his eternal suffering. I want him dead, and I want to be the one who ends him.

"We can make his death a very painful one," I say. Part of me feels like a stranger for saying it; ladies aren't supposed to think such violent thoughts. I should feel ashamed, but I'm too heartbroken, too vindictive to care.

Ethan lowers his gaze. Then, in a subdued rage that mirrors my own, he whispers, "I could break every bone and set each of his limbs on fire, and it still wouldn't be enough."

He lifts his eyes to look at me when I remain silent and must see the desperation in my face.

"He *will* die. I promise you." His hands take hold of mine, and his eyes bore into me, pleading and demanding. "Death should be his release, not his punishment."

Frustration builds in my chest. That isn't what I want. But I know Ethan will have his way, whether I like it or not.

"Then make him pay."

12

Connor

Villagers gather under the early morning sun, bathed in its subtle warmth and brightness, the noise and clamor of the previous day reduced to a memory among the colorless faces, and the scaffold they so willfully ignored now their focal point. Atop it, Flynn, the noose around his neck, looks on with the blank gaze of a man resigned to his fate. Asher couldn't let his friend die alone, and I couldn't let him come by himself. If I had, Raven would be here in my place. I recognize the woman next to Flynn. Her terrified, tear-streaked face is the same one that cried for her missing son yesterday at the market. What's her crime? Demanding the return of her child? How can they stand for this?

Asher and I push through the crowd, discreetly making our way to the front. Flynn sees us before we make it there. His eyes rake over me for only a second before they settle on Asher, and the two exchange small, discreet nods, a muted acceptance of the cards of fate, or the will of their Gods, as they like to say. But unlike Flynn, the woman pleads incessantly to the skies, to the averting eyes of the crowd, searching for salvation, and I feel my knuckles turn white.

There's nothing you can do.

A man with a stone-cold expression and white hair strides up the platform. Missing the infamous red cloak and armor, he dons a simple dark leather tabard over a tunic. This must be the commander the redcloaks spoke of. The crowd was silent before, but now it seems even the wind has stopped dead in its tracks. Even the helpless woman has lulled to feeble whimpers.

The commander faces the crowd, a hand to the pommel of his sword, a dispassionate look on his long face. "Behold the fate of those who oppose our emperor," he exclaims as one of the soldiers joins him on the scaffold, stepping to the woman, who has regained her voice and uses it once more to let the world hear her panic. But the soldier kicks away the step her feet desperately cling to, and her screams are cut short with a choked cry.

I try and fail to swallow the revulsion inside me. But I make myself watch. When Flynn's turn comes, his body resists, clutching to that innate desire to live. His feet kick, struggling for that elusive step just out of reach, but his eyes are as resolute as they were before the noose went taut around his neck, and they hold on to Asher as though he's the one who will guide Flynn to the other side.

Amid the morbid silence of death, the commander surveys the faces in the crowd, eying the villagers with a calculated gaze, as though choosing his next victim . . .

And catches me watching.

I swiftly avert my gaze. As I wait, the silence ensues and I imagine those eyes lingering. I still my breath.

"That is all for today," the commander says. "Let this be a lesson to you all."

With those parting words, the commander marches down and takes his leave on horseback. The villagers stir, eyes downcast as they disperse.

Asher finally turns to me, faring even worse than the villagers do. A look of death stamps his ashen face as he staggers past me, quick to seek the support of Beast's frame.

Asher pulls Beast on and makes his way to his first customer as best he can. I keep a close distance but give him breadth to sort himself. The villagers who purchase our product utter as few words as possible. Some hands tremble as they provide him their coin. I search the shaken villagers for signs of outrage, for any trace of rebellion, and come up empty. These people are broken, mangled with the same fear I heard in the woman's pleas.

After two hours of bartering, Asher decides to call an end to his miserable day, leaving three full sacks left unsold in Beast's cart. He moves with purpose now, eager to leave the village behind us. I tag behind him like a shadow, keeping tabs on the soldiers we pass.

But trouble isn't done with me yet.

I find it just outside the village, in the form of a scraggly young boy.

Pip. The boy from the brush. He's fighting against the clutches of a soldier who taunts him with a ham bone. A gaunt, fragile-looking woman defends him. "Please, he's just hungry—he meant nothing by it—"

One of the other three soldiers strikes a hand across her face.

"Mama!" Pip squeals, squirming in the soldier's grasp.

"Connor." Asher's call is a warning. I ignore it, inching closer to the unfolding scene, when I feel his hand at my shoulder. "This is folly. We can't help them."

Pip's mother tries again for her son. She flings herself at the man who holds him captive. She tugs at his arm with a force only a mother in fear for her child could possess, prying Pip free, but the pair doesn't get a chance to run. The soldier turns. I see his face now. It's disfigured, a canvas of angry scars. In two fast strokes, he unsheathes his sword and plunges it into the mother's back. The blade slices clean through her torso.

Blood thumps loud in my ears, but nothing can drown the sound of Pip's screams.

The shrieking wails trigger a flash of memory: I'm hiding under a bed. I see a pair of bare feet, the hem of a chemise hovering over them like a curtain.

I blink and shelve the shred of memory. Now is not the time.

"Hurry home, Asher," I say over my shoulder as I shrug his hand off.

There's four of them, but a few shouts and the rest of the patrol will be alerted, so I have to be quick.

Tension coils my muscles as I creep up. The soldiers are distracted with Pip, enjoying his torment. The scarred one mocks the boy, and they laugh.

"Don't you worry, little rat, you'll join your mommy very soon," one of them says, but Pip has stopped crying. His bloodshot eyes fix on me as I come up from behind. My hands clasp the unsuspecting soldier's head. He flinches at my touch, and I snap his neck before he gets a chance to turn around.

The scarred one throws Pip aside and comes at me with his sword, still dripping with the woman's blood, while the other two paw at their scabbards. I unsheathe the sword from the dead man and throw the limp body at the scrambling soldier to my left, parrying the scarred one. Our weapons crash with sparks. He growls and tries for me again, arms slashing recklessly. I duck and twist out of the way, shoving him to the floor with a kick just as another soldier attacks. He swings his blade through the air. I lean away, but the tip of his sword manages to slice through my side.

I see Asher reaching for a stunned Pip. Then I snap back to block a strike, shoving a fist into the soldier's nose, feeling the crack of bones beneath my knuckles. I rush to slice at his torso, but the blade bites into leather and mail. The redcloak takes a step back, vulnerable. It's my chance to finish him, but the scarred one swoops back in. I block his sword inches from my face, and we circle each other. He bares his teeth, making him look more animal than human.

And then he charges.

His thrusts come at me seconds apart, relentless and fast, sweeping and slashing like a beast born from violence. My muscles burn as I continue to parry his blows, my clothes and hair sticking to the sweat on my skin. But another sword sweeps into my periphery. I lean back, parrying one blade and dodging the other, seeking the third soldier. He's limping toward the village.

Not good.

The scarred soldier rages on, but I don't have time for him to tire. The other soldier is coming at me from my right, sword pointed at my chest like a lance. Sword to sword, I push against the scarred one with all my strength, teeth grating, knuckles white, and swivel out of his way. His sword catches my shoulder, and I feel the burn of the cut as he stumbles forward, his throat connecting with the point of a sword meant for me, killing him instantly. Ignoring my stinging shoulder, I pivot and drive my sword into the other redcloak's belly. He's still shocked at seeing his own weapon through the scarred soldier's throat.

He lets out a hellish wail.

And I'm not the only one that hears it.

Soldiers have already been dispatched. Their boots thump toward me. I press my foot against the soldier's torso, pull the sword from his body, and kick him to the dirt. Wiping my brow, I let myself take a breath and assess my surroundings. Asher and Pip are gone.

Approaching soldiers' angry shouts ring louder and louder. I've got only a minute or two until a stampede of mail comes into view. I consider the road. Nothing but shrubby vegetation. Even with a head start, I'll be an easy target with nowhere to hide. And if any of the soldiers are smart enough to be riding a horse, there'll be no outrunning them then.

I drift back to the dead soldiers at my feet. The scarred one is on his knees, eyes vacant, mouth gaping and drooling blood, sword sticking like a rod through his neck. The other lies on his side over a bed of blood and filth, twitching and breathing his last breaths.

And it comes to me then.

It's risky, and there's no guarantee it will work, but it's my best chance.

13

Meredith

I stare listlessly into the dark under the warm fur covers of my bed as the sky outside my balcony lightens with the approaching dawn. It's been hours. Every time I close my eyes, I see Elijah's face, I see that smirk, and my resentment surges back, warding off sleep.

This hate . . . it's taken hold of me . . . it's all I have.

Ethan's proposition weighs heavy on my thoughts. I've run circles around it all night. If we let Elijah live so that he may suffer, I worry that with time, Ethan will convince himself not to end him, and to let him rot in jail instead.

But Elijah must die.

I will not be at peace until he does. And though I fear what will become of me when that day arrives, if carrying out my vengeance leaves me a soulless wretch, then so be it. It's a price I'm willing to pay; I'll drag Elijah to hell myself if I have to.

A loud, urgent pounding comes at my door. I swing my legs off the bed, scrambling, not pausing to grab a coat.

It's a guard. "My lady, your presence is required immediately in the king's office."

"Is something wrong?" I ask stupidly after him, but he disappears into the shadows as if he didn't hear me. The urgency in the guard's voice made it clear I shouldn't even consider waiting for Lorette to arrive, so I don't waste time trying to put on a dress, but at least I have the good sense to grab the long sleeveless fur coat folded over the chair and swing my arms through it. Not a minute later, I am rushing out the door, clumsily tying a leather belt around my waist as I scurry through the halls, taking sharp turns as I go, thinking the worst. Has Elijah escaped? Or have the king's troops returned with news from the Borderlands? Is King Perceval about to order me to pack my belongings and go home?

The empty halls are eerily quiet. Only a few servants cross my path; courtiers are not accustomed to rising before first light. My breath comes hard and my lungs beg me to slow down, but I urge my feet forward.

The ward, expecting me, moves to open the door when he sees me bend the corner. Lead-footed, I follow him into the chamber. The sun teases the dawning sky outside, its subtle light reaching through the windows, lighting the councilors' black robes. They're assembled around the king, their hard-nosed expressions absent. If the council was summoned, this must indeed be serious. There are no servants. Only Captain Offa and four of his men are present. Cups of wine litter the spacious map table, but I get the sense their contents have scarcely been touched. Among the men stands a dark-haired stranger in a maroon cape. Half of his mahogany hair is tied behind his head in a pigtail, the rest draping below his shoulders. He swivels to the sound of my entrance, and I see his face. A trimmed beard shadows the bottom of his chin, paired with an elegant mustache. My arrival stops him midsentence. His hooded silver eyes find me at the echo of the closing door, and for a split second, I think I'm staring at my father. I watch him approach, distracted by his armor, a fitted, eye-catching black set lined with gold, decorated with elaborate carvings of elegant patterns, with two dragons on each side of his breastplate and a golden bevor around his collarbone. He looks like a king ready for battle.

Ethan is beside me suddenly. He stands so close our arms brush, and I can feel just how tense he is, his hand ready at the hilt. A deep frown carves the space between his eyes, and his mouth is set in a grim line, a clear sign the caped stranger's presence is not welcome. The stranger addresses me, his canny voice echoing against the silence. "Meredith." My name rolls off his tongue like a purr as his gray eyes sweep over me. He takes my hand and brings it his to his lips, the tips of his mustache gently brushing my knuckles as he plants a small kiss. "At last we meet." He looks up at me from under his short lashes. "I see you have been blessed with Olivia's looks."

Hearing him say my mother's name is jarring, and I pull my hand away from his soft grip. I take in his incisive eyes, which seem to absorb me into a void, and the neatly combed hair specked with grays at the sides of his temple.

"Who are you?" I ask.

A smile forms underneath the mustache. "I'm your uncle."

I blink at him, mind whirring. Reading my face, he says, "I was never a favorite at your father's court, so I'm not surprised Edgard didn't mention me. In those days, people knew me as Theodore." He flashes a wry smile that fills me with unease. "But you may call me Theros."

What?

His voice sweeps like a chill over my skin. I stare at him in horror. Helplessly, my mind wonders if perhaps I'm imagining this. Was my sleepless night and the knock at my door all a dream? Is it possible I could be asleep still, tossing and turning in my bed at this very moment? Outlandish as that thought is, it's certainly more believable than the reality in front of me, and I desperately want to squeeze my eyes shut and wake up in my room. But I can hardly blink. And the longer I stare, the less and less I believe this is a figment of my imagination. The Theros of my nightmares looks nothing like the man before my eyes, who has so much of my father in him. Theodore. The bastard brother father cast away from Stonefall when he was but a boy.

The man I've feared for years. The man who made me flee for my life, running away from home. It's really *him*. Standing mere inches from me. And he's . . .

My own flesh and blood.

I think I might vomit.

I try to back away and stumble into Ethan, who steps around me, shielding my body with his.

"There's no need to be afraid," Theros murmurs as his eyes

slither to Ethan. "I didn't come for you."

"Y-you tried to have me killed," I rasp, hating the quiver in my voice.

"My apologies. You were a means to an end, but you can rest assured your death would serve me no purpose now," he says, adding insult to injury.

"Then why are you here?" I ask through my teeth.

"That's what we'd all like to know," King Perceval demands from across the table, reminding me we're not alone.

Theros keeps his attention on Ethan and me as he answers, "I am here to collect my son."

"Your son?" repeats the king, looking as bewildered as everyone else in the room.

"Who is being held prisoner at the behest of yours."

I feel my lips part, drawing a sharp breath.

Elijah is Theros's son?

The king's expression coils with outrage and reproach. "A *prince* in my prison, Ethan? What is this, some kind of joke?" Perceval demands, and all eyes shift to Ethan. I see my dread mirrored in him. Confusion seeps into the lines of his face.

The mercenaries delivered Elijah to Milus only hours ago. How is it that Theros is here already, demanding his release? Was he plucked from Talos in plain sight? It doesn't make any sense.

Ethan's hesitation plunges the room into a strained silence, and all I can focus on are the erratic thuds of my heart.

Finally, Ethan speaks. "You denied me the chance to hunt

him down for Connor's murder, so I did what I had to." At the king's long stare, he adds bitterly, "I didn't know he was a prince."

The king lets out a long, heavy sigh. If years of exhaustion could be distilled into one sound, it would be that. "Is he still alive?"

Ethan shoots me a look before nodding. Then, to my horror and disbelief, the king signals to the guards and commands Elijah's release. "Bring him here at once."

14

Connor

I steady my breath, inhaling the metallic scent of blood. They are only a few yards away now, and my senses are sharp with anticipation. The dirt crunches underneath their boots as they approach, dust and rocks kicking up.

"They're dead!" someone calls out in disbelief.

I feel a predictable stab of pain in my gut, and I surrender to the force of the soldier's kick, my limbs loose and heavy as my body rolls over like a rag doll. At least he missed the wound. Breathing slow, I keep my eyelids deathly still under the bright glare of the sun above me.

A breeze whisks by, cooling my sweat-and blood-soaked shirt.

I feel a foot on my right hand, crushing three of my fingers under its weight. I grit my teeth.

"Anyone know this bastard?"

"We must inform the commander," a young, uncertain voice mutters.

"No," comes a stern voice, "he just left for the fort; he won't be pleased if we summon him back."

"Darius is right," says another. "The commander will think us fools."

Someone kicks me in the ribs, and it catches me off guard. My eyes flutter open for an instance, glimpsing pairs of leather greaves and dust-flecked boots.

"You let this dog kill Blythe and Torbin?" asks an angry voice. "Look at you—your face is a bloody mess. Did you even *do* anything? Or did you just run like the frightened imp you are?" The questions are met with a snarl and the sudden shuffle of feet. I suppress a groan. I don't know how much I'll be able to endure if they start trampling me; it's hard enough with the one foot smashing my fingers numb. But to my good fortune, some of the soldiers are smart enough to see the absurdity of a fight, and their warnings dissuade the insulted soldier before he can act on his wounded pride.

"He was well trained," he finally says in his defense, his voice heated with disdain.

"Aye, a match for Blythe," another mutters in his defense.

"Why did he attack?" asks the one called Darius.

"I think he was after the little rascal that tried to steal from Blythe."

"And where is this rascal?" someone else asks.

"Does it look like I know?"

"You *should* know, Julius."

"I was busy trying to get help," Julius scoffs.

Another laughs. "Busy running away is more like it."

"Whole lot of good it did," a new voice mocks.

"Enough," Darius interjects. "Get our fallen ready for burial."

"What about him?" Julius asks.

The foot stepping on my fingers gives way, and I feel the blood rush back into them. They throb with pain, jutting into the air like gnarled, twisted twigs.

The one who first taunted Julius speaks. "We should burn the bastard."

No.

"Throw him in the pit," Darius answers finally.

Can't blow my cover yet . . .

"Gorgos." Darius says the name like a command, and a second later, two large hands clamp my torso from under my arms and carelessly haul me up to a shoulder. Needles of pain shoot from the slash in my abdomen. The superficial wound isn't deadly, but it's deep enough to make my knees go weak from the agony. I knew the moment I cut into my own skin it would need stitches, and there is always a risk it might fester, but I needed the wound to look real.

Dangling off Gorgos, head drooped, I open my eyes—just barely—and see his massive back. Mounds of muscle strain his leather armor, powerful and deadly. He could snap my spine easily enough, I realize, feeling like a gnat in his grip.

I can smell the pit before we get there. Even at a distance, the sickening scent of rotting flesh is overpowering.

Rotted flesh. Not burnt flesh.

How deep is this hole? I won't find out until I hit the bed of dead bodies. If I'm lucky, I won't break anything on the way down.

Gorgos halts his heavy steps, and I have a split second of respite before my body is plummeting toward the pungent stench of death and the swarming buzz of flies. I brace for impact, gritting my teeth and straining every muscle, hoping I don't land on any jutting pieces of broken bones.

My body hits the bottom with a thud, and the pain is instant, blooming from my neck and back until it's all I can feel. I struggle to draw in a breath, making me gasp and gulp down the putrid air into my lungs. Revolting smells assault me from all sides—rotting flesh and gases to urine and feces.

I remain still, eyes closed. I can't risk Gorgos catching me in my lie.

As the seconds turn into minutes, I listen to the flies buzzing around me. *The sound of death,* I think. I hear the occasional breeze overhead, giving me momentary relief from the stench of the pit. Is Gorgos standing over the edge, peering down at me?

I'm not sure how many minutes pass before I dare to open my eyes. The sun's white glare greets me.

There is no sign of Gorgos.

The pit is about six feet deep, and it's just as revolting as it smells. Over a dozen bodies lie under me. Most are nothing but carcasses, the bones frayed from the pecking of vultures, but some are still bloated and decomposing, their skin violet and black, covered in maggots.

I fight the pain and pull myself up, ready to climb out of this pit of death, but I stop short when I see Flynn's body at my feet. Inches away is the woman who hanged with him this morning, their skins pale and marked with purple blotches, but otherwise still intact.

Carrying Flynn out of here is neither logical nor practical, but I can't leave him to rot with the rest of them.

"Sorry," I mutter as I lift Flynn's body. I haul him to my good shoulder, groaning from the effort. Fresh blood wets my midsection.

I give myself a moment's breath before I hurl Flynn's body out of the pit. His chest collides with the edge and starts to slink back in. I break the fall and let out another groan as I thrust his legs up. The body snags at an angle, half outside the pit, half dangling over its wall. Then I jump, feeling blood trickle down my abdomen and groin as I do. I grab on to the ledge, pulling myself up and, at last, out.

Panting, I drop to a crouch over one of Gorgos's oversized footprints, and eyeball his trail back to the village, which is less than a mile away. Above it, a mass of dark clouds gather. A gust of wind fans the land, drying the sweat and blood on my face. Heavy rain should provide some cover, but I'll have to steer well around the village just to be safe. With the warning rumble of thunder in the distance, I crouch and hoist Flynn's body to my shoulder once more, baring my teeth at the searing pain. His added weight makes running impossible, but I fight the urge to leave him behind and trudge onward as fast as my legs allow.

Lightning blasts the darkened skies, illuminating the cottage up ahead. It must be near dusk by now, but the storm's chased the sun away, leaving only enough light to blanket the landscape in a wet, blurry gloom. I am soaked through. Most of the blood has washed off, and the rain water helped chased the thirst away, but I'm exhausted. With the cottage in sight, I finally slow my pace.

I splash through puddles and mud to the door. My knocks silence the muffled voices within.

Moments later, Asher appears. His brows lift at the sight of me, his expression filling with shock and relief. Then his eyes fall to the body in my burning arms.

"It's Flynn."

Surprise crosses his face. "Get inside!"

A pair of strangers are seated at the table. A square-built man with a bushy mustache and deep lines, and a much younger, lither companion with a broken nose. They're as dry as hay, which tells me they've been here awhile.

Raven gasps when she sees me, almost dropping the cup in her hand, spilling some of its contents on the floor. She quickly sets it down on the kitchen table and runs over to me.

"You're hurt," she says, looking at the dark-red stain on my shirt.

Asher locks the door and gestures at Flynn's body. "Set him on the table."

The two men step away from their chairs as I gently lay Flynn down. I turn to Asher. "Where's the boy?"

"In your room, sleeping," Raven cuts in, taking my hand in hers and examining it. "Let me clean those wounds."

The older guest looks like he's about to object, but Raven silences him with a look before she draws me away to her room.

"Take off your shirt," she commands as she lights a candle.

I gingerly lift the soaked fabric over my head. It falls with a splat on the floorboards. By candlelight, Raven inspects my wounds up close. Water drips from my hair, falling on the candle, its flame flickering in protest.

"Just a nick," she mutters at the cut on my shoulder. She brings back the candle to my torso and sighs through her nose. "I think you'll live."

"Who are those men?" I ask.

Her eyes darken. "Sit," she orders, pointing with her chin at the bed.

As I do, she hands me the candle. Then she fetches a clay pot from her bed stand. Using a wooden spatula, she smears its pasty contents across the glaring red gash on my abdomen. The open skin flares with pain, burning as though she's poured liquid fire onto me.

"They're part of a resistance movement," she answers, spreading the paste.

"The Brotherhood," I mutter. *So much for their secrecy.*

She pauses, needle and thread in hand. A look of hurt flashes across her eyes. "You knew?"

"Since yesterday." She nods absentmindedly, connecting dots in her head. Lightning flashes through the window, followed by the loud crack of thunder. Raven blinks her thoughts away, tending to my wound. "Why are they here?"

"I think Papa sent word t' them about Flynn," she says without looking up. "Was he one o' them, too?"

"Yes."

A pause. "They were talking about you," Raven whispers.

I narrow my eyes at her. "Why?"

"Not sure. I was in your room looking after the boy, so I couldn't work out all they were saying."

Right. The boy.

"How's Pip doing?"

Raven jabs the needle through my skin. I wince, biting off the pain. "You know him? He's struggling t' cope . . . buried himself in a corner and cried for hours. Must have passed out from exhaustion; I couldn't get him t' eat anything." She shakes her head, thinking. "It won't be easy for him, waking up t' reality tomorrow."

"I'll watch over him tonight."

She pulls the needle and thread through my wound, slowly making her way across. "Papa would have left Pip t' his fate if it wasn't for you," she says, glancing up at me with steady eyes.

"Asher chose to save the boy's life," I say in his defense. *Hurry home* was all I'd asked of him. "How well does he know the boy?"

Raven cuts the extra thread with a small knife. "Only a little, same as I. His mother always kept t' herself, didn't talk much t' anyone . . ." She seems lost in concentration as she wraps a cloth around my torso. "There, all better now."

"Thank you."

"Working the grove might pull the stitches, so ya best stay in and rest tomorrow," she instructs as we both stand. I pick up my soppy shirt and follow her to the door, but before she steps into the corridor, she turns to face me, lips pressed in a thoughtful line. "I'm glad you're all right."

The storm rages on outside, beating against the roof and windows, shaking the cottage with the boom of thunder.

Flynn lies on the table as though in peaceful sleep, arms folded at his chest. Asher and the two visitors stand vigil over his body, their bowed heads rising at the thud of my wet boots. Asher walks over to me when I enter. His hand falls on my shoulder. "Flynn will get a proper burial, thanks to you," he tells me in a quiet voice filled with emotion. "I won't forget this, lad."

"Thank you for bringing Pip home with you," I answer with equal gratitude.

"I make a point not to intervene in strangers' matters. They often bring more harm than good," he says, his tone abruptly cold. "I was convinced you'd signed your death sentence . . ."

"I knew the risks."

"Aye. And it didn't stop you, did it?" He sighs, studying me. "I understand why you did it. More than you know." His tired eyes linger a moment longer before he directs my attention to the older guest at the table. "Connor, this is Uther, leader of the Brotherhood."

Uther joins us in two strides and extends a hand, giving mine a firm shake. He gets right to the point.

In a refined Sunderian accent, he says, "I'd like you to join us."

15

Meredith

I hold back a gasp when Elijah limps through the door. His face is the epitome of revenge. The myriad of contusions seem to have festered overnight, swelling and darkening in ugly shades of green and purple. His left eye, which all but provoked me last night, is now a slit, threatening to swell shut like the other. But in spite of his marred features, Elijah seems pleased with himself. His cut, raw lips curve into a knowing smile, shoving the bruises aside, unflinching, as though it doesn't even hurt.

The realization that he's my cousin curdles my blood.

"Is this how you treat all your royal guests?" Theros asks the king, whose face is growing redder by the second, looking as though he might suffer a stroke.

When the king finally reins his temper, he answers, "I do not condone my son's actions. But let us not forget Talos is the enemy of Alder's only ally. And prince though he be, your son spilled Alderian blood, and as such, his release is a courtesy on our part."

Theros remains expressionless. "If His Majesty is indeed as wise as tidings claim, he would take great care not to offend me."

The implied threat seems to suck the air out of the room.

"Are you so foolish as to threaten me in my own castle?" Perceval asks.

"Tell me, mighty king," Theros starts with a polite smile, clasping his hands at his back, "have you heard of the blue fever?"

Perceval stares, impassive. I scrounge my own thoughts, unfamiliar with the name. Milus, who stands at the king's left, dips his head to whisper something in his ear. On the king's right, Rowan is oddly quiet.

"You might recall it as the plague that ended my adoptive father's conquest of the west," Theros continues, "but like most rumors, it was only that: a rumor. In fact, not only did he survive the plague, he brought it home for me to play with."

The plague that ravaged the Western Continent and thrust Theros into power. I never knew it had a name. But never mind that. He's saying it can be controlled?

Perceval frowns, skeptical. "If the Mad King lives, why do you claim the crown of Talos?"

"My father was an exceptional man, but not even exceptional men are immortal. Age is the one adversary he could not defeat."

"Exceptional?" Ethan mutters with a snort of disgust. "He was insane."

From the way Theros looks at Ethan, he doesn't appear the slightest bit offended. "The simpleminded call it madness because they themselves do not understand it."

"If there is a point you are trying to make, Theros, now would be the time to make it," the king prods, growing impatient.

Whatever entertaining notion held Theros to his charms and polite smiles, it's certainly gone now. His gaze turns icy. "My point, Perceval, is that I have a plague at my disposal, and unless you want it unleashed on your people, you will do exactly as I say."

Silence.

My chest tightens as the two kings stare at each other, surrounded by breathless and wide-eyed spectators, waiting for the spark of war to ignite and burn us all. Captain Offa and his guards are itching to reach for their hilts, a mere signal away from pouncing on Theros. Elijah, smirking, looks as amused as ever.

Perceval's eyes narrow like the sharp edge of a blade. "Do you expect I'll let you or your son leave with your heads still attached to your bodies after spewing such vitriol?"

Surrounded as he is, Theros remains unfazed. "Unless you want blue fever to run rampant in your streets, then yes, I expect that and more," he drawls.

"And how would you manage that if you're dead?" The king all but growls, but the certainty in Theros's gaze is telling. Ethan brings me momentary comfort. I feel the anxiety in his hand as it clutches tightly over mine. Together, though, we hold steady.

Theros shakes his head, disappointed. "I suppose I can't hold your ignorance against you, mighty king. We've only just met, but you'll know me well enough after today . . ." He's distracted by the decanter on the table and proceeds to pour himself a glass.

"My actions are never thoughtless. In your eyes, I may seem powerless, which, in the physical sense, I am." Briefly, he studies the wine in his cup and sniffs it before taking a sip. "I waltzed through your gates knowing I'd have to leave my men behind. Thus, I made arrangements An insurance policy, so to speak." After another drink from his cup, he smiles and says, "Should I fail to return in due course, I've left someone here very specific instructions to release the blue fever into your wells and your rivers, contaminating all of Alder City's water supply."

"That's preposterous!" the king rebukes. "Plagues cannot be wielded like weapons—mankind does not possess such power!"

"I don't bluff, Perceval," Theros says dryly.

The king's wrinkles seem to deepen with disbelief. "Say I don't strike you dead where you stand. Say I keep you and your son locked in my prison. Will you welcome this plague of yours into my city then?"

The wicked glint in Elijah's eyes is answer enough, but Theros says, "It would certainly prove more interesting to witness the demise of your kingdom firsthand than to read about it in my general's report."

"Are you telling me you are willing to sacrifice your lives to get your way?"

"I was raised by the Mad King, was I not?"

When King Perceval signals to Offa to take them away, Theros raises an open hand and says, "Before you make the worst mistake of your life, I suggest you fetch a stable hand who goes by the name Ash."

The king glowers, looking ready to dismiss Theros, but decides against it. "You heard him," the king tells the guards.

Captain Offa dispatches two guards out of the room, and while the council, Ethan, and I remain apprehensive, Theros turns to the window, content with taking in the view. Aware of his audience, he brings the wine cup to his lips and swallows in slow gulps, clearly enjoying every second. "I must say, this wine is exquisite," he says to no one in particular.

The apple doesn't fall far from the tree, I think, glancing at Elijah. He's every bit Theros's son.

Elijah's mocking gaze gravitates to me, and I take great care to hide my fear behind my curled lips, but this only seems to please him. Only he can pull off a smug look with such a battered face. The silence endures, with only a few whispers exchanged between the members of the council. I would have imagined, of all the councilors, Rowan would be the most furious with the knowledge that I am Theros's niece, but when I search for his glare, I'm surprised at how stricken he looks. The sadness in his otherwise scowling eyes is disconcerting.

Then, when the guards return with the stable hand, Theros's motives become clear.

He's only a boy, and he struggles to stand on his own, swaying on weak legs. His skin is pallid and glossy with sweat, his eyes unfocused and foggy. But it's his lips that draw my attention. They're dark blue, almost purple.

"I thanked him with some of my own wine when he took my horse in this morning," Theros says.

Disbelief and outrage spread over Ethan's features. "You *infected* him?"

"I knew your father would want proof," Theros tells Ethan. "And you should be glad he did, or this boy's death would have been for naught."

King Perceval stares at the stableboy with horror in his eyes. "How?" he asks, aghast, turning to Theros. "How is this possible?"

Theros smiles. "You would be amazed at the things an unsound mind can accomplish."

No longer able to support himself, the boy drops to one knee, moaning weakly as he tries and fails to get back on his feet.

"Unless you want the fever to spread," Theros quips, "I suggest you do away with that boy before he starts coughing."

The guards haven't yet left the room with the sick boy when the king bares his teeth. "What is it you want?"

Theros's brow rises slowly. "That wasn't so hard, was it?" As he lets that sink in, the king's jaw twitches. "As you may already suspect, Elijah isn't the only reason I am here. In fact, I've been meaning to pay you a visit for some time. This circumstance"—he gestures flippantly at the air with his hands—"only expedited my trip. Besides collecting my son, I've come to make you an offer."

The king quirks a petulant eyebrow. "Which is?"

"It is no secret that my interests lie in Stonefall, so it should come as no surprise that Alder poses a problem. You've been a pebble in my shoe all these years, Perceval, the only king with both power and reason to stop me. But"—he lifts a finger—"to my good fortune, my brother's negligence has proved very useful. You can't deny that he's made Stonefall undesirable in your eyes and the eyes of your people. So my proposition to you is this." He steeples his fingers at his lips, entreating the king with the illusion of choice. "Stay out of my way, and I will let you be. It's that simple. If you cross me, I will know it, and I will order my source to unleash the blue fever upon your lands. What do you say?"

Before the king can respond, I blurt out, "What will you do with Stonefall?"

Theros turns to me. "Princess, from whence do you think I hail? You don't believe I would travel through your lovely kingdom without stopping to say hello, do you?"

"What?" I stammer, feeling the blood drain from my face.

"My father's already paid them a visit," Elijah answers with a crooked smile, but he isn't done salting my wounds. "And we shall return once we're through with our business here."

"Would you care to join us, little niece?" Theros asks, and Elijah scoffs, an affronted look crossing his bruised features.

"What have you done?" I whisper, afraid to hear his answer.

Theros steps close once more. He leans in. "I have merely righted wrongs."

An overwhelming fear consumes me. Charles is the first person on my mind. Beth. Anabella.

And Father, who's wronged Theros most of all. To think he might be in danger leaves me at odds with my newfound hate. For all his faults, Father is nothing like the monstrous Theros; no amount of resentment would have me wish him harm. "Please don't hurt my family."

Theros's smile is bitter. "How can you call them that? You're only a pawn to them."

"Am I not a pawn to you?" I ask, defiant, trying and failing to keep calm. "You're just like *him*."

"I am nothing like him," Theros seethes. "You are useless to me, yet here I stand, offering you the world, and you swat it away because you can't swallow your own pride. Foolish girl."

"You're a tyrant," Ethan answers for me.

"I'd watch my tongue if I were you," Elijah mutters.

Tension fills the silence, stretching through the room, until finally King Perceval makes a decision.

"For the sake of Alder, I am willing to break off the alliance with Stonefall."

Maker. No.

My chest heaves, clawing at my throat. I rush to the table, facing King Perceval head on. "You can't do this. Please don't do this!"

"You forget your place, Princess," Rowan warns.

Is King Perceval simply going to hand Stonefall over to Theros like it's some underloved garden plot? My shaking fingers run cold on the table. It feels like my life is plunging down a slippery slope, pulled by a single loose thread, unraveling before my eyes, and I am helpless to stop it.

"Your Majesty, please—," I try, but the king is quick to silence me.

"I'll do what I must for the sake of my kingdom."

"Excellent," Theros says, stepping behind me. "And before we conclude our business, there is one last thing I will ask of you."

For once, I'm too numb to cower under the king's glare. "What is it?"

"I will require an audience with your lords and ladies."

"An audience?" Perceval repeats. "What for?"

"So they may bear witness as I bestow upon your son the same courtesy that he's bestowed upon mine."

16

Connor

Pip's appetite returns at the sight of the boiled oats Raven sets on the table. She took a break from harvesting after filling her first basket to cook him breakfast. I watch Pip slurp the spoon hungrily, content to see him eating. But Raven is more interested in the dark circles under my eyes.

"Those wounds are never going to heal if ya don't rest," she reprimands when I catch her stare.

I sigh, glancing back at Pip. He's scraping the bowl now, digging for a few last bites. "I tried."

Raven bites her lower lip. "Have you decided anything?"

I couldn't give Uther an answer last night, so he urged me to think it over. "No," I say.

"It's because of her, isn't it?"

As if summoned, the golden-haired girl materializes in the darkest corner of the room, the intensity of her amber eyes throwing me off guard. Does she wait for me to speak? To admit how much she rattles me? It's irrational, because I have no idea who she is, but I *know* she matters to me.

"I can't commit myself to a cause I might abandon," I tell Raven as the girl's shadow fades.

Thump. Thump. Thump.

All eyes dart to the front door.

"Open up!"

Instinct takes over, cutting through the fog in my head.

I lift a frozen Pip out of the chair and rush him to Asher's room, lifting the floorboards and ushering him underneath them. He curls his tense body within the cramped space and blinks at me with an anxious set of eyes. "Is it the redcloaks?"

I bring a finger to my lips, then fetch a short sword and a dagger from the weapon stash and quickly shut the trapdoor. When I return, Raven is ready by the door, hiding a kitchen knife behind her back.

The door rattles in its frame from the pounding on the other side. It won't hold much longer if they keep that up. I scoot out of way, pressing my body flat against the wall by the door's hinges. Raven's free hand slides the lock with a loud chink, and she opens the door a quarter of the way. Her armed left hand slides behind the door, holding three fingers for me to see.

Three soldiers. I look through the slit between the hinges and see a familiar bony face. It's Julius, the coward who ran away.

"Where is Asher?" he demands.

Raven remains sure of her ground. "He's gone on business t' the village, same as every day."

"You think we didn't start there?" he scoffs.

"What is it you want with him?" Raven asks, icy.

"A witness confessed, said Asher aided a little thief yesterday.

Mind if we have a look?"

Julius pushes his way in and Raven adjusts, attaching herself to the door as she swings it open.

I crouch behind the door, and a flash of pain burns through my stitched wound.

"Watch her," barks one of them, and two pairs of boots march inside, splitting up at the end of the corridor to search the rooms. Julius remains sentry, blocking the door, should Raven decide to make a run for it. If things go astray, I can't have her standing between me and Julius. She'll only get in the way. Slowly, I nudge Raven's calf. Understanding, she hides the knife in the waist of her skirt and moves from the door, treading just a few steps toward the echo of crashing objects. Those two must be realizing Raven isn't lying, and they aren't happy about it. That's a good sign; a hotheaded soldier is less likely to find the trapdoor than a methodical one. The slew of crashing and clattering goes on for another minute, at which point the empty-handed pair return to redirect their dissatisfaction at Raven.

"*Where* is he?" one of them growls.

"I've already told ya, he left for the village."

The wood creaks under the shuffle of feet as they approach her. "Then we'll remain here until he returns."

"You can wait outside," Raven bites back, unwavering.

Another step. "We'll wait right here." The rage in the soldier's voice eases into a snake-like charm. "Get inside," he calls to Julius. "And close that door."

Julius snickers and steps into the entryway.

I spring to my feet, slamming my right foot into the door. It swings hard against him, shoving him back. A scuffle breaks out behind me, but my focus is fast at the door. Julius is recovering, his hand reaching in through the opening. I slam the door on his wrist with a bang. Julius cries out and his hand disappears. I slide the bolt before he tries a third time, and feel his fist reverberate through the wood just as I turn to the crash of boots behind me.

A sword swings.

I block with the dagger in my left and jab with the sword in my right, driving it hard into the soldier's midsection, feeling it break through leather and mail. I twist the sword, tearing through innards, and yank it out.

He staggers back, gurgling curses as he slashes his sword through the air. I catch his wrist and bash it against the door's frame; his hand opens up, fingers gnarled, dropping the weapon. He slides down the wall, eyes rolling back in his head as his last breath slips away.

Raven stares from the other end of the corridor, chest heaving. The second soldier lies sprawled on the corridor in a pool of blood. "Are you hurt?" she breathes, her healer instinct breaking through the shock.

At the onset of silence, I spin around and unlatch the door.

Julius, no longer attempting to break in, is climbing up on one the horses. His head snaps at the sound of the door, and our eyes meet. Recognition flares in the whites of his eyes, and he bares his teeth, glaring like a scorned weasel.

Come on, you coward, fight me!

But once again, Julius decides to flee. He lifts the reins and wheels the horse around, kicking up a circle of dust around him.

I sprint after him.

Pain shoots up my side and I hiss through gritted teeth when I feel the stitches give. Warm blood blooms on my skin, soaking through my shirt. I curse and push harder, tasting sweat. There's no way I'll catch him on foot. I toss the sword. Using momentum, I adjust my grip on the dagger I'm still holding and arch my torso, pulling my arm back, feeling the pain double. I throw the blade. It spins through the air and spears Julius's shoulder. He doubles over, but it's not enough to throw him off the horse. Breath ragged and bleeding, I watch him get away, as he did before, to bring reinforcements.

17

Meredith

It's astonishing how quickly news travels of a public flogging—and how rapidly people flock to it. And of their crown prince, no less. Out in the entrance to the gardens, guards have just finished tying Ethan's wrists to a branch when courtiers start to gather. Some even stumble in their hurry, as though worried they will miss the show, their expressions both horrified and eager. Confused castle servants flank the bulging congregation in small groups of their own.

This is Theros's idea of an apology.

Ethan's feet barely touch the ground; the whole weight of his body pulls on his wrists. His coat and shirt lay crumpled in a heap on the stone, his sinewy torso exposed to the frosty morning air.

He must be freezing.

I'm still reeling from it all: meeting Theros, learning he and Elijah are my kin, losing my kingdom . . . and now this. King Perceval gave away the alliance at the bat of an eyelash, yet balked at Theros's demand to publicly humiliate his son.

Lief stands rigid at my side like my own personal guard, but his welcomed presence fails to bring me any comfort. Are Heloise and her brothers here yet? A cursory glance reveals only strangers in all manners of state of mind. But my attention returns to Theros when he produces a rolled-up whip from under his coat, garnering sharp breaths from the gathered courtiers. Nine long leather tails sprout from the implement, each tied with several knots throughout. The sight of it brings ghost pains across my back, reminding me of my own punishment for helping Holt and James escape the palace all those months ago.

My eyes affix to Theros as he watches the growing crowd, his intent clear in the serene set of his lips. He wants to mortify the king in front of his own court while Ethan endures the cold and submits to his lashes. From the corner of my eye, I see Elijah watching me intently, and I can't help but be drawn to his stare. As our gazes meet, his marred face breaks into a sardonic smile.

He knew, I realize. *He knew.*

Elijah knew Theros would come for him. He knew we would be punished. And yet it's Ethan who will answer for it, when I am just as responsible for bringing Elijah here. I would have killed him if Ethan hadn't stopped me. What would Theros have done then? Would he have demanded Ethan's life as payment? A pang squeezes my insides at the thought, and I can't discern if it's borne solely of guilt.

For as long as I can remember, I was convinced Theros's motives were fueled by greed. It frightened me, thinking what such a man would do to get what he wanted. But greed is selfish, its course can change. Revenge, on the other hand, is an entirely different evil. Ruthless and unrelenting. It knows nothing save for its own desire. I know this because I, too, feed on it. It sustains me like nothing else does. A despondent chuckle titters in my throat. What a cruel twist of fate it is to understand my enemy, to realize we bleed from familial veins.

You are nothing like Theros, a small voice echoes in my head, but I'm not so sure I believe it.

I thought I was strong enough to watch, but my fortitude vanishes at the first strike of the lash. Ethan's screams tear through my skin like sharp claws, and cringe as I might, I can't shut them out. Eyes squeezed shut, my fingernails dig into my palms, and I welcome the pain. Anything to distract me from the present. Then I hear the queen's cries from a distance; they ring with the wrath of a mother scared for her child. She races toward the garden, the stomp of her shoes echoing loudly against the stone steps.

The king had intended to shield her from all this, ordering Captain Offa to stand guard outside her quarters. But apparently, not even the captain can stand in a mother's way.

"Stop this at once!" she demands, barging in with all her ladies trailing after her. She barrels past the king, who fails to stop her, and tries to throw herself between Ethan and the whip, but Captain Offa and a guard grab her by the arms.

"I'm glad you've decided to join us," Theros says to the queen in a honeyed voice. His whip strikes again, sending the queen into a frenzy. The murderous glint in her glare would make any man quake in his boots. If strong arms weren't there to hold her back, I don't doubt she would end Theros where he stands.

But Theros seems to relish the queen's rage. Amid the lashes and Ethan's cries of pain, Edith wails helplessly with fury and desperation, her pain bared like a wound for all to see. I don't know which suffering is harder to witness. I keep my head down, jaw tight and hands clenched at my sides, and I don't dare look until it ends.

And then I wish I hadn't.

Ethan's head droops. He's blacked out. The whole of his back now looks like it belongs in a butcher shop, doused in blood and ripped skin.

"Not so brave after all, are you, *cousin*?"

I bristle, realizing Elijah has slithered to my side, and I don't know how I keep my hands from flying at his throat, but I do. I meet his eye, no longer feeling satisfaction at the trail of damage left on his face. My voice is a scathing whisper. "You will never be family to me."

He gives me a pitying look. "Even if I'm the only cousin you have left?"

My eyes flare open. I stop myself from screaming at him. If he's harmed Charles . . .

Maker, I can't even think it.

Somehow, I strangle my anger. Knowing Elijah, he could be bluffing, and if I threaten him, he might consider it a challenge. When I finally have the strength not to speak what's in my heart, I choke on an uncomfortable swallow and say, "They're your family, too."

He grins as though he can see right through me, peeling my mask of indifference with a knowing look and staring straight into my discomfort. "You should know better than anyone: that hasn't stopped me in the past."

I remember the sharp and burning pain of his blade like it was yesterday. He could have done away with me on numerous occasions. A slash to the throat or stab to the chest would have done the job, but Elijah's penchant for flair and spectacle got in the way of his intentions; I doubt I'd be alive if it hadn't been for his arrogance.

"Oh, don't worry. I haven't hurt them," Elijah confesses in mock sympathy, and my knees wobble with relief, which must show on my face, because Elijah doesn't hesitate to dampen it. "Though, frankly, the thought has crossed my mind on more than one occasion. Charles hasn't been as good a friend as he used to be. He's a sanctimonious prig these days, too good to keep me company. Can you believe it? Now, his sister . . ." He gives a soft whistle. "She's as infatuated as ever."

Why am I not surprised? Charlotte always was a self-serving witch. And with Theros taking over, Elijah is the most obvious target to sink her claws into. But how could she? Elijah poisoned the wine that killed her best friend. She blamed me after it happened, but that was before Elijah revealed himself the night of the ball. That was the last time I saw Charlotte. The memory is marked like ink in my thoughts. I can still see the rage and grief in her eyes. She made me believe I was responsible for my mother's death out of pure spite. I thought I would never forgive her for that, but none of it matters to me now.

"Is . . . ," I begin to ask in spite of myself, struggling to form the words. I hate having to do it, especially if I can't trust that he'll tell me the truth, but I have to know. "Is my father alive?"

"For now," he says, watching me with interest. "I'm surprised you care. I didn't think you two were close."

"We're not," I say quickly, glad that I don't have to lie. Elijah would see right through it.

Elijah chuckles. "Then you won't mind when we put his head on a pike."

I blink, startled at the brutality of Elijah's casually spoken words. Is that what he and Theros are planning? My stomach sours, sickened by the thought. But is that all I would feel if I lost Father? I'd like to think a part of me still cares, however small it may be.

By now, servants have finished untying Ethan's wrists, and the queen, released, rushes to his slumped body, swatting servants away as she falls to her knees. His blood stains the skirt of her gold and green dress, but she doesn't seem to care.

"How did Theros learn of your kidnapping?"

I don't know why I bother to ask. Honesty is the last thing I expect from Elijah, but I know that he will brag and gloat any chance he gets.

And gloat he does.

Elijah can't resist a scoff. "You think I'd let those oafs kidnap me? How naive you are, Meredith. All I had to do was double their offer," he admits with a shrug. Then, smiling, he leans in, his breath warm against my cold-bitten cheek, and I clamp down the urge to recoil. He's so close I could stab him in the throat. "That's the problem with mercenaries. Their loyalty is to the silver."

Maker. It was all a ruse.

A wave of nausea roils in my belly. "The bruises were all for show," I whisper bitterly.

"You misunderstand, Princess," Elijah drawls. He points me to his face, which, for all its wounds, is surprisingly menacing. "*This* was the ploy for *that*." His slitted eyes trail to where Ethan and the queen should be, only they're hidden behind the body of servants tending to them. Beyond the ruckus, where Ethan's blood doesn't stain the stone, Theros is busy exchanging words with the hard-faced king.

"I could have killed you," I say.

Elijah shrugs, nonchalant. "No risk, no reward." His gratification is appalling.

I look back at Elijah. Though my pulse hammers away, though my skin burns hot with hatred, my voice comes in an unflappable, breathless whisper.

"I will kill you."

His fair brows twitch. "Is that a threat, Princess?"

"It's a promise."

Elijah stares back, a slow smile pulling his split and swollen lips.

While King Perceval remains a shadow in the background, Theros addresses the crowd as though they are his subjects, as though *he* is their leader. "People of Alder, I am Theros, king of Talos. Let it be known that all of you remain alive and in good health because *I* allow it, and that it is through my grace alone that you shall continue to live in peace." He points his whip behind him, toward Ethan. "Speak of what you have witnessed here today. Tell your families, your friends, let them all heed my warning, for if your king decides to cross me, my mercy will run dry, and nothing—not even your Maker—will stop me." He takes one arresting step toward the deathly still crowd.

Still holding the attention of everyone present, Theros makes his next move. He comes to me, pulling my unwilling hand to his lips, and I feel my face contort with disgust as he kisses my strained-white knuckles. "Beloved niece," he says, louder than necessary, drawing gasps from the crowd. "It's been a pleasure." Then he places the whip in my hand, forcing my grip around it, and whispers, "A token . . . for your mistake."

The whip doesn't last more than a few seconds in my hand before I let it fall to my feet. But it makes no difference. Every courtier is looking at me now, and suddenly, I realize what Theros has done. They stare, blatant and deliberate, their eyes making a unanimous accusation.

Traitor.

18

Connor

We travel north, weaving through beech trees under the sunset's slanting golden light, keeping a hurried pace until we lose sight of the road. There was no time to pack but for a change of clothes, Raven's healing herbs, and the stash of weapons. Asher returned from the village within minutes of Julius's escape, relieved to find us still alive. Some brave soul had tipped Asher off about the guards hunting him down; he was forced to abandon Beast and the cart where he stood, and lurked his way back behind the cover of bushes and rocks, avoiding the road.

Raven is quieter than usual, troubled about leaving her home behind. She was hurrying to finish restitching my wound when Asher decided our only choice was to seek refuge with the Brotherhood, and although she kept quiet, I saw the way her eyes glistened. As I watch the slender frame of her back, overloaded with the weight of the bag slung across it, she pauses to survey the distance we've traveled. Her chest rises and falls. "We're never going back, are we?" she asks in a quiet voice.

Asher, walking ahead to guide us uphill, stops to turn and face Raven. "I'm sorry, my girl. I know how much the grove means to you. I never meant for any of this to happen."

This, I think, *is entirely my fault.* But one look at Pip, who struggles a few paces behind me to keep up with the terrain's incline, is all the affirmation I need. I'd do it all over again if I had to.

Raven meets my eye and, perhaps sensing my guilt, says, "None of us did."

We climb the first hill in the stifling dusk, and as the dotted light fades and my eyes adjust to the encroaching darkness, I see the ground ahead, an uneven web of steep slopes, blanketed in dry, fallen leaves and broken branches. It isn't long before Pip's muffled grunts almost drown out the whir of insects and the nearby rustle of bracken and bramble. Not ten minutes later, when his breathing runs haggard with fatigue, I haul him onto my back, his bony arms circling my sweat-drenched neck.

"Are you certain the Brotherhood won't turn us away?" I ask Asher.

"Yes, but we'll have to pull our weight in exchange for food and shelter." He phrases the statement like a question, as though waiting for my agreement.

"I wasn't expecting them to help out of the goodness of their hearts," I say dryly.

After an hour of climbing, when my aching legs threaten to buckle under me, Asher huffs, "We are close."

I search for the light of fires or the smell of smoke, but there are no signs of life, only moonlit blackness and the crumple of leaves under our boots. Perhaps this is how their camp remains hidden.

But then Asher is speaking to the trees. "At ease, keepers."

Branches crack and leaves rustle, and three hooded figures jump down from their covers, each holding a spear. They pull back their hoods to reveal the bearded faces of men easily twice my age.

"You might give us a lil warning next time, Asher," one of them complains.

"What's this?" the second keeper juts in. "A woman and child?"

The third keeper steps closer. "Why have you come?"

"I must speak with Uther," Asher says.

The keepers exchange glances. "You'll have t' wait till morning," the first keeper says.

Asher shakes his head. "We aren't prepared to sleep in the woods; we left in haste."

The second keeper scoffs. "Might as well wake Uther 'n; he'll skin our heads if we let you into camp for the night without his approval."

Begrudgingly, the others agree.

The third keeper, who Asher introduces as Zen, leads us up to the foot of a large rock formation. It looks like limestone, but I can't be sure without the light of day. We trace the formation, circling around it, and come to a cavity slightly wider than the average torso. Zen leads us inside in single file. It's pitch-dark, but the passage is so narrow the rock walls sand the fabric at my shoulders. At least I don't have to worry about any of us getting lost. The dim, uneven trail begins to widen as we progress, and the darkness lessens. I can vaguely discern the back of Pip's head in front of me. Every ten steps or so, the temperature plunges, cooling the damp, stagnant air that clings to my clothes and skin. A water source must be nearby. We eventually step out into an expanse that spans hundreds of feet, with an impressive height three times its width. A cave within a mountain. Below, a firelit campsite sits on the sandy floor bordering a subterranean lake. Above, a black starlit sky pours down from sinkholes in the cavern's roof, ringed by stalactite clusters.

We make our way down the rocky slope. The tents are spread across the sand, separated by a designated congregation area, set up with long tables and a makeshift stand made of rods, with pots that dangle from hooks. For a faction that calls itself the Brotherhood, its scant number of tents isn't promising. A few men sit by the fires, drinking or sharpening blades. Some acknowledge the keeper as we cross camp, exchanging nods and watching us pass with vigilant gazes.

Zen asks us to wait outside a pavilion-style tent before slipping in through the folds. Seconds later, a small light comes to life, creating shadows within the tent, followed by muffled whispers before the keeper reappears to grant us entrance.

A half-dressed, bedraggled Uther is lighting the rest of his iron candelabras when the four of us step inside. He sets a fully lit one on a plank that serves as a table, topped with a stack of worn books, a half-filled ceramic stein, and a stained map with splotches of ink and strategic markings.

"Please, sit," he offers, groggy, pointing us to the three mismatched sand stools circling the table.

Raven is the first to move. She crosses the stained rug that covers most of the tent's floor and settles on one of the stools. Asher follows, sighing with relief to get off his feet.

Raven motions to Pip, patting the remaining stool, but Pip shakes his head, inching closer to me instead.

Uther laces his hands together and shifts to Asher. "What's happened?"

"The redcloaks know I took the boy. They're looking for him," Asher explains.

Uther processes the information, massaging his temple. "Were you followed?"

"No. We left in good time."

Uther shakes his head, incredulous. "You have refused me for years, Asher. Yet here you are, forced by the Gods. I never thought I'd live to see the day."

Asher cracks a tired smile. "You and me both."

Uther slaps a sympathetic hand on Asher's shoulder. "I am glad you're here, old friend, truly." His eyes wander briefly to Raven and Pip. "But you know well as I do your guests put me in a quandary."

"What d'ya mean?" Raven asks, suddenly alert.

"Our rations are limited," Uther says with a wave of his hand.

"If you want to eat, you must provide—"

"Connor and I will share our portions with them," Asher cuts him off.

"I can mend wounds. And I can cook," Raven offers, eyes darting uncertainly to her father.

"I am aware of your talents," Uther says softly. "And they might prove useful, as I do not have a healer. But this camp has rules. If you want our food and shelter, you have to earn them with a sword."

Asher clearly kept this to himself. I can tell he feels my eyes on him, see his discomfort in the way he shifts on the stool, but he doesn't look at me.

Raven blinks a few times before she speaks. "Well, I'm no fighter, but I can learn."

Asher shakes his head. "No."

"You don't have enough men to be waging battles against an army," I cut in. "So what is it you want us to fight, exactly?"

"We fight for survival, lad."

I keep my gaze on Uther. "I thought the whole point of this was to free your kingdom."

Uther stares with a distant smile on his lips. "Free Sunder? I'll be long dead by then," he says. "No. Our work ensures the kingdom doesn't crumble under the Usurper's ruin, as others have." He unfolds his steepled hands to press them flat on the table. "What we do here helps prevent that from happening. We take from the Usurper what wasn't his to begin with. We steal from the collectors and give the coin back to the people."

I make an effort to keep my voice controlled as I say to Asher, "This is what Flynn died for? What you risked your life for? An organization of *righteous thieves*?"

Uther squares his shoulders. "I only have a hundred men. The Usurper has an empire." He watches my face. "You may disapprove now, but you are young, lad. When your hair is as gray as mine, you won't be so emboldened with ideals." Faced with my silence, he says, "You may speak your mind freely."

"Your intentions are noble," I say after a moment.

"But?"

Opting not to remark on the futility of his cause, I ask, "Haven't you considered an alliance? There's bound to be other kingdoms who want freedom same as you. Empires don't create themselves. If Theros built one for himself, others can, too."

"Aye, but we would need many, and as far as we know, not one ruler has dared rise against him." Uther sighs in exhaustion. "The only kingdom with an army large enough to stop him has been ruled by isolationists for generations, and they've done nothing."

"Is Theros not a threat to this kingdom?"

"They have fifteen battalions under their command," Uther scoffs. "Even if the Usurper conquers the whole damn continent, he still won't have enough men to overtake Alder."

The name flickers in a landscape that fogs my thoughts. Evergreens—a sea of them—and large, snow-capped mountains.

Alder.

"I know that place," I mutter under my breath.

"It *is* a northern kingdom," Uther comments offhandedly. "And you have a northerner's skin and tongue." Then he flicks his attention to Asher. "What do you think, old friend. Does he look like one of you?"

Something like hope flickers inside me. "Alder was your home?" I ask Asher, seeking his reluctant gaze.

"It's his old hunting ground," Uther answers when Asher doesn't.

"That was a lifetime ago," Asher finally speaks. Unease creeps into his expression, and I realize Alder must be part of his dark past.

Uther swigs his ale, leaving traces of it on his mustache, and sets the empty stein back on the tenuous table. "Let's get back to the matter at hand, shall we?"

"There is nothing to discuss," Asher tells him. "Connor and I will pledge our swords to you and share our keep with Raven and Pip."

But Raven isn't having it. "I can be of more value than any of your men," she points out, ignoring Asher's glare. Uther leans forward, listening. "How many men have you lost because you did not tend t' their wounds in time?" she asks. Uther doesn't answer the question, but he stares at Raven as though her offer is worth considering. "From what I've seen, you have few as it is. If I'm out there with your men, I can see t' their wounds before it's too late," she adds.

Asher is shaking his head. "And what happens when it's you who's wounded, Raven? What good are you then?" he asks. "I won't have Uther consider this. You will not fight, and that is final."

"And what should I do if it's you who's killed?" Her brow rises higher than I've ever seen. "Should Connor split his share with me as well?"

"I'd be a cockered arse if I wasted your talents, lass," Uther interrupts them and holds up a silencing hand at Asher, who teeters on the verge of a tirade. "But I can't dishonor your father's wishes."

Raven grits her teeth. "I'm not a child. I can make my own decisions."

"You may do as you like when I'm dead!" Asher barks, loud enough to be heard outside Uther's pavilion. "Until then, you'll do as I say!" His harsh words lack their usual self-control, and they hit Raven like a whip. She shrinks back on her stool, staring at her father in disbelief, and I sense this is the first time he's raised his voice at her.

Uther clears his throat, an attempt to dispel the charge in the air.

"I'll have my men set up tents for you in the morning," he says. "For now, try to make yourselves comfortable. I would offer food, but as you know, our supply is strictly rationed." He gestures to his stein. "There's plenty of drink to be had, though, if you are thirsty."

Raven gets to her feet in one sharp motion, marching past me and Pip, swiping angrily at the tent's folds as she exits.

The rest of us follow, leaving Uther to resume his slumber, and perch on logs around a dying fire. Asher picks up a branch with a scorched tip and stokes the wreathlike flames, bringing them back to life. Raven keeps to her anger, glaring at the flames in silent protest, hands crossed tightly over her chest. Pip nods off the moment he rests his head on my arm, his body slumped at my side like dead weight.

It's not until Raven's light snores can be heard that Asher breaks his silence.

"Would you have left us . . . if you'd known?" he asks, mincing words.

I think about leaving. I could travel north, where my skin and tongue won't be considered foreign. I could travel to Alder. A familiar place might help jar my memory. Maybe someone would recognize me. It's a tempting idea. But I doubt Asher can stretch his rations to feed all three of them. I would have to take Pip with me. I glance at the boy's ragged face as Asher waits for my answer, at the dark circles under his eyes. He's still weak from years of hunger, and has yet to develop proper fat and muscle. He is in no condition for a journey like that. "No," I finally say.

Asher nods, licking his dry lips. "I misjudged you." At my silence, he goes on. "Ever since the Takeover, life has been bleak 'round here. But Raven and I had the grove, and we were happy enough, all things considered. I didn't want to take the chance at a normal life away from her, as normal a life as that could be, but the Gods had other plans for us." He turns away from the fire, and I feel his drained gaze on me. "And for you, it seems."

"I don't believe in your Gods."

He is nodding again. "Aye. The people of the North believe in one god."

The Maker, I think. Reading, writing, crafting and shooting arrows—like all other learned things, religion is not lost on me.

"What is it you believe in, lad?" Asher asks after a long pause.

I let out a tired breath. There are no real answers for me in this dark, dank hole. What does a ghost believe in? I see the mountains again, towering shadows that break the sky and give depth to the landscape.

"I believe I'm meant to be elsewhere."

19

Meredith

I swipe my sword with an angry thrust. Lief skips out of the way, curling around to whack me in the back.

"You can't train like this, my lady," he pants.

I recover and answer with another strike, determined to land a blow. Again, I miss. I'm winded. Sweat dampens my skin, and my heart wallops in my chest, but I don't yield. I grunt, frustrated, swinging back and forth. Reckless. Desperate.

Lief remains quick on his feet, expecting my every move no matter how many times I try. When I finally land a hit, I realize it's because he's no longer fighting back. His wooden sword falls freely from his hand, disappearing in the snow-covered weeds.

"Pick it up," I huff between breaths.

"Thrash me if you must," he says, still panting. "I won't fight you. Not like this."

I groan, annoyed. He suggests a walk in the garden with Heloise might do me good, but the garden is the last place I want to be right now. Even the servants shy away from it, after Ethan's flogging. The memory makes my insides recoil. I've been burrowed in my rooms for the past two days, waiting for the dust to settle. Heloise, my only visitor, keeps me informed. Just as Theros intended, he planted seeds of doubt and distrust, and now the entire city seems to be under the impression that I am his pawn. In a way, I suppose I am. An unwilling, unassuming pawn who led the wolf to the hens. Like the whip Theros publicly gifted to me, I, too, am a token for the misfortune that has befallen Alder. All these months of toeing the line, training in secret, attending tea parties and card games. *And for what?* I think bitterly.

The king is my only saving grace. He saw Theros's machinations for what they were, and had the good sense to speak of them when he addressed the assembled lords and ladies shortly after Theros and Elijah made their exit. It's the only reason why I am still here, why I haven't been exiled, or worse, executed for treason. But it's hardly a relief. The alliance is off, as is the wedding. My worst nightmare is coming true, after all. I've never felt so lost.

"Do not fear," Perceval said confidently to the stunned crowd before he followed after his wife, who'd left with the entourage of servants carrying Ethan's unconscious body. "Alder will persevere."

Whether he believed it or not, the people did. At least for now, the king's brief words of reassurance have been enough to soften the worried looks on their faces.

I still can't believe Theros is my uncle. And *Maker*, he wanted me to join him.

Did he really think there was a chance I'd agree? Or was that just another of his calculated moves?

I think of the stableboy he infected. The physician had him quarantined, kept him fed by sliding bowls of food under his door; he didn't live past the third day.

Theros can't get away with this. Though it feels hopeless, I can't simply give up. I have to right the wrongs somehow. I may not have a fully formed plan, but I can think of a good place to start.

"It's time I pay Ethan a visit," I say to Lief, dismissing his idea of a walk.

He is said to be recovering well, although that could simply be what the king and queen want the court to believe. I should have visited Ethan as soon as the physician had seen to his wounds, to be there for him when he came to, but I wasn't sure that he'd want me there, to see him like that, wounded and weak. I thought I'd wait a few more days, but I've run out of patience.

Not wasting another minute, I part ways with Lief and stalk to Ethan's rooms. The courtiers I cross paths with in the hallway are quick to avoid me, hushing their conversations and casting nervous glances in my direction as I tread past them.

The devil's niece, Heloise told me. *That's what they're calling you.*

When the doorward lets me in to Ethan's rooms, I'm so hasty to get out of the public eye that I almost bump into Ethan's steward and a young servant girl carrying a bowl of soiled bandages.

It takes me a second to remember the steward's name. "Sir Wallis," I say in greeting, as the servant girl with the bandages bows her way past me. "I'm here to speak with the prince."

The steward bows his head. "He's been expecting you, my lady."

I blink in confusion. "He has?"

The steward blinks back, seeming just as confused. "Is that not why you're here, my lady?"

"Yes," I say slowly, still unsure.

Nodding, the steward steps aside to let me through. I smile awkwardly and weave my way to Ethan's bedroom.

I shared tea with Ethan and the queen here once, on my second day at the castle. It was nothing more than a formality to become better acquainted.

The door is ajar, and the odd mix of onions and honey soaks the cold, stuffy air. Candles burn low on a mahogany nightstand, bathing the room with a dim, golden glow. A pair of maroon curtains is drawn; hiding what I'm guessing is a pair of doors that leads to his balcony. Ethan lies face down on a large bed, covered to the waist in layers of fine blankets. The queen sits at the foot of the bed, looking down on her son, patting the lump of his feet as she speaks to him in a soft voice I can't make out. Strips of soaked linen cover Ethan's bare back.

Ethan notices me come in, locking eyes with me. He looks exhausted, but even so, he still pulls off a smile. The queen's gaze follows, and her lips tighten for an instant before she smooths the stern expression from her face. I should have known she'd be here. She probably spends the majority of her days and nights by

Ethan's side. Although, if she's had little sleep, it doesn't show. Edith looks as fierce and elegant as ever, leaving no trace of the wounded woman I saw two days ago.

I fold in an awkward curtsy. "I didn't mean to interrupt. I'll come by another time."

Ethan's voice is a hoarse whisper. "Wait—don't go. Mother, would you give us a minute?"

The queen acquiesces with a reluctant nod.

"Very well. I'll return for supper." She pats his leg. "Try to get some rest, sweetheart."

I bow as she strolls out of the room, feeling her accusing eyes on me as she does, and then take up the chair at Ethan's side.

"I was starting to think my mother never sent for you," Ethan says when the queen is gone, greeting me with a wan smile.

Well, that explains things. "I'm sorry I didn't come sooner," I whisper.

"You're here now," he says, his smile not quite gone.

"Are you feeling better?"

He nods. "They're only flesh wounds."

Painful flesh wounds. His back must be on fire. "They could get infected."

"Not with that awful onion concoction, they won't; it's going to take weeks to get its smell out of my rooms."

"And your clothes," I tease, glad to see him in good spirits. "People will smell you coming."

He chuckles, and then we both fall silent, seeming to guess at each other's thoughts.

"Everyone thinks I'm in league with Theros," I venture, unsure of his feelings. Does he doubt me, too?

His chestnut-brown eyes target mine with such directness that it scatters my thoughts.

"Not everyone does."

I break from his spell, staring at the shadows in a corner. Ethan saw the darkest side of me in the prison, my penchant for violence. "Theros is my uncle," I remind him.

"You say that like it's your fault."

His hand reaches for mine. It's softer than I imagined. Unwittingly, I relish in the warmth of his skin as he caresses my knuckles with his thumb. I'm thinking I ought to pull my hand free, but the guilt I see in his eyes stops me.

"How can you look so contrite when you're the one lying wounded in bed?"

"Wounded and shamed, yes," he murmurs, his hand still steadfast on mine. "But you lost Stonefall. You expected my father to uphold the alliance, and he betrayed your trust."

A lump lodges in the back of my throat. I suddenly feel small. I pull away, crossing my arms tightly at my chest. "There's nothing anyone could have done." Despite my candor, there is bitterness in my voice.

"Isn't there?"

I blink. "What are you saying?"

He tries to sit up, and blanches, gasping back onto the bed.

"Would you mind?" he asks, bashful.

Carefully, I clasp onto his shoulder and help him up. Then I remember he's not wearing a shirt and, suddenly, I have to make a conscious effort to keep my eyes on his face.

"What if we expose Theros's 'insurance policy'? What if we get to him first?" he asks.

My breath hitches. Is that even possible?

"But how? We have no leads."

"Theros said his lackey would release the plague whether or not Theros survived. He seemed confident that person would have access to Alder."

"Are you saying it's someone we know?"

"Someone here in the castle. Someone with easy access to information."

"But that could be anyone. A lord, an adviser, a servant even," I argue, afraid of the hope building in my chest; I'm not sure which of us I'm trying to convince more.

"True. But regardless of who it could be, we need two things: coin and secrecy," Ethan says, holding up a pair of fingers. "Milus has men under his employment, men who've procured sensitive information for him in the past. Discreetly. He can help us."

"Is that wise?" I ask. "If it's someone within the castle, doesn't that make Milus a suspect?" I hate questioning the councilman's trustworthiness when he's the only one who stood up for me at the meeting.

"Milus is like a second father to me—I trust him," Ethan assures me in a steady voice. I'm about to say that his gut instinct may not be enough to go on, but he must see the doubt in my expression because he quickly adds, "I understand Milus is a stranger to you, but you should know he is the only member of the council who insisted on a war against the Mad King when news of his conquests first reached us years ago. And I can attest that his opinion remained unchanged after Theros took the throne, but no one would hear a word of it. Not the council, and certainly not my father. Not even I could agree with it because it goes against Alderian rule." He pinches the bridge of his nose as he lets that sink in. "If we had listened, none of this would be happening." He takes in a slow breath and sighs. "Isolation has been our greatest strength for generations, but the world changed, and we didn't change with it." A grimace twists Ethan's pallid features. "It's hard for me to recognize that's become our greatest weakness."

I can't help but agree. With fifteen infantry battalions of five thousand soldiers each, Alder has the most powerful army known to man. But not even that is enough to defeat a plague.

"I trust you, Ethan," I confess. "If you believe Milus can help us, then I'll support your decision."

Ethan's face lights up with that contagious grin of his. "Thank you."

I clear my throat. "So, how do I help?"

"For now, by continuing your training and being patient."

A groan rolls off my throat. Sitting by is all I've done since I arrived. I want to be useful, to feel like I'm doing something—*anything*—to help my people.

Then Ethan's expression sobers. In a quiet voice, he says, "If this fails . . . I want you to know that you are welcome to stay here. You don't have to go back. Ever." The look he gives me is genuine and steadfast, and it pierces me with warmth.

It's a generous offer, but I can't accept it.

A Theros-ruled Stonefall is the last place I should ever return to, but I won't abandon my people. And even though it frightens me, I think I would rather die trying to help them than remain here, hiding like some coward.

"Thank you," I say after a short pause. "But if it ever comes down to that, I couldn't simply look away and forget about Stonefall."

Ethan bites his lower lip, thoughtful. "You would return to Stonefall?"

I nod.

"And what would you do once there?"

"I would . . . ," I start, shrugging and searching for an answer on the wall. "I hardly know."

"You haven't given this much thought, have you?"

I inhale deeply, letting my shoulders sag as I sigh. "None."

Ethan falls silent, and I'm suddenly wary of his thoughts. "It's foolish, I know."

"No," he rushes to say. "I think it's admirable. But Theros would get the better end of any deal you could hope to make. The only way you'll get your kingdom back is by force." He levels a determined gaze on me. "Alder can give you that."

"But your father—"

"It doesn't matter what my father says. *I* want to help you. And I want to help my own kingdom. Perhaps we'll have to wait until I'm king to do anything about it. But that doesn't mean we have to give up. Alder has more men at its disposal than all other eastern kingdoms combined."

I blink at him as gratitude flows through me. "You would do that for me?" I ask when I finally find my voice.

"It's the right thing to do, for both our kingdoms. It's what Connor would have done," he says, his voice thoughtful. "So what do you say, Princess? Do we have an agreement?" he asks, his hand waiting for mine.

Unsure as I am, I smile and shake his hand. "We do."

20

Connor

I blink away the blur of sleep as I rub at a kink at the back of my neck; I must have slept with my head bent on the log. A few fires burn still, enough to light the outlines of the cave. Pip, Raven, and Asher are sound asleep, huddled around the black mound of ash where the fire burned last night. There's no trace of smoke left, which tells me it's been out for hours.

The camp is coming alive. Tinkering metal objects clash, echoing against the rocky walls, and as silhouettes emerge from their tents, more fires are lighted. I get up and shake sand off my trousers. Dried sweat and grime and crusted blood cling to my skin. A bath is long overdue. I glance down at the pile of ash. It's enough to make soap, but that would take time. A rinse will have to do for now.

I make for the underground basin, leaving a trail of footprints in the compact sand. At the edge of the lake, a crouched man gets back on his feet, lifting a bucket out of the water. He glances over his shoulder at my approach, shooting me a look laden with distrust and skepticism. I ignore him. The aquamarine water is cool to the touch and carries a strong mineral scent. A source of water like this is a lifeline; the Brotherhood wouldn't be able to camp so high up the mountain without it.

Just as I'm about to cup water in my hands, the man with the bucket breaks his silence. "Don't drink it," he says in a gruff voice. His free hand points up. My gaze hikes to the cave's ceiling, where dark shadows cover the space in between the stalactites. Bats. Hanging directly above the subterranean lake. The water isn't safe to drink, I realize, not without boiling it first. I nod my thanks at the man before he walks off with his haul. I'll have to follow his trail later to quench my parched tongue. For now, a bath will do. It takes me seconds to remove my clothes and dive in.

The water is like a cool balm on my skin.

Hell. I could stay in here for hours.

Once I've rinsed off, I force myself out. Perched on a rock, I'm pulling on a boot when I spy Pip walking toward me, sleepy-eyed and sluggish.

"You shouldn't wander around," I say when he's close enough to hear, but he's lost in the view of the lake, staring through desolate eyes and a sobering expression on his dirty face.

"Mama would have liked it here," Pip mumbles in a quiet voice.

"If she were here, she'd probably tell you to take a bath," I say, running a hand through his matted mop of hair.

A small grin breaks through his glum façade. "Is it safe t' drink?" he asks as he drops to his knees.

"No. It will make you very ill if you do, so be careful not to swallow any when you wash up."

"It looks . . . deep," he whispers.

I register the alarm in his voice. "You can't swim?"

He looks up at me, and the shame in his eyes answers for him.

"I'll teach you," I say, shrugging off his embarrassment.

Pip glances at the water, then back at me. He shifts nervously on his knees, as though I'm about to push him in.

"I don't like being in the water. Please don't make me."

"I'm not—"

The sound of feet sifting sand hushes me.

Two men approach the lake, slowing at our presence, studying me with dissatisfaction as they murmur past us.

"They don't want us here, do they?" Pip asks in a low voice, his weary eyes on the retreating pair.

"I sense it's me they don't like. But keep your distance all the same."

We head back, and as promised, Uther has ordered two tents to be set for us. Unlike his pavilion, these tents are practical, as are all the others. The pair of wicker cots inside takes most of the space, leaving little room for anything else. Raven inspects the tent assigned to her and Asher in a standoffish silence. Asher mutters something to her, and her head turns away sharply. Judging from the looks of it, I doubt she's said a word to him since last night.

Uther makes an appearance to survey his men's work, towing the young fellow who was with him at Asher's cottage; the only other member in this group who doesn't seem to have a decade on me. There's no grit about this one. His lop of curly black hair is too perfectly combed, his fingernails too clean, and the way he carries himself . . . he's not like the others.

"Welcome to camp," Uther says from behind me. "I didn't get a chance to say so last night, but I'm pleased you've joined us, despite the circumstances." He points me to his companion. "Rhys here will show you the ropes."

Rhys's small and moody eyes stare icily at me.

Asher—who seems eager to leave Raven's side—gifts Rhys with his weapon stash without reservation. "This is all."

Rhys takes the blade-filled sack, and I follow him around camp to the armory, where an array of long swords, axes, and bows rests on wooden stands, shields propped against them. Rhys drops to one knee and adds Asher's blades to the stockpile. When he's finished, he looks up, expectant. I raise a brow and he points at my back. "Hand me your bow," he says impatiently.

I take one glance at the bows they have on the stand. Rudimentary at best. I'm not about to give up the much finer one Flynn gave me. "I keep my bow."

"It wasn't a suggestion," he says, standing. "Your weapons belong t' the group now."

"I keep my bow."

Rhys steps close, his manner all arrogance and confidence. He means to intimidate me, but he's an inch too short to pull that off. "You can leave it here now or have it removed later. Your choice."

"Like I said, I'm keeping the bow."

"Uther won't be happy when he hears about this," Rhys clips.

"I'll take my chances."

My gaze follows him as he stalks off.

That afternoon, the whole camp is summoned to the gathering place near the cave's lake, a mostly flat section of sandy floor bestrewn with stumps of limestone where the men sit and prop their legs.

The group is silent like a pack of wolves awaiting the instruction of their alpha male, and they remain so when Uther calls for Asher and me to join to him at the front. Rhys stands with his arms crossed, tapping an irked foot on the sand. He wears the same glare from before. I doubt giving up my bow up would have lessened his hostility. The fellow disliked me from the start.

"Brothers, tonight we welcome two new members to our family." He draws Asher to him. "As you all well know, Asher has been a loyal supporter to our cause for years. But tonight he becomes one of us." Uther faces Asher. "Tonight, you give yourself to a cause greater than yourself, and inasmuch as we gain a brother, you gain a family. Brother, we welcome you."

Oh, hell. An induction ceremony.

Uther asks Asher to repeat after him. "From this night, I pledge my life and sword to the Brotherhood; I will fight as one with my brothers; their mission is my mission; their fight is my fight; and only death shall set me free."

Once the words are spoken, the cave thunders with a chorus of stomps and the echo of a slurred chant. I meet Rhys's glare—anchored to me without fail—and in my mind the pretentious oath boils down to a simple sentence: *Their loot shall be my loot.* They carry on with the racket as Uther takes Asher's hand and glides the point of a knife across it. When the men finally quiet down, Uther motions for me.

"Our brother Asher took Connor under his wing, into his home, and Connor proved himself loyal. He brought honor to our fallen brother Flynn, allowing us to give him a proper burial. And here he stands tonight, willing to fight our fight. So let us welcome him."

I repeat the binding words, hating every second of it. I don't know these men, and I don't much care for them or a cause that leaves much to be desired, but I deeply dislike pledging an oath I will ultimately break.

Uther turns my left hand over, pausing to look at the beastly scar that must have once been painful; another mark without a story. "This'll be interesting," he mutters under his breath.

The stomping chant returns, and as the knife cuts my palm, I catch a flicker of golden hair within the crowd.

The girl, emerging again from my impenetrable memory, moves among them, watching me, a silent reminder of my true allegiance. A reminder of where I belong. Her eyes linger on the knife cutting my palm, telling me this is a mistake, and the sting of it is suddenly an afterthought. I need to go to her. My arms tingle with the aching urge to wrap themselves around her, to cup her face in my hands . . .

Who are *you?*

The crowd is breaking up, and they're in my way. They block my view, slapping my back and uttering felicitations. I don't care for any of it. I want to shove them aside and run to her. But she's gone.

21

Meredith

The fear of plague spreads through the city like fire, sparking unrest and protests at the castle gate. Inside the castle walls, the mood is subdued but no different. Fearing an outbreak, many of the lords leave court to return to their country estates, taking their families with them. Those that remain carry on their daily routines, albeit their demeanors are understandably darker and more somber. Thankfully, Heloise and her family forgo returning to their chateau for the time being. With the queen's frequent absence from court, and the egress of courtiers to the provinces, Heloise's only obligation is tea with her mother at noon, to which she's always late. We spend most afternoons together at our leisure, though mostly in the confines of my room. We share supper there, usually followed by a game of Justice Quicksand, Hel's favorite Alderian game of cards. It involves matching and outsmarting, which Heloise does with ease, until we've played enough hands for me to learn the tricks behind her strategy.

Being patient is a struggle. It leaves me to wonder what's become of Stonefall. Of Charles. Of Father. If anything, waiting for news from Milus's spies seems to make my mood grow darker and more impatient with each day. I visit Ethan often, much to the chagrin of the queen, hoping he might have news. I make a point of visiting him after training, so as to abate my discontent and avoid accidentally assailing the crown prince with it. Now that we're not engaged, I find it surprisingly easy to be around Ethan. Even in his pain and discomfort, he is far more pleasant company than I could ever be, were I in his condition. Still, I keep my visits brief. I carry on this way, waking anxious each morning and suppressing my disappointment through a glass of wine and Hel's company in the evenings. Uneventful days turn into long weeks, and the best I can do is bite my nails down to the quick.

When Ethan's wounds heal and set him free of his rooms, the king orders fliers to be distributed around the city. Today, when the clock strikes noon, he will address the people at the central district, the heart of the city. Ethan was quick to suggest I attend discreetly on account of the stigma that follows me now. "Crowds can be unpredictable," he said. "If you stand with us during my father's address, there's a chance your presence could agitate them and get in the way of his message."

I agreed. And though condemnation from the aristocracy wasn't anything new, I couldn't help the twinge of resentment at the people's disapproval.

Thus, with the royal family departed, Lief and I prepare to head out on our own, removed from the usual entourage and the attending courtiers. Lief gathers saddles from a stable hand as I make a beeline for Daisy and Diago, comforted by the familiar scent of hay and horse manure. I find them grooming each other across their stalls.

"Hello, beautiful," I whisper to Daisy when she nuzzles my face. Diago, too, is happy to see me. I ignore the bittersweet ache in my throat and stroke his neck when he dips his head toward me. Being around him never gets any easier. "I'm sorry I don't come see you both more often."

"I hear he doesn't let anyone ride him," Lief says, coming up from behind, a saddle dangling from each hand. He looks up at Diago in awe, as though appraising him for the first time. "I'd forgotten about him. He's quite the horse, isn't he? A fitting steed for a man like Westwend."

My eyes sting. I turn away. I was ravaged with pain the first time Lief spoke of his admiration for Connor, and I couldn't stand to hear it; I'm glad that's no longer the case.

"Did you hear that, Diago? It means he likes you."

Lief drops one of the saddles and stretches a cautious hand toward Diago's nuzzle, but quickly draws it back when the horse snorts angrily at him.

"I don't think he fancies *me*."

"You ride Daisy, then."

"I believe you are one saddle short," comes a singsong voice.

Heloise struts into the stables, hair up in an immaculate crown of braids, wearing a form-fitting gray woolen coat, with red stitching from chest to foot.

"You're coming?"

"No, I'm only here to smell the horse dung," she declares, inhaling the air.

"But you said your mother forbade you to—"

"Humphrey came to my rescue, told my mother he needed me for a social call with some girl he's wooing."

"And your mother believed it?" Even I know Humphrey is the least likely of her brothers to adhere to courtliness.

Heloise laughs as she calls on a stableboy to fetch her horse. "I think she wants to believe it."

"If I'd known you were coming, I would have told you not to overdress." I take in her red sleeves and thigh-high boots.

She looks look at my dress then, a plain garb of murky green Lorette spruced up for me. Perfectly forgettable. And completely pointless with her around.

"This old thing?" She casts a glance down her coat. "Nonsense. I'm a nameless lady traveling with her maid and guard."

"You want the princess to play your maid?" An affronted sound rolls from Lief's throat.

"It wouldn't be the first time," I mutter ruefully, remembering the day I ventured into town in search of Beth. The day I met *him.* I fit my foot through Diago's stirrup, pushing the memory away as I haul my body onto the saddle with a huff.

Heloise's eyes widen a little. "Now that's a story I'd love to hear."

"Perhaps I'll tell you all about it if you win the next round of Justice Quicksand."

"In that case, prepare to lose."

The stableboy returns with Heloise's horse, an ebony steed resembling Diago, only not quite as large. Once fully saddled, we exit the portcullis and cross the drawbridge, then head south to the city districts. As it is through my balcony, the view from up above is stunning, a sloping facade of spires and clusters of buildings, with sunlight glinting off the snow-coated mountains that surround the city. Winter suits this place. The snow paints the myriad of roofs in dazzling white. In the streets, it peppers the corners of ladders and barrels and carts. But even the snow's brightness can't strip the city of its dark mood. Those lingering in the streets move about with hunched shoulders and darting eyes, looking suspicious of everyone, as though there might be someone out there already feeling symptoms of blue fever.

We round a corner onto Mill Street, which feeds directly into the central district, but the crowd is so large that it spills into the street, blocking our advance; nearly every citizen in the vicinity must be present. I steer Diago right behind Heloise and Lief, listening to the garbled echo of Perceval's voice that carries in the brisk air. The king and his entourage are nothing more than blurry figures at a distance. They stand on a platform of sorts. An outdoor theater perhaps? People surround them on all sides, gazing at the king in rapt silence. I knew Ethan was right to err on the side of caution, but seeing the crowd, it prickles my skin. Imagine what an angry mob that size could do.

I inch forward on the saddle, straining to hear, but I can't discern enough words to piece the king's sentences together. I notice the people on foot around me do the same, frowning in silence, ears perked for crumbs of understanding. A girl among them catches my eye. She stands with the crowd but her head is turned, her attention fixed on me. I look away and clear my throat. But I can't help my gaze when it drifts back to the girl. She's still staring. Does she know who I am? Before I can look away again, she moves through the crowd with off-the-shoulder glances in my direction.

She wants me to follow.

The first and most obvious thought that comes to mind is that she's a thief. If that's the case, she'll be sorely surprised to feel the point of my hidden dagger. But if she means to rob someone, why isn't she vying for Hel's attention? She's the one bedazzled in finery. Instinct tells me to stay put, but my increased pulse begs me to do otherwise. The girl slows her pace up the street, turning every so often. I get the feeling she might disappear at any moment.

If I'm going to take the bait, I must be smart about it. I call to Lief and Heloise to follow me as I pull on Diago's reins and turn him around. The girl scurries east through the mostly deserted streets. I resist the urge to get closer. I don't want to run into anything unprepared.

Hel trots to my side. "Why are we following that girl?" she asks.

"That's what I intend to find out."

Hearing our conversation, Lief cuts in from behind, "It's likely a trap, my lady. We should turn back."

"You have nothing to fear, Lief. I'll keep you safe." Heloise smiles, pleased with her barb.

Out the corner of my eye, I see Lief's face go tight, but whatever his flattened lips wish to say, he keeps to himself.

"As much as I would love to see you in action," I say to Heloise, "it's not worth ruining your reputation." But she shrugs it off.

"There's hardly anyone in the streets, and the few who are don't know who I am," she reasons, unconcerned.

I turn my gaze back to the girl just as she turns into an alley too narrow for the horses.

Lief beats me to dismount. "Let me go first," he says, sword ready in his grip by the time my boots hit the cobbles.

I nod, probing the inside of my boot for my dagger. "I'll be right behind you." I turn to Heloise. "Watch the horses."

She's disappointed with being left behind. "Scream for help if you need me."

Lief hesitates, probably trying to decide if she's capable of defending herself should someone think her vulnerable. Not that I blame him; we've yet to see her wield a weapon. But with all that confidence she exudes, I wonder if there's anything she's unprepared to do.

Sensing his concern, Heloise moves her coat to reveal the gilded hilt at her hip. "I'll keep watch."

Lief stares at Hel for a moment with what looks like an odd

mix of awe and chagrin, to which she responds with a wink that turns Lief's cheeks a deep red. It's enough to get Lief walking. I follow him into the alley. The girl's silhouette waits for me in its shadows. Lief takes six steps forward. "What is it you want?" he asks her.

"I'll only speak with the princess," the girl says in a raspy voice.

So she knows who I am.

"She could be armed," Lief warns in my ear.

"If she is," I whisper back, "her blade will meet mine."

Keeping my dagger tucked against my wrist, I inch toward her, close enough for privacy while still out of her reach.

"You are the Stonefall princess, are you not?"

"Who wants to know?"

I see a flash of teeth. "I will take you to someone who has the answers you seek . . . for the right price."

Though her words spark a fizz of curiosity, I can't help the skepticism in my voice. "The answers I seek?"

"Someone in the castle wants this information."

My heart thuds. "Who?"

The girl turns her palm to me, open and waiting. She wants payment.

"I don't have any coin."

"Your choker will do." She says this like she was expecting my answer. Or perhaps she set her eyes on my choker the moment she found me in the crowd. Instinctively, my fingers graze the thread around my neck, feeling the small stone affixed to it. I don't even remember what it looks like, only that Lorette put it on me this morning, insisting I might as well walk out naked if I wasn't going to wear any jewelry.

Parting ways with it does not trouble me, but I don't want to hand it over if she's just going to play me for a fool. "You've yet to convince me that I want what you're selling," I say.

The girl comes closer. Too close. I can see she's young, not much older than I. "I know the prince wants it," she whispers.

"And how would you know what the prince wants?"

"His councilor pet has his spies on the prowl, does he not?" she purrs seductively, confident that I want what she's withholding.

My neck stiffens. Are Milus's spies so easily noticed? My gaze flits around the alley as though I'm expecting to find others lurking about in the shadows. "Who else knows this?"

Her furtive gaze points me to her waiting palm. Wordlessly, I unfasten the choker and hold it over her palm. She snatches it, marveling greedily over it, eyes gleaming with excitement, before she stuffs it in her skirt pocket.

"Meet me at the King's Head in one hour."

Warning bells chime in my head. I tighten my gaze. "Why not now? I can follow you there." I couldn't care less about losing the choker. But if the girl is speaking the truth, I'd rather not lose sight of her.

"No one's there now. And you can't follow me," she says,

growing serious. "They might see."

"Who?"

She scoffs at my question. "The spies," she says through gritted teeth. "We don't trust them."

"We?" I'm beginning to feel like a birdbrain, and by the look she gives me, the girl might agree.

"In one hour," she repeats, making her exit at the other end of the alley, but not before she turns around to give me one last instruction. "Lose the pretty dress."

22

Connor

It's near dawn when Rhys's head slips through the slit of the tent. He seems surprised to find me awake, but he regains his glare quickly enough.

"Uther wants you," he snaps, and disappears.

Pip's fast asleep, curled up into himself. Careful not to wake him, I reach for my bow from under the cot and sling it over my shoulder; Uther's summon probably has everything to do with my bout with Rhys in the armory yesterday. I cut through the tents and fires of the slumbering camp with the comforting feel of the bow between my shoulder blades. Uther will likely order me to hand it over, but why should I? My aim won't do me any good with a shoddy bow. The smell of boiled grain warms the confined air of the cave, making my stomach grumble. I trace the scent to a large kettle pot cooking over a fire. A thin, long-limbed fellow stirs it, staring blankly at the simmering food as I pass. He's a far cry from the rest of the pack—a strong wind might snap him in two—and it makes me wonder how better skilled he is at handling a ladle over a sword.

I find Uther absorbed in the poorly illuminated map at his table. He looks up, dark shadows under his eyes, and fixes on the bowstring affixed to my shoulder for a second before he clears his throat and bids me to come in.

I take a seat on the stool across the table and glance down at the map. Dots penned with town and village names speckle the paper. *Fhalbo* catches my eye. Near it is a large red *X*. Unnamed. Areas outside the towns are circled, some of them with question marks, and others crossed out with a slash.

"These raids," I prod, assuming that's what the circles mean, "are they individual missions?"

Uther gives a pleased nod. "The number of raiders I assign depends on the collection they're after." He taps his index finger on a question-marked circle. "Each town and village is assigned a pair of collectors to make the rounds. I send scouts first to learn their routes and get a head count beforehand, then we use that information to come up with the best plan of attack."

"How many missions have failed?"

"None yet; we don't bite off more than we can chew. And we don't get greedy. The scouting reports have shown an increase in redcloaks over the past year, but it's not cause for concern yet." He scratches at his temple, and his eyes dart away with a thought. "They either believe we are too small a group of petty bandits to bother hunting us, or their resources are spread thin."

I point to the *X* on the map. "What's this?"

"A possible location for the commander's fort; Vishal is his name. We're not sure exactly where it is"—he taps the circle with his finger—"but we suspect it's near this area."

I remember the commander clearly from the day of Flynn's hanging. The oppressor in charge. "Are you planning to pillage the fort?" I ask.

"I seek its location so my men know to avoid it; the commander isn't a man I ever want to cross paths with." The underlying fear in his voice makes me frown.

"Why's that?"

Uther eyes me cautiously before asking, "Do you know what the people of Sunder call the commander?" At my shrug, he says, "Soul Reaper." Uther looks reluctant to go on, but he does. "Rumors say he steals the souls of men and turns them into his puppets. There are also whispers that he feeds on the blood of missing children."

I give him a blank look, keeping my brows in place. He's serious. "You believe these rumors?"

Uther raises his hands, shrugging as he does. "I know how it sounds, lad. But I've been around a while. The way I see it, all rumors are borne of truths, and, well, let's just say I'm not keen on finding out how much truth there is to this particular rumor." I continue to stare, incredulous, which prompts Uther to move things along. "Now, superstitions aside, Vishal's fort is the heart of the Usurper's operations in Sunder. From what little we know, it's equipped with more men and resources than we can handle. Attacking the fort would be suicide."

"Overpowering an enemy isn't the only way to win a battle."

"Aye. But without the backing of an army capable of waging

a full-scale war, winning a battle is meaningless. Even if I could slaughter every last one of them—and believe me I want to—it would only be a matter of time before the dead were replaced. Going after a commander's fort would put Theros on alert, and that's the opposite of what I'm trying to do here." He leans back on his stool, crossing his arms and gauging me curiously. "You seem to have some grasp on military strategy. We can put that experience to good use here." He glances over my shoulder. "But before we get into that, I wanted a word with you about a different matter. Rhys tells me you refused to give up the bow."

"An archer is only as good as his bow; the ones in your armory are junk."

He blinks. "Agreed. But why should we deny the others the opportunity to wield a better weapon?"

I point my chin at the scimitar across the pavilion. I don't have to get close to know it's a fine weapon; the golden carvings on the pommel give it away. "By that logic, that sword should be in the armory."

"The armory has a fine selection of swords and knives—courtesy of our deceased comrade—so I'm not depriving my men out of a good blade in keeping this one for myself."

"You keep that sword because you have adapted to it," I say. "Its weight, its length, the grooves of its hilt. Your body is trained to fight with *that* sword. You could use another and still be effective in a fight, but where bows and arrows are concerned, precision is key."

Uther sits in stunned silence, and I wonder if my bluntness has finally pierced his patience.

I get off the stool before he decides anything and offer a compromise. "You keep your sword, I keep my bow."

He gives me a long, stiff look before his mouth twists in a hard smile. "I like you, Connor. And I see great potential in you, so I will let this one slide . . ." Uther inclines his head. "Under one condition."

"Do I have a choice?"

"Not if you want to keep the bow."

"Speak then, what's your condition?"

"You teach your new brothers to shoot. Keepers first, of course. Tros, Zen, and Amos . . . you've met them, yes? They're the ones who keep watch outside the cave. They'll have better aim than the others."

Words fail me for a moment. "Your sentries aren't trained with the bow?"

"Is that so surprising? The keepers have good eyes, and can handle any target that comes close. But I won't lie. They are brutes, just like the rest of their brothers. Stabbing and butchering comes natural to them. Hitting a target from a distance takes . . . finesse." His eyes glint with approval. "Improving the keepers' skills will strengthen the camp's security, and if you can teach the raiders how to shoot, it'll make the raids easier."

Teaching untrained men to handle a new weapon will take some time, more than I planned to remain in this place. But they clearly need this. And in helping these men, I may be able to aid Asher and Raven in the long run.

I sigh in resignation. “Then I hope your arrows are straight.”

23

Meredith

I don't think I've ever seen Lief's face so scrunched up. "It's quite a stink, isn't it?" I grimace at the dried brown stains on the unsightly apron. The hem is no better, blackened with caked dirt and cow dung. Manure alone is not too hard to endure, but mixed with the scent of fresh milk, it's a tough stench to stomach. Hiding behind the cover of a cow while a milkmaid helped me out of my dress was an interesting ordeal, to say the least. I don't doubt the maid felt as odd as I did when it was my turn to tie my corset on her. It took more effort than I thought to convince her that I was serious about swapping clothes.

"I've smelled worse, my lady," Lief says, and I realize my face is frozen in a grimace.

"I still can't believe she thought your dress was pretty," Heloise chimes, holding a hand over her nose and mouth.

"And I still think the princess shouldn't go to the tavern alone." Concern furrows Lief's brow.

"If what that girl said is true—about the information—I'd rather not risk my guise. It's too important. And besides, I don't have anything worth stealing, so no one should pay me any mind," I say, but Lief is unconvinced.

"You are still a woman, my lady," he says, casting his scowl at his feet.

"Are you implying all her training has been for naught?" Heloise parries. "Because if it has, I'll be glad to take over the lessons."

Lief's breath erupts from his chest. "I am responsible for her well-being. If something happens—"

"I'll keep my dagger ready the whole time," I promise.

Lief tries a smile that says he isn't sold on the idea.

Before he can think of some other way to object, Heloise wraps a reassuring hand on Lief's arm and tells me, "If anything goes wrong, you make a run for the door; we'll be keeping watch outside."

The King's Head is a loud hole in the wall. A cacophony of howls of laughter carries into the street. You would think they were having a feast in there; Perceval's speech must have lifted their spirits. I glance over my shoulder. Up the street, Lief and Heloise remain at a close distance. Just enough so people won't suspect we belong to thc same party.

Then the tavern door flies open, making me jump. Two red-faced laughing men stumble into the street, and I have to scurry out of the way to avoid running into them, but they don't even notice me, engrossed in their conversation, and it bolsters my confidence. With any luck, everyone else inside will ignore me, too. I dash inside.

Patrons clutter the first floor of the tavern. They fill rows of candlelit tables, surrounded by barrels of wine and ale. Baskets and small clay bowls hang off each wooden beam, tied by a network of ropes that crisscross over the ceiling and through the metal chains supporting chandeliers made of large wagon wheels flipped on their sides.

In the midst of the banter, I hear the strings of a lute—probably a bard—but the sound is almost consumed by the commotion, making it impossible to hear its tune.

"Well done," a voice whispers in my ear.

It's the girl from the alley. She eyes me from head to foot with a slightly curved lip.

"I almost didn't recognize you."

"I'm surprised you recognized me at all. How did you know who I was?"

"I saw you once," she whispers. "Months ago, on that same horse you rode today. You looked worse than I do on a bad day. But you don't forget the face of a princess. Which, by the way, is looking too clean for a milkmaid. Come."

Taking note, I tilt my head down and keep my eyes on the back of her skirt as she leads me up a short flight of neglected stairs that groan with each of our steps.

She takes me to a table at the back of the room, to a man who squints at me with an air of disbelief. The first thing I notice are his scars. They mark his left cheek, down to the bottom of his chin, in deep, angry slashes, earning him the look of a battle-hardened man. My first impression of this man is that he's a savage, but his long gray hair, neatly pulled up and tied at the back of his head, suggests more civility than that.

"Sit," alley girl orders. As I do, I make room, expecting her to follow suit, but instead, she walks away, headed back for the stairs without another word.

"She's not the one you want to talk to," says the scarred man from across the table.

Under the table, I squeeze the hilt of my dagger, letting the feel of it comfort me.

"Who are you?"

"Who I am is of no importance," he answers, looking up from his pewter tankard, which he holds in both hands like a precious object. His next words are spoken so low I can barely hear them. "You are here for information on the blue fever."

I feel my pulse jump.

"I am," I hurry to say. "But . . . why me? Why not request to speak with the king?"

"You are the only one whose interests I can trust. I've been trying to find a way to contact you without alerting anyone. There was no way to do it without others finding out. But the Maker answered my prayers and put you in my daughter's path . . . and here you are."

Alley girl is his daughter? A barmaid comes with a refill for the scarred man's tankard. "Any poison for you, girl?" she asks, her voice gruff and gravelly.

"No, thank you."

"Suit yourself," she mutters, on her way to the next table.

"What interests do you speak of?" I ask once she is out of ear-shot.

"Your kingdom's interests; word on the street is the alliance is off."

I raise my chin. He hasn't the faintest clue how much that stings. Voice clipped, I ask, "What would that matter to you?"

He keeps his gaze on me. "Stonefall is of no consequence to me."

I can't help but feel defensive, as though I am here to prove Stonefall's worth. "So it's Alder you're concerned about?" It's the only other assumption I can make, although he doesn't strike me as the patriotic sort.

"I care for Alder's future because it's akin to my own. Alene—my daughter—is all that matters to me." He taps the table with his index finger. "And if this Theros character is threatening to endanger her life with a plague, it is my obligation as a father to do something about it."

"I'm seeking Theros's mole." My stomach churns. "The one who could release the plague in his stead."

He looks at the people seated at the tables around us, and I find his hesitation agonizing.

"I believe I know someone who might know who that is," he finally whispers. Not a very promising answer, but I'll take what I can get. He goes on, "I once knew a woman named Ella, who spouted warnings about a plague that would be unleashed in the city. She begged me to leave with her all those years ago. All this time, I figured she wasn't right in the head, missing a few marbles. But then I heard the news, and thought maybe she didn't babble nonsense after all." By now, I can barely sit still. "Last week, I went looking for her. I knew she wouldn't be happy to see me, but I thought . . . never mind what I thought. She played it all off, claimed it was a coincidence, that hers were the desperate ramblings of a foolish girl who wanted to leave this place and make a life elsewhere."

"You don't believe her?"

"No one rambles about a plague like that." He sets his drink aside, resting his forearms on the table, leveling his eyes at me. "I could have pushed her for the truth, but Ella is as spiteful and stubborn as she is opportunistic. I figured it was better if she thought she'd fooled me."

I anxiously wait for him, but he just stares at me, brows raised, expectant.

"You want *me* to speak with her?" I ask, and he nods, slowly, as if that will somchow help me digest his request better. "What makes you think she'll be honest with me?"

"You are a princess," he whispers. "You have both the power to intimidate her and the resources to tempt her."

"And you think she can be bought?"

He nods. "If she believes she is in trouble with the crown, she might be amenable. A pardon from the king along with some coin to sweeten the pot should suffice."

Glancing around the tavern, he reaches into his pocket and pulls out a folded piece of paper. He hands it over to me. I unfold it. The scrawled handwriting reads: *Ella Rew. Hut at the riverbank.*

I slip the piece of paper into the safety of my boot. I have what I need, but I still don't have an answer to the question that's been nagging me since my conversation with Alene in the alley. "How is it you and your daughter know about the spies?"

The man stiffens. For a moment, I think he's going to stand and walk away. But then, slowly, he speaks. "I was one of them." He looks away, as if ashamed to admit it, but his hatred is plain as day.

Alene's words in the alley come back to me. *We don't trust them.* She meant her and her father, I realize.

"What happened?" I ask, but the sharp sound of something breaking steals our attention. A slew of yelled curses follow, accompanied by the echo of shattering objects and toppling chairs.

The scarred man gives me a look. "Best get on out of here before you're spotted. The place tends to get a bit rowdy around now."

"Thank you," I say before I turn to leave, wishing I had a name to call him by.

"Take care, Princess. And good luck to you."

Keeping my blade hidden within my tight grip, I walk past the curious patrons leaning on the railing to get a view of the fight below and quickly slip down the stairs.

From the landing, I see a table bumped out of place in the middle of the tavern, its chairs scattered across the ale-splattered floor. Three pairs of inebriated men fight each other amid pieces of broken tankards, yelling obscenities and throwing punches that set them off balance. Their scuffle is met by a mix of amusement and annoyance from the seated patrons around them, who seem to pay no mind to the filthy milkmaid scurrying through a row of tables to the entrance.

At the end of the long street, Heloise sits straight on her saddle, looking as bored as ever, while Lief stands stone-faced, his hand glued to the hilt of his sword. His rigid posture relaxes a little when he spots me coming up the cobbled road.

"See? I told you she'd be fine," Heloise drawls as I walk up, inspecting her perfectly trimmed nails.

Lief gives her a look. "I gather you've never been inside a tavern, Lady Cresten? Men of questionable morals frequent such establishments."

Amusement stirs in Heloise's eyes. "Better to face a man who doesn't hide his questionable morals behind lavish clothes and happy manners, though, wouldn't you agree?" she muses with a wink. Then, before Lief has a mind to respond, she turns to me. "What I'm dying to know is if this tedious adventure was worth smelling like a barn?"

I'm not entirely sure it was, but I don't let the doubt dampen my spirits. I exhale, grinning up at my companions despite the pulsing pain in my head. “I think so.”

24

Connor

"Eyes closed?"

The one called Tros frowns at me like I've gone mad.

"Already griping, Tros? We haven't even started," says Amos next to him. To Amos's right, Zen tugs on his bowstring, testing the draw. Three upright logs dragged from one of the campfires stand ready for their arrows five yards ahead. At close range, they are easy targets.

If the keepers can't hit them, I'll have my work cut out for me.

"Know your release," I tell Tros. "You can't be a good archer if you can't shoot by feel. You want the release of the arrow to become second nature. Closing your eyes forces you to focus on form. So, again, draw your bows and take aim, shut your eyes, and shoot."

Zen is the first to follow my instructions. His stance is wrong, but the correction can wait for another lesson. They must learn the motions of shooting before I teach them anything else.

Amos shrugs at Tros and closes his eyes, but Tros cocks his head, annoyed. I sense he doesn't like taking orders from someone half his age. "Focus on your grip and the tension of the string.

You want your body—not your mind—to anticipate the shot. Focus on the exact pressure required to release the arrow."

The men shoot. Their arrows fly almost in unison. All three arrows miss the logs, shooting a couple hundred yards across empty sand.

I stifle a sigh.

It's their first day, I remind myself.

"Again. Your release should be smooth. No jerking. No flinching," I instruct, ignoring their surly grumbles.

About ten minutes in, half a dozen rebels have gathered behind us to watch.

"We'll never hit anything shooting blind," Tros gripes, aware of his audience.

"This isn't about the target," I remind him as Raven, Asher, and Pip walk up to watch. "Not yet."

I look at their quivers, packed full of arrows. Not enough for the hours of training these men will need. Twenty blind shots later, I send them to fetch their arrows. The respite should give their arms time to rest. Conversation picks up behind me as the small gathering of onlookers grow bored waiting. The pair I saw at the lake yesterday is among them, their animosity gone. The taller of the two acknowledges me with a nod.

Asher leaves his place and joins me. "You're proving your worth to them," he says. He stands, hands at his back, squinting at the trio of keepers hunting after arrows.

"I'm not doing this for their approval."

"But you'll earn it just the same."

Until I abandon their hopeless cause . . .

"They'll approve of Raven as well when she saves their lives" I say.

Asher drops his chin and loses a heavy sigh. "Raven is a talented healer, but I have no quarrel wasting her gifts if it keeps her safe; no life is more precious than hers . . . she is everything to me."

My eyes cut to Raven. She's at the edge of the crowd, crouched at Pip's side, smiling at his words. "Healing is all she has left."

"There will be wounds for her to mend here," he says, shoulders stiff.

Flesh wounds and bruises, perhaps; no rebel will make it back to camp with a life-threatening injury. But Asher's mind is already made up. Nothing I can say will change that, so I drop it.

Tros returns first, glaring under a sweat-beaded brow. "We wouldn't have t' chase these damned things if you'd let us shoot with our eyes open."

"That's what happens when you put an amateur in charge."

I follow the snide remark to Rhys, who's just appeared.

No longer crouching, Raven pointedly asks, "Don't ya have something better t' do?"

A scowl shows through Rhys's smirk. "I do." He turns his smug gaze to the rest of the crowd. "As do all o' you. This ain't a show, lads," he snaps. "Get back t' your stations."

His command is met with glares, but they do as he says and disperse back into the camp. Raven takes hold of Pip's hand and leads him back to the tents.

"That's how you follow orders," Rhys goads me, flicking an irked look at my bow, probably wondering why it's still in my possession. He's itching to pick a fight, but I won't meet his anger with my own today.

"Carry on with this silly charade 'n." Rhys waves dismissively. "I've got more important things t' oversee."

"You sure about that, Rhys?" Amos asks. "It might do ya good t' learn how t' shoot."

Rhys's jaw sharpens. "I can shoot better 'n all of you numskulls." He doesn't wait for a response. Watching his undignified retreat, I hear Tros chuckle.

"If that turd don't like you, you're doing something right, lad."

Why would Uther grant command to someone despised by his men? I wonder, watching Zen and Amos return with their arrows.

"D'you bore the crowd with your griping?" Amos asks Tros.

"Turd showed up to squash the fun," Tros says, earning a groan from Amos.

Four hours later, the keepers have learned the proper stance, but their arms are spent, so I send them off to rest for tomorrow's lesson; a couple more days should suffice to improve their aim. But the rest of the camp will be more of a challenge. Unlike the keepers, the raiders' familiarity with weapons is limited to those used for close combat. They've never handled a bow or shot at a target; I'll be lucky if I can train them to shoot at close range before the week is over.

Training the raiders is worse than I expected. Three weeks in, progress is still slow and my patience is waning. The men draw like beasts, too hard and too fast and too far, bending the bows beyond their limits and breaking them. During the second week of training, the bowstrings start snapping from overuse. I can't fix the bows fast enough, and with a decreased arsenal, I'm forced to train fewer men at a time. Half of the men can't listen and the other half chooses not to, bent on disregarding my instruction to learn through their own trial and error. It's a small miracle they haven't been caught by redcloaks before now.

But over these weeks, I've noticed their resistance lessening somewhat. They hold a seat for me around their fire at supper and share their stories with me. Farmers, merchants, fishermen, artisans. Simple folk who lived quiet, ordinary lives before the Takeover. Their families murdered, their homes burned or stolen, given to traitors who pledged allegiance to the Usurper to save their own skins. I meet the brash twin brothers, Axel and Jace, who lent a hand to a failing raid before they joined the Brotherhood. Then there's Tros and Amos. They tell me they met as orphans in the streets, turned from begging for food to stealing it, and fell in with a group of bandits who saw their potential. They were among the first to join Uther's cause, eager to offer the tricks of their trade.

The Brotherhood is new family for them all.

But I'm not the only one who's noticed a change. The camp's attitude toward Raven and Pip has improved as well. They were seen as burdens when we first arrived, but Raven was smart to insist on helping with the meals. Though the stores are limited to porridge and gruel, her knowledge of seasoning outshines that of the camp's cook. The first time she asked to prepare breakfast, she took care not to divulge that information to the men, letting their bellies make the decision for them before bias clouded their judgment. Though she's still angry at Asher, cooking keeps her occupied, and she's still employed with Pip. He's fit enough to travel now, and yet I remain here.

I'll leave when the training is finished, I decide, *not a day later.*

"Relax your grip," I tell a man named Bardo when his arrow misses.

The flinch of his release keeps throwing his aim. Bardo wrinkles his rounded nose, frustrated. The other trainees have all managed to hit the log at least once so far; even Tick, named so after his twitching left eye, has shown prowess. But Bardo has missed every shot.

He pulls another arrow and draws again. I dissect every detail, looking for mistakes. Grip, stance, anchor, form. I'm anticipating a better shot this time, but he jerks at release, distracted by high-pitched voices.

"Someone's getting their chops busted," Bardo mutters as we look on.

Maro, the oldest of the bunch, chuckles. His voice is as raspy as his face is wrinkled. "Hope it's Rhys."

"Best not meddle 'n," Tick replies, "or Uther will be busting *our* chops."

I shift on my feet, listening to the indistinct echoes. A brawl shouldn't scare them. It should entertain them, if nothing else.

So why do I sense alarm?

"Keep practicing," I say to the group. "I won't be long."

"Don't say I didn't warn ya," Tick shouts out.

I trot back to the camp and make for the lake. A quarter of the rebels remain at their stations, apathetic to the commotion. I deliberately walk the path to the camp's kitchen. A half-peeled potato lies abandoned on the table, and the pots are left unattended over the fire, clouds of steam gushing out of them, the water boiling.

My eyes snap to the lake.

I'm running through sand, leaping over moss-slick rocks and skidding around tables and tents and foraged piles of mushrooms, nuts, and horsetail weeds. A woodchopper halts his ax midair as I race past and veer in between a pair of tents.

I skid to a stop behind the crowd and maneuver my way in to get a better view, nudging shoulders to let me pass.

Asher holds Pip at the foot of the lake, tilting his body downward so that his head dangles a few inches off the wet rock. Raven holds his mouth open with one hand and presses on his stomach with the other.

I rush to my knees beside her. "How can I help?"

Too overwhelmed to speak, Raven merely shakes her head, her features set as she massages Pip's abdomen, pushing down toward his lungs, eyes solid with determination. With each stroke, her hand moves faster, pushing deeper.

And then Pip is coughing up water.

Raven flops back on her legs, letting out a huge breath, as though she held it the entire time. Asher lays Pip down on the rocky surface, rolling him to his side as he vomits more water and gulps air. When he finally stops, his small, reddened eyes blink up, confused to find the whole camp looking at him.

"What happened?" I ask.

"Rhys pushed him," Raven says bitterly.

"I was teaching the boy how t' swim." Rhys swaggers out of the crowd, looking down his crooked nose at me.

I'm on my feet in an instant. Asher grabs my shoulder, trying to keep me at bay. I swat his hand away.

Fussing over his tunic, Rhys says, "He was gonna have t' learn eventually."

I lunge, throwing Rhys to the sand, pinning him with my body. The men part around us, yelling excitedly as my shaking hands clench into fists and pound Rhys's jaw over and over, intent on turning his arrogant face into a pulp.

But arms clamp around my torso, pulling me off him.

Rhys wipes the blood off his nose and lips, and taunts me with a cold smile as I struggle to get free, itching for more blood.

"You are better than this," Asher whispers in my ear.

I grit my teeth. He's strong for a man his age. "You know nothing about me," I hiss, shaking him off.

Rhys gets up and dusts his tunic. "Is that all you've got, *Northerner*?" He stresses the word like it's an insult, like I'm a trespasser. But I'm no idiot. He wants this. Rhys risked Pip's life just to provoke me. And I played right into it. He hasn't landed a single blow on me; he hasn't even tried.

"Thank your Gods he didn't drown," I growl.

Rhys's snide smile disappears when Uther pushes through the men and points at us.

"You two, come with me."

The command is docile, but the hard line of his jaw is hard to miss.

"He's the one who attacked me," Rhys complains, reminding everyone of his age.

Uther silences Rhys with a stony gaze. Then he addresses the gathered men. "Get back to work."

The crowd scatters, and Uther retreats to his pavilion, with Rhys hobbling after him. If he had a tail, it'd be tucked between his short legs.

Raven is beside me. "I don't care what Papa says. You did right by Pip."

I look over at Pip. He's nodding at Asher, wiping tears off his face with the back of his hand. "Keep an eye on him," I say to Raven, and at her nod, I turn on my heel toward the pavilion.

Rhys and Uther are in the middle of an argument when I pull back the flap of the tent and step inside.

"What you've taught—"

Rhys cuts himself off when he hears me come in.

The angles on Uther's face are drawn tight. He taps an impatient finger on his table, his incensed eyes flicking back and forth between Rhys and me. "Whatever that was back there, it's the last time it happens."

"Tell that t' *him*," Rhys whines.

Uther's tapping hand slams against the wood, knocking his stein, ale spilling down the edge and onto the ground, splashing Rhys's legs. Spots of color appear on Uther's cheeks, and the vein on his temple threatens to burst. "Another word and I'll finish what he started!"

That shuts him up.

"Whether you like it or not," he continues, pointing a finger at no one in particular, "you are brothers now. And you will work out your differences, or so help me, I will throw you to the redcloaks myself."

Uther gives himself a moment to cool off, drawing in a long breath through his nose. He clasps his fingers over the spilled ale, and finally, he says, "I'm sending the two of you on a scouting mission. You leave at dawn."

25

Meredith

I was hoping I'd get the chance to clean up before giving Ethan the good news, but I find him waiting for me in my room when I rush in. He sits by my desk, forearms braced on his knees, staring at the cracks in the flagstone between his feet.

"Ethan? What are you doing here?"

His mouth goes slack when he sees me, aghast at my appearance. He's looking at me like I'm completely mad. "The guards said you hadn't returned from the city."

He was worried.

I should be flattered, but somehow, it unnerves me.

I'm mumbling incoherent words that made sense in my head, but then Ethan leans back against the chair, nose wrinkling, probably affronted with the awful odor of my hem, which, thankfully, I can no longer smell.

"What in the Maker's Gate are you wearing?"

"In case you couldn't tell by the smell, it's a milkmaid's dress," I say, feeling amused and embarrassed at the same time.

He covers his nose, half grimacing and half smiling. "I'm afraid to ask what possessed you to dress like one, but I assume there's an explanation."

"There is!" I'm brimming with enthusiasm. "I was going to tell you straightaway. Once I bathed. But, well, here you are."

Not bothering to sit, I tell him everything, speaking so fast that my tongue struggles to keep up with my brain, stumbling over the words. He listens, his expression growing more and more weary as I continue. For a moment, his face scrunches in disapproval, and his mouth works like he's about to interrupt me. But I rush to get the words out, and as I speak of my conversation with the scarred man, I see in him the same hope I felt, the same eagerness to hear what the man had to say. A frown furrows between his eyes when I mention Milus's spies and how the scarred man said he used to be one of them, but the glint of hope lingers.

I'm out of breath by the time I finish.

Ethan stands, blinking disbelief. He steeples his hands, fingertips at his lips. "This is great news, indeed," he says, pacing from one corner of the room to another, and I can almost see the wheels of his head turning. He stops to grab my hands. Squeezes them hard. "If the lady he speaks of can point us to the mole—if we find him—we can bring an end to all of this."

He's smiling at me and I'm smiling back at him, our hands locked.

And then he breaks the spell.

"But first, I must have a word with Milus about his spies."

I pull away from him. "No. We can't speak of this to Milus. The man's daughter said they don't trust—"

"The spies. Not Milus. I promise you he is not our enemy,

Meredith," he stresses. "But if his spies are double-crossing him, he needs to know."

My lips press into a grimace. "Fine," I bite back. "But we find the mole first."

Ethan runs a hand through his hair and sighs, not looking inclined to agree, leaving a tuft out of place. I ignore the desire to reach out and fix it.

"Even if he is as trustworthy as you say," I begin, "don't you think it's best if we leave him out of this? Milus commands the spies, and if they suspect something has changed—"

"Fine," he says tightly, raising his hands in a gesture of surrender.

I fight the relief tugging my lips; I don't want to push my luck.

"So what happens next?" I ask.

"We pay Ella a visit."

"Now?"

"Tomorrow." He pauses, making a face. "I will send Lorette to draw you a bath. We can talk more after dinner."

"That's all right." I chuckle. "Lief will be fetching her by now."

"Good. I'll leave you then." With a nod good-bye, he makes for the door.

"Ethan?"

He half turns, his expression filled with hope and all its possibilities.

"I'm sorry for making you worry," I say in earnest.

His voice is light and teasing, but his eyes are thoughtful. "Don't be. I like worrying about you." Then he must think better of it, as he pulls the handle and says, "But I would prefer not to make a habit out of it."

We travel back to the city the next day. Ethan signals to dismount just outside the market in the central district. He turns to face his guards, who have followed us like shadows since the castle gates. He addresses the sergeant. "The princess and I will continue on foot. Alone."

"*Alone,* Your Highness?" the sergeant objects.

After dinner last night, Ethan and I brainstormed how we would pay Ella Rew a visit without unwanted eyes trailing our every move. A rather hard task when you're royalty. Naturally, I suggested he forego the excursion and let me go with Lief instead, to which he replied with a resounding and final no.

"What's it to be, then?" I asked him. "We can't very well dress under our station. Ella will never believe who we are."

His only answer: "I have an idea." Which he didn't bother to elaborate, sending me off to bed pouting, making me wonder if he actually had the first clue what to do.

"I can take care of myself," Ethan assures the sergeant. "We will meet you back here in a few hours." He hands the man a small coin purse. "Take the men to the King's Head. Let them have a drink on me." His eyes sneak to me for a half second. "I hear the patrons are lively in there."

The sergeant rubs his chin, his expression blank as he stares at the coin purse in his hand. "Is this a test, Your Highness?"

"Of what, Sergeant? Your distaste for ale?" At the sergeant's lack of response, Ethan offers his arm to me. "My fair lady," he teases with dramatic flair. "Shall we?"

I hook my arm around his and we parade through South Main Street, which leads into the crowded area that makes up the square. Tenant farmers sell the very winter vegetables they harvested on their landlords' estates. Stalls piled high with parsnips, leeks, carrots, and turnips trick my nose into thinking I'm standing in a garden. We step inside the square, and the remote silvery tunes of flutes and bagpipes immediately snare my attention. Quite the contrast from yesterday's deserted streets. A quartet of minstrels plays on a raised stage at the opposite end of the square.

"It was good of your father to come and speak. The people seem better for it."

"He's good with words. I only wish they were more than empty reassurances," he admits. "Did you get a chance to listen to any of it?"

I shake my head softly. "I was too far away to hear." After a pause, I say, "Is this the part where you finally tell me what we're doing here?"

I don't even ask why he forced me to wear the azure cape dragging dirt at my heels, or why he's wearing an exact replica; I doubt it's because he wanted us to match.

He gives me a no-nonsense look. "We are *shopping*."

"I had no idea you were such a spendthrift," I say dryly.

Ethan smiles at a gray-haired woman shuffling across our path, swinging a basket of flowers I don't recognize at her elbow. Ethan digs out a coin from his pocket and gives it to the woman in exchange for a flower. "I'm not, but I think this is rather pretty," he says, presenting me with the delicate flower. It's small and white with a green center. The fully bloomed bud droops away from the stem, as other flowers might when wilting, but this one looks healthy, its petals bright.

"What kind of flower is this?"

"Snowdrop," Ethan quips. "They bloom in winter. You should see them on the ground. There are woods covered in them outside the city. You'll think them snow if you don't look too closely."

"I shouldn't hold on to it," I say, wishing for a small vase with water. "I'm too clumsy. I'll crush it without thinking."

Ethan angles his body to face me, his breath warm against my cold cheek as he takes the flower and tucks it behind my ear. "There. Safe and sound."

I attempt a nonchalant smile. "Thank you," I stammer.

We continue through the market, where stalls offer pastries, salts and spices, textiles, and iron ore. Peddlers call out to the buzzing square, hoping to catch a customer. Those who can't afford a stall sell from baskets, like the flower lady, or spread cloth on the ground along walking paths to display their wares. "I've never seen a market this size," I say in wonder.

"It's the largest of the district markets in the city. And the oldest. The other markets were built as the city grew to accommodate the demand. As the kingdom's capital, and as a large city, Alder City attracts scores of peddlers and merchants, especially with it being in close proximity to the Ganes River; trade benefits greatly from it."

"It's almost . . . chaotic," I say. "Is it strange that I feel more relaxed here than I do in the castle?"

Ethan grins. "It doesn't surprise me. I figured you would appreciate the anonymity. But make no mistake, people are aware of our presence. They're simply too busy to mind. It's one of the advantages of the central market. It's only when my father visits that their dealings get disrupted."

The paths are so crowded that it takes us several minutes to cross the market, making frequent stops to let others pass. Those who struggle to get around us pay enough attention to acknowledge their prince, offering respectful nods and smiles before moving on with their busy day. "I thought we were shopping," I say when Ethan takes us outside the market.

"We are."

At the first intersection, Ethan pulls me out of the cobbled street and into a shop with a neatly carved sign that I don't get a chance to read. The aromatic smell of fresh-cut wood peppers the air inside. A carpenter's shop. Wood shavings litter the floor, forming heaps around the tables. A large wagon wheel rests on the far wall, along with stacks of countless planks of wood. On the right, small, sharp tools are hung, while the saws and other large cutting tools I have no names for dangle from ceiling beams. Two boys work on one, assembling with hammer and nail what looks to be a window frame, while an older man—probably the carpenter—shaves an ornately carved spindle. The three workers freeze when they realize who their patron is.

"Your Highness!" The carpenter bows his head with surprise. Then, suddenly animated, he claps his hands together, smiling expectantly at us. "How can I be of service?"

"I'm in urgent need of a cart," Ethan tells him.

From the carpenter's expression, I can tell he wasn't expecting this answer. But he recovers quickly. "How urgent would that be, sire?" he asks, as though treading on eggshells.

"This instant," Ethan clarifies, and the carpenter's face falls for a second. But then he recovers, slapping on a wide grin.

"I have just the thing."

While the two young workers resume their tasks, the carpenter shows us to his shed. A worn, four-wheeled cart takes up half the space. The rest of it serves as a stable for the carpenter's lanky brown horse and its hay.

"It's seen better days, but it gets the job done," the carpenter says as he waits for the approval of his prince.

"There's no need to leave you without a cart of your own, not when your business depends on it." Ethan slaps a confident hand on the carpenter's shoulder. "I'll pay to borrow it. And your horse."

This gives the carpenter pause. "My horse, sire?"

"I give you my word I will return them both this afternoon."

Accepting a generous purse from Ethan, the carpenter and his two assistants rush to saddle the horse and hitch the empty cart. As we stand by and wait, Ethan moves to unfasten my cape from my shoulders. I watch him flip it inside out, turning the blue cape into a hooded black cloak. Ethan steps to face me, his arms curling around me to tie the cloak at my collar bone. "I'm not saying your milkmaid guise wasn't clever, but I prefer the mysterious merchant look. It's a lot easier to shed . . . and easier on the nose," he whispers.

Understanding finally dawns on me: we are shopping for a disguise. We couldn't simply take a horse to find Ella; we would stick out like the royal thumbs that we are. But as far as the guards—or any other interested party—knows, Ethan and I are spending the day at the market with a pair of very bright and noticeable blue capes attached to our backs. On foot. But now, draped in drab cloaks, we are just another pair of peddlers making a living along the cold winter roads of Alder. I can't help the smile on my lips as I watch Ethan tie his cloak in turn. His lips hitch slyly at the corner when he finds me watching, and then he pulls the hood up, covering his face.

It's not until we leave the city behind that I allow myself to relax, filling my lungs with a deep breath. If it weren't for pretenses, Ethan would probably have us barreling forth at a full gallop. I wouldn't mind getting to Ella's house sooner, but I'm glad we're not pushing the carpenter's horse too hard; he's less than half the size of Diago. Even my Daisy is a sturdier mount.

Prompted by the cold wind on my face, I slide in the seat and press against the warmth of Ethan's side, keenly aware of his arm brushing mine as he handles the reins. But cold as I am, the gentle pull of the horse helps to calm me.

The farther we get from the city, the closer the snow- and pine-tree-covered mountains get to the road, becoming more than a shadowed, majestic backdrop now. We follow the Ganes River, which cuts through the snowy landscape. Huts blot the field, but there are only a handful of them, set too far apart from one another to be considered a community. It doesn't escape my notice that none are near the river's bank. *Hut at the riverbank.* For a moment, I'm back at the tavern, reading the scribbled note. I had wondered how we would determine which hut's door to knock at, but I'm beginning to understand now.

When Ella's hut appears like a speck in the distance, I feel my body tense again. Are we really so close to freeing Alder from Theros's clutches? Logic tells me things are never so easy. But why couldn't they be? The scarred man is convinced Ella is the answer, and I can't shake the feeling that he's right. We just need a name. That's all. Apprehensive hope swells inside me, growing in my chest like roots the closer we get, and I have to remind myself not to hold my breath.

The only sign of life within the hut is the thin trail of smoke pouring out from the chimney. It looks smaller than the other homes we passed, but it's well kept. The thatched roof looks uniform and dense, free of holes or uneven patches. At a short walking distance, the constant and soothing flow of the river trickles over a sea of pebbles. It's close enough to make water-hauling trips easy, and far enough to be safe from the high summer tide. Having the water seems like a luxury, though it does make the frost in the air more prominent. A deep, wet cold sinks into my bones. I glance up again at the chimney. Ella Rew must have that fire going day and night to keep the chill at bay.

Ethan questions me with his eyes after he helps me off the cart. *Ready?* they seem to ask. I nod at the unvoiced question and hover close behind him, pulling at the thread of my cloak to keep my hood up as an icy gust swoops by. Footprints of different sizes mark the snow to Ella's hut. More traffic than I would have expected. Ethan knocks a few times with no luck. He glances over his shoulder at me. From what I gathered from the scarred man, Ella lives alone. So she must be out, doing whatever it is that allows her to put food on her table each day.

"How long do we have before the market closes?" I ask, thinking of Ethan's guards awaiting our return.

"About three hours." He scans the white landscape. The tip of his nose is pink from the cold. From the numbing feel of it, mine is too. He rubs his gloved hands together to try and keep warm. "Her chimney is still smoking so she hasn't been gone long. We can wait by the bank upriver and build a fire, close enough to keep an eye on the hut but not so close that we draw attention."

"And if she doesn't return in time?"

He presses his lips into a reticent line. "If there is no sign of her before then, we'll have to head back empty-handed." I let out a heavy breath, expecting that to be the case. "But we'll try again if we have to," he says, reading my disappointment. "I doubt the sergeant will protest another round of free drinks." He starts to make his way back to the horse but stops when he notices I'm fixed to the snow-white dirt at my feet. Waiting out in the cold for Ella's return is a reasonable plan, but it feels like such a waste of valuable time. My pinched gaze strays back to the door, to the small cavity that makes the keyhole.

"We can gather branches from the trees," Ethan calls, but my hand is on the rusted iron handle. The cold metal bites through my gloves as my fingers curl around it. I push lightly, expecting the clink of the lock to resist me, but the door inches softly inward. I can feel the warmth of the fire popping and crackling inside through the crack in the door.

"It's unlocked," I mutter.

"Then she can't be far," Ethan warns me. "We should move on before she sees us breaking into her home."

"You're the crown prince. What's she going to do? Have you arrested?"

"She might flee if she sees us."

"Then let's wait inside where it's warm."

I let myself in . . .

And I hold back a scream, unable to make a sound.

Three bodies sway suspended, hung by ropes that loop at their necks. Two women and one man. Their heads sag, still and lifeless, and though their hair obscures their faces, the jeweled choker I spot on one of the women is all I need to see to crush what little hope I had.

26

Connor

Rhys and I sit in the back of an artisan's cart, feeling every pebble in the road vibrate through the wood. Our hooded capes come down just below the shoulders over the large pale-yellow tunics tied at the waist by frayed strings of rope; the loose-fitting clothes hide my skin from the sun and obscure the dagger strapped to my leg.

All this fabric and I still feel exposed without my bow and quiver.

Uther assured me his scouts have yet to rely on their daggers, but it's Rhys I have to watch out for. After what the bastard did to Pip, I doubt there's' anything he wouldn't do. The animosity between us makes the two-day trip to the village of Locke feel like a week. Uther's decision to pair Rhys and I was drastic. The mission could fail because of it. I should have left the camp with Pip last night and saved myself the trouble. But I couldn't risk it. Not after he swallowed all that water. He needs to recover. There was no sign of fever when I left this morning, which was promising, and knowing Raven will be there to look after him made my departure easier.

On the road, travelers are scant. Less than a handful cross our path; the Usurper is choking trade to its bare bones. The artisan—who introduced himself as Walden—stops in the middle of the road to exchange words with a merchant pulling a cart with a couple of wine barrels. Like Flynn and Asher, Walden is another of Uther's aides, who uses his trade as a front to serve the Brotherhood. Walden trades him silvers for a wine sack. The merchant thanks him and continues on his way toward Fhalbo, throwing curious glances at Rhys and me. The merchant stares at my face with that look people get when they recognize you, but eventually he turns and disappears down the road.

We move at a dogtrot's pace along the winding dirt path. Walden hums a merry tune, flicking the mule's reins whenever it stops to chew on weeds sprouting in the road. When he's not humming, he's making comments on the shapes and colors of boulders and the way bushes grow in clumps around stunted trees, talking as though Rhys and I are enthralled. Hours pass before we arrive at Locke.

It's another farming community, and not much different than Fhalbo. Though the faces are different, soldiers patrol like tyrants around the market, and the residents bear the same signs of oppression. We stop the cart at the square so Walden can set up his wares.

Rhys jumps off and pulls out the ripped piece of paper with Uther's hand-drawn map. I watch him inspect it, knowing it would be wasted breath to ask about it. If he wants to figure it out on his own, that's fine by me.

Walden removes the cloth from the back of his cart, revealing a stack of scrolls. He unfolds one. It's a canvas. A painted landscape with a river that slices through the center.

"What d'you think?" Walden asks when he catches me looking.

I step up and take a closer look. The brushstrokes are broad, blurring the finer details, but the essence is there; now I understand his obsession with rocks and scrubby bushes. "You have an eye for scenery."

"Only eye anyone 'round here's allowed t' have."

"There's a law against art?"

Walden nods, his long mustache and beard moving with his head. "Places like these, art's dangerous. It has the power t' inspire others." His voice lowers an octave. "'Tis why the Usurper banned portraits. The only portraits 'round here are those o' wanted men." Walden's attention cuts behind me. "You might want t' catch up with the lad before he disappears."

I turn. Rhys has walked off on his own. I sigh, shaking my head as I pace after him. He walks fast, as though it will make a difference. I'm gaining ground when I notice someone following Rhys. A woman. She hurries to keep up, looking conspicuous as she scans her left and right. There's nothing peculiar about her: black hair, olive skin, same as every other girl walking around the square.

But I recognize the confident gait.

"What are you doing here?" I whisper behind her shoulder.

Raven's surprise melts into relief when she sees me, pressing a hand to her stomach and uttering something under her breath. "Keep moving," I say, eyes back on Rhys. Raven's hurried steps fall in line with mine. "What are you doing here?" I ask again.

"I don't trust him," she says, eyes ahead.

"That doesn't answer my question."

She takes her time to answer. "I don't know . . . I woke up with this bad feeling in my bones."

She came all this way on a *hunch*? I have to bite my tongue to keep from snapping at her. "What about Pip?"

"He'll be fine. I left the cook a regimen o' tonics, should he need 'em."

"Raven—" I start to protest, but she doesn't let me finish.

"Pip will be fine," she insists in a heated whisper. "I wouldn't have left if I thought otherwise. The tonics will strengthen his defenses and keep him hydrated, but his body will have t' do most o' the work fighting off an infection from that contaminated water. The cook promised t' look after him, so don't worry too much."

"I wasn't worried until I saw you."

"Well, I came all this way because I was worried about *you*. Then I come here and find Rhys alone, and I think—"

"What, that he slit my throat? I can look after myself, Raven."

"I'm aware o' that," she scoffs. "But an extra pair o' eyes can't hurt, can it?"

A fair point. Except now I will have to watch her back as

well. “How did you get here?”

“Same as you. I hitched a ride from a neighbor . . . he owed me a few favors. Only he travels by horse.” I can hear the smirk in her voice, pleased with herself.

The throng of villagers dwindles as we carry on past the square. The patrols seem to follow the crowd. No soldiers roam outside the market, but I sense someone staring at me. I make eye contact with a villager who leans against an empty post, mindlessly chewing on something that sticks out of his mouth. He doesn’t look away.

“Keepers let you leave camp?” I ask Raven.

“I told ’em I was foraging wild berries.”

“You’re going to give your father a stroke.”

“He’ll live.”

I know that tone. She’s still angry with him.

We follow Rhys out of the village and venture into the hill country. The wheel-carved road spans across the grassy slopes like a snake, lined by stretches of dense, bushy trees. Looming ahead, a flat-topped ridge of boulders and dirt, baked dry under the harsh glare of the sun.

“What is *she* doing here?” Rhys says through his teeth when we join him in the trees.

“I’m here t’ make sure there are no . . .”—she sizes him up with fiery eyes—“hiccups.”

Rhys snorts. “The only thing you’ll do is get in the way.”

Raven crosses her arms. “Go on and laugh. I’m not leaving.”

"We only have provisions for two." His grip on the sack hanging from his shoulder tightens. "If you stay, one o' you will go hungry."

"I glanced at our provisions before we left," I say. "We could make do if we're frugal."

Raven shakes her head. "There's no need for that." She unfastens a pouch from a fold under her skirt. "I brought my own."

Rhys knows he can't win this argument without my support. The smile on his face doesn't reach his eyes. "Try t' keep up then, sweet face. Just let me be clear: I'm not responsible for ya," he declares, jabbing an angry finger at her collarbone. His head inclines to me. "If something happens t' her, it's on you."

Two days of hiding out in this heat has sapped our water supply. We haven't run out yet, but there's not much left, and we need to make it last. Uther expected the collectors to pass through yesterday, but they didn't. It's possible they're changing schedules to keep from getting robbed.

At the first sign of movement, I pick up my legs and find my footing on the sturdy branch of the tree that faces the road, feeling the flow of blood chase away the prickling numbness of sitting too long in one position; I would have more room to stretch on the ground, but the tree provides a better vantage point. I squint through the foliage. Shadows move in the distance.

Below, Rhys jumps to his feet, alerted to their approach. Raven doesn't bother getting up this time. She was eager before, but her excitement has waned with each false alarm.

"Is it them?" Rhys asks.

"No. Four travelers on foot." Peasants, by the looks of them. I watch them, expecting them to pass our hiding spot, but the closer they get, the more their steps veer to the edge of the road. I lean back. "I think they're headed this way."

Rhys curses in annoyance. "I'll handle 'em."

Looking down, I watch him step out of the shadows to meet the strangers.

Rhys folds his arms and takes up an uninviting stance. "This spot's taken, lads."

Instead of words, the reply comes as a fist. Rhys's head jerks sideways from the blow, and three of the men rush him. The other jumps to the shadows.

Raven cries out. My eyes cut toward the sound. One of the men has her pinned with a knife to the throat.

If only I had my bow.

When the men point their own weapons at him, Rhys stops fighting and raises his arms.

Just don't look up.

One of the men crouches, digging through our supplies while still pointing his knife. If I get the angle right, I can land on him. The distraction should buy Raven and Rhys a few seconds.

Rhys's open arms suggest surrender, but his tone is anything but docile. "We don't have any coin."

"Where's ye friend?" asks the ruffian who has Raven.

How long have they been watching us?

The man is done fumbling with the sack and is back on his feet. If I jump on him now, I'm hoping it will break his neck. But even if I miss, it will still create a distraction. The real risk is the landing itself. One false move, and it might give them the upper hand.

"There's no one else," Rhys replies.

"Don't play with us, lad. The scarred one." He grips Raven's chin and shakes her head. "I saw him with this pretty thing in the village. Where'd he run off t'?"

I jump.

My feet miss his head by a few inches, crashing on the ruffian's back. My weight smashes him flat on the ground with a thud, and his head bangs hard, but not enough to knock him out. I pin his arms with my knees, and he groans under me as I reach for my dagger. One second I am stabbing his spine and his struggling limbs go limp under me, the next I am pulling the dagger out and charging the man fighting Raven. I push him off and slam his face against the tree. He's the man I saw observing us in the village. He drops his knife, too dazed to grip the handle. Then I drive my dagger in his belly. He moans, eyes flashing open. "Here I am," I say and yank my dagger out.

Rhys is kicking one of the two bodies at his feet. The man is dead but that doesn't stop Rhys. Holding his bleeding arm, he growls at the dead man, venting anger that's likely been building since the day I stepped foot in his camp.

Raven resists her healer instincts for no more than a minute. She claims the dead man's knife, tucking it in her skirt, and asks Rhys, "Can I take a look?"

"It's just a scratch."

"That's a lot of blood for a scratch," she says, digging items out of her pouch. She reaches for his bleeding arm. He pulls away at first, but Raven proves more stubborn than his pride.

"Did you have anything to do with this?" I ask him.

Rhys's stare goes cold. "You think *I* put 'em up t' this?" There was hardly time in the village for Rhys to have planned something like this, but I didn't have my eyes on him the entire time.

"Are you surprised?" Raven asks. "You've given him plenty o' reasons not t' trust you. My being here is proof o' that."

Rhys licks his thinned lips, his gaze darting between us. "I dislike ya, it's true," he says, nodding at me. "And I don't have a problem playing dirty, either. But I'd never jeopardize a mission." His gaze falls on the dead bodies before he turns to me. "I had no business with these tramps."

"Why would anyone target peasants with nothing to steal?"

Rhys glowers at me through winces as Raven cleans his wound. "Hell if know!"

His frustration seems genuine . . . but is it? A talented liar could fool anyone, even me.

"Perhaps it's a sign that things are getting worse—that people are desperate," Raven weighs in, but her voice lacks confidence.

Raven finishes with Rhys's wound. She rolls the bloodied sleeve down and stares at it a moment. "This is going t' draw attention."

"Roll it back up," I tell her. "There isn't much else we can do." The look we briefly share hints at more than just the obvious. If Rhys hired these men, we have no way of proving it.

Rhys notices the exchange with a curled lip, aware, looking as though he's about to object, but the sound of a carriage stops him. I crouch to the edge of the shadows, with Rhys a step behind. We trace the thumping noise to two hundred yards away: two officials driving the coin wagon, flanked by four pairs of soldiers on horseback. Raven's skirts rustle as she joins us.

"That's them," Rhys mutters. "Eight soldiers. That's twice as many as usual."

"Seems like the commander is tired of losing his taxes to thieves," I say.

"Aye. This many soldiers will make the raids difficult," Rhys mutters.

The collectors finally pass through, headed for Locke, blind to the eyes that watch them from the shadows; no bodies drag from their wagon yet.

"We have what we need," Rhys says evenly once the collectors are out of sight. "Let's get back t' Walden." He stalks off without us, making it clear he's still miffed.

Raven and I collect our supplies and follow suit a few yards behind, baking under the sun as we make our way back through the uneven road. "All things considered," I say to Raven, "that went better than expected."

"Aye, and you didn't need my help once." A sigh. "You were right. I shouldn't have come . . . I used t' swear by my hunches; I'm getting rusty."

Pebbles crunch and scrape under our boots, the only sound around us in the arid afternoon.

"I would have preferred that you stayed with Pip, but for what it's worth, I'm glad you're here."

"Stop worrying about the little lad, will ya?" Ahead, Rhys follows the turn of the road around a hill, hiding him from view while we catch up. Raven frowns in his direction. "You really think he had something t' do with that?" she asks.

"If he did, I doubt he'll try anything else, so it doesn't matter now."

We wind the turn of the road around the hill . . .

And come face-to-face with the collector's coin wagon, parked just to the side of the road. The soldiers have their swords drawn and ready, aimed at us. They have Rhys. He's on his knees, head bowed and arms raised at his sides.

27

Meredith

Sometimes anger is a good thing. Before today, I'd been careful. Mindful. Secretive. *Discreet.* I let myself be constrained by norms and opinions. Not anymore. Today I wear my sword in the open, at my hip. Though the blue hooded cape Ethan gave me does a good job of covering it, the metal flashes in the sun as I stride, visible to inquisitive eyes.

Ella was our only lead. And she's dead. But I refuse to give up. After witnessing the gruesome scene in Ella's hut, neither Ethan nor I had the frame of mind to step inside. The answers we sought were irretrievable, lost to a noose. But what if Ella knew her life was in danger? What if she left a clue that could lead us to her killer? A note, perhaps, or a letter. Or perhaps the killer left incriminating evidence. It seems unlikely, but I can't disregard the possibility, not when there's so much at stake.

I saddle Daisy and canter to the portcullis.

"Godfrey will accompany you, my lady," says the guard in charge of the winch, gesturing to one of the men.

Knowing they won't let me through alone, I grudgingly agree. I could have avoided this by asking Lief to come along. But my mood is too foul today to be worthy of company. Lief would put up with me, but I'd rather be alone. At least I won't have to talk to Godfrey.

A stable hand brings a black and white horse for Godfrey. Once he's mounted, the guard at the winch draws the gate to let us through. I draw my hood up over my head as we enter the bustling city, and I keep it on until we are well away from its southern entrance, past the last of the paved roads that give way to sludge and snow.

Up ahead, Ella's hut beckons me, teasing me with its mystery. I dismount with an uncertain sigh. What will I do if there's nothing in there for me to find? Where will I go from there? Godfrey remains at the door, tight-lipped and vigilant as I take a step inside the dark and cold hut. The image of the three hanged bodies appears like a ghost in the empty room, haunting me; I don't envy the person dispatched by the city authorities to handle their removal and burial.

Alene and her father were right to be fearful. But their precautions were for naught. They weren't careful enough. Or perhaps it was by my clumsy hand that they were found out. I'll never know.

I venture inside Ella's hut. The floorboards creak and groan under my boots as I search the small room. There's no desk. No papers to rummage through. The only surface Ella used is grease stained and scarred with chopping marks—a kitchen table. Though the fire that burned in the hearth yesterday has long died, its smoky scent remains in the ashes.

My fading hope ushers me to Ella's bed. I pat the cotton blanket, feeling only straw. A peek underneath the flimsy bedding reveals a dead mouse and its droppings.

There's nothing here.

Frustrated and a tad disgusted, I tramp out of the hut to Daisy's side. Godfrey regards me with detached eyes. I want to scream my lungs out. I feel like I'm standing at the edge of a precipice, waiting to fall. I glance down at the pommel of my sword. Stonefall's crest burns my eyes with angry tears. Even if Alder remains safe, Stonefall is not. And now I've lost my only chance to save it; I can't bring myself to accept it.

Godfrey is probably expecting to return to the castle, but I'm not ready to go back. *Should have let me come alone,* I think bitterly with a scowl in his direction as I guide Daisy toward the trees at the foot of the mountains.

The fragrant scent of the evergreens sharpens and the air grows colder under the canopy, denied the sun's warmth. It's serene, like stepping through a painting. An abandoned masterpiece with no birds flapping their wings, no critters to disturb the silence.

Ethan and I were both silent on our way back to the market yesterday, shocked out of words. He tried to comfort me once we returned to the castle, and though I know he meant well, the pity in his eyes did me in. I couldn't stand it, so I pushed him away, told him to leave be me. It came out harsher than I intended. I should have apologized.

Daisy snorts, pulling me from my dark thoughts. Her ears flick back and forth, alert.

I stroke her crest. "What is it, girl?"

Whoosh.

I look over my shoulder, startled by the sound. And my mouth falls open.

The guard stares at me, his face frozen in pain and shock. The point of a spear sticks out from his chest. I jump off the saddle, drawing my sword. Everything is still. My eyes flit through the snow-peppered trees, ears pricked for the spear that will end me.

Then I hear it—a faint scraping sound; if it wasn't for the perfect quiet of the woods, I would have missed it. The noise comes again and I flinch. I look around, trying to pinpoint its direction.

Crunch.

I whirl.

The snow shifts. It takes me a second glance to see what's before me. A shadow flies through the trees toward Godfrey's hunched body on the saddle. A boy, silver haired and pale-skinned, garbed in snow-covered garments that look primitive. He's young, not a day older than twelve, but his uncanny bright-blue eyes hold no innocence. They glint like an animal's.

Then I notice the bloody spear in his hands, plucked from Godfrey's body. The weapon seems long for his height, like it belonged to someone else, but that doesn't seem to hinder him. He grips the shaft with confidence, angling the sharpened stone tip in my direction. I struggle to rationalize that this boy just speared the guard. Why?

I raise my free hand. "I mean you no harm," I say, cautious, taking a step away from Daisy; if he throws that thing, I don't want her anywhere near me. The boy cocks his head like a bird, the fiendish eyes curious for a moment. "Please," I try again, and slowly lower my sword. If he doesn't understand words, he should understand a gesture of peace. The boy's frame seems to loosen a bit, and I am halfway through an exhale of relief when he twists the spear in his grip and throws it.

I drop to the icy ground, feeling my veins throb with shock, and jerk my head up with just enough time to see the boy racing toward me, a large dagger in hand. I scramble to one knee, lifting my sword to his dagger as it whooshes in the air, and meeting it with a loud clang that sends me back to the ground. His strength is surprising. The wild boy slashes down at me again, relentless and feverish. I don't know how I manage to block him, but I do. Barely. Half of me can't rationalize that I'm fighting a child, afraid of wounding him, trying to make him stop. But he doesn't. And the hunger in his face crawls like a spider up my spine. He looks at me as though I am his prey. As though he intends to pry the meat off my bones.

Breathless, I coil my legs in and kick, slamming into his shins.

He teeters back a few steps, and I jump to my feet. The boy growls, angry at my resistance. He charges, his knife cutting the space between us in brisk strokes. Despite the cold, a sheen of sweat dampens my skin. My eyes strain to follow the blur of the blade. Daisy's anxious snorts fill my ears. Slash after slash, the dagger comes, clashing and scraping against my sword. My arms burn, demanding a reprieve. And then the boy kicks my left knee. I yelp as hot pain bursts in my leg. I lose my balance, wavering.

The boy swings at me again, and I respond in kind to block, but I am too slow. I feel the dagger slice across the back of my hand and I lose my grip on the hilt of my sword. I don't have time to recover it. Blood drips down my arm as I catch hold of the boy's wrists above my head, the tip of his blade digging into my forearm. I scream, clearing my mind of reservations as a desperate sense of survival roots in my body and takes over. Through the nauseating pain, I squeeze his wrist and push with all I have, the both of us grunting with effort in a tug of war. In seconds, half of my arm is streaked with blood. The metallic scent is overpowering, mixing with the fetid odor coming from the boy. Neither of us gives in, but I can feel my strength waning. If I don't do something, we'll stay like this until my wounds catch up to me and I can't fight him off any longer. He knows it, too, his savage features set with determination as he grits his teeth at me. He's close enough that I can smell his rank breath. Close enough that . . .

I bash my head against his, seeing stars. The boy's head bobs and I yank the dagger off his fingers. Jaw clenched tight, I point it at him. He lets out a feral hiss. I'm expecting—praying—he'll make a run for it. As wild and menacing as he looks, he is still just a boy, and I'm not sure I can bring myself to end his life.

But he makes the choice for me.

He lunges, taking me down with him, biting my bloodied hand. I'm screaming, his grip manipulating mine, pointing the sharp end of the dagger at my neck. In that split second, I see Holt, fighting for his life as Elijah brings his knife down on him, and an anguished snarl rumbles out of me. I feed off my hate, pushing the boy off to the side. I roll over and stab the dagger deep in his stomach.

The boy's ferocity is replaced with wide-eyed confusion. His eerily blue eyes meet mine, and for once, they look like the eyes of a boy, and I see fear in them. Pure, undiluted fear. And as his blood blooms underneath him, turning the snow a dark crimson, he stares at me as though I might do something to help him. But all I can do is stare back, numb with shock. I remain on my knees, breathless and horrified, unable to break his gaze.

It takes me a while to realize I've been staring at the eyes of a dead boy.

28

Connor

"Wait," I whisper to Raven when her hand moves to the hidden knife in the folds of her skirt, eyes on the approaching soldiers. There's eight of them. They have swords and armor, we have daggers. Fighting must be our last resort.

"I told you I saw something move in those trees," a smirking redcloak says to the one leading the pack.

They surround us. We raise our arms in surrender, but that doesn't stop them from smashing the pummels of their swords on our temples, forcing us to our knees and binding our hands with rope at our backs.

Raven's head bleeds from the blow. "What's our crime?" she dares to ask.

"Ask another question, and I'll knock your teeth out, thieving wench," barks the one binding her hands.

I look up at Rhys. His face is ashen, his body coiled as though he might take off running. There's a storm of unease in his eyes, and for once, he doesn't sneer.

The redcloaks parade us back to Locke like cattle ready for slaughter. Villagers scurry out of the way like rats, giving us a wide berth. The soldiers lead us to the village lockup: a freestanding jail cell built from large stones with a spire-shaped roof and a single iron door. We are shoved inside, the door slammed shut behind us, followed by the scrape of a sliding bolt. The slit in the door provides enough light to discern the stack of hay pressed against the wall. It smells faintly of piss and vomit. And the heat. *Maker's hell.* It's worse than a bathhouse in here. Jails like these aren't meant for more than one prisoner. We stand like fish in a school, boots overlapping. Raven climbs up the hay to give us more room.

"Are you going t' blame me for this too?"

Rhys's sarcasm is lost to the shake in his voice.

"Keep it together, Rhys." I kneel and reach inside my trousers for the dagger.

It takes me a few tries to grip the weapon's hilt in my bound hands. "Cut your ropes if you can, just take care not to cut all the way."

Sweat drips into my eyes while my fingers strain to seesaw the blade, working through the pounding headache building in the side of my head. It's a rough go, but little by little, I slice into the rope fibers. One at a time it feels like. Rhys's impatience gets the best of him. Thrice, he drops his dagger, muttering curses each time.

Raven can't reach for the knife at her waist. "The redcloak called me a thief like he knew we were scouting . . . does that mean they know about the Brotherhood?

"I don't see how," Rhys answers through grunts. "Someone

on the inside would have t' give us up, and our brothers would never betray the Brotherhood."

"But there are others," I say. "Men like Flynn and Walden. If there's a weak link, it's probably someone in Uther's network of spies." I'm almost free. "How good are you with the dagger?" I ask Rhys.

We are crammed so close I can hear the nervous swallow in his throat. "Good enough."

I can't tell if it's the nerves or if he's just a bad liar.

"Can we really fight our way out o' this?" Raven says doubtfully. "There's only three o' us and eight o' them. And that's not counting the village patrols."

Just a few more strands.

"We can't fight eight of them all at once with daggers," I agree. "We'll have to wait for a lucky break."

Any way I look at it, our odds aren't good, but worrying is useless.

We hear the stomp of soldiers outside.

Focus.

Rhys goes still and Raven backs up into the corner, pressing herself against the wall. My hands are bound by a thread, just as I intended. I stand, knees sore from kneeling, and face the door as the jail cell darkens to near pitch black, the light from the slit blocked by the redcloak standing outside.

Rhys is a jittery lump on the floor. "Get up," I hiss.

Metal clinks and scrapes on the other side.

The door opens, and blinding bright light floods in.

"Out, you leeches," comes the gruff command from the soldier.

I step forward—dagger ready in my sweaty fingers—and halt at the entryway, letting my eyes adjust. All eight redcloaks are back. I could get away with killing two, maybe. But then what? The market is crawling with packs of them.

A few paces back, the collectors remain at the helm of the coin wagon, fanning their faces against the heat. Attached behind them is a smaller wagon—a cage, slitted with iron bars all around, its metal door swung open, waiting for prisoners.

The redcloak standing before me, a tall soldier with long dark hair and an overgrown beard, claps my shoulder and hustles me forward, unaware of the frayed rope at the small of my back. I push the dagger into the narrow space between my wrists, hiding it from view. As I near the wagon, I home in on the hinges . . . welded. The lock seems too small for my dagger to pick, but I know I'll try anyway first chance I get. I climb up the step and tuck my head in. There are no seats, only the nailed planks of the wagon's bottom.

Rhys stumbles when his turn comes, pushed by the smirking redcloak at his back, and falls flat on his face. The redcloak laughs and hauls him up by the elbow, and pushes him again. Rhys is ready for it, though. His legs teeter but he keeps his balance.

"Don't think we'll be catching a lucky break locked in here," he whispers.

Then Raven steps out into the light. She makes her way, moving quickly, but not quick enough. The soldier who pushed Rhys smacks her bottom as she climbs into the wagon, causing a slew of snickers. I grit my teeth, glaring at their lot as Raven clambers to my side, incensed and terrified.

"Any idea where they're taking us?" she whispers after the wagon is locked and the soldiers have mounted their horses.

Rhys answers, looking much paler than he did before. "Where all collectors go . . . Vishal's fort."

29

Meredith

The bailey, full of courtiers and merchants, erupts in a rumble of gossip as I limp across it on my good knee, looking as though I've just returned from battle. I suppose I have. Alarm, disdain, concern, revulsion—it doesn't matter what I see plastered on people's faces. It's all noise, muffled by the image of a pair of dead eyes staring back at me. The guards at the portcullis, at least, were quick to overcome their shock and send a patrol to the woods to collect their fallen guardsman; I couldn't bring myself to tell them who attacked me, but they'll soon see for themselves.

I brush away the matted tresses that stick to my sweat-dampened face and stagger past the castle foyer, through the cold corridors, keeping a hand on the steel that dangles from my hip. The solid weight of it, the cool of its hilt against my skin, is more reassuring than anything. I'm still reeling from the deadly encounter. I could have died in those snowy woods. I *would* have, if I didn't have the sword Ethan gave me. This is what I wanted, isn't it? To fight my own battles? To save myself? It certainly doesn't feel as heroic as I thought it would.

I cross paths with a servant who drops his coal bucket at the sight of me. "M' lady," he says as his arm steadies me.

"Thank you," I heave, grateful.

News of my grisly return spread like wildfire, which, it turns out, is much faster than I can hop; Ethan is knocking at my door by the time the servant and I round the hallway to my room, a cross-looking Heloise pacing behind him.

Their heads jerks back when they see me, like they hadn't really expected it to be true. Ethan rushes to my side, his gaze scanning my bloody arm.

The coal servant hands me to Ethan, who thanks him before he returns to his duties.

"This castle is too big," I complain, wincing from the pain in my knee and the burning muscles of my leg; I must have hopped thousands of steps.

"Where are you wounded?"

"It's just my hand," I say and lift my arm to show him the gash. I don't bother mentioning the cut in my forearm; it's not deep.

He slips his arm under my shoulders and we hobble to my door.

"What happened?" Heloise asks in alarm. It's the first time I see worry in her face.

Touched by her concern, I give her a wan smile. "I'll be all right, Hel."

"Lady Cresten, would you please fetch a handmaid?" Ethan asks. "Have her bring clean cloth for Meredith's wound."

Heloise casts a hesitant glance my way before nodding. "Of

course, Your Highness."

With a sharp bow, she stalks off down the hallway.

Ethan helps me to my room. Carefully, he lowers me to the foot of my bed. I let out a sigh of relief.

"What's the matter with your leg?"

"My knee," I rasp, pointing at the culprit.

"Do you mind if I have a look?"

I shake my head and he reaches for my ankle, gently slipping my boot off. His fleeting touch is soft and gentle against my icy skin as he flips the bottom of my skirts up to reveal a reddened, swollen knee, about twice its normal size.

"Did you fall off your horse?"

"I was"—I gulp—"attacked."

His brow shoots up, eyes going wide. *"Attacked?"* The word slips like a horrified whisper over his lips. "By whom?"

Hot tears burn the backs of my eyes. "I didn't want to hurt him, I swear it!" I blurt out, my voice cracking. "But he—he killed the guard," I say. "He would have killed me, too."

Concern deepens the lines on Ethan's face. He lowers my foot slowly back to the ground and clasps onto the edge of the bed at my sides, his arms straddling me. When he asks again, his voice echoes that of the king's, ringing with authority. "Who attacked you?"

"I don't know. He was so strange . . . some sort of savage."

Ethan's eyes stop blinking.

"What?" I ask after his stiff silence.

He stares blankly at me for an entire minute before he mutters in awe, "How are you alive?"

I scoff. "All these months of training, and you still think me incapable of self-defense." Exhausted as I am, I shouldn't take offense. Besides, Ethan rarely trains with me. How could he really know what I'm capable of?

But Ethan shakes his head. "Your attacker . . . his skin, was it unusually pale?"

I'm staring at those dead eyes again, their azure brilliance faded. *Child murderer.* I blink it away and focus on Ethan. "Yes," I mutter suspiciously, feeling like I'm missing something. The boy's skin had been white as snow.

He watches me for a moment, muscles rigid, before he responds. "Where, exactly, did you go?"

"I went back to Ella's hut. I was hoping I'd learn something. But I didn't." I pause. Ethan waits in patient silence, a worried frown frozen on his brow. "I was angry and I didn't know what else to do."

Ethan's frown deepens. His eyes stray to the side for a moment, weighing my words. "That can't be," he says in a low voice laden with concern.

I lean forward, close enough to feel his warmth, to smell the soapy sage on his skin. "I killed him," I say through tight lips.

Ethan practically gapes at me, and for a second, I wonder if he already knows, but then I realize his mouth isn't slack with condemnation, but amazement. And then he's frowning again.

"Weren't there others?"

The thought of facing more than one makes me shudder. "I wouldn't be here talking to you if there had been."

"That's . . . odd."

Odd is the last word I would use to describe it.

"He was just a child," I confess, my voice barely a whisper, but Ethan is close enough that he can probably hear me. I thought saying it out loud would ease the ache in my chest. It doesn't.

Retracting his arms to his sides, Ethan's gaze fills with understanding.

"It was you or him." That much is true, but how he could know that? He wasn't there. He didn't see the fear in that boy's face as his life slipped away from him. The life that I took. I'm shaking my head, rejecting his words, when his fingers still my chin, drawing my eyes to his. There are flecks of gold in his irises I hadn't noticed before. "Meredith, that boy was Lucari. I spoke of them the night of the feast, do you remember? They are violent people," he stresses, his warm eyes pinning me with resolve. "Even the children are violent. They are raised to be so."

The cannibals. I recall the way the boy was looking at me. Like he was hungry, like he wanted to eat me. A sick feeling settles in my stomach, making my toes curl.

"He was going to eat me," I mutter under my breath. Instinctively, I'd known this. I'd seen the hunger. I'd felt it. I'd felt like prey. But I didn't—couldn't—believe it.

"The Lucari are fierce warriors. You are fortunate it was a

child that crossed your path and not a man."

Conjuring up an image of a hungry, snow-pale grown savage pricks the hairs on my neck.

"Why was he there—in the woods?" I ask. "Didn't you say their territory was up in the mountains?"

He gives a grave nod. "Those woods aren't part of their territory. No one's ever seen a Lucari there before . . ." His face pinches with thought, as though trying to figure something out. After some deliberation, he says, "Lucari hunt in groups, and yet you say this one was alone."

"Could he have lost his way?"

"Perhaps . . . either way, the area should be patrolled."

"A group of guards left to investigate when I—" I close my knees together without thinking and yelp at the raw throb that lances through me.

Ethan shoots to his feet. "Forgive me, I—you're in pain. We can discuss this later. I'll send for the physician."

"Yes, well, faced with the knowledge I was almost eaten alive, the pain is rather forgettable."

He tries to hide a smile. "Nevertheless, your wounds need tending. And you'll need more than a cloth and clean water."

Ethan opens the door to find someone on the other side. I can't see who it is from where I'm sitting, but I assume it's Heloise and the handmaid.

"Your Highness," echoes the voice of a man. Probably a guard. "A messenger has arrived seeking an audience with the princess."

My breath catches in my throat.

A messenger for me can only mean one thing: news from home.

I rush to stand, but my knee rebels.

"She is indisposed at the moment. Make arrangements for the messenger to stay the night, and she'll see to him tomorrow."

There is a pause.

"He said it's urgent, sire."

"Did he say who sent him?" I call out from the bed before Ethan can refuse him again.

Please. Please. Please.

"Yes, my lady, he's come to see you on the orders of a gentleman who goes by the name Charles of Elsham."

30

Connor

My legs are numb from sitting and my arms ache to move. The redcloaks ride two abreast, flaunting their flasks each time they take a swig, knowing we're parched in this heat. By the position of the sun, it's well past noon.

"We must drink. We're no use t' you dead," Raven says to the redcloak I dubbed Smirk, for obvious reasons. If I were free, I'd wipe it off his face.

"Hold that tongue, wench, or I'll cut it off!" another soldier yells.

But hours later, Smirk steers his horse to the cage and offers us water. I let Raven and Rhys take their fill before I quaff the rest. At dusk, they stop to set up camp, and finally let us out so we don't soil ourselves.

Smirk walks me to a spot a few yards away, and when he reaches to untie the rope, I feel it rip apart in his hands.

I curse just as he digs the point of his sword into my spine. "Hand the dagger over."

One look at the expanse of grassy plains squelches any thought of slicing his throat and making a run for it. There's nowhere to go. Even if there was, I can't leave without Raven. Taking on the redcloaks all at once would be reckless, and with their group huddled together setting up camp, taking them out quietly one by one is out of the question.

Dammit.

I open my wrists and let the dagger fall to the grass.

"Turn around. Slowly," Smirk commands. "And walk back five paces."

Once I obey, he kneels and snatches the dagger, tucking it into his belt.

And then he takes those five paces and slams a fist in my mouth.

I spit blood and look sideways at Smirk. It would take nothing to dodge him, punch him, steal his sword, and stab him with it. Easy. And stupid.

Smirk finds twine to bind my wrists, and we return to the jail wagon. Rhys levels his swelling eye on me, doubtless surmising the same thing I am: the frayed hemp gave us both away.

"Did they search you?" I whisper to Raven when they bring her back.

She shakes her head once, and I sag against the iron bars.

One blade left . . . It'll have to do.

The sun sets, leaving most of its heat behind to keep us sweating through the night. Huddled on the planks with our backs digging into the bars, we don't say another word until the redcloaks and the collectors are lying around their campfire.

"We can't escape on foot," Raven murmurs, her tired eyes

scanning the blackness.

Rhys chuckles, the sound bitter and resentful. "We can't escape in any manner." His left eye is swollen shut by now.

"I still have my knife, Rhys," she says in an attempt to comfort him, being mindful of enemy ears as she does.

"And what do you plan t' do with it? Stab all eight o' them and gallop away?"

"Don't be absurd," Raven bites back.

"Thinking we'll escape is absurd."

I study Rhys until he notices, and when he proceeds to avoid my stare, I speak my mind.

"You're afraid of fighting them. Why?"

Rhys snorts, but his voice becomes tight. "I'm no more afraid than any man."

Raven sees through the lie. "You're not any man . . . You're a *trained* man, trained t' fight redcloaks and steal their silver. So why does the sight o' them make you shake in your boots?"

Red flushes up his cheeks—violet under the moonlight. If his arms were not bound, I imagine they'd be crossed. Raven and I exchange a look, and Rhys mumbles from over his hunched shoulder, "Fear keeps me alive."

I stay awake that night, listening to the crackle of the fire and the howl of coyotes in the distance. Raven's sleep is restless. She lies on her side, her head nestled on my outstretched leg, waking often to readjust. Rhys is half sitting across the wagon; his body leaned against the corner. It puzzles me that Uther would allow someone like him into his camp. Knowing he's a coward certainly changes things. If we try to escape and things go south . . . I can't rely on him.

Our journey resumes at dawn.

The redcloaks give us water after midday, when the sun burns its hottest, and let us out of the wagon late afternoon, before tying the reins of their horses and building a fire. But no food. And after the second day, I'm fighting headaches and muscle cramps in my legs from hunger, or dehydration, or both. Once, one of the collectors parades around our wagon with a sly glance and a piece of crisped meat in his hand, chewing loudly, the smell of it teasing our hollowed bellies. Bastard.

We get a much-needed rinse when the rain comes. Thick gray clouds hide the sun, flashing white with lightning, and a cooling gust sweeps by. Thunder booms in the sky, and the trickle of raindrops abruptly becomes a dense downpour, washing the salt and caked dirt off my skin and the stink of sweat off my tunic. The three of us stick our heads out through the bars, mouths open, quenching our raw throats and cracked lips.

Blissful as it is, rain does have its drawbacks.

Once the drops stop coming and the clouds part, the sun returns with a vengeance, its heat suffocating. Smirk doesn't bring us water that day.

Each day that passes is a day closer to Vishal's fort, shortening our window of escape. But with no opportunities to seize, Raven's knife goes unused. The plains are never ending, nothing but sun and grass and sparse fields with a few rolling hills. No forests. No mountains. Escaping out here would be a death sentence. But we grow weaker each day. We can't go much longer without food and still have the energy to kill and run. I realize that's why we are not fed when there are rations to be shared.

Because weaklings don't escape; Rhys was right to claim we wouldn't.

Perhaps he isn't as pigheaded as I thought.

31

Meredith

I shoot off the bed, injured knee be damned. I'll hop through the entire castle if I have to for news from Charles.

"Take me to him," I blurt to the guard, but one look at my wincing face and Ethan blocks my exit.

"Fetch the messenger. The princess will see him here," he instructs.

The guard nods. "As you wish, sire."

Alone once again, Ethan helps me back to the bed. "You're persistent, I'll give you that."

News from Charles.

I let that sink in, bringing my hand to cover the slow smile tugging on my lips. I have to believe that it's good news. Ever since Theros and Elijah left, the worry has been constant, burrowing inside like a parasite until it became part of me; I hadn't realized just how much until now.

"This Charles . . . he's important to you?" Ethan asks, sitting beside me at the edge of the bed.

I lower my chin and nod, remembering the sound of Charles's laugh. He's a bright, untainted part of my life. A part that doesn't hurt to think about. And yet, I didn't. Ethan doesn't know of

Anabella or Beth either, and he knows nothing of Holt aside from his name and that he was a dear friend. I wonder what Alder's crown prince would make of my peculiar friendships. "Charles is my cousin. He's the best man I know."

We sink into silence, Ethan to his thoughts and I to my restlessness. Then, after a moment, his solemn voice brings me back. "It can't be easy knowing your family is living under a tyrant . . . I don't know what I'd do if I were in your situation; my family is everything. They're the legs I stand on."

"You are lucky to have them both." *And their love.*

Ethan cups my shoulder, the weight of his hand as reassuring as his words. "Don't give up hope. We'll find a way to make things right."

Waiting for the messenger is mentally taxing. My good leg jitters helplessly against the floor as my sweaty fingers fuss with the folds of my pleated, pale-green dress. The silk fabric is wrinkled and torn and smeared with blood. What a sight I must be. After a few minutes, Ethan stands and starts to pace across the room, growing anxious himself. I sit up straighter when a knock comes at the door. Ethan flings it open.

But it's only Heloise and the handmaid Ethan sent her to fetch.

They step inside; the maid lays a clay receptacle full of water at my feet.

"What sort of trouble did you get into this time?" Heloise asks, kneeling at my side as the maid wipes the blood around my wounds with a wet cloth.

"The Lucari sort," Ethan answers for me, crossing his arms at his chest.

The handmaid gasps. Heloise's mouth drops in wonder and dread. Ethan goes on to explain so that I don't have to. Thankfully, he doesn't tell them it was a young boy who attacked me, mindful of my guilt.

Heloise's brow creases as she grapples with this information. "I can't believe it." She trails off like she wants to say more. Perhaps it's Ethan's presence that holds her back. Would she have fared any better against the savage boy?

"Lief's training seems to have paid off," I say.

"He'll be a proud sort when he hears," Heloise muses.

"I wouldn't have survived without my sword," I say, sensing Ethan's remorse; I know he would have trained me himself, had his schedule allowed it. Ethan's gaze darts to my birthday gift. He stares at the pommel and grip, both smudged with blood. I don't know if it's mine or the boy's. Probably both.

Finished dressing my wounds, the handmaid picks up the receptacle, its water pink with my blood, and turns to Ethan. "Her knee will require healing salves, sire. Should I call on the physician?"

"Yes, thank you."

Heloise follows the maid to the door. "I'd stay awhile, but I'm late for tea," she announces, sounding faintly disappointed.

"One of these days, your mother's going to snap," I warn her.

She holds a hand over her heart and laughs. "If she does, I promise you'll be the first to know."

Alone again, Ethan resumes his seat on the bed. He doesn't say anything, looking as though he's uncomfortable with his thoughts. Then, when the silence grows, his eyes focus on my temple. "Did you hit your head?" He reaches with his thumb.

I flinch away from his touch. "Ow."

Ethan coils his hand away, his face cringing in apology. "Sorry."

"I had to use my head in the fight. Literally."

Ethan chuckles at that, and I smile in spite of all the aches in my body and all the anxiety broiling inside me. We sit there, smiling at each other, until suddenly, our smiles have drifted away and the air around us feels heady.

Knock knock knock.

The door swings open.

And then my beat-skipping heart freezes.

Chancellor Ulric?

He's a stark, unkempt version of the pompous weasel I remember. There are dark bags under his eyes, and even his attire is modestly plain, but he is still the same short, bald man who mercilessly whipped me on my father's orders and scarred me for life.

"*You're* the messenger?" I ask as he bows. I can't hide my disdain. Of all the staff at my father's disposal, why would Charles send *him*?

I can feel Ethan staring out of the corner of my eye, trying to read between the lines.

"Your Highness," Ulric says grandiosely, "it is very good to see you. I trust—"

"Is Theros in Stonefall?"

Oh, the pleasure of seeing that pointed nose wrinkle.

The chancellor clears his throat. "He was, Your Highness. He returned to Talos shortly after the siege. His men, however, continue to reside in the palace grounds."

My breath catches. A siege. I feared as much, but hearing it from the chancellor's lips makes it true. I can barely bring myself to ask, "How is my father?"

"Alive," he assures me.

Relief burns my throat. I sigh. "Tell me everything."

"King Edgard surrendered. He acquiesced to all of Theros's demands," Ulric deadpans, like he's delivering a report on an estate. Then, after a brief pause, he concludes, "Stonefall is now under the rule of the Talosian Empire."

Empire?

The news is painful to hear. For the longest moment, all I can hear is the sound of my heartbeat in my ears. But something in my expression compels the unfeeling chancellor to add, "It was an unfortunate turn of events. But that is not why I am here, Your Highness."

As much as I hate the man, I am desperate to hear what he has to say. "Go on."

Ulric clears his throat. "I've come to deliver an urgent message from Lord Charles of Elsham." The chancellor glances hesitantly at Ethan. "He insisted this information was for your ears alone, Your Highness."

"The prince stays," I say. "Now out with it, Chancellor."

The chancellor sighs through his nose. "Very well, Your Highness." He produces a yellowed and tarnished missive from his coat pocket and hands it to me. I take the creased paper with feverish fingers. Unfolding it, I'm greeted with only three words that are hardly legible, as though penned in haste.

There's a cure.

It's Charles's handwriting, a dastardly version of his otherwise elegant cursive, but it's his all right. My gaze strays back to the chancellor. "A cure?" I ask, exchanging a glance with Ethan. It can't be. "Does he mean . . . ?"

"I believe it's the plague he's referring to, Your Highness."

"A cure for the blue fever? How is that even possible?"

Ethan finds his voice before I can find mine. "Well, come on, man!" he urges Ulric. "What is it?"

"If I knew that, I would have said as much."

I scoff at his reply. "You've come all this way to tell me there is a cure you know nothing of?"

"This is all His lordship was able to provide, Your Highness."

"Why did Charles write *only* this?" I hold up the small missive. The few words in it don't warrant being written when the chancellor could have simply repeated them himself. "What exactly did he say when he gave this to you?"

"He could only manage to ask that I give it to you, Your Highness."

I feel myself go very still. Something isn't right here. "Speak plainly, chancellor."

"Sir Charles was imprisoned, Your Highness."

"Imprisoned?" I mutter weakly under my breath. "On what charges?"

"Espionage. Elijah's men intercepted a letter addressed to you containing Talosian Empire secrets, which I now believe are related to this matter of a cure; he was bound for the dungeon when he slipped the note in my pocket."

Something snaps inside me. I teeter off the bed, clutching the chancellor's collar as I stumble into him. If it wasn't for the wall behind him, we would've crashed on the floor. "What have they done to him?"

"Y-your Highness—there is no need for alarm. The duke interceded on his son's behalf," he stammers under my grasp, his palms raised in surrender at his sides. "He won't be harmed!"

"No need for alarm? Do you hear yourself, chancellor?" My voice unhinges. "My kingdom is lost to a madman, my cousin is in prison, and you think there is no need for alarm?"

"Please, Your Highness," the chancellor beseeches me. "I am here to help turn the tide in our favor."

I release him, reluctant to limp back to the bed. "And how are we going to accomplish that?" I throw my arms out in frustration. "Am I to march to the palace and demand they hand me the cure?"

The chancellor straightens. "Precisely, Your Highness. With Alder's army, we can take back the palace and free Sir Charles."

"My father's army can't be mobilized without alerting Theros," Ethan cuts in, leaning against the closed balcony doors with his arms crossed. "He's planted a mole in the city who will unleash the plague if we take action."

This doesn't deter the chancellor, however. He digs in his pocket once more, retrieving yet another piece of paper. He steps toward the bed and offers it to me. It's a folded letter, its edges worn and carved with wrinkles. I open it. My eyes can't read fast enough. I skim through its contents with hungry eyes. Paragraphs upon paragraphs of military intelligence: the number of regiments in the Alderian army, names of commanders, and their locations within the kingdom.

"How did you get this?" I ask.

Ulric clasps his hands at his back. Seeming to recover his self-importance, he boasts, "It came from a contact in Stonefall's palace in possession of official correspondence from Alder. It was bound for Elijah Gannon's desk. I believe the mole you seek is the author of that letter."

My eyes drop to the paper. The name is written only once, at the bottom of the page. A signature of the traitor who gave away every possible detail about Alder's army.

Councilor Milus.

I close my eyes, taking a deep, pained breath.

When I open them, I meet Ethan's expectant gaze. I hate it when he pities me, and yet here I am, pitying him. Part of me wants to keep it from him, to protect him somehow, because I know this will destroy him.

"What is it?" he asks when I keep quiet, his frown growing with concern.

For a moment, I just stand there, holding the letter between my hands like it's a snake bearing its fangs.

Ethan takes a step toward me. "Meredith?"

I hand him the letter. His eyes travel down the paper as eagerly as mine did . . . .

His eyes widen. The color drains from his face. "This must be a mistake . . ." He's shaking his head. "Maker, it can't be true."

"Ethan," I hesitate to ask, "did you tell the councilor about the man in the tavern?"

The look he gives me sends a pang low in my belly. "No, of course not," he shoots back.

"Then how did he find out? Could he have followed us without you knowing?"

Ethan rubs a flustered hand through his hair. "Milus is not our enemy," he insists, and the conflicted glint in his eyes tears at my insides. Despite his doubt, he adds, "His name might be in that report, but we have no reason to believe its authenticity."

"Is that not his signature?" I ask.

As Ethan inspects the letter one more time, a slow, hard swallow makes its way down his throat. "It's a forgery—it has to be."

"If I may," Ulric breaks in, reminding us of his presence, "His Lordship Charles intercepted that letter and gave it to me for safekeeping."

Ethan works the muscles of his jaw as his eyes narrow at the chancellor. "How did you manage to leave Stonefall with this letter in your possession?"

"Through the secret passage behind King Edgard's rooms," Ulric easily replies. "As of the time of my departure, Theros's men were not yet aware of its existence." He gestures at me. "Her Highness herself escaped the palace by way of this passage."

Ethan stares down the chancellor before turning to me. "Do you trust him?"

"I trust Charles. I trust him with my life. If he wanted me to have this—"

"That doesn't prove anything."

"Then we should speak with the king," I suggest. "He should be the one to compare the signature in this letter to that of Councilor Milus and decide how to proceed." Ethan stares into my eyes and says nothing. So I get up slowly and inch toward him, grimacing at the throb in my knee. Ethan watches me approach with a wary look in his eye, as though he doesn't want to hear what I have to say, but I don't hold back. "I know this is difficult," I whisper, "but we can't walk away from it. There is too much at stake."

Ethan gives me a long, pained look. It's the first time I've seen frailty in him. "If the roles were reversed," he says quietly, "if it was your cousin's name on that letter, would you believe it? Would you let him hang for it without being absolutely certain he was guilty?" His solemn eyes seek mine for an answer.

I bite my bottom lip, breaking away from his gaze. *Charles would never do such a thing,* I almost say, before I realize the same reasoning is echoing in Ethan's thoughts. *Family is everything,* his earlier words echo in my head. To Ethan, Milus is family. He's a second father to him.

"No," I admit, my voice too quiet. "I wouldn't."

King Perceval is no less hesitant to take action. Ethan and I wait for his response across the wood-slab table. A past council meeting's document lays on it. Near the bottom of the paper are the elegant signatures of all councilmen present at said meeting. Given the delicate nature of our discussion, both servants and guards were swiftly dismissed upon our barging into the king's office. Ethan is deathly still, his wary, unblinking gaze affixed to his father. After minutes of staring at the intercepted letter, the king folds the paper and tucks it inside his vest. Then he clasps his hands behind his back and walks slowly along the length of the table, stopping at the window to peer down at the city.

His voice is flat. "This is grave news, indeed."

"It's a lie," Ethan rushes to say. But even as he denies it, I can hear the shred of doubt in his words.

The king glances over his shoulder and shares an emphatic look with his son. "I struggle to believe it myself. Milus has loyally served our family since infancy, as his father did before him . . ."

"He's been much more than a servant and you know it."

"Yes."

"We should summon him, let him speak for himself," Ethan pleads with the king, who is staring out the window again, looking down on his city.

"And what good will that do? He'll deny everything. Guilty or innocent."

Lines of disbelief and defiance sketch Ethan's face. He makes the four strides to the table in two. "Father, you can't arrest him!"

Impassive, the king turns to face us and holds up the letter to Ethan. "Can you discern a difference in the handwriting and signature? Because I can't." Ethan stares at his father with hooded eyes, unable to object. "What is our creed, son?" Seconds pass. Ethan hangs his head. Watching him, I can't help but wilt a little.

"We serve the people," Ethan finally gives in, despondent and without conviction, aware of the direction his father is taking.

"And by that creed, what is the proper course of action?"

Ethan doesn't answer.

The king lets out a sigh laced with pity and disappointment. "It pains me to say it, son. But the evidence is too incriminating to ignore. We'll have to arrest him quietly to avoid alerting anyone who may be working for him." He pauses, giving Ethan time to assimilate this; by the colorless look on his face, he's taking it as well as he can. Perceval rejoins us around the table. "Once Milus is behind bars, there should be no further threat of plague in the immediate future. The next step would be to try and obtain information of this supposed cure from him, which I suspect, if there is one, we'll likely find it in Stonefall."

"And what shall we do if Milus gives us nothing?" Ethan insists in a tight voice.

"We continue as planned: we march to Stonefall and obtain the information from Princess Meredith's kin."

I pause. Then, in a held breath, I ask, "You'll free my kingdom from Theros, Your Majesty?" Whether the king realizes it or not, my whole existence orbits around the answer to that question.

The king directs his steely features to me and, in an even voice, says, "I will reclaim Stonefall under two conditions: First, that you wed my son. And second, that you bequeath me as sovereign of the kingdom until my death, upon which Ethan will be crowned king and continue my rule, with you as his queen."

It takes me a moment to find my voice. "You want me to overthrow my own father?" I stammer.

Not one to mince words, the king replies, "Your father has proved himself unfit to rule time and time again. He squandered his kingdom and left it to rot so he could indulge himself in the pleasures of extravagance. I will not lose men to save a crumbling kingdom." Though it's my father he speaks ill of, I can't help but flinch, feeling as though it's me he's reprimanding. "If you want to do right by your people, your father must never be allowed to rule again."

The king knows he cannot wage a war without a cure, and he'll likely need Charles's help to get it. But the king must also know I have Stonefall's best interest at heart, and that I would see the logic in his argument. Alder has prospered for generations under the Caster dynasty, after all. I want that for Stonefall. I want it more than anything.

I want it badly enough to betray my father.

Despite his anguish over Councilor Milus, Ethan returns my searching gaze with a determined look in his eyes. *I'm willing if you are,* he seems to say.

I have no desire to marry him, as I'm sure he has no desire to marry me. But isn't that why I am here? My lifelong purpose? My duty? Ethan, too, is driven by his duty to his people and his kingdom, and he's just proved he's willing to imprison someone dear to him for that very cause.

Why, then, do I feel so grim?

Because you're a miserable wretch with a spiteful, shriveled heart, a voice rasps in my head. *You will never be the wife and queen he needs you to be, and he will resent you for it.*

I take a deep breath.

"I'll do it."

32

Connor

Two days of traveling south leads us to a small fishing village where huts with thatched roofs snake around the rain-bogged road to a Great Hall made of wattle and daub. The mud is too deep for the wagons, so the collectors climb down from their seats and continue on foot, mudding their green tunics. Half the redcloaks follow them to the first hut on the right, where a woman weaves threads of yarn into a cloth out front and sheep bleat 'round back. The woman runs inside at the soldiers' approach. A second later, a weary man—the weaver's husband perhaps—appears at the door to drop his coin into the collector's sack.

"They're the real thieves," Raven grumbles next to me, watching with tight lips.

But my gaze keeps straying east to the tranquil river at the edge of the village.

The collectors go from hut to hut, taking what little the villagers have to fill their deep pockets. King Theros will chip this land to its bare bones soon enough. And to what end? Why is the Usurper so pressed for wealth?

Screams in the distance.

Up the mud path, coming from the Great Hall on the hill's

mound, the collectors and the redcloaks return with a girl. Behind them, at the hall's opened doors, a woman kneels, her arm reaching in front of her.

Raven grips the iron bars with white knuckles, her eyes oozing concern. "Gods have mercy."

Villagers gawk from their huts. Mothers hold on to their children, fearing a similar fate. Two fishermen gripping spears trot from the river, drawn by the commotion. But the soldiers don't tie the girl's feet to the wagon. The bearded redcloak binds her wrists and drags her to our cage, shoving her inside. Seeing her up close, I understand why they took her. She's a pretty thing, with a long neck and full, rounded lips. And doesn't look a day over fourteen. Her brown eyes are red with tears, and her thin black hair sticks to the wet streaks on her cheeks. She isn't the only thing the redcloaks took. One of them has his arm hooked around a rundlet of ale.

"What's your name?" Raven asks the girl quietly.

The girl casts wary glances at the three of us. "Khalia," she whispers after a pause.

"That's a pretty name. I'm Raven." She gestures with her head toward me. "This is Connor . . . and Rhys."

Rhys hardly bothers to acknowledge her, keeping to his corner in sullen silence.

More tears slide down the girl's face, falling down to her rough woven tunic. Raven's eyes flash with pity.

I watch the redcloaks ride the weedy fields on their horses a few yards from the bank, drinking freely from their flasks now that they have a water source to refill their supply.

"Khalia, does that river keep south?" I ask.

Rhys stirs, meeting my eye for the first time in two days. The question seems to distract Khalia. Her trembling chin stills while she thinks, then nods.

Indeed, the river keeps south . . .

We leave the fishing village behind soon after. Khalia leans her stricken face against the bars as the redcloaks lead us down the riverbank and her village shrinks in the distance. Raven offers kind words that go unheard, though who could blame the girl.

It rains again that afternoon, bringing on an insufferable night. I'm dreaming of mountains and amber eyes when I wake to find Khalia's stare, noting Raven's head on my shoulder. But when Khalia finds me awake, she quickly diverts her curious gaze outside the wagon.

A frail girl like her complicates things. She can't fight, nor can she defend herself, which makes her a liability, one more person to look out for. "Can you swim?" I ask her.

Her expression is so intent that I wonder if I've said the wrong thing. I can hardly hear her whispering voice over Rhys's snoring. "The river isn't safe."

"Neither is this."

I lean my head against the bars and peer at the stars through the gaps in the clouds, listening to the loud buzz of bush crickets. Asher is probably losing his mind, wondering where Raven ran off to. He may have connected the dots and realized what she did, though it won't do him any good. Without word from us, the rebels will think us dead. I hope Pip is all right. I think on my promise to him that I would return. I'd hate to break that promise. *I'll try my best, Pip*, I wordlessly swear. But if I'm to die, it won't be like this, tied up and caged. If I go down, I'll go down fighting, and I'll be damned if I don't take half these redcloaks to the grave with me.

"We won't have t' swim," Khalia says, bringing me back to the cage. It's the first time she speaks without being prompted. "My father will come for me. He's a good tracker. He'll find us."

"Your father is a tracker?"

I feel Raven rouse on my shoulder, blinking off deep sleep. She lifts her head and straightens against the bars.

"He's lord o' our village," Khalia says, watching my face for a reaction. At my impassive silence, she says, "His vassals will come with 'im."

I try not to pity the encouraging smile on her lips.

"Fishermen," I say. It's not a question, but Khalia nods anyway.

I remember the men who watched Khalia be dragged away. Simple folk unequipped to fight ruthless soldiers; they'd need strength in numbers. Though, if her father does come with a handful of men, that could prove useful. *If*, I think. And most importantly: *When?*

Time is not on our side.

The next afternoon, the redcloaks drink the stolen ale. Traveling with prisoners and collected coin, I expected they would drink with more restraint. By the lewd conversations and occasional bickering, I take it they've likely emptied the rundlet, drinking themselves stewed to the tunes of a flute one of the collectors plays. It makes for another difficult night's sleep, so we are all awake when Smirk clambers to open our wagon. If my hands weren't bound, this would be the perfect opportunity to take him down and make a run for it.

Smirk curls his finger at Khalia. "Come dance for us, pretty flower," he slurs. Naturally, Khalia scrambles to the back of the wagon, trying to hide behind Rhys. The redcloak draws his sword with clumsy hands, making patterns in the air as he tries to point it at Khalia. "I'm not asking, little girl."

"Please," is all Khalia can say through her whimpering.

"*Don't,*" I hiss at Raven, wishing I had a free arm to hold her back, but she's on the move.

"I'll dance for you," she says to Smirk.

Maker's hell.

Smirk's brows rise appreciatively. "Will you now?"

It's more than concern for her well-being that sinks my stomach. If they get their hands on Raven . . .

"They'll find the knife," I warn in her ear.

Before she steps off the wagon, she whispers, "I'm counting on it."

33

Meredith

"I've found the perfect gown!" Heloise gushes over dinner. Even she can't help but feel the wedding excitement, despite knowing the bride and groom share none of it. She and her family are enough to fill up the royal table as the honored guests, as Heloise's father, the Count of Ambrosia, gifted King Perceval the head of a great snow bear as congratulations for the upcoming nuptials. Three seats to my right, the count shares a laugh with the king, and I catch snippets of hunting lingo. The countess listens to the queen, smiling Heloise's smile, only not as wolfish. The vegetables on her plate are all but gone, leaving a small ring of boiled sprouts around the untouched bear meat. At the king's table, the Cresten brothers carry on as they always do. Only Humphrey keeps his colorful personality in check. He's cautiously soft-spoken tonight, carrying on with a disarming smile. He's as poised as Arthur, though not withdrawn like Tristan, who only speaks when spoken to.

"I can't wait to see it," I say to Heloise, chasing my words with a forkful of stewed potato, and steal a quick glance in Ethan's direction. He's deep in conversation with Marcus. Fatigue stains under his eyes, and there is stiffness to his posture that wasn't there before. And despite how often he touches his knife and fork, his plate is never empty.

No appetite again.

Once more, he and I are troubled by twin woes: worried sick over a loved one behind bars.

Councilor Milus's arrest was carried out by Captain Offa and his most trusted men in the dead of night, leaving both the court and the members of the council to wonder at his sudden disappearance. So far, it is as Ethan feared. The councilor refuses to divulge information, insisting on his innocence. But without proof of it, there is only room for doubt and suspicion. The most we can do is hope Councilor Milus was working alone. Ethan hasn't had the heart to question Milus, let alone visit him. "I couldn't bear to see him in a cell," he'd said to me. I didn't bother to reply. What could I say? I'd practically put Milus in jail myself.

It's been twelve days since our fated meeting with the king, and we've scarcely talked. Ethan spends his days with the king and the council, and retires to his rooms not long after, avoiding company. The few times he makes an appearance for supper, he hardly eats anything. I hate knowing that I've pushed this misery on him. Most of all, I hate how it eats at him, chipping at his heart bit by bit. I don't want him to end up like me. But broken hearts and disappointed hopes should be the least of my worries. I can't let that distract me from the danger Councilor Milus poses. If blue fever is ever unleashed in the kingdom, it will be a death sentence for all of us. Having the councilor locked in a cell is no guarantee that it won't happen, but at least it will give us a fighting chance.

As for Chancellor Ulric, the king decided to pay for his room and board at a city inn until further notice, provided that he keeps his identity to himself, both for his own safety and to avoid unwanted attention. It's a good thing the king ordered him out of the castle. I could hardly tolerate his presence, brief though as it was. Knowing he traveled all this way to help Charles has done little to change my feelings about the man.

"I must say, if the two of you don't change your attitudes, you may go down in the history books as the most miserable bride and groom that ever graced the temple," Heloise comments, pulling me from my dark thoughts.

"Can you blame him? He has to marry the devil's niece," I jest, trying to lighten my own mood, pretending there isn't any truth to my words.

"You don't really believe that nonsense, do you?" She points a perfectly arched brow at me.

I know the councilor's imprisonment is the reason for Ethan's misery, and yet, I've caught myself wondering if Ethan blames me for it on more than one occasion. If I hadn't insisted on bringing the matter to the king, none of this would have happened.

I feel the weight of Ethan's stare. Our eyes meet across the table, and my smile fades. He hasn't looked at me for days. But he looks at me now, eyes unreadable, and I feel strange that he caught me smiling.

"I'm surprised Katrina has the gall to speak ill of you," Heloise prattles on, unaware of our exchange. "What with the news of you butchering a Lucari and all; I think the ladies are more afraid of you now than they ever were of me," she says, envious.

Icy blue eyes flash in my mind. I hold back a shiver. "I didn't *butcher* him."

It's a relief that none beside Ethan knows just how young that Lucari was. What would they think of me then? Though there have been no other sightings of Lucari, patrols remain in and around those woods even now.

Heloise takes a delicate sip from her golden flute. "That's the thing about gossip. It's never a true account." She drops her voice to a surly whisper. "And why is it that I'm never around for these thrilling encounters of yours?"

"Perhaps it's a sign from the Maker that sword fighting is not your calling," I whisper back as I cut into the meat.

Heloise turns her head to me in a slow, calculated motion. Lifting my fork to my mouth, I slyly look her way. She stares at me, her lips parted in a mock gesture of hurt. It occurs to me that, unlike other ladies, the coming war will likely be exciting news to Heloise, even as her carefully guarded reputation forbids her to partake. The king's sealed letters must be well on their way to the battalion commanders throughout the kingdom. Within them, the order to summon their contracted soldiers and march south. Though the king keeps the order a secret from the council, the summoning of an army will not go unnoticed for long. But there is nothing to be done to avoid it. The cities and towns in their path will be the first to know. Word will spread eventually. And once the battalions arrive at Alder City's garrison, everyone will know. I have yet to tell Heloise and Lief about it, worried someone might overhear. Lief will surely march with us, and if Heloise could, I'm certain she'd volunteer without hesitation. A part of me envies her for it. There is no telling what will go down at the siege of the palace, and as ready and willing as I am to take back my kingdom at all costs, underneath all the patched-up layers that thicken my skin, I am terrified.

Having said our good-nights at supper, I'm not expecting any visits from Heloise, so I'm surprised when I hear a knock at my door. As soft as it is, the sound is jarring.

I can't imagine Ethan's here to patch things up. From what I gathered of his hasty exit at supper's end, he couldn't be more relieved to get away from everyone. Myself included.

When I open the door, I see the grim face of Queen Edith.

"Are you just going to stand there, or will you invite me in?" the queen asks as I continue to stare. She hasn't changed out of the finery she wore to supper, bedecked in silver and silk.

I scoot against the open door to let her pass.

"Your room is quite small," she mutters when I close the door.

I fumble with my hands, at a loss to her presence. "It's more than enough. I don't have much use for large rooms."

"Yes, we both know you much prefer the outdoors."

I stare at her stone-gray velvet coat in the ensuing silence. Her elegant neck rises out of it like a planted rose. "Your Majesty, to what do I owe this honor?"

She swivels to face me, straightening her shoulders and clasping her hands together as she sets her unyielding eyes on me. "Do you love my son?"

I blink at her, unable to think for a moment. The intensity of her gaze pushes an uncomfortable swallow down my throat. Whether or not I love Ethan isn't the question she should be asking. I can't deny that I've come to care for Ethan. I realized as much the day of his flogging. But love? My wilted heart, which stubbornly clings to a ghost, stiffens at the prospect. "I hardly know him."

The queen draws her lips into a tight line. "That's not what I was hoping to hear. Nevertheless, I appreciate your honesty; seldom is it given freely when you sit on a throne." She tucks her right arm below her chest, holding her left elbow atop it to cradle her chin with two fingers as she regards me coolly. "I hope you realize you came to be here because of me."

Ethan told me as much the day we met. "Yes," I start, but Edith goes on as if I hadn't spoken.

"The king was ready to forgo the alliance and annul your betrothal when I interceded on your behalf. I thought it unfair that you should take the blame for your father's failings." Her eyes drop to my feet and then back to my face. "I thought you deserved a chance."

"I am very grate—"

"Seeing you when you first arrived, beaten and tattered as you were, a poor, helpless princess in need of help"—her eyes are ice—"I thought I'd made the right choice. But then your *uncle* came to visit." She emphasizes her disgust at the word.

My marriage to Ethan will make Theros part of her family, too.

"I am queen. But I am a mother first. Always and forever. And after what that monster did to my son . . ." A flicker of rage tightens the fine lines of her elegant face. "I'm left wondering if perhaps you aren't as helpless as I thought." She paces slowly across my room, much like Ethan does when he has something on his mind. "It is said Theros overthrows kings from within, like a wolf that hides its teeth, infecting wounds that fester and grow. I wonder if this"—the queen twirls her finger to gesture at my person—"is all but a ruse. I wonder if *you* are the pus that needs cleansing."

The words hit me like a slap to the face, just as she intended. It isn't her opinion of me that I find surprising—she'd given me plenty of cold looks after Ethan's lashing to come to that conclusion—but to hear her say it so bluntly . . .

A cold, quiet anger takes hold, seeping into my voice. "Your Majesty, Theros and I may share the same blood, but we are *not* family. That, we will never be." Theros has taken so much from me. Too much. Just thinking about it churns my stomach. "I would never consider him anything other than my enemy."

The queen tilts her head and narrows her eyes with discerning scrutiny. "I thought you'd say something to that effect. Both the king and my son believe you speak the truth, and perhaps you do," she considers, coming closer. Hints of her sweet perfume fill the space around us. "If you are sincere, I extend my deepest apologies for speaking against your character." She takes another step. "But if you are lying to me, if more harm comes to my family, if anything else happens to my son because of your doing, I swear to the Maker I will rip your beating heart out and feed it to the wolves."

I stare at the queen. I don't think I've ever heard a threat uttered so delicately, which makes it all the more menacing. Except I have no reason feel threatened. Time will prove to her what my words cannot.

When the queen leaves my room, I am left with the strangest sensation, one she can't have intended to evoke.

Yearning.

I envy Ethan.

What I wouldn't give for the love of a mother like his.

34

Connor

I stick my head out through the iron bars, fists tight at my back as I watch Smirk shuffle Raven toward the campfire. The soldiers shout and whistle at her presence, goading her.

"She's going t' get herself killed," Rhys mutters, his tone disapproving.

"Or she might save your cowardly pelt."

I ignore his glare. My eyes are on Raven, heart racing in my rigid body. It's to her advantage that the men are drunk, but there's eight of them—ten if you consider the collectors—and only one of her. She doesn't stand a chance.

Dammit, Raven!

I strain against my bounds, my exhaustion forgotten, frantic for a way to break free.

"She made her choice," Rhys deadpans, observing my frustration. "You can't help her."

Smirk drops the rope at Raven's feet and roughly positions her near the fire, where every man can get a good look at her. Khalia is still whimpering, eyes squeezed shut so she doesn't see. The collector is playing his flute again, prompting Raven to start dancing. She moves to the mellow tune, moving in fluid but controlled motions.

Rhys gives a low, appreciative whistle that makes me want to bang his head against the bars. "The lass can dance."

The redcloaks are enchanted by the elegant twirl of Raven's arms and the graceful thrust of her hips. Distracted *and* drunk. Raven's feet travel smoothly toward a staunch-looking redcloak—the bearded one—as though it's all part of her dance. Watching the scene unfold is nerve-racking. Raven sits on the soldier's lap, undulating and whipping her head, her dark hair flipping about the bearded redcloak's face. The others watch intently, hooting and whistling.

Raven's arms dart to her sides and her head flips back in one motion. In a second, she's on her feet, gyrating around the fire toward another soldier. With their attention on her, they don't notice the dark gash on the soldier's neck behind her . . .

Until his body falls backward.

My hands are numb from straining when the first shout of alarm breaks the music.

The campfire explodes like a rat's nest.

Redcloaks spring from their seats, sober enough to lunge after Raven. The collectors flee toward the bank. Raven bares her teeth, her knife pointed at the redcloak who would have been her next victim had the others not pried her off him so quickly. They disarm her and throw her to the ground. The redcloaks begin to kick her.

"*Gods*," I hear Rhys whisper, empathetic for once.

It doesn't matter if they don't mean to kill Raven. Drunk as they are, the soldiers won't check themselves, won't even realize how hard they kick.

"We have to distract them," I say.

Rhys shoots me a look. "And turn them on us? Are you mad?"

"Hey!" I'm shouting at the top of my lungs. "HEY!"

Rhys crawls toward a crying Khalia, distancing himself from me. *Coward.* I keep shouting, but the soldiers don't let up, stabbing their boots into Raven's side.

My blood becomes ice.

She's going to die.

The thought sinks like an anchor, dragging my guts with it to my feet. She saved my life, nursed me back to health, and I can't even return the favor. The helplessness is maddening. I strain and buck against my binds, feeling the rope dig into my skin—

A gargled scream makes me go still.

One of the redcloaks falls, clutching at a spear that sticks out from his chest . . . and the kicking stops.

Shadows rush through the weeds. The fishermen. Seven, maybe more. A flurry of spears flies across the field. The soldiers are screaming at each other, their weapons drawn, but without shields, the spears strike freely, piercing torsos and legs.

Growls and cries of pain erupt.

Rhys is back at my side, wearing a stupid smile of surprise. I assess the chaos. Two redcloaks limp around the campfire; one calls for help, belly punctured—he won't make it much longer—the other screams as he tries to remove the spear lodged in his thigh. Another lies twitching on the floor, beyond saving. The remaining four soldiers have spotted the fishermen and are on the attack. Smirk is among them, barking orders while he sprints.

Footfalls crash toward our wagon.

"Khalia!"

The girl all but jumps from her cowered slouch. "Papa—I'm here!"

Khalia's father is running to the wagon, his unkempt shoulder-length hair plastered with sweat to the sides of his age-lined face. A crude ax gleams in his right hand. He scans the barred wagon with harried eyes, searching for Khalia, and lets out a tired breath at the sight of her.

Time is running out. But Khalia's father shifts his focus from the wagon's lock toward the cries of his men, indecisive.

"You won't survive those swords!" I shout over the commotion. "Let me help." The man's gaze cuts to me, and his pause hardens my stomach. "Hurry!" I urge through my teeth.

Blinking, Khalia's father scuttles into motion. His ax slams onto the lock with a loud chink. He roars, hammering the metal, and I hold my breath, praying the ax doesn't break before the lock does.

Chink. Chink. Chink. Chink.

A plea for mercy echoes within the scuffle of soldiers and fishermen, followed by a faint groan. The fight is a flurry of clashes and grunts and butchering, but I don't need to see. I already know how it will end. And soon.

At last, the lock gives. Panting, Khalia's father lurches two steps back to swing the door open. I jump out and thrust my bound hands into his view. "Cut the rope!"

Rhys stumbles down the wagon and moves to get his rope cut next, but at the stomp of charging boots, he breaks into a run, darting into the darkness where the firelight won't give him away.

Khalia's father cuts the rope with one clean swing, and I pull my arms free just as I register the glint of swords. I lay eyes on Smirk. He's barreling toward me, teeth bared, his sword aiming at my chest.

But I'm faster.

I shirk from the swat of his longsword, edging the blade. I upend his next strike, smashing my fist into his elbow. The pummel bangs his head as I slam another fist to his chest, hurling him to the calf-high weeds. Smirk loses his sword midfall. In one swoop, I catch it and swerve right. The side of the blade cleaves into an incoming redcloak's ribs, catching him with his arms raised above his head, the falchion sword in his grip a second from striking me down. I ram my elbow into his throat and kick him down.

Khalia's father is lumbering away from his opponent, hardly parrying the blows. Blood dribbles down his left arm, which sags limp at his side, made useless by the wound on his shoulder.

Breathing hard, I swap the longsword for the single-handed falchion and lunge to his aid. I'm on them in three strides, and my blade ripples through the air, its curved point cleanly severing the redcloak's head from his body.

And Khalia's father is throwing his ax at me.

But the weapon spins inches from my ear. I whirl just as it splits Smirk's head with a sickening crunch, stopping him in his tracks. The longsword falls from his grip for the last time. Smirk makes three waddling steps before his body flops to the grass.

In the aftermath of a slaughter, the fishermen are either dead or dying, their bodies hidden in the dark and weedy field . . . I had been right to assume they were no match for redcloaks—even drunk ones—but I did not account for their skilled aim.

I run to the campfire, rushing to Raven's side. She lies as they left her, crumpled on the dirt. I crouch beside her and gently roll her to her back. Her sleek hair blankets her face. I brush it aside. Her eyes open to slits, barely conscious.

Rhys's shout echoes from the bank.

"The collectors—kill them before they get away!"

Water splashes. They're trying to swim across the river. I'm debating if I have the gall to kill defenseless men. But collectors are crafty, and letting them escape could bring dire consequences to Khalia's village.

Across the bank, someone shrieks in horror.

When I leap off my knees, a hand clamps my shoulder.

Through the screams, Khalia's father murmurs, "No need lad. The crocodiles will do the work for us."

35

Meredith

Bells chime across the city every few minutes, announcing the royal wedding as though someone could possibly forget it's taking place today. Lorette and five royal handmaids buzz around me like worker bees, scrubbing my skin, brushing the tangles out of my hair, and trimming my nails. The dizzying attention has been constant from the moment they woke me and ushered me to dunk my body in a petal-strewn bath. What I wouldn't give to exchange the lot of them for Anabella. Has she fared any better than Charles? Has Beth? I've told myself a hundred times over that it's pointless to worry, but without news, knowing they live under Theros's rule nauseates me. I've seen his cruelty firsthand, but I can only imagine what life must be like for those constantly near him.

I will be home soon, I silently promise them.

I will make things right. Today marks the first step in that direction, and I will see it through, no matter what. After the queen's visit to my room, I decided my guilt and reservations could wait for a time when I have nothing else to occupy my thoughts.

The maids dress me in an ivory gown with a fitted bodice

covered in lace that runs from the sleeves to the train below the tulle skirts. I watch through the mirror as my tresses are pinned just above the neckline into an elegant bun of braids and pearls and floral accents. Red dye-smeared fingertips pinch my cheeks and stain my lips while another maid carefully places a circlet of pearls across my temple. It takes three of the ladies to slip my arms into a cream-colored sleeveless fur coat. The coat's train trails an inch past that of my gown's, and the weight of it instantly tugs down on my shoulders. Once the skin on my neck is generously scented with the pale yellow petals of winter sweet flowers and every inch of me is inspected, Lorette finally deems me ready.

I stare at my reflection. The girl in the mirror stares back, looking very much like a bride.

My stomach tightens with anticipation. I grip my snowdrop bouquet as I stand behind Lorette and the procession of white-gowned handmaids.

This is it, I think.

The day I've dreaded since I was a little girl has finally come to pass.

"Wait," I say, before the maids cross through the door. I move to my desk, pulling the left drawer open. With my free hand, I take my silver dagger, drawing soft gasps from the girls, and lift my skirts to tuck it in the garter at my thigh.

"You won't be needing that, my lady," a frowning Lorette assures me, her eyes pleading with me to put the dagger back. But the dagger isn't for protection.

"I'll feel better with it on my person."

Lorette stares like she might insist, but she bows her head in a curt nod instead and turns to face the handmaids, signaling them to move. Skirts swishing with each step, I am paraded toward the main hall through the hauntingly silent castle, where the entire staff has gathered to see me off. Aside from the guards, they are the only people left within the stone walls and polished doors. Everyone else is probably seated in the pews of the city's temple. Is Ethan standing there now, awaiting my arrival? Is he as fidgety as I am? It seems we were closer when the wedding was off than we are now. I had hoped we'd have a moment to talk before today, to try and patch up this sudden rift between us. But Ethan maintained his distance, and I never worked up the courage to seek him out.

Outside, the midday sun burns bright, unhindered in a clear blue sky, keeping the cold at bay. A large carriage bedecked in ribbons of blue and gold awaits with open doors. Atop it, the coachman is dressed in fine black silks and a matching feathered hat. A troop of minstrels and lute players stand behind the coach, ready for the procession. Lief is there, looking the same as any other day, only today he can't stop smiling at me. Though I don't share his excitement, his presence helps quell my nerves. I return his beaming grin with a shy smile of my own as he takes my hand to help me up the folding step. Handmaids rush to my side, careful with the mass of gown and fur as they deposit me in the spacious velvet passenger seats. With Lorette and the rest of the ladies inside, Lief closes the carriage door and climbs to join the coachman up front. Moments later, we are off to the city.

Colorful tapestries decorate the streets, where all manner of people line up to watch the procession. Some stand in their doorways, craning their necks to get a glimpse of their future queen as the spokes of the carriage turn down the path. I look at their curious faces and wonder how many of them have an unfavorable opinion of me. These people will one day be my subjects, so I know I must make an effort to prove there's more to me than hearsay.

Ahead, the high temple cuts into the sky like a stone mountain. We turn into its heavily guarded courtyard, free of spectators, and I stick my adorned head out the window. Someone must have been watching for the carriage, because an echo of the temple's choir song spills from atop the steps, signaling my arrival. Mouth dry, I exit the carriage like a hesitant animal offered freedom from its cage, and suppress the uncanny desire to flee. Lorette instructs a pair of handmaids to the trains of fabric that sprawl behind me, and they lift the heavy hems off the cold pebbled ground as Lorette and the other three ladies lead the way. Lief remains on the carriage seat with the driver, smiling me on, unaware of the apprehension building in my chest.

Breathe, I tell myself. *Just breathe.*

I count each step in my head to give my thoughts something to do besides fret. When I get to sixty, the inside of the temple comes into view. King Perceval's entire court—over three hundred people—rises and pivots toward me. So many strangers dressed in finery, dissecting me with their eyes. Judging me, the foreign princess who trains with swords, daughter of a fool, the devil's niece.

If I were them, I wouldn't know what to make of myself, either.

Atop the dais, at the end of a seemingly endless red carpet runner, Ethan stands next to the golden-robed priest, garbed in a maroon tunic. I can't make out his face from here, but I can feel his eyes on me. Behind him, on a second-story landing, a faceless bronze statue of the Maker spans from floor to ceiling, covering most of the back wall and its narrow stained windows. The choir of young apprentices sings from up there, perched by the Maker's feet. Bronze statues of the Maker's twelve heralds edge the walls. Incense burners dangle from the ends of their staffs, hovering above the pews and wafting fading tendrils of smoke.

I take careful steps, and though my face is a blanket of composure, inside my heart thrashes against my ribcage. I grip my bouquet as though it's the hilt of a sword, feeling every step, every heartbeat, every breath. As I close the distance to the altar, Ethan's silhouette sharpens, and I can see the gold trimmings that accentuate his brocaded doublet and the golden collar of state around his shoulders. He stands as still as the statue behind him.

My handmaids come around me at the dais and move with practiced grace to either side of the church. I stand alone, frozen with uncertainty as I face my future. *Stonefall's future*. Red rims Ethan's eyes as though he didn't catch a minute of sleep. He takes my hand and manages to pull off that flawless, charming smile of his. It's been weeks since I last saw it. I hold on to that smile, finding some comfort in it.

Then, as the choir's song ends, the priest begins the ceremony.

I dare a glance at the guests. The king and queen sit stiff in the front pew to Ethan's side. The king's face is void of expression, stoic and inscrutable. But Queen Edith wears her feelings like a mask. I've never seen her look so grim, as though attending a funeral. And she's not the only one. Councilor Rowan sits beside her, face and neck red with hate, his glare pinned on me. I find a friendlier face two pews back, where Heloise sits between her brothers. She winks at me, a sly smirk on her face, easing my tension in those brief seconds.

The priest reads from a tattered, ancient-looking copy of the book of the Maker, its passages handwritten, the paper yellowed and uneven, stained with ink at the corners. I try to focus on his mouth as he reads, but his words blur in my ears. My mind is elsewhere, thinking of a pair of brooding dark-blue eyes. I can almost see them, peering into my soul as though it's an open window. Will the ghost of his memory haunt me for the rest of my days?

A request brings me back to the temple.

The priest has closed the leather-bound book and asked that

we each press our hands on the holy book. Ethan's cold hand covers mine.

"The Maker receives thee, the Maker binds thee, and two become one, wholly and completely, in life and beyond His gate. For what the Maker sows together, man can never destroy."

Another priest steps forward to hand each of us a gold ring.

Ethan takes my damp hand. "With this ring I thee wed," he says, slipping the band on my ring finger.

"I receive thee," I say, my voice barely above a trembling whisper. And then it's my turn. Ethan's hands, unlike mine, are dry and steady. Through all this, I somehow manage not to drop the bouquet clutched in my right hand.

"With this ring I thee wed."

"I receive thee."

Looking pleased, the priest's announcement booms across the temple. "By the Maker's grace, I declare you man and wife."

Ethan's throat bobs. His hand falls on my cheek like a feather. Tentatively, he dips his head closer. Ever so lightly, his bow-shaped lips brush mine, sweet and gentle and foreign. In that briefest of moments, my face, neck, and ears burn hot, and I become aware of my own heartbeat again, racing away in my ears like a galloping horse. Our chaste kiss prompts the choir above us to resume their celestial song. With my hand still in his, Ethan turns to face the court, and all at once, bells ring in the streets once more, announcing our union to the city.

36

Connor

"I'll be fine." It's the first thing out of Raven's mouth when I walk in the hut. I knew she'd be awake. The bickering outside is loud enough to keep anyone from rest. "It's only bruises."

I hissed when I saw those bruises last night. Her abdomen, her legs, her arms—they were covered in them. They must look worse now. She slept on our way back to the fishing village, and through most of the day after we arrived, so I was hoping she would fare a little better, but every movement makes her wince and groan. Sitting up on the hay-stuffed bed is a struggle for her.

"I didn't say anything."

"You don't have t'; your face says it all."

"It wasn't easy watching you take that beating."

Her eyes look up at me. "Least I got one o' those redcloak scum."

My lips twitch. "It was . . . impressive."

"What d'you think o' the dance?" She tilts her head. A strand of hair falls into her face, but she blows it away.

"Stressful. Rhys liked it, though."

She laughs. Just then, the village squabble grows louder. "What's going on out there?"

"Half the village's men died last night rescuing Khalia," I explain. "Some of the women think it was selfish of Osberd to sacrifice their husbands for his daughter."

Raven sighs. "If the fishermen hadn't come t' Khalia's rescue, we'd still be locked in that wagon . . . Nothing comes without cost in these lands."

"Rhys and I would still be locked in that wagon. *You*," I chide, "would be dead."

Raven closes her eyes, taking a long, pained breath. "For a minute there, I thought I was." She shivers despite the sweltering heat. "It was foolish o' me, I know." She slowly looks at me, her expression sober. "I couldn't let them hurt Khalia."

"It was reckless, but I can't blame you for trying to do the right thing."

I trail off into my thoughts.

"Something the matter?" Raven asks, observant.

"I feel like you remind me of someone, but I don't know who." A bitter smile tugs at the corner of my mouth, longing to remember.

"The Brotherhood's wrong for you, Connor," Raven says quietly after a thoughtful pause. "You belong in the North."

I sit on the ground across from her, letting my weight sink me to the packed mud. "Then you'll understand when I leave."

"When . . . not if?"

I nod. Something like sadness fills her eyes.

"As long as Pip is in good health."

Her hands stray to her chest. "You're taking him with ya?"

The Brotherhood's rationing policy leaves me no choice, but it's the way Raven asks that makes me hesitate.

"You don't think I should?"

Raven wraps her arms around herself, her full lips thoughtful. "No, you should. He'll be safer away from this place. It's just . . . I think I'll feel very lonely without you and Pip."

"You're welcome to join us."

She nods, but her eyes are glum. "Asher will never leave the Brotherhood."

"And you will never leave Asher," I finish for her.

She nods again, absently biting her lip this time. "Shouldn't you wait for more memories?" she asks a moment later.

I shake my head. "I've done enough of that. Not knowing is eating me alive. I have to try something else; seeing familiar lands might help."

After another long pause of staring at the thatched wall, she takes a breath and lets it out slowly. "You'll have t' leave in secret. We don't want your new brothers t' skin ya for deserting."

Rhys drinks himself nearly to death that night. I'm watching over Raven while she rests, listening to the river's distant burbling when I hear snippets of his hoots and ramblings. I find him weaving by the coin wagon, as though it's discovered treasure, a clay stein in his tenuous grip. *Is that all he's had to drink?* I wonder, searching for the barrel. Someone must have served him the drink, thinking one wouldn't do any harm, but Rhys hasn't rested. He's remained alert and on his feet since we returned, as I have. But I'm smart enough to stay away from ale.

"Ah, Connor, my hero!" he bellows when I draw near, a sloppy smile on his face. "Have a drink with me."

Faces peek from the huts nearby, their eyes glinting with torchlight, curious about the inebriated stranger in their village. Rhys aside, it's peaceful here at night. I can't see the river, but I can hear the water lap gently along the pebbled bank as it ebbs and flows.

"I think you've had enough, Rhys."

He curls an arm around my shoulders and hiccups in my ear. "Such a soddy wench, you are." His hot breath reeks of ale. "We should be celebrating! Uther sent us scouting, and we'll return with the whole bounty. He'll be impressed."

"We're leaving the loot with Osberd. Isn't that what the Brotherhood does—give it back to the people it's taken from?"

"Not a tenth of that is theirs," Rhys scoffs.

I remove his arm. "This village needs the coin, Rhys. They've lost half their men rescuing us."

"They weren't rescuing *us*! We just happened t' be locked in the same wagon as the girl."

"We are free all the same."

"The dead don't care what we do with the coin," Rhys says with a sly grin. Then he downs his stein and kicks it to the side, breaking it in two.

I glare at him and consider slamming his blotchy face in the mud.

"The families of the dead do."

Rhys fails to swat a loose curl out of his eyes. "*The families o' the dead*?" he sneers. His words slur, but the anger is clear. "These people know nothing about pain. They haven't suffered as I've suffered." He pushes a finger in my chest, almost falling. "You pity their loss . . ." It takes him a minute to finish. He sways slightly on his feet. The faces that stared are gone, tucked back into their huts. "Those are flesh wounds," he continues. "I've been cut deeper—I've endured worse."

The ale has loosened his tongue.

He tries to shuffle away but stumbles on a trestle table piled with weir traps. The stack topples, rolling one to my foot, wafting the faint, briny stench from its last catch.

"What happened to you?" I pry.

Leaning on the table, Rhys shifts to face me head on. A cynical laugh bursts out of him.

I wait out his amusement, watching him silently.

He doesn't look at me when his smile fades, turning to the table. His throat bobs. "He made me do it."

I step to the edge of the table. "Who made you do what?"

"It's been three years," Rhys murmurs hoarsely. His head bobs subtly back and forth to find balance, clearly drunk, but his eyes are sober. "It feels like days . . . never gets easier, does it?" He keeps staring at the table. "I'd give anything t' forget."

A rustling noise turns my head toward the huts. Twenty yards away, an elderly woman fiddles with the leaves of a bush outside her door, pretending not to stare at us.

"Why did Uther recruit you?" I ask.

There's an ugly twist to his mouth. "T' keep his promise t' my dead father."

"And he knows you can't fight?"

A nonchalant shrug. "I can do something none o' the other rebels can."

"What's that?"

"Here's a little tale for you." His head wobbles like it's too heavy for his shoulders. He speaks slowly, eyes half-lidded, with the flair you'd expect from a drunk. "Uther used t' be a royal mercenary. He and my father worked for the king." A wave of the hand. "Minor skirmishes that could be carried out discreetly . . . Our king maintained order that way." A hiccup. "The king compensated the mercenaries well for years, earned their loyalty. The right hands o' the king—they called 'emselves—which is why the Usurper came straight for 'em during the Takeover. Uther survived, but the redcloaks killed his family."

"So he disappeared and formed his band of rebels?"

Rhys barely has the strength to nod. "Aye. But losing his son took the life out o' him. He was a dead man walking. But then I came along and made everything better."

I stare at the drunken smugness all over Rhys's face. "He loves me like a son," he says. When I don't respond, he pushes off the table and lurches toward me, bringing the stench of ale back with him. "Uther favors *me.* He will *always* favor me."

I lift my brows, seeing the fear hidden underneath the jealousy.

This is what's been pricking his thumb all this time? It's both absurd and disconcerting that he feels this way about Uther's approval; perhaps he grew up without a father's affection.

"I'm not your competition, Rhys."

"You're a good liar." He laughs, sounding half-mad. "You're a mighty fine killer, too. But who says I'm worried?" He spins away in a huff, offended yet again.

And then he vomits his guts out.

37

Meredith

Hours later, Ethan is drunk. Beside me at the royal table, and in view of the entire assembly before us in the Feast Hall, he swirls his goblet of spiced wine and signals loudly to a servant girl for a refill.

How many will this make? Seven? Eight? I lost count. He drained his first one after the king's toast, to which the nobles cheered: "Long live the prince and his bride!"

At only arm's length, Ethan's never felt so distant. He hasn't bothered pretending with the fork tonight. The untouched roasted mutton and pickled vegetables on his plate are probably cold by now. I can't say my food fared any better. I forced a few bites though my stomach rebelled; it didn't feel right to let my wedding meal be a complete waste.

Ten feet from the dais, a dance troupe performs to a lively melody of harps and flutes, skipping and kicking and leaping, their synchronized steps chiming from the bells looped at their knees. They're the third set of entertainers to perform for the royal table this evening. Presently, Ethan is more interested in his slurred conversation with his favorite Cresten brother. Marcus is a tad inebriated himself, only he scarfed down his food, which staved off the effects of the wine. The king and queen pretend not to notice their drunken banter, but the nobles sitting near the head table can't help but stare at their newlywed prince swaying and floundering in his chair. Courtiers flick their eyes to the bride at his side, the telltale root of his unseemly behavior. Embarrassed as I am, I can't blame Ethan for chasing wine like water.

After the wedding ceremony, our silence in the carriage ride back to the castle hadn't been as awkward as I'd thought it would be. The bells tolled the whole way and continued for another hour. The spirit of celebration seemed to have taken hold in the streets, livening the people; they too would be enjoying good food and music down in the central district at the expense of the king. But the festive spirit stopped at the walls of the carriage. I could tell something was wrong with Ethan, something besides the same troubles that have plagued him since the councilor's arrest. I could see the bleakness in his glassy eyes. So when I worked up the courage to inquire if it was the wedding that had him in such a state, he didn't hesitate to reveal his concerns and placate mine.

"Milus will be executed at dawn," he choked out in a strained voice.

The words caught my breath. "He confessed?"

Ethan nodded. "Under torture." His throat bobbed. I could tell he was making an effort to keep his composure. "My father gave me his word he wouldn't resort to that."

Guessing his thoughts, I dared to ask, "You think Milus lied to make the pain stop?"

Minutes went by before he looked at me with those distraught brown eyes. "I don't know what to think anymore," he whispered. "He claimed to be working alone, and said that he kept a contaminated wine decanter in his quarters. But when they found the decanter, there was a half-poured cup next to it. If it truly is tainted wine, Milus wouldn't drink it, would he?"

I bit my lip. "That *is* odd."

"My mind's been running circles around it." He looked at me. "It makes no sense. There is no reason anyone would suspect anything from an untouched wine decanter."

"So why bother with pretenses," I say, coming to the same conclusion.

Ethan leans forward, forearms braced on his thighs. "Milus *is* lying—I'd be willing to drink that wine to prove it. I just don't know if he lies because he's innocent, or because he doesn't want us to find the plague."

He sat there, shoulders stiff, looking like he was suffocating in his anguish. Not knowing what else to do, I pushed closer on the velvet seat and reached for his arm. I held on, my body pressed to his, hoping my touch would comfort him, if only a little. Couldn't the execution be delayed? I wondered. It was the simplest solution for both the decanter conundrum and Ethan's sanity. After a moment, I said, "The king's timing for the execution seems a bit callous." *More than callous, it's cruel. Ethan loves Milus like a father, and the king knows it. He knows what this is doing to him.*

Ethan chuckled bitterly at that. "My father's timing was intentional. He thinks our wedding night bliss will distract me."

The words sank, leaving me flushed and tongue-tied, and it took every cell in my body not to pull away. The silence stretched, settling once again like an invisible companion between us. I was too mortified to come up with a response. Even now, the thought makes my cheeks burn. At some point before we arrived at the castle, I muttered a meek apology, which Ethan accepted with a solemn nod. *I know*, it seemed to say, though I could sense from the rigid set of muscles of his arm that he didn't want my pity.

The wine seems to be doing its job, I think as I watch Ethan now, his arm slung over Marcus's shoulders, sharing a laugh with him.

"Congratulations, Your Highness."

I'm surprised to see Rose curtsying across from me, a shy smile on her powdered face. She looks lovely in a regalia of weaved blue damask and silver silk. For once, she is alone, free of her sister's shadow. She steals a longing glance in Ethan's direction, and for a second, in that bittersweet glint of her eyes, I think she might be imagining the life that almost was. The life that could have been, had I not come along. But then, Rose drops her eyes to the garlands decorating the table and surprises me yet again when she says, "You'll make a more fitting ruler than I could ever aspire to be."

The compliment catches me off guard, but her humble manner suggests she means it. She's not her sister, after all. That shyness, that gentle innocence . . . it reminds me so much of Beth. Perhaps, under different circumstances, Rose and I could have been good friends.

I smile. "I—thank you, Rose."

She looks up. "It was an honor to earn the king's consideration. It's simply that I . . . I don't have the heart of a queen," she says softly, careful that others might not overhear, outspoken and discreet all at once. *I'm not so sure I do, either*, I want to admit, but it's not like I have a choice, only the illusion of one; Stonefall needs me to be a queen. "But you're different," Rose goes on, her eyes a pair of candid orbs. "You're not afraid."

"I'm flattered you think me so fearless," I say. "I hope I don't let you down."

Rose starts to speak, but just then, Katrina swoops in like a bear protecting her cubs.

"Mother would like a word, Rose," she says tightly. If she had claws, they would undoubtedly be drawn and pointed at me.

"Of course," Rose replies, ignoring her sister's ire as she takes her time to curtsy once more.

Katrina remains a moment longer, looking between Ethan and me. Her lips twist in a smug smile. "You make quite the happy couple, Your Highness," she drawls. Though Ethan happens to be all drunken smiles at the moment, I know her remark is meant as a barb.

Funny. Rose reminds me of Beth, and Katrina . . .

I force a smile, which is harder to do when all my face wants to do is glower. "It's a shame my cousin Charlotte wasn't invited. She would love you."

"My, she sounds awful, Your Highness," someone says from behind Katrina.

Heloise struts to Katrina's side wearing an embroidered pearl corset and a long, flowing golden skirt, her lustrous hair tucked in an intricate side braid, lips glossy and crimson red.

"Can't wait to meet her," she adds, giving Katrina a disdainful once-over.

Katrina scowls into a shallow curtsy and disappears behind the dancers.

"I thought I'd come by and shoo the flies away," Heloise quips.

I chuckle. "You do it so well."

She beams at me, a flash of pearly teeth and bright-red lips. "I'd say congratulations if I wasn't the hundredth person to tell you so."

"Coming from you, it would mean something," I admit.

"Are you implying you haven't tired of receiving contrived compliments? I have a list-long set of them memorized in my head if you'd like to hear them."

I bite back a snort. "Flattery never did anyone any harm."

"Tell that to Marcus." Hel's feline gaze falls on her brother. "Just look at him. He's drowned himself in wine."

Indeed, Marcus and Ethan are bragging of sparring victories

and the fine metal of their swords, loud and obnoxious. As I watch, the queen's eyes flick to me, ominous and vigilant. It can't be easy entertaining guests while the one she loves most drinks himself numb. Within our silent exchange, Edith's fixed stare conveys what we discussed in my room, what she promised she would do if I hurt Ethan. I will myself to hold her iron gaze, not in defiance, but in promise.

"I'll drag him away if you like."

I slide my eyes away from the queen and blink up at Heloise. "What?"

"My brother," she clarifies, blinking disapproval at Marcus.

"Oh." I shake my head, watching the cup bearer refill their drinks. "No, there's no need to spoil their fun. Leave them be."

Heloise shifts her weight to one side, resting a fist on her hip. "Should I drag *you* away, Your Highness?"

I want that more than anything. To escape my own wedding. Though I don't say anything, I think the look on my face is answer enough.

Wordlessly, Heloise walks to the king and queen, saying words I cannot hear that prompt a brief glance in my direction. Then, to my sudden relief, she returns to fetch me. "I've explained to Their Majesties how exhausted you are." She waves at a table near the back wall, signaling to Lorette and her coterie of handmaids to come forward. "Lorette and I will help you to the prince's quarters."

And just like that, my relief turns into a wave of jitters.

Not my room.

Ethan's rooms.

Maker. I am not ready for this.

Inside Ethan's private quarters, I fetch a bucket from his bathing room with only seconds to spare. Not ten seconds later, Ethan is hurling the contents of an empty stomach into it on the crimson rug at the foot of his bed. This would not have proved an easy task with my wedding gown on; even Heloise had to lend a hand to the handmaids to pluck me out of that sea of fabric. Kneeling next to Ethan, I cross my arms at my chest, both from the chill of the room and the thin cotton of my shift.

Not that Ethan is in any state to notice.

Done vomiting, he leans back with a muted grimace, eyes closed and frowning, slumping down the side of the bed in his crumpled doublet.

When I'm certain he's done emptying his stomach, I pick him up from under his armpits, grunting as I struggle to lift him to the bed.

"Maker, you are heavier than you look," I gasp, breaking a sweat despite the cold.

Unsuccessful, I kneel on the edge of the bed for purchase and try to pull him up. He's still heavier than a sack of potatoes, but once his torso is over the edge, I let myself fall backward on the bed, huffing as I bring us both down onto the feather mattress and silk sheets. Ethan falls like dead weight on top of me. I take a moment to catch my breath and then roll him off to the side. He's lost to his dreams, snoring softly. I drag a pillow under his head as gently as I can. Not that he'll wake up if I'm brusque. At this point, I'm pretty sure I could throw him off the bed and he wouldn't stir. I observe him under the flicker of firelight, taking in his peacefully passed-out state, a drastic change from the grief that drowned him earlier. His public display of intoxication will probably have tongues wagging for the next fortnight. But it's better this way. Tomorrow will be hard for him. Hopefully, after all that wine, he'll sleep through most of it. And, if I'm honest, I'm more than relieved about not having to fret over our *wedding night bliss*.

Blushing a little, I push off the bed and cross the room to the fireplace, picking a couple of logs and feeding them to the flames. I lay on the bare stone, legs crossed, feeling my skin warm as I listen to the crackling fire. My mind whirs with the significance of today's events. It's a disquieting feeling, as though a prophecy has been fulfilled, setting the wheels of fate into motion.

For once, Father would be pleased.

I shake my head. Even now I seek his approval.

But oh, the irony. The one thing Father raised me for—the only reason I ever mattered to him—has all been for naught. He's going to lose his throne. And I'll go down in history as the princess who betrayed her king. Father will be furious. Furious *and* powerless. Deep in my gut, I know it's the right thing to do. He deserves to be dethroned. Still, I won't get satisfaction from it.

Because no matter how much I resent my father, I can't help caring for him. Part of me always will, I see that now. The worry in my heart at what Elijah said when he was here, what he threatened to do . . . I despise my father. And I love him. I don't know why, but I do. Maybe it's because even though I find fault with everything he's done, he's the closest thing to my mother, whom he loved above all else. And she loved him, which must mean there's a good man in there somewhere. A man worthy of her love.

Drained by my thoughts, I curl up on the fire-warmed floor and fall asleep to the sound of Ethan's light snores.

When I wake, the room is dark and cold.

There's no smoke coming from the fireplace. It must have gone out a while ago. That's odd. Ethan's steward is supposed to return every few hours to check on it. Blinking through the sluggishness of sleep, I sit up, limbs stiff and numb. My skin feels like ice under the shift as I try to rub warmth to my arms. I've just picked up a log to throw in the fireplace when I hear a noise. The sound is muffled, but within the dead silence of the bedroom, my ears pick up on it.

I wait with bated breath for more.

Silence.

It's probably nothing.

Creak.

The groan of a door comes from the sitting room, slow and

faint. Someone's in the other room. The steward, then? Perhaps he overslept. So why does the hair on my neck stand on end? My head snaps to Ethan for a second. He's sprawled on the bed, just as I left him, oblivious to the cold. I'm holding my breath again, staring at the closed bedroom door, expecting it to open in the next instant.

Log still in hand, I slink to the door, flattening myself against the wall at its hinges.

If it really is the steward, I'll simply . . . hand him the log.

Hushed footfalls come from the other side of the wall. Fear hammers my chest. I grip the log tighter, palm and fingers aching from the awkward grasp.

Slowly. Too slowly, the knob twists, metal scratching on wood as it rotates, the movement hardly visible in the dark. The door opens one inch at a time, swinging toward me.

A broad shadow enters, floating quietly toward the bed like a dark cloud.

Not to the fireplace.

Toward Ethan.

I don't see it, but I hear it.

The sound of steel being drawn.

I lunge for the silhouette, slamming the log against what I assume is its head.

The figure groans and stumbles sideways over the bed.

Breath bursting in and out of me, I remember my dagger. I fumble with jittery hands for the garter still looped around my thigh.

The shadow stands and hurls forward, swinging around the bed.

Panic tramples me, sending my heart into a frenzy, and suddenly, I'm once again the helpless girl, afraid and ready to flee to safety.

No.

That's not who I am anymore.

I am strong.

I am a fighter.

The trespasser clamps one hand around my neck, the other—meant to finish me with his blade—jabs toward my midsection. Struggling with the force crushing my windpipe, I swat blindly with my left arm, deflect the blow, and jam my dagger into the arm that chokes me, feeling it cut through leather.

He's wearing armor. A guard?

The shadow hisses, releasing me.

I don't waste a breath. Still coughing, I throw myself at my attacker, and we careen to the floor, landing hard. My palm just misses the padded rug, and my wrist connects with stone. I scream as a warm burst of pain radiates up my forearm, followed by the crack of bone. At first, I think it's my wrist that's broken, but then I feel the trespasser go still under me. Something wet and sticky soaks my fingers.

"Meredith?"

Ethan is upright on the bed, but groggy.

I climb to my knees, dazed and panting, gently pressing my fingers around my sore wrist to assess the damage. Nothing feels broken that I can tell.

"Someone wants us dead," I rasp.

"What?" Ethan's grogginess seems to vanish when he notices the form pinned under me.

He rushes off the mattress.

"Is that—who the hell is *that*?"

"Let's find out," I breathe, crawling to my feet. I pick up the log I used as a weapon and throw it in the fireplace. My fingers trace the mantelpiece for the steel striker and flint. Ethan is on the floor before the first trace of flames come alive, trying to inspect the body in the dark.

"He attacked you?"

"I think he was after you," I say.

We're both staring at the body in stunned silence as firelight begins to color the room. A crown of blood surrounds the man's head. The dead assassin is stocky and bald, with pierced ears and a beard twisted into a pair of short braids beneath his chin. As I expected, he's covered in armor, but it isn't that of a guard.

I take a long breath and close my eyes for a moment, swallowing a twinge of guilt. My third kill . . .

Ethan glances from the dead man to me. Now that the shock seems to be wearing off, he takes in my frazzled state. His eyes trail down to my hand, to the dagger I haven't bothered to drop. "Did he hurt you?"

"I'm fine."

I hear him sigh. "I should have protected you." He looks down at his hands, his head shaking.

I set down the dagger on the mantle and go to him, kneeling at his side. Ethan's rumpled wedding clothes, his skin—they're sweetened with the nutmeg and cloves of the spiced wine. I clasp his cold hand in mine. "We protect each other," I whisper. He lifts his face to look at me, his lips pressed in a thin line. Then he cups my face with his free hand, his thumb stroking my cheek.

"We protect each other," he agrees in a soft voice. His hand lingers on my face as we breathe in silence under the firelight, locked in the moment. I catch the subtle shift of his eyes as they fall to my mouth, then lower, to my sheer underthings.

I pull away, awkwardly folding my arms at my chest. "We should wake the king," I rush to say.

Ethan clears his throat. "Yes." He nods. "We should."

He leans down to pick up the assassin's short sword, and I fetch my dagger from the mantle. I lift my leg onto the nearest chair and slide the dagger back in the garter, hoping I won't have to use it again any time soon. I don't realize Ethan's been watching me until I straighten. The shift falls back in place to my ankles, and his parted lips clamp shut. He looks away, rubbing the back of his neck.

I hurry into my wedding coat, mentally cursing its ridiculous weight.

Out in the hallway, the door sentry lies unconscious, slumped against the wall as though he fell asleep, no blood or sign of a struggle.

I scan the partial darkness while Ethan crouches to check the guard's pulse. The candelabras and torches crackle and pop, their yellow and orange flames dancing against the stonework.

"He's dead," Ethan whispers, tipping his head in respect. But something catches his eye. He frowns and plucks something from the guard's neck. He pivots toward the torchlight, holding the item between two fingers at eye level. A dart.

"Look." I point at the puncture wound. The skin around it is stained violet, too bright and vivid for a bruise.

Ethan stands. "It must be some kind of poison." He gazes down at the guard, a shadow settling over his features.

But something doesn't add up.

If the assassin had poisoned darts, why did he draw his sword?

I fall in beside Ethan and push my legs to match his break-neck pace down the corridor, a challenging feat when you're dragging pounds of fabric. Gusts of wind whistle through the loophole windows, bringing the cold with them and threatening to blow out the flickering torches on the wall. We trod to the king's quarters, sharing anxious glances as we go. Our footfalls on the slate are the only echo to be heard until we run across a pair of guards on patrol coming the opposite direction. Alarm widens their eyes when they see their prince wielding a sword in the middle of the night.

"Come with us," Ethan orders them.

They pick up our tail several feet back so as to not step on the train of my coat.

A gnawing feeling churns my stomach. None of this makes any sense. Why go after Ethan when it's the king who holds all the power?

But as we turn the corner, we careen to a halt.

The sentries posted outside the king's rooms lie crumpled on the floor.

38

Connor

We're on the road the following morning, supplies restocked, bodies rested and bellies full of fish soup. The wind's up. It whistles loudly, blowing the smell of warm earth and sunlight in my face and rustling my hair from my eyes. Rhys's sour mood is the worst I've seen, thanks to his overindulgence of ale and the fact he's been deprived of the collector stash; by the time I woke Rhys, Osberd had already unloaded the wagon and hid the pile of coins, so Rhys had no choice but to cut his losses and keep his swearing to himself.

"Uther should be pleased we left the silver with the villagers," Raven quips from her redcloak horse—stripped of its winged leather breast collars in case we run into more soldiers. She claims she feels much better today, but the strained set of her mouth says she's still hurting all over, riding that horse.

"*Pleased?*" Rhys balks at Raven. "You'll think him pleased that we had a raid's worth in our hands and we brought none o' it back with us?" He scoffs. "Rebels don't live off goodwill alone, ya cow."

"Call me that again," Raven says evenly, "and I'll rip out your tongue."

"I'd like t' see you try."

I squash their feud before Raven follows through with her threat. "We have enough to get us back to Fhalbo. We can sell the horses there; they'll fetch a good price."

"And there'll be other raids," Raven adds with flared nostrils in Rhys's direction. "We'll make do."

"Will we? In case you two forgot, those redcloaks at Locke were onto us," Rhys counters. "They've figured out the raids are connected."

"So we change tactics," I say.

I feel Rhys's glare shift to me. "Oh, that's great. I bet Uther will be frothing at the mouth t' hear your ideas. Perhaps you could sit us all down 'round a nice fire and tell us how t' run things."

Raven puffs an irked sigh. "How can you be such a sorehead day after day? Don't ya find it exhausting?"

"Being around your lot's what's exhausting."

"Best hurry your horse 'n," Raven tells him. "Because we've got a ways t' go."

We ride northeast for half a day, until we reach the city of Arkah, a walled labyrinth of roads barely seven feet wide, flanked by compacted timber post-and-beam tenements. Locke is a fox's hole, compared to this place. The framed housetops sag into the street. Most of the houses have shop signs on their windows, their living quarters built above them. A throng of townsfolk, sheep, and mules choke the unpaved sloping street, and it takes the better part of half an hour to reach the commercial quarter, where the street opens up. Roaming chickens squawk around our feet as we make our retreat to a two-story inn called the Tipsy Rabbit, nestled west of the main square.

Mindful of our scant funds, we ask the innkeeper for one room on the ground floor, but he seems reluctant to take our silver and dallies with the key as he plucks it from the master ring. He stares at me, his pressed lips considering.

"Are ya going t' pussyfoot with that key till the roosters crow?" Rhys asks him.

The innkeeper shrugs off his hesitation with a too-quick smile. "The room includes supper for one," he says in a scruffy voice as he places the key in Rhys's waiting palm, "but you all go on ahead and fill those bellies—gruel's aplenty tonight."

After untacking the horses at the inn's stables, we file inside the commons for supper. It's dim despite the double set of open windows, and the dark-stained rosewood walls and floors make the place seem even smaller. There are no tables, only benches, but the place is as crowded as the town's streets.

"Arkah's pick o' the litter," Rhys mutters, scanning the room full of beards and scars and shrouded eyes; we've walked into a den of scoundrels.

"A place without redcloaks is as good as any," says Raven.

A sweat-soaked maid offers us ladles of gruel in a stale hollowed loaf of bread. We eat on our feet in the least desirable spot, pressed to the wall by the cauldron. The stifling heat of the flames quickens our pace. Rhys discards his spoon and slurps his meal instead, his belch lost to the throng of banter. Finished with the gruel myself, I try a bite of the bread bowl; it's sour and hard but I chew it anyway.

"They treat this place like a tavern," Raven mumbles between hurried gulps.

Rhys snorts. "Ya think they ought t' come for the food?"

Our room for the night is no more desirable than the bland gruel and stale bread. Rats scurry out of sight when we first open the door, their beady eyes gleaming briefly under the dancing flame of the lantern in Raven's grip. The smell of mold and rotted wood greets us. Four moldy walls, no windows. A worn sheepskin blankets a pile of hay crammed against the wall, barely enough for one person, its lost needles littering the unswept floorboards.

Raven doesn't hesitate to hand me the lantern and claim the bed. The stacked hay loses half its height as she sprawls on it, arms spread out at her sides, her body spent from healing its bruises. She's asleep in seconds. I set the lantern down and find a spot on the floor. With my back pressed to the wall, I draw my knees up to rest my hands on them, watching Rhys gather the loose hay needles into something of a pillow before curling on his side on the floor, his back to me.

Muted shouts and cackles from the commons echo through the wall. I listen for a good minute before Rhys's loud snores come. The journey hasn't been long, but it might as well have.

Those hours under the scorching sun sapped my strength. I should be fast asleep, snoring like Rhys, but I'm ill at ease. I keep thinking of the innkeeper's peculiar stare. Lately, it feels as though everyone is shooting second glances my way. Something about my face is drawing attention. But it can't be my scar. There's a half dozen men in the commons with marks on their faces, some worse than mine. Is my northern appearance that obvious? I can't think that it is. Months of working the grove have darkened my skin enough to blend in.

When my eyelids grow heavy, I dip the back of my head on the wall and let sleep drag me away. The last of the candle's wick burns, casting the room in a shade of deep, golden amber.

Like her eyes, I think, before . . .

I wake to the sound of hasty steps. More than one pair, drawing near; they don't sound like the footfalls of patrons making their way to their rooms. The corridor's faint light spills from under the door, allowing me to see in the windowless room. I hear no chatter from the commons. How long have I been asleep? I pull my new dagger out of my mud-ringed boot. Soft on my feet, I bolt to the door, weapon ready.

Not a second later, it's kicked open.

Hearing the scrape of steel, I sidestep away from the swinging door as a flash of a red cape charges in. The corridor is crammed with redcloaks—four soldiers, from what I glimpse through the doorway, probably more.

Behind me, I hear Raven and Rhys scramble awake, just as I

plunge my dagger into leather and ribs. Two more soldiers have squeezed through the doorway, and I count six other swords in the corridor, blocking our only exit.

I snatch the sword from the stunned and bleeding redcloak as he falls in my arms. I may lose this fight, but I'll be damned if I don't give Raven and Rhys a chance. Using the soldier's body as a shield, I ram into the others before they strike, thrusting the sword as I do, its point finding flesh. Those in front careen backward into the corridor, clearing the doorway and crashing down on the other soldiers; I fall down with them.

To my left, the corridor is clear.

"Go! Run!" I shout over my shoulder at Raven.

Something pricks my neck. A faint stab that burns. I bring a hand up and feel a dart between my fingers. Within seconds, a dizziness takes hold, running in my veins like liquid twilight. The redcloaks under me push me off, their legs kicking me to the wall. I try to get up, but my feet drag. There's another soldier a few feet back, likely the one who shot me with the dart, but my eyes can't focus. The redcloaks are on their feet now. They're coming for me. Everything seems to move so slowly. I search with numb hands for a sword—I'm too foggy.

A blinding white light consumes the corridor, and I lose myself in it.

39

Meredith

I can't believe my eyes.

The king and queen are dead.

They lie peacefully in their canopied bed, under thick blankets of wool and fur as if in a deep sleep, like the fallen guards outside their door. Ethan's pleas do nothing to rouse them. Nothing does. Their bed is a grave.

The flames burn low in the fireplace, enveloping the spacious room in a haunting light. Ethan is shaking the queen by her shoulders, desperately calling her name, when Sir Dormon rushes in. The bottle-nosed royal physician Ethan sent for is clad in his undergarments, a startled look on his face as he makes a beeline for the king.

I round the bed and approach the physician. His back is to me, hunched over the king. "There were darts on their necks," I say. Ethan removed them, thinking it might help; I didn't have the heart to tell him otherwise. I peer over the physician's shoulder when he proceeds to inspect the king's neck, dabbing a finger over the violet stain. He brings it to his nose.

"*Nex tacitus.*"

"What?" I ask.

Ethan looks up, eyes red with tears, his mother's body cradled against him, her swanlike neck dangling off his arm. Her fair hair, which she always wore up so elegantly, droops like a brushed curtain of shiny satin over Ethan's bent knees.

The great rulers of Alder are dead, murdered in their sleep.

"The silent death, Your Highness; the violet stain is a telltale sign." The physician sniffs his fingers again, now faintly stained with the mark of the poison. "It's sweet to the nose and harmless to the touch, but in the blood it makes you sleep, never to wake."

Ethan's chest heaves in absolute despair. "Is there an antidote?" His voice is a choked whisper; he's barely holding it together.

The physician is noticeably contrite as he says, "None that we possess knowledge of, Your Highness. But even if there was one . . . it is already too late, sire."

Ethan looks down at the queen's lifeless form, his expression twisting in anguish and despair as a broken sob escapes him. He squeezes his eyes shut and touches his forehead to hers, rocking her in his arms. I look away, blinking aside the tiny pins that prick my eyes.

"I will return with my assistant to prepare the bodies," the physician whispers to me.

"Of course," I say softly before he ducks through the doorway.

With the guards waiting outside, only I remain in the room with Ethan. Suddenly, I feel like I'm intruding, witnessing a moment I should not0 be privy to. He clings to his mother, shoulders shaking with sobs. Watching the tears stream down his face, I have to hold back my own, feeling a thickness in my throat. I want to tell him how sorry I am, but words seem insignificant.

I can't decide if Ethan wants me to stay or go. Floundering, I hug my own shoulders. I don't know what else to do.

Eventually the sobs lessen, and his tears slow to glistening streaks on his cheeks. He gently rests the queen's head atop her pillow. I approach him then, eager to mitigate his pain somehow. Finally aware of my presence, Ethan lifts his gaze to mine. The pain in his eyes—it's so wretched, I can hardly look at him.

"They're gone," he whispers, and the crack in his voice clenches my heart. I throw my arms around him, and he pulls me close and buries his face in my shoulder. He holds me so tightly it almost hurts, but I don't mind. I let him hold on as he gives in to his despair once more. My hands travel across his back in slow, consoling strokes. All the while, disbelief continues to echo in my head.

There is no doubt in my mind that Theros is behind this. But that can only mean there are others working for him, and if that's true, then Councilor Milus is our only lead. And he's to be executed at dawn.

"Ethan," I say with a start. He draws back. Despite his torment, he hears the urgency in my voice. A wrinkle of concern creases his temple.

But then, someone's at the door, arguing loudly with the

guard.

"Let me pass!" demands the surly voice of Councilor Rowan.

Ethan collects himself as best he can. He stands and crosses the bedroom in three strides and disappears into the parlor. I follow.

The councilor is still yelling at the guard when Ethan opens the door.

"I'm the grand councilor, you buffoon—Your Highness! There you are. We must call a council meeting at once," he spouts.

"The meeting can wait," Ethan says icily.

"Forgive me, sire, but it cannot. It's a matter of absolute urgency."

Ethan's puffy, red-rimmed eyes narrow, scrutinizing the councilor for several seconds. "It better be, Rowan," he rasps. "Gather the councilors."

"I already have, Your Highness. We shall be waiting for you."

Ethan closes the door and turns, pressing his back against it, eyes on the ceiling. Then he rubs at his temple as if warding off a headache. "Would you like to change?" he asks.

"You want me to attend the meeting?" I'm not sure why, but I hadn't expected him to include me.

He gives me a look through his veil of misery. "Of course I do."

"Well, I best put on a dress," I breathe. Then, remembering, "And you best order Captain Offa to stop the execution before that sun rises."

Though the long night has gone, deep in my bones, I know this nightmare is far from over.

Bells have been tolling for the last hour down in the city. They chimed for a wedding only yesterday, enlivening with the joy of celebration. Now they wake people from their sleep, laden with loss and mourning.

No longer in my underthings, I make haste alongside Ethan to the council chamber in a beige-colored linen dress over a thickly-lined gray shift; Ethan's still in his wrinkled wedding regalia.

"Did you see Councilor Milus?" I ask. There had been no change in his demeanor when he returned from the jail to fetch me; he told me the execution was postponed indefinitely but nothing else.

Darkness lines his face. "I didn't think it wise."

He's probably right. Questioning the councilor while in such a troubled state of mind wouldn't help.

We walk in to a heated conversation among the councilors at the council chamber. Dawn has not yet climbed completely through the honeycombed windows. The shadows shroud Milus's empty chair like a bad omen, and though candelabras burn at each corner, they give off no warmth. Ethan and I take a seat, he at the end—the king's chair—and I to his left.

I notice goblets of wine on the table; it's never too early to drink at times like these. One filled to the rim is awaiting me at my seat, as well as Ethan's. After all the drinks he inhaled last night, I expect him to be repulsed by the wine, but not a second from sitting, he picks up his goblet and takes a sip. I consider following suit, my eyes on the goblet, but the idea sours my stomach. If Ethan drinks as he did last night, all the more reason for me to remain sober; one of us has to keep a clear head.

Rowan stands at the opposite end of the table, ink-stained fingertips propped on the edge. "Your Highnesses. Councilmen," he says in somber greeting, his attention shifting between the many faces on the table. "I've called this meeting in light of a troubling report I received hours ago . . . There is no easy way to broach this." He licks his lips and casts his eyes into the shadows, toiling with his news before he finally directs himself at Ethan and declares, "Our battalions have been infected with plague."

Disbelieving gasps ring across the table.

I sit there, fixed on Councilor Rowan as if in a trance, frozen; I feel like I'm falling, and I can't look away.

This can't be happening.

Everything that could go wrong *has* gone wrong.

Out the corner of my eye, I see Ethan close his eyes for a second to absorb the blow. "How many battalions?" he asks, sounding exhausted and faraway.

Rowan's mouth twists in a grimace. "Nine that we know of, Your Highness."

"We are ruined," one councilman mutters, throwing his hands up in the air.

Then, all at once, the panic spreads around the table, and they all turn to Ethan—their new sovereign—for guidance, bombarding him with questions and hasty proposals that get lost in their own cacophony.

And I'm still staring at Rowan. At his ink-stained fingers.

That's not ink, a voice in my head tells me.

Rowan slams a flat palm against the wood, quelling the frenzy of voices. "Gentlemen, calm yourselves! This is perilous news indeed, but we cannot lose our heads." He points an outstretched arm at Ethan. "Need I remind you what His Highness has been through in the past few hours? He and his bride survived an assassination attempt, and he lost his parents—all in one night. Our full support and guidance is the least he deserves, so please, I beg of you, act reasonably."

"Guidance?" one councilor scoffs. "More than half our army is lost! What guidance could we impart other than surrender to the enemy?"

The men bicker, their tempers and fears set free. The racket breaks my spell, but I'm left with a nagging feeling I can't shake. I blink as though that will somehow give me clarity. Ethan says nothing. Stares at nothing. His hand, still gripping the stem of his goblet, rises absently to bring it to his lips—

I slap it away before he takes another sip.

The heavy goblet bounces on the table, splashing wine all over him and rolling to the floor with a loud clang.

Startled out of his stupor, Ethan's dulled chestnut eyes widen at me.

"Don't drink the wine!" I shout to the rest of the councilors, darting keen glances at their goblets. Some of which, I notice in alarm, are empty.

The council members gape as though I've gone mad.

But I'm not wrong. Am I?

Inadvertently, it occurs to me to look through the shadows of the chamber for the servant who served the wine. I find him hovering a respectable distance away from the table, head bent low. I think he feels my stare, because he suddenly looks up, our eyes meeting through the flock of black bangs that hang over his temple. He's young. And afraid. He looks at me as though I'm one second away from asking for his head.

"Meredith?" Ethan's hand touches mine, bringing my startled gaze back to him. He leans in to whisper, "What are you saying? You think it poisoned?"

I stare at him, at his frown and his frazzled eyes, at the deep stain of wine on his wrinkled doublet. Ethan waits for me to speak, and I second-guess myself. But my doubt isn't enough to ease that nagging feeling in my gut; it won't let me betray my own instincts.

I jerk my head to Rowan.

"How did you know?" I ask. My anger does little to keep the shakiness from my voice. "How did you know someone attacked us?"

"The guard at the king's door told me everything," Rowan answers calmly, no sign of distress in his shrewd gaze, nothing to suggest he feels threatened.

I feel my skin flush. Have I just accused an innocent man?

But Ethan is sliding his hand away from mine on the table, slowly rising to his feet like a coiled lion. "No. He didn't," he says. "I recall you yelling at him the entire time to let you in."

Unflappable, Rowan doesn't budge. "That was after the fact, Your Highness. I can assure you that he did," he confidently replies.

The guard is one of the only two people besides Ethan and me that knew of the attack. Rowan's either innocent, or he's a very good liar, and I'm not good enough at reading people to tell the difference.

Ethan looks to me, his lips pressed flat with suspicion, and then at the toppled goblet of wine on the floor. He scrutinizes the rest of the goblets. If the wine is indeed poisoned, he should have felt something by now. I dip my head to my goblet and sniff. It smells of sour oak. No sweetness.

Perhaps . . . perhaps it really isn't poisoned.

I stalk to the other end of the table to Rowan, feeling all eyes on me as I do. I reach for one of his hands, trying to inspect it up close, but the councilor wrenches his arm away, tucking it behind him.

"What is this?" he scoffs, as though offended by my touch.

He can't hide it this time. I see it in the rapid blinks of his eyes.

"It was *you*," I hiss as he sneers down at me. "It was him," I say, louder this time so they can all hear me. So Ethan can hear me. But when I turn, the victorious smile on my lips disappears.

Ethan is gripping the table, doubled over like he's about to retch.

He starts to dry-heave, and he clutches at his stomach, groaning in pain.

I wasn't wrong after all.

40

Connor

Warm water splashes on my face. It stirs my senses, wrenching me from the peaceful dark. I stink of dried blood, sweat, and grime. I'm thirsty. So thirsty.

A voice tells me to drink, but I want to sleep.

The voice asks again.

I can't open my mouth. I can't move. The link between my body and my mind is broken. A hand grips my chin. It parts my lips without resistance. I fight to open my eyes. They're as heavy as an iron gate.

"Drink, you oaf!"

Water floods my mouth, crashing into my throat. I'm coughing. Bright light floods my slitted vision. It dims and sharpens into a cloudless blue sky. Reddish-blond hair and angry eyes greet me.

He shoves the waterskin in my face. "You're as stubborn as a mule. Drink, or I'll slit your throat." My own body fights me, refuses to listen. It takes everything in me to hold the leather bag. I bring it to my lips with unsteady hands and take a slow sip. It tastes of leather and goes like a lifeline down my throat. "I've wasted all my stash on you ... should have ended you in Far Water," he mutters under his breath while I take a second sip.

"But you're no use to me dead." He jerks the waterskin from my feeble grip. "That's enough—don't want you pissing your trousers in your sleep."

"Where are you taking me?" My voice is hoarse with disuse.

A wry smile. Then a slap on my neck, the movement too fast, gone before I can blink. The last thing I remember before the darkness beckons is the sound of his stilted voice: "Now that's more like it."

I wake tied to a chair, arms wrapped around it with rope that digs into my skin. I'm weak. Lightheaded. Thirsty. Even thought is a struggle. How long have I been here? I squint up at the beam of sunlight glaring down on me from a manufactured hole in the thatch, its heat scorching my skin.

I'm in a room of undulating sand-colored cob walls and a pounded earth floor. In front of me is an empty table, its thick wood marred with scratches and holes. Several paces ahead is a door enforced with rusted iron, likely locked. My memory is foggy, but bit by bit, the disorientation ebbs and I begin to recover my thoughts. Hazy flashes of the inn's corridor . . . an ambush. How did they find us? We'd stripped the horses of redcloak garments. I search my scrambled thoughts, retracing our steps back to the fishing village. The villagers are the only ones who could have given us up, but it's unlikely, not when they'd kept all that coin. They'd hang for such a theft.

I can't remember if Raven and Rhys made it out. I can't remember if they even tried. It all happened so fast.

As I sit and sweat, my thoughts keep returning to the night at the inn. The innkeeper directed the redcloaks to our room, no doubt. But was he the one who summoned them? Why would he? I'd known something wasn't right by the odd look on his face. But if the sight of me tipped him off, it means someone was searching for me. Hunting me. Someone who knows what I look like, and that could only be—

Metal scrapes against wood, and the door opens.

Julius's spindly shadow saunters in, a rolled piece of paper in his grip and the look of victory spread across his face.

The redcloaks keeping watch outside lock the door behind him. "Awake at last." He closes the distance in two strides, plunging a fist in my gut, taking the wind out of me. I look up to the sneer of his hooked nose. "That's for making me look like a fool. *Twice*."

My breath comes ragged. "You did that all on your own."

"Ah, but the third time's the charm," he croons through clenched teeth. "You won't win now."

"Untie me and say that to me again," I challenge; I'm too weak to be any good, but I'd still love to try.

Julius sinks another fist in my stomach.

"I can't wait to see what the commander has planned for you," he snarls over my coughs. "He'll make you wish I killed you the first time we met."

The Soul Reaper, Uther's voice echoes.

So that's where I am—the commander's fort.

Julius raises the paper in his hand to his face and uncoils it. He inspects it for a moment, his bony head cocked.

"The weasel did a fine job, wouldn't you agree?" he asks, turning it over so that I can see. It's a penciled portrait . . .

Of me.

Above my drawn face, the word *WANTED* is boldly penned. A generous offer of fifty silvers inks the space below, more than enough to feed a starving family for months.

That's why the innkeeper recognized me. And he was looking to cash in. It all makes sense now. The thieves we ran into at Locke were likely after the bounty on my head as well. If that's true, I owe Rhys an apology.

Gotta make it out of here first.

"This is his best one," Julius remarks, turning the paper over again to inspect it some more. "First one he drew for me, too. By the time he was finished with a few hundred of them, the quality just wasn't there. Perhaps it was the lack of food and drink that sapped his talent." He rolls up the portrait, carefully slipping it inside his breast pocket. Then he leans his hands on his knees to level his gaze with mine. "I promised him we'd let him live if his portraits led to your capture. I lied, of course, but the commander wants him around a while longer . . . We may yet have other portraits to commission in Fhalbo." Menace rims his narrowed eyes. "Say, where's that little thieving rat you saved?"

"Safe."

Julius smirks. "Won't be long before we find him."

"You won't."

"Oh yes, we *will.* And you're going to lead us straight to him."

"Your commander will bleed me to death before he pries a word out of me."

He snorts, eyes lit with mischief, but his amusement is cut short by the sound of the door.

The man from Flynn's hanging—Commander Vishal—towers over the doorway, wearing a gaze that could slice a man in half. Cold and hard and sharp as a blade. A mallet hangs loose between the fingers of his right hand, a pair of pincers clutched in his left, the sleeves of his brown tunic rolled at the elbows, ready to get his hands dirty.

Maker's hell, I silently hiss, feeling my scalp prickle.

Julius straightens and dips his head in a respectful nod. "My lord."

But one pointed look from Vishal has Julius scampering out like a roach through the open door. The commander doesn't spare him another glance as he approaches and drops the mallet and pincers on the table like a smith would his hammer and tongs. Hands clasped at his back, his dead eyes rove over me, pausing on the coin around my neck. "Connor, is it?" I can tell I'm something to be studied, something he doesn't understand. Then his eyes flash with recognition, flattening his deeply lined brow. "You were there," he muses, his expression shifting with understanding. "At the square. The day we hanged your friend."

"He wasn't my friend."

Vishal's thin mouth twitches, suggesting he doesn't believe my truth. "Is there no kinship between accomplices these days?"

The tingle in my skin tells me something is very wrong here. What does he know?

He pushes the corners of the table forward until it meets the armrests that bind me, perfectly level. Designed to be so, I realize, as the commander spreads my fingers flat on the table; the subtlety of his touch is unnerving.

"What is a northerner doing in Sunder of all places?" The commander produces a yellowed cloth from inside his tabard and reaches for the pincers with his free hand. I stare at the roughened grips as he absently wipes the tool; anticipating the pain is almost as distressing as the pain itself. Without an answer, he goes on, "People typically migrate out of Sunder, not into it. Even before the emperor's Takeover—that's what you people call it, isn't it? Sunder was never an inviting place. The land holds no beauty, and the kingdom never recovered from the drought. Most citizens are beggars, or serfs, or impoverished farmers," he elaborates, waving the pincers in the air. "I'll accept that King Seram was a man of the people, but he wasn't keen on trade and fiscal affairs. A true leader would have restored this place to its former glory."

Watching him prepare his tools, I can no longer tell how much of the sweat on my body is from the heat.

"But where King Seram failed, Theros succeeded," he casually informs me, inspecting the pincers at eye level. "With eight eastern kingdoms and the Western Continent under his command, he duly proclaimed himself emperor of the new Talosian Empire."

Eight kingdoms. Eight undisputed coups. *Hell.*

"What compelled you to come here?" the commander asks, snapping me back to his callous eyes, wider now, glinting with mild curiosity.

"Why does that matter?"

"I don't suppose it does." Vishal's cold eyes search me. "Most men faced with torture do everything in their power to keep me interested, but you"—he blinks down at me, an appraising smirk bringing life to his unfeeling visage—"you'd rather get it over with, wouldn't you?"

I'd rather kill you. "All this to find a child?"

It takes the commander a moment to catch on. "The young thief? No. That's Julius's concern. I have bigger fish to catch."

To catch . . .

He's still looking. For whom?

"You will answer my questions, or I will rip out your nails," he explains objectively, no different than he might command his soldiers. Losing my nails doesn't sound as hellish as losing my soul, but I find no comfort in either. My hand is splayed on the table, clammy with cold sweat. "We'll start with your left. If losing fingernails isn't enough to persuade you, we'll give the mallet a try." The commander opens and closes the pincers twice, the rusted metal clinking a warning in my ears. "Tell me: Where is the Brotherhood hideout?"

41

Meredith

I draw my dagger and shove Rowan to the wall. The blade's edge pins him there. "Guards!" I screech, so loud my throat burns. A second later, three guards burst into the room, weapons drawn.

"Bring the physician!" I call over my shoulder to them.

The voice in my head tells me it's pointless. The physician said it himself. There is no antidote. But I can't help myself. I think I understand Ethan's desperation now, the desire for a miracle to save his dead parents, because even when reality stares you in the face, you still have to try.

Then a racket of scratching chairs erupts as the councilmen break free of their dazed states. Most scramble about the room, yelling uselessly at each other. Some flock to Ethan, who groans through labored breaths. A few remain where they stand, staring flabbergasted at the dagger pressed to Rowan's neck.

"If he dies," I warn Rowan, voice shaking with pure, white anger, "I *will* kill you."

"I didn't serve the wine," Rowan grumbles, eyeing the blade at his throat like it's a snake ready to bite.

I press the dagger harder, drawing a drop of blood. My face is inches from his. "We both know you poisoned it," I hiss in his ear, and as his nostrils flare with hatred, I throw him into the custody of one of the guards.

Justice can wait.

The councilmen around Ethan make way for me as I rush to his side. His blanched skin shines with sweat; he's in pain. I throw a guarded glance at the councilors. No one else seems affected by the poison. Ethan shudders under my touch, his eyes glazed and unreadable. He can't even look at me when I call his name.

Maker, not him. Please, not him.

Rowan protests within the guard's grip, clamoring for the attention of his fellow councilors. "I have committed no crime," he blusters, but I have no mind to hear him.

Ethan staggers on his feet, clutching the table's edge for support. I lower him gently back on the chair as my mind races for a solution. It's too late to make him empty his stomach, but the spilled wine on the floor reminds me he didn't drink it all. How much is too much? I know nothing of the poison aside from what the physician mentioned earlier. Was he supposed to down the whole goblet? Or will a single sip prove deadly?

"Stay with me," I whisper. I take his hand. It's cold and clammy, and it twitches in my grasp. I'm biting back panic. I kneel beside him, touching my head to his, and plead into his ear. "Please, Ethan. I can't do this without you." As I speak the unbidden words out loud, I become aware that I mean it, awakening a part of me I thought long gone. There is no denying the truth now: losing Ethan would shatter my patched-up heart to pieces.

Ethan doesn't seem to hear me, and it dawns on me then that his hand no longer trembles. It's gone dreadfully still. I watch in horror as his eyes roll back into his head.

"Ethan?" His name is a frightened prayer in my tongue. My pulse thunders so that it makes me dizzy, and though I am screaming inside, I find the will to focus, to steady my breath.

The longest moments of my life pass before the slow rise and fall of his chest tells me he's alive. My held breath comes out in a whoosh. I grip Ethan's face, willing him to wake up. *Maker, he's too pale.*

Finally, Sir Dormon arrives, dressed this time. But he doesn't come alone. A worry-stricken Lief is with him; relief washes over me at the sight of them.

"The silent death," I rush to tell the physician, unable to recall the poison's true name. I point to the mess on the table. "In the wine—he drank some of it." Even as I speak, I'm dreading that same look of sympathy Sir Dormon gave Ethan hours ago. I can almost hear the words rolling off his tongue, crushing what little hope I have.

The physician touches a hand to Ethan's temple. "He drank it, you say?"

I blink, leaning toward the physician. "Yes," I breathe, nodding hastily.

The physician closes his eyes and sighs in what I'm hoping is relief.

"His Highness will be very sick, to be sure, but he'll live," he says. Though I think I must have heard wrong, my legs still buckle under me, suddenly weak. "Nex tacitus is deadly in the blood," Sir Dormon goes on. "But it reacts differently in the stomach. It is believed the acids counteract with the poison, limiting its effects on the body."

I snap a look at Rowan, whose eyes are protruding from his skull. He didn't know. He wouldn't have gone through the trouble of poisoning the wine if he did.

"I'll make him a tonic to ease his stomach, Your Highness," the physician adds with a wrinkled, reassuring smile.

I take the physician's hand and kiss it. "Thank you," I say from the depths of my heart. Then, I lower my voice and speak for his ears only. "If I may, I would ask that you remain a while longer." At the physician's consent, I straighten and walk to the center of the chamber to address the guards awaiting command. "The prince needs rest; take him to his rooms." Then I whisper to Lief, "Watch over him."

The guards nod. Two of them lift an unconscious Ethan out of the chair. His head lolls as they prop his arms around their shoulders. When the door shuts behind them, the councilmen remain anxiously silent, waiting for me to speak.

Rowan no longer struggles against the guard who holds him. He watches me warily, his lips curled with hatred.

"Why?" I demand.

"I have done no wrong. The councilmen can attest that I did

not serve the wine." Rowan juts his chin at the cupbearer, who hasn't dared leave the room. "*He* did."

My eyes return to the servant. This time he doesn't look up, knowing every pair of eyes in the room is homed in on him. He's shaking. From where I stand, I consider the possibility that he may have aided Rowan, committed the crime for him under coercion or bribery. I come before the young servant and take his trembling hands in mine. They're wet with nerves. He shies from my touch at first, confused as to what I'm doing, but he doesn't pull away. At close inspection, the only thing on his fingers is the grime under his nails; he didn't handle the poison.

My mind churns.

I look back at the decanter. It stands nearly empty in the middle of the table.

It wasn't the wine that was poisoned, I realize. It was the goblets.

"Sir Dormon, would you examine Councilor Rowan's fingers?" I ask.

Limited by the guard's strong arms, Rowan can't jerk away this time, though he still puts up a fight, doing what he can to keep his hands balled into fists. When he doesn't give in to Sir Dormon's polite request, the physician applies pressure to the side of Rowan's leg just above his knee cap, forcing his hands open.

It only takes a quick glance. "Nex tacitus," the physician asserts.

"Nonsense!" Rowan decries. "He's working for her!" He frantically searches the room for support. Met with skeptical silence, Rowan asks, "Must I remind you she is the *devil's niece*? Can't you see? She's planned this all herself—she's trying to frame me!"

To my shock, a few of the councilors shoot evaluating glances my way.

"Careful, Rowan," a stumpy council member with bushy, grayed brows warns. "Those are treasonous words you speak."

"She's the treasonous one!" Rowan barks, spittle coming out of his fevered mouth. The man is cunning, but his anger seems to be getting the best of him.

Bang!

One of the double doors slams open, a hand splayed against its metal-enforced wood. Ethan stands in the doorway, shoulders bent and breathless. Lief and the other guards crowd the space behind him, ready to catch him should he lose his footing. Though his skin's still pale and shiny with sweat, Ethan's expression is wrathful; I've never seen him like this. His steps falter as he scrambles toward Rowan, weakened by the poison. I dread his balance might fail him at any moment. When he finally gets close enough, he musters the strength to yank the scruff of the councilor's tunic. "*You duplicitous bastard.*" Ethan's voice trembles with rage. "It was you all along, wasn't it? You're the mole."

Rowan's eyes grow wide as saucers. "Sire, this is a terrible misunderstanding!" His eyes point at me once again. "She's the trai—"

Ethan pulls hard on the scruff.

"*She* is *my wife*! Accuse her again, and I will cut off your tongue." He lets go of Rowan's tunic, straightening it for him with menacing fingers. Then, between labored breaths, Ethan voices his demands: "You will answer all my questions . . . tell me everything I need to know . . . and I will grant you a quick death. Lie to me once . . . and I will make you wish you were never born."

Dawn has come and gone. The sun's rays now shine brightly through the windows, bringing much-needed warmth to the room. The council chamber has emptied of councilmen, filled instead with a plethora of guards. Rowan sits on the very chair from which he watched Ethan sip his poisoned goblet. The councilor has finally abandoned his stubborn charade, glaring at the table while he awaits the interrogation.

Ethan's mouth is hard-set as Lief and I help him into a chair. Even through his doublet, I can feel his fevered skin. The physician attempted to order Ethan to bed before departing, saying he shouldn't be anywhere else. But Ethan was as pliable as iron ore, and try as he might, the physician had no power over him. "Sir Dormon is right. You need rest," I whisper to him over his shoulder.

I'm met with a look of grim determination. The hoarseness in his voice sounds painful. "I'll have no peace until I'm through with him," he says. There will be no convincing him otherwise, so I abstain from trying again. Beside his chair, I rest my hand on his tight shoulder, hoping he sees the gesture for what it is. *I'm here.*

Ethan's first question is one I'm not expecting.

"Is Milus your accomplice?"

I should have known he would want confirmation; it still eats at him to think Milus a traitor.

Confusion flashes in Rowan's face. "Councilor Milus?" Deep wrinkles split his temples, as though he can't believe his ears. Then he seems to remember something. "Ah, the spies, is it? No, no. Milus is unaware of their allegiance to me," he says by way of explanation, though it only adds to my confusion, and by the look on Ethan's ashen face, he's struggling to make sense of it as well.

"Answer the question, Rowan. Is Milus your accomplice?"

"Your Highness, Milus is a most loyal man. He would never betray you," Rowan answers emphatically. I scrutinize the councilor. Is this merely a gesture of camaraderie, an attempt to save Milus in the hopes he will succeed where Rowan failed? Then, understanding fills Rowan's face. "He didn't disappear, did he?" He looks straight at Ethan. "What have you done with him, sire?"

Ethan ignores the question. "Why was his signature on the letter?" he asks, and confusion returns to Rowan's aged features.

"What letter?"

Ethan's fist slams on the table—surprisingly hard for his current state—making the remaining goblets on the table closest to him jump. "Do not trifle with me, Rowan!"

"Your Highness, please, I am completely ignorant of this letter you speak of." Rowan licks his lip, debating. "Perhaps, if you would enlighten me—"

"An intelligence letter with the ins and outs of our army." Ethan speaks in a rush of impatience. "Intercepted in Stonefall."

Rowan's eyes narrow. "Intercepted by whom, sire?"

"The chancellor of Stonefall Palace. He delivered the letter to us himself."

For the first time, I regret that King Perceval sent Ulric to the city. His presence would have proved useful for the interrogation.

Rowan stares, blinking as though he doesn't understand. "Milus's signature is on this letter?" At Ethan's nod, Rowan shakes his head. "That can't be, sire. It must be some sort of forgery." As he says it, the councilor lifts his chin to me, but he's smart enough not to voice his false accusations again.

"We compared the signatures. They were a match." From Ethan's clipped tone, I can tell his impatience is growing.

"Was my name on that letter?" Rowan asks, which, up until now, had not crossed my mind. Ethan's silence suggests he hadn't, either. Rowan goes on, "I have no way to prove this to you, sire, but believe me when I say I'm not afflicted by loyalty to Milus. I'm telling you the truth. He is innocent. If that letter was authentic, it would have my signature on it, not his."

A chill shoots through me. If what he says is true . . .

"Are you suggesting Milus was framed?" Ethan asks, hopeful.

"That appears to be the case, Your Highness."

"To what end? And why Milus? Why him?"

The councilor gnaws on his cheek, deliberating an answer. "That I don't know, sire. Did the man who gave you the letter say how he came upon it?"

"Vaguely."

Rowan's brows rise. "Interesting," he ponders. "Did he say or give you anything else besides this letter, sire?"

I give Ethan's shoulders a light squeeze. Though I don't expect the guards to leak this information, I can't help worrying that it might get out, and that harm might come to Charles because of it. Ethan debates for a moment before answering. "He spoke of a cure for the blue fever."

Rowan's hands go limp on the table, his posture sagging like he's figured something out. He starts to laugh then, and at first, I think he's laughing at our naïveté for believing in a cure, but there is an edge in his tone. It brings me back to the day father had me whipped, when I was in pain both from the lacerations on my skin and the gashes in my heart . . . and I couldn't stop laughing.

"You find this amusing, Rowan?" Ethan asks.

Abruptly, the councilor sobers up with a grim expression. He swallows, his Adam's apple bobbing ominously.

"Sire, I believe we've all been played."

42

Connor

White-hot, throbbing pain; nausea heaving in my stomach; the smell of blood . . . It's hard not to lose sight of yourself during torture, to forget why you're enduring it. The commander has pried hours of excruciating agony out of me, but not answers, and after five mangled fingernails and some broken bones, he finally relents.

"Impressive," Vishal remarks, but I'm still slipping in and out of consciousness.

I'm too far gone to make out his retreat or hear the clang of the door. A light touch tends to the raw damage wreaked by the mallet and pincers. In my muddled state, I wonder if those glimpses of hands belong to Raven, thinking she's here to patch me up yet again. But I know that can't be. My throat and lungs ache, sore from the screams; the entire fort must have heard them. It had been my only recourse. I grasped for lies to give Vishal—anything but the truth—but all I could do was scream and endure the pain.

Stooped on the chair, on the verge of nothingness, I piece together Vishal's words, feeling the broken bones in my hand snap into place as I do. The commander spoke of Asher and Flynn, but not once did he ask about Raven, and I was glad of it; I'd hate to see her in this chair, yielding to Vishal's torture.

How long can I go on without giving him what he wants? He's too smart to bleed me to death. Worse, he's having his men patch me up so he can do it again.

I open my eyes, seeking a glimpse of my healer, but I'm not in the fort anymore.

Cold seeps down to my bones, and the distinctive sharp scent of pine permeates the air.

Steely, narrowed eyes watch me.

A sprawling lake hedged in evergreen ripples with the gentle breeze. At its bank, a water mill churns. Tree-covered mountains sweep the sky, nestled under a majestic snow-capped summit.

Home. This is home.

I'd hug those mountains if I could.

The man steps away from his saddled horse to kneel before me, his plate armor clanking with the motions. A trimmed black beard frames his strong jaw. Blue and gold paint the tabard that spills from under his breastplate, covering his bent legs.

"Won't you bid me farewell?"

My gaze trails to the patchy grass under my mud-covered boots. I sense that it will be a long time before I see the man again, and a swallow plunges down my throat.

"Son, look at me." The command is firm, but also affectionate. The smiling lines around his eyes deepen when I meet his gaze. "I need you to look after your mother while I'm gone."

"Yes, sir," I hear myself say in a mousy voice, head bobbing fiercely.

The man claps my shoulder and smiles down at me with pride in his eyes. "That's my boy."

I watch him mount his horse and gallop down the sloping road that cuts through the grass, past the other manors and their farms. He becomes an indiscernible speck moving in the breathtaking landscape and disappears into the mass of green hills below the looming castle that cuts the sky like a mountain.

I may have looked on forever, breathing pine and feeling the early morning breeze on my skin, but without warning, a dull ache in my left hand spikes into hundreds of sharp needles, and the sun bursts.

It dissolves the landscape in the blink of an eye, forcing me back to the fort's jail.

The pain and the heat and sweat come back all at once.

A crouched boy not older than thirteen inspects my hand. The linen robe he wears is yellowed and ratty, but mostly clean. He feels me move and looks up from his handiwork. "I had to snap your finger back in place," he says in a voice that bears no Sunderian inflection. My eyes fall on my left hand, to the blood that soaks through the bandages on the tips of my fingers where my nails used to be. Three fingers are swollen to twice their size. Bad as it is, I'm glad Vishal didn't go for my dominant hand. On the table, a clumped cloth floats inside a clay pot, sullied from the wiped blood. Beside it is a wooden mortar with a transparent gelatinous paste.

"One more and we're done," says the boy, and before I can brace for it, his small hands seize my ring finger and pop it back to alignment. The motion is sharp and quick, no more than a second, but the pain flares and explodes ten times that before subsiding. I'm still holding back a growl behind my gritted my teeth when the boy tells me, "You should have given the commander what he wanted, saved you all this trouble."

I slump back in the chair, head lopped forward. "Are you his slave?" I ask gruffly, reminded of the missing children.

"No." He lifts a cup of water from the table to my lips. I gulp it down, and the boy exchanges the empty cup for the mortar and its minty, green-tinged goop. He massages the gel-like salve on my inflamed hand, mindful of my pain. "I'm the fort's healer."

"You look a little young for a healer."

"I was only an apprentice when I came here with my master, but he taught me well."

I strain to raise my head and stare at him. "You serve Vishal willingly?" The boy nods, ignoring my surprise. There are no bruises on his supple skin, no darkness under his eyes. No signs of abuse. He must be Talosian.

"You disapprove," he observes as he works to remove the soaked bandages, unrolling them one at a time, revealing a gruesome mass of raw flesh.

"You seem decent. Decent people don't work for despots willingly."

"Vishal may seem ruthless to you, but I see a man who isn't afraid to do what he must."

"Including taking children hostage?"

His hands pause on the mortar. He looks up. "Yes."

"What does he want with children?"

Dipping his fingers, he daubs more of the gelatinous salve on my hand. Not so gently this time.

"It isn't my business to know."

Or to care . . .

The sharp burning in my hand eases slowly. Too slowly. "Would you make it your business if these were children of Talos?" I ask through my clenched jaw.

A crease knits his youthful features. "I don't know. I don't remember much of Talos," he says offhandedly. "I've lived in this fort for most of my life . . . my name's Felix, by the way." From the table, he unfolds strips of cotton to redress my wounds. "But you're right—I don't much care for Sunderians. I did once. I won't make that mistake again." He finishes tending to my hand. It throbs under the bandages, burning as if I've held my fingers in flames. "Your wounds are clean. They won't fester so long as you leave the bandages on. I'll leave you the table to rest that hand flat."

"What happens next?" I ask as Felix gathers his materials.

"You heal," he answers simply.

"I still have another hand to mangle," I probe, searching Felix's earnest face.

To my disbelief, the boy says, “The commander won’t torture you again.”

He turns on his heel, careful not to drop anything.

“I haven’t given him what he wants.”

He turns, eyes lidded with sympathy. “You will.”

43

Meredith

The councilor perks up in his chair and glints back at Ethan with newfound interest. "It seems to me Elijah has chosen Milus as his scapegoat; someone else needed to take the blame so I'd be free from suspicion."

A deep frown furrows Ethan's brow. "Why Milus?"

"I should think it's quite obvious, sire," Rowan replies in a soft voice.

"To get to me?" Ethan gleans in disgust. "And how would they know that, Rowan? Did the enemy ask, or did you share that information out of pure generosity?"

The councilor's eyes sink to the floor. "No detail was spared, sire," he admits.

Ethan glares at the councilor, his tired eyes glinting with anger as he grips the armrests of his chair as if to hold himself back. Then his glare narrows. "You knew Milus would be framed," he says darkly.

"No, sire."

Ethan's glare searches the councilor's face. "Then what makes you so sure?"

Rowan lets out a defeated breath through his nose. "The mention of the cure, sire. Believing there is one is the only logical reason you'd mobilize your army. They knew that."

"Are you saying there isn't a cure?" I cut in. I could believe his lies if news of the cure had come from Chancellor Ulric himself, but the handwriting on the missive was undoubtedly Charles's.

Rowan clenches his jaw as he lifts his head to regard me. It takes him a moment to answer calmly. "There is a cure . . . of sorts." He elaborates with his hands in the air. "An immunity, if you will."

Ethan shifts in his chair. "Theros demanded we yield to him. Why would he want us to defy him?"

"Not Theros, sire," Rowan says, his lips a sad line. "Elijah."

"Elijah?" Ethan spits the name back at Rowan.

"King Theros may be a lot of things, Your Highness, but a fool isn't one of them; only Elijah would dare risk losing their leverage over Alder."

"But why?" I ask. "What's Elijah after?"

I am surprised at the sadness that flashes in the councilor's eyes.

"That's what I'm trying to sort out. Elijah's motivations elude me. What's clear is that he meant for you to learn of the cure so you would take action, and in so doing, force my hand to fulfill my end of the bargain."

"Your end of the bargain with Theros," Ethan says.

Not a question, a statement.

The councilor darkens with shame. I have to wonder if it's all an act. After all he's done, it's hard to believe he has a conscience. But if he's so heartless, why would he care if Milus takes the fall with him?

Ethan leans his face in his hand, rubbing his eyes with the heel of it. Then he drags his hand through his hair. It comes down to the nape of his neck and reaches for my hand on his shoulder, his fingers curling around mine. "How long have you been working for Theros?"

"Since you were a boy, Your Highness."

"How could you?" Ethan snarls, or at least tries to. What little strength he has is waning.

"Your Highness, I had no choice. That is how Theros takes control." Rowan looks down at his hands. "He sends his sleepers to other kingdoms, and they immerse themselves in our lives. They watch us and learn everything they can, and when Theros finds a weakness, he exploits it. He blackmails those in power and steals thrones from kings. He poisons from within, unnoticed, until it is too late."

Ethan leans in too fast and winces, holding his stomach for purchase. "And you simply went along with his extortion? Why didn't you come to us—to my father?" he hisses through gritted teeth. "We would have helped you!"

But Rowan is shaking his head. In a heavy voice, he says, "Theros took my son, Your Highness."

His son. The one Ethan mentioned the night of Wintertide.

The one who disappeared.

Rowan levels a zealous gaze on Ethan. "His life was in my hands, sire. I did everything that was asked of me—against my own wishes—so that he would live."

Silence falls in the council chamber.

"I'm sorry you were placed in such a difficult position," Ethan says finally. In spite of everything, he still finds it in his heart to pity the man. "What became of your son?"

"Theros kept his word, Your Highness. He let my son live, took him under his wing, and gave him the life of a prince." Rowan seems to struggle with himself a moment, his lower lip trembling slightly. "I needed proof, of course, needed to see it for myself. In my absence all those years ago, when I told your father I was embarking on a search for my son, I set a course for Talos. It was then when I met Theros. I could finally put a face to the man who had taken everything from me. My boy was still himself then. I was so relieved to see him. He was happy . . ." Rowan trails off, looking away for a moment. "There is treachery to everything Theros does; he kept his word and gave my son a good life, but he rotted his soul in the process."

Uneasiness crawls across my skin as I place the resemblance. I noticed it before—the first time I laid eyes on Rowan—I couldn't grasp it for what it was then.

"Who is your son?" I hear myself whisper.

Rowan doesn't meet my weary gaze when he answers.

"Elijah."

Ethan lets out a heavy breath and lays back on the chair as I gape at the councilor, my mind blank with shock.

If Elijah is truly Rowan's son, then that means . . .

Elijah isn't my kin.

"I tried to speak with him when he was here, to appeal to him," Rowan goes on, "but he wouldn't even look at me."

"You saw what he'd become, and yet you still did Theros's bidding," I say. "For a monster who used to be your son? A monster who doesn't even acknowledge you as his father."

Rowan shakes his head ever so slightly. "He may be a monster, but he's my *son*." His pleading eyes fall from me to Ethan. "I cannot ask for your forgiveness, sire, but I would ask for your understanding."

Elijah is as sinister as they come. That anyone could find room in their heart to care for him is beyond comprehension. But, somehow, grudgingly, a part of me does understand. It would be self-righteous of me not to, what with my own irrational feelings for my father.

"I understand family is everything," Ethan says with a fading thread of sympathy. "But you robbed me of mine, councilor. So I, too, ask that you understand their deaths will not go unpunished."

Rowan's throat bobs. This time he doesn't look away. "I do, sire," he says wearily.

"And there is also the matter of the battalions. How many have you infected?"

The councilor squirms in his chair, and it takes a painfully long moment for him to answer. "All of them, sire; my hand was forced the moment King Perceval summoned them."

The moment he summoned them. But the order was carried out in secret. "How did you discover he'd sent those orders?" I ask.

"Because I was the one person the king entrusted with the task." There is no pleasure in the councilor's admission. "Theros didn't choose me as his agent without cause."

Ethan is deathly still under the desolate squeeze of my hand. "Can any of it be stopped?" he asks, but Rowan shakes his head.

"It is too late, Your Highness."

It's an overwhelming concept to grasp. The revered army of Alder. Seventy-five thousand men will be lost in a matter of days. And with them, our only hope of defeating Theros.

I feel Ethan's muscles quiver, his knuckles turning white against the curve of the armrests.

"And what of the cure?" I ask, desperate for a solution. "Can it save any of them?"

"As I said before, it isn't a cure. It does not heal the infection," Rowan explains. "It inoculates the body—makes one immune to the plague—but it doesn't work if the body is already infected."

"Inoculates how?" Ethan asks.

"The fever causes pustules within the mouth. When the host dies, they become scabs, which are pestled into a paste that is applied to a superficial wound—a scratch, if you will. It's effective but not infallible. On rare occasions, if the plague is still alive in the scabs, it can infect the host."

"Theros and Elijah are immune, aren't they?" Ethan mutters.

"As are all his soldiers, Your Highness. The Mad King discovered this immunity on his voyage home from the Western Continent. He learned some of his crew members were infected after they set sail. The Mad King isolated himself with a supply of food and wine in his cabin, and through the window, he watched the disease spread among most of his crew. But where others might only see death and disease, the Mad King saw opportunity. When only a handful of men remained alive, he ventured out of his cabin to inspect the dead. Madman that he was, he crushed a pustule with his fingers and inoculated himself on a whim, curious to see how it would affect him. But days passed without sign of infection, so he dared tend after those who hadn't yet succumbed, willfully exposing himself. Three months later, he arrived at the shores of Talos in perfect health."

And with a ship brimming with plague—a weapon to conquer the world.

The beginning of the end.

You would be amazed at the things an unsound mind can accomplish.

The tale casts the room in an uncanny silence. Even the guards stand uneasy.

Ethan is quiet for a long moment. Then, hesitantly, as though still working out his thoughts, he asks, "Does the plague live on in the dead? Is that how Theros harvests it?"

"In a recently dead host, yes, sire. But from what the Mad King learned during his sail across the Blue Abyss, to harvest the disease, for it to live, you need the saliva of the infected while they are still alive. If stored properly, the plague will remain in a dormant state until exposed to a body."

"We would have to infect people in order to inoculate others against the disease," I whisper.

Revulsion creases Ethan's features. "How did the Mad King come to that conclusion?"

"He collected saliva from one of the sick, kept it hidden in his cabin. Before their journey ended, the king surreptitiously tested it on his own soldiers, men who'd been lucky enough to avoid infection.

"Is there any left in your possession?" Ethan asks once the astonishment wears off.

"It's all gone, sire."

"What about Elijah?" I ask. "Wouldn't Theros leave some in his charge?"

Rowan deliberates. "Possibly, but I can't say for certain."

"How many enemy soldiers are stationed in Stonefall?" Ethan asks.

"One hundred soldiers, sire."

At this, Ethan leans back, skeptical. "So few?"

"They have control of Stonefall's army now, sire."

A faint nausea turns my stomach. I consider asking after Charles and father, wondering if he knows anything, but I can't bring myself to do it. I'm terrified of what Rowan might say.

Ethan goes on. "And what of the Borderlands?"

"The Borderlords are under Theros's command, as well, Your Highness."

"That's two hundred, give or take," Ethan says to no one in particular. "And Stonefall's army?" He turns his head to look up at me.

"Five thousand," I answer.

"I want a list of all the traitors in your employ," Ethan says to Rowan, signaling the guards for ink and paper.

"Of course, sire."

"When he's finished," Ethan says flatly to the captain, "send him to the executioner."

Rowan absorbs his fate with a single, heavy gulp. To his credit, he accepts it without pleading for his life.

Instead, he leans toward Ethan. "It was an honor to serve your father for as long as I did, Your Highness. Alder was truly magnificent. I take no pleasure from its undoing. Please believe that I did what I could to prevent it." At that, the councilor gives me a dark look, and his lips press together stubbornly. What little redemption his words had just now, he undoes when he continues. "For years, I tried to convince your father to break the alliance with Stonefall. Had he listened, Theros would have never set foot in our kingdom. But then she showed up and ruined everything! She's the only reason—"

Ethan jumps off his chair and tries to lunge at Rowan, knocking goblets over. But he's too weak. He falters to one knee.

I go to him, but he holds up a hand, refusing my help, and hoists himself back on his feet through labored breaths.

"Meredith didn't poison my parents," Ethan wheezes at Rowan, who is now plastered to the back of his chair, creating what distance he can between himself and Ethan. "She didn't infect our soldiers. *You* did." Ethan's finger shakes as he jabs it in Rowan's chest, eyes sharp as daggers. "This is on you, councilor. If Alder falls, it will be because of your actions. Remember that, while you still have a head attached to your neck."

44

Connor

The sun is gone when I wake, but its heat lingers on my skin. A crescent moon and a handful of stars peek through the hole in the roof. There's enough light to see the dried blood on my bandages. The swelling hasn't gone down and my fingers still hurt like hell, but it could be worse. Outside the door, I hear the voices of the guards. I turn over Felix's words. What leverage does Vishal have if not torture?

Raven? Rhys? My mind whirs.

I swear silently. Giving Vishal the location of the camp would doom the Brotherhood and endanger Pip and Asher. If Vishal has Raven captive, do I have the guts to refuse him so he can unleash his barbarism on her? So he can torture her to death? I can't bring myself to answer that question.

I have to get out of this room.

First, I need to free myself of this chair, then I can worry about what do to next.

I give gnawing the rope to my right a try, clamping into the rough fibers and spitting them out. Minutes in, my teeth and jaw start to tire from all the pulling. But I'm not one to sit around, so I take short breaks and keep going. After a time, I pause to survey my progress. I've cut through the outermost layers—far from a clean cut—fraying the fibers around it. It will take hours at this rate, and someone is bound to check on me. But I have to try. Keeping an ear on the guards for rotation changes, I pull and twist and spit all through the night, until the darkness begins to shy away, cast out by the impending dawn, alighting the walls that cage me.

And with the dawn comes Vishal.

Only a third of the rope around my wrist is gnawed off and in plain view.

Damn.

Felix accompanies the commander. He holds a loaf of bread and a cup of water.

The commander's brow rises a fraction when he notices the rope. "You are persistent." A simple observation, bereft of anger or any other emotion I expected. He signals Felix to come forward. The boy walks to me and offers the loaf of bread. *I need my strength*, I think as I bite into the crust with a sore jaw. It's warm. Fresh out of the oven. Felix brings the water to my lips before I finish chewing. I take a sip. For a split second, I hesitate, tasting something bitter in the water. Poison? Felix tilts the cup so that I continue, and I gulp the drink on impulse, defying myself. It goes down my throat like liquid gold.

I cough. "What is that?"

"Noxtail," Vishal answers, hands clasped behind him. "It has none of the mess that comes with torture . . . and none of the charm."

They both watch me intently. I feel different there and then, a euphoric sensation that sets my nerves aflame.

"My lord, I think he's drank it before," Felix informs him. "His eyes are dilated—he's responding to it."

"He's acclimated?" Vishal studies me. "Interesting."

"What's happening to me?" I gasp.

"You don't know?" Felix's question holds no surprise.

"You'll find out soon enough," says Vishal.

A chilled breeze blows over my skin, turning my sweat cold within the muggy jail. But as quickly as it came, the cold grows tepid, like I've been dunked in a warm bath. Exhaustion erodes to numbness, and a buzz fogs my head. It pushes me out—the essence of me, of my mind—like a crashing wave, tossing me ashore. I feel . . . distant. Suddenly, I'm a stranger to my own thoughts, forced to watch from a faraway window. I can sense my body, feel what it feels—the pain in my hand is still there . . .

But I am no longer in control.

Worst of all is the familiarity. The darkness welcomes me back.

Vishal's question is a muffled echo. "Did someone give you this before?"

"I don't remember."

Hearing my voice, spoken flatly and of its own volition, spears me with shock.

A shock that my body doesn't respond to. It all seems surreal, like a nightmare I can't wake from.

"What's the last thing you remember before the blackout?" Felix asks.

"I remember nothing of my life. My memories were lost to an injury."

From the dark corner in which I exist, I see the whites of Felix's eyes grow. "Amnesia?" he mutters, his gaze darting to the commander. "How long have you been like this?"

"Six months."

"Can you heal him of this condition?" Vishal asks him.

Felix shakes his head. "No, my lord, herbs wouldn't help him. The mind is complicated. Like a labyrinth. If it can mend, it will do so of its own accord."

Vishal's displeasure is obvious. I expect him to lash out, to strike Felix. He doesn't. "I want to be informed the moment he recovers those memories," the commander tells Felix before approaching me. "Amnesia will only keep so much from me." Up close, his unyielding eyes inspect me. "Where is the Brotherhood's hideout?"

NO! I scream the word, and yet there is no sound, absorbed in the dark cocoon that holds me hostage. I have no voice, only a deep sense of desperation. Betrayal flows out of my mouth without reservation. "Inside a cave hidden in a mountain northwest of the village of Fhalbo."

So this is how the Soul Reaper pries it all out of me—an herb that turns me into a snitch.

The rumors were wrong. Vishal doesn't steal souls, he cages them.

If this is his leverage, perhaps Raven and Rhys did escape.

"Excellent. And how large is this camp?"

"Not a hundred strong."

"So few?" In his eyes, victory is his. The enemy he seeks is not a threat, it's a nuisance, nothing more than ants to squash with a stomp of his boot.

Vishal isn't looking for an answer, but like a mindless slave, I nod.

"What is it these rebels aim to do with such dismal numbers?"

"To reclaim the coin you steal and give it back to the people."

Any other redcloak might have laughed, but Vishal does not. "Is that all?" he asks. "There is no plan of attack against the emperor?"

By now, I am beyond trying to stop my own mouth from running.

"The leader of the Brotherhood believes it impossible to win back the kingdom. His only concern is to impede the starvation of the Sunderian people."

The commander hikes an eyebrow. "A philanthropist? He's twenty years too late."

Julius returns minutes after the commander and Felix exit, seeking the pleasure of seeing me as I am: a slave.

With a smirk on his face, he unsheathes his sword and cuts

the ropes around my wrists and ankles.

He turns the sword's hilt to me, offering it. "Take it." The blade falls limp in my right hand despite the frenzy raging within. "Stand up."

My body answers the call, obedient, Julius's sword dangling uselessly at my side. Escaping without control of my body is impossible.

How long will I be like this?

Julius looks me up and down, gloating. "Not so tough now, are you?" He leans in to whisper, "You're nothing but a dog now. A *loyal* dog. I could ask you to clean my chamber pots and shine my boots, and you'd do it. Better yet, I could tell you to slice your hand off, and you'd do that, too! You'd bleed and stand there like an idiot, waiting for me to give you something else to do." He laughs. "Might be something to look forward to when the commander's through with you, eh?" He snatches the sword from my willing hand and slides it back in its scabbard. "Dog. Isn't that fitting? I think I'll call you that. Come with me, *Dog*."

I follow Julius outside, indeed like a dog. I don't even need a leash. The morning air clings with the smell of burned wood. Servants young and old whisk by, covered in soot, carrying pails that spill in their hurry. Sentry archers keep watch along the rampart, stationed fifty yards apart. *If only I could get my hands on one of those bows.* I count three archers before my body turns a corner to follow Julius, taking us deeper into the fort's maze.

Servants enter a structure that's larger than the surrounding buildings. Through its opened doors, I catch glimpses of beds and tables. Redcloaks roam inside, unburdened of their armor, manners relaxed. Pairs of them play cards around tables, seated on stools too small for their frames. Others fill the beds, dozed off. *Barracks*. Every soldier not on duty is in there.

When we reach the western edge of the fort, Julius leads me to a doorless hut with a balding roof of dilapidated thatch. Inside, an elderly man flinches at our entrance. He lowers his head in forced respect. and his bloodshot eyes plummet to the beaten earth beneath his feet.

Julius sidesteps to the wall so that I have an unrestricted view of the old man. "Dog, meet Maggot. You're going to help him draw a new portrait." The painter looks up slowly. Recognition sharpens his wary gaze—he knows me from his drawings; I gauge he's penciled my face more times than he can count.

In a wanton display of power, Julius grabs me by the scruff of the neck like I'm a rag doll. "You will tell Maggot every aspect of the Brotherhood leader's face, and you will not let him rest until he draws an exact match. Is that understood?"

"Yes."

He releases me. "Good. Now get to work. If Maggot isn't finished when I return," he says to me in warning, "it will be your fist that breaks his nose."

The painter's fear leaves with Julius. He stares at me a while, taking me in between blinks. "Young lad," he finally says, voice hoarse. "I am sorry they caught you. What is your name?"

"Connor."

"I wish we were meeting in better circumstances. I'm Irven." He extends a hand. It trembles in the air as he waits for me to shake it. He frowns when I don't, doubling the wrinkles on his face. "Did they make you drink the herb?"

"Yes."

He nods, pitying me. "They don't waste it on helpless men like me." Sighing, he lowers himself on the unbalanced stool behind him. I watch him pick up his pen and flick the excess ink back into the small glass bottle. "What does this poor fool look like?" With his back to me, his hand moves over a piece of paper as I describe Uther's features. The sound of my voice is torture. Worse than any physical pain Vishal could have inflicted. I'd rather he cut me to pieces than make me live the rest of my life subdued like this.

Irven's hands move fast with what can only be years of experience. The scratch of his pen against the paper comes in short, repeated strokes. He's done in less than ten minutes.

He shows me the finished portrait, seeking my approval. "Is there a resemblance?"

I stare at Uther's inked image, his hooded eyes accusing me of treason. The likeness is uncanny. Had I possession of my tongue, I might have praised Irven's talent.

"Yes."

Irven smiles, revealing a row of decaying teeth. "It's easier when I have precise details." Aware that my drugged self has nothing to say, Irven doesn't wait for a response. His foot pushes an open box from under the table. "These are the reason I'm here," Irven says, unapologetic, pointing to the contents: rolled canvases, like Walden's. "The commander said he won't burn them if I do as he asks." He smiles again, proud this time. "He gave me his word he wouldn't destroy them when I'm gone," he says without a shred of fear or dread in his voice. Irven takes one of his canvases, unfolding it with care. The woman inside smiles in her finery, her jeweled hands folded in her lap. Irven stares longingly at his own art. "Marquess Larew of Thiel Nors. Isn't she something?" He rolls it up after a moment's admiration, hurrying for another. And another. All portraits of regal monarchs in the kingdoms he's traversed. Then he unfolds a man holding a pitchfork. "I drew this farmer as a challenge to myself. I wanted to prove there was beauty in hardship. Don't you agree?" he asks with a glance in my direction. "It is unfortunate serfdom leaves little time for leisure. This man was the only one I could find who dared leave his work for half a day to let me paint him; I remember his wife wasn't very happy about it."

Irven's pride in his work must be what sustains him, I think as I remain a statue in his company, watching him dig in the bottom of the box for yet another canvas. "Ah. This is one of my earlier works," he says, slightly out of breath. A family portrait. A royal one, I gather from the crowns. They peer back at me as if they know me, exuding their presence through the oiled linen.

And their son . . .

Somewhere deep within the void of my psyche, a hairline crack of light ruptures. I see glimpses of the boy—a disarray of half-second flashes.

Amused brown eyes peer at me over the boy's shoulder. He runs on a grassy field, laughing as I bridge the distance. He pushes his legs to sprint faster, but he's no match for me. I run past him. Ahead, a boulder marks the finish line. I'm in the lead when the boy rams into me, and we careen in a heap of arms and legs through the turf.

"One of these days I'm going to leave you in the dust," the boy pants, climbing to his feet.

"You'll have to grow longer legs first."

"Oh, I will! Just wait till I'm all grown up. I'll be the tallest, most light-footed king that ever lived!"

Shock reels control of my body in the span of a second. I draw in a clipped breath, feeling like it's the first time I've filled my lungs in ages.

Irven goes on, unaware. "King Perceval and Queen Edith. Most powerful monarchs of our era." He scratches at his temple. "The wee prince was a nice little lad . . . I forget his name."

The boy's memory is alive in my thoughts. It remains like an echo long after my foreign mouth speaks his name.

"Ethan."

45

Meredith

Councilor Rowan is executed at dawn.

I am propping pillows at Ethan's back so he can sit and drink another mouthful of Sir Dormon's tonic when Captain Offa comes to inform us the order has been carried out. I wasn't sure if I'd be relieved or saddened, but to my surprise, I feel nothing; I try not to think about what that means.

"Bounty hunters are trailing the councilor's mercenaries and the subordinates who carried out his commands, Your Highness. They have orders to bring them in dead or alive." The captain's words echo in the room, bouncing off the stone fireplace, where Ethan's steward works to keep the flames strong; the poor man's left temple is purple and green from a blow to the head . . . but better that than a poisoned dart.

Ethan accepts the report with a grim nod. After the first mouthful of tonic and a hot bath, his condition seemed to improve. Now, clean and clad in fresh undergarments, I can start to see color return to his complexion. "And Chancellor Ulric? Have you found him yet?" He assumed Ulric had been another pawn in Elijah's game, tricked into believing he had intercepted information Elijah meant for him to find, but I wasn't so sure.

"My men are looking for him as we speak, Your Highness."

"Have them wait at the inn; he'll turn up."

"I doubt that, Your Highness. The innkeeper said he packed up and left weeks ago."

"What?" The word slips from my tongue.

"He's journeying back to Stonefall," Ethan infers.

"Should I send bounty hunters south, Your Highness?"

Ethan looks to me, silently asking for my thoughts. "No," I say bitterly. I would love nothing more than for him to be caught and dragged back here to face me, but it's too late; he could be far from the city now. "There's no point in wasting our resources."

"There you have it," Ethan tells the captain. "Is there anything else?"

"Yes. There are a couple other matters to discuss, Your Highness," the captain says before Ethan lays his head back onto the pillows.

"Go on."

"Another two of my guards were found dead by poisoned dart. Their bodies were hidden under a flight of stairs."

"Be sure their family names are included in my bereavement list," Ethan says darkly.

"I believe their deaths might explain why the assassin did not poison you as he did all the others, Your Highness," the captain adds.

Ethan looks back at the captain. "How so?"

"They were off duty, Your Highness."

"The assassin wasn't expecting to cross paths with them . . ." My voice trails off as awareness takes root. Those guards died in our place.

Ethan bows his head, shutting his eyes a moment. "Thank you, captain. What else do you have for me?" He asks the question as though bracing for the answer, expecting more bad news.

"The fifth battalion's field marshal reported at the gates half an hour ago. His troops arrived at the garrison early this morning."

Silence befalls the room. We stare at the captain.

"They're not infected?" Ethan asks, finding his voice.

Offa shakes his head. "There have been no signs of sickness, Your Highness."

I realize I've become quite the cynic, as I find the good news hard to believe. Rowan was convinced there would be no troops left, and I believed him. But as evidenced by our continued existence, Rowan's plans were not foolproof, there were cracks he did not foresee, and the fifth battalion slipped right through them.

"Praise the Maker," Ethan mutters. He takes another moment to let his relief sink in. "Did the marshal say how they managed to avoid infection?"

"The battalion changed course to avoid a blizzard, Your Highness; they bypassed the first outpost at Evergreen Pass."

Ethan squints at the captain. "A blizzard?"

"Yes, Your Highness."

To add to my confusion, the captain breaks into a grin, something I've never seen the man do before. Ethan smiles back at his captain, and my mouth quirks, wanting to join in myself—glad to see something other than gloom on Ethan's face—but all I can do is flick my blank stare between them. I feel as though I should understand.

"Was that all, then, captain?" Ethan asks after a moment, a shadow of a smile lingering on his lips.

The captain bows and turns on his heel.

"Oh, and captain?" Ethan asks before Offa makes his exit. "Release Councilor Milus from his cell at once. Bring him to me."

I give Ethan a puzzled smile when the captain leaves. "What was that about?"

"Remember that old story I told you at Wintertide?"

I nod. "The Battle of the Snow," I recall.

Ethan's eyes are expectant as they stare into mine . . .

And then I piece it together, remembering what he'd said.

The battle would have been the end of Alder, had it not been stopped by a blizzard.

"That's quite the coincidence," I marvel.

Ethan's smile widens. "Well, it *is* winter." He shrugs. "But we Alderians are a superstitious bunch when it comes to winter storms."

A whole battalion. Five thousand soldiers.

"Whatever it is, I'm grateful."

Ethan leans on his pillows, regarding me appraisingly. "It's about time we had some good news."

"Does this mean . . ." I begin to ask, treading around the question. It's enough men for a fight to the teeth against Stonefall's army. But to think I may have to fight my own soldiers is inconceivable. I shun the possibility. It's Theros we should be fighting, not each other.

"We can fight for Stonefall." Ethan beams as though he's in perfect health, infecting me with confidence. "And who knows, other soldiers might have survived. Two battalions would be enough to avoid a battle with Stonefall altogether."

"And if there are no others?" I hate to cloud his newfound positivity, but the last thing I want is false hope.

"We'll try for diplomacy regardless," Ethan assures me, reading into my fears. "We need as many soldiers as we can get to fight Theros. If we join forces with Stonefall, we'd be at least ten thousand men strong. That, and our knowledge of a cure gives us a better chance at convincing other kingdoms to fight with us."

I blink at him. "You make it sound so easy."

He chuckles. "Plans are often easy. The difficult part is fulfilling them." My gaze goes to the hand resting at his side, to the golden band on his finger. The fact that we are married is almost as hard to believe as the deaths of Alder's rulers.

And to think, I almost lost him today.

I'm toiling with that horrible thought when Ethan sits up straighter, and his hand closes on mine. "I wish I could say that everything will be all right," he says, misreading the concern on my face. "But whatever the future holds, know that I'll be right by your side."

I nod, grateful. "Together."

Half an hour later, Milus is bowing at the door, covered in soot, his gray hair blackened and plastered to his head, reeking of jail. Captain Offa stands at attention at the councilor's side, his assertive eyes locked on the wall behind me.

Milus raises his head a fraction, but doesn't quite look up at his prince. "You asked to see me, Your Highness?" he asks hoarsely.

Ethan's throat bobs. "Milus, I've brought you here to beg your forgiveness." The councilor's stunned gaze lifts to Ethan then, hope glazing his eyes. "You devoted your life to this kingdom," Ethan goes on. "To me, to my family, and at the first test of honor . . ." Ethan's shoulders seem to curl over his chest. He lowers his head, but his eyes don't shy away from the councilor. "I'm sorry."

Wrinkles crease the corners of Milus's watery eyes as his mouth turns up in a soft smile. "There is nothing to forgive, Your Highness. Misled though you were, I understand you and the king acted in the kingdom's best interest."

Ethan presses his eyes closed, shaking his head. "It was Rowan who should have been imprisoned. He was the real traitor." Ethan is shaking his head again. "I made a grave mistake, and it cost me everything."

"Councilor Rowan?" Milus's mouth drops. He takes a step

forward. "What's happened, Your Highness?"

"The king and queen are dead, Milus," Ethan says evenly, though not without effort.

The councilor's eyes widen, and his face pales from one instant to the next.

"There's much to discuss," Ethan rushes to say, fighting what looks like a wave of emotion. "For now, get cleaned up and rest. We'll talk later."

Milus nods and bows through his shock, unable to utter a word, and follows Captain Offa out the door.

Ethan's blank stare lingers on the empty doorway after they depart. And then he's shaking his head again, first rubbing his closed eyes and then pinching the bridge of his nose. He cups his hand over his eyes. "I should have believed him." The shame in his voice is clear as water.

I inch closer to him on the bed and pull his hand from his eyes, seeking his reluctant gaze. "A part of you always did," I say, tracing reassuring circles over his knuckles with my thumb. "I'm the one who pushed you to doubt, so if you're going to blame anyone, it should be me."

Ethan's eyes shift to our hands, and then back at me. He leans off the pillows to cup my cheek, bringing his face close to mine, close enough that I can smell the mint and lavender water from his bath.

"You and Milus are all I have left," he whispers, his warm eyes longing and grieving, searching my own. There is so much of the late queen in those eyes—same shape, same color—but where hers were knowing and calculating, his are expressive and kind. After everything that's been taken from him, it's a wonder there is kindness in them still. "I could not have lived through last night without you."

His thumb caresses my cheek with a feather-light touch, moving slowly to my chin and pausing just below my bottom lip. I hold my breath, surprised at the wanting that kindles in the pit of my stomach. I'd been dreading this for months, convinced I was hollow beyond repair, but now that it's staring me in the face, it's the emptiness that makes me long for him, for a reprieve from all the hurt and suffering. Ethan tugs me to him, his hand clenching fistfuls of fabric at my waist.

Not breaking our stare, he tells the steward, "Wallis, please leave us."

"Of course, sire," comes the steward's prompt reply.

Flushed, I listen to Wallis's rushed footfalls across the stone and rug. He's not yet at the door when Ethan brings his lips to mine, soft and hungry. His tongue parts my lips, craving to discover me, to unravel me, silencing my thoughts as our shallow breaths meld with the snap of the flames. I twist into him, and my hands come around his neck, pulling him closer. His mouth travels down my neck, sending shivers up my spine. I soak up the feel of his chest and shoulders, reveling in the hard, sinewy muscles under my palms, wanting him all the more. He tugs me against him, and I wrap my hands at his back. Without warning, my fingers catch the scarred ridges of skin and—unwittingly—I flinch, feeling the illusory strike of Theros's whip.

Ethan pulls away slightly, creating just enough space between us so he can meet my eye.

"Ghastly, I know," he mutters apologetically, as if somehow his scars could make him lesser.

"No," I whisper. "No," I say again, firmer this time, holding his gaze as I try for the right words. "Our scars do not define us."

He blinks at me. "*Our* scars?"

I turn my back to him, guiding one of his hands to the laces of my bodice. Ever so slowly, he starts untying my dress.

It only takes a few loosened laces for him to see.

His intake of breath is more a hiss than a gasp. I feel his fingers on my skin. On my scars. He undoes the rest of the lacing and takes it all in.

"Maker . . . who did this?"

"Chancellor Ulric," I mutter over my shoulder. "On my father's orders." Though the truth of it was, in a way, crueler than the strike of the whip, it no longer pains me to say it.

Out of the corner of my eye, I catch the disbelieving shake of Ethan's head. "What could you possibly have done to deserve this?"

His questions bring unbidden memories to the surface. A lump grows in my throat. I focus on the mantle, glowing with the flames below it, and savor the tranquility of the room and the warmth of Ethan's hands on my shoulders . . .

I start from the beginning, explaining everything. Well, almost everything. I tell him who Holt really was, and how our friendship—his and Beth's—taught me that you can find the truest of friends in the most unlikely places. How my childhood was filled with memories of them. I tell him about Anabella's motherly love and her perpetual scolding . . . what I wouldn't give to hear her lecture me now. I relive the day of the rehearsal. The day everything changed. The echo of screams surrounds me as Geneve's bleeding face comes alive. Connor is there too, but I don't speak of him. I can't. Not without revealing what I keep buried in my darkest depths. Instead, I divert to James and Holt's imprisonment, and my father's order to execute them. I tell Ethan about Jackson and the other jailer whose name I never learned, who were both killed because of me. The words flow as though I'm reading them off the pages of a book, except I feel every bit of them as I speak them, though, admittedly, the pain they bring is now a fragment of what it once was. The fear, the sorrow, the guilt . . . it all comes back in bitter shreds.

When I have no more to say and the room grows quiet again, I feel Ethan's lips on my back, kissing the raised white lumps of my scars, as if to mend them.

"Now I understand your behavior toward the chancellor," he breathes against my skin, sending chills through my arms. "He better hope I never lay eyes on him again."

I turn to face him. He's looking at me in concern, his eyes an open book, hiding nothing.

"If I'd known he was under Elijah's command, I would have done a number on him myself."

Ethan chuckles softly. "You would," he agrees.

Then our eyes fall into place, like two pieces of a puzzle, locked together like magnets. In the silence that ensues, his concern evaporates, displaced by a kindling in his expression, a yearning stirring in his bright gaze that quickens my pulse. We are broken, him and I, but I realize it's that very brokenness, that sense of loss and heartache, that unites us. Our wounds have formed jagged patterns only he and I can understand. This bond between us . . . I can't grasp or define it, but I can feel it.

His hands hold my face, and I lean in to his touch. He swallows hard. The need that burns in his eyes makes my blood race. But underneath the need, there is hesitation. Doubt. He whispers my name like a question, waiting for an answer.

I pull him to me, breathing him in, and he answers my call, his lips crushing mine. His hands fall like burning coals on my bared shoulders. It doesn't seem possible for my heart to beat faster, but it does. Our first kiss at the church had been curious and brief. Gentle. Borne of traditions and obligations.

But this . . . is different.

This is giving in.

It's letting go.

His hands roam over me, zealous, longing to forget his demons. My palms press against his chest, tracing the corded muscles underneath his shirt, seeking the feel of him. Ethan's arms wrap tighter around me, and he kisses me deeply, desperately. I want to ease his pain as much as I want him to take mine away. And he does. Fate and war. Loss and oblivion. None of it matters in this moment. The reprieve is almost as intoxicating as the fire thrumming through my veins. And in the rasp of our ragged breaths, I let myself forget.

The world dulls as my broken half melds into his. I give myself to him without reserve, utterly and completely, and the woes of my heart dim to nothingness.

46

Connor

My body stands upright and unmoving, shackled to the back wall of the jail cell. The memories are coming back. They were there all along. Ethan's painted image jolted open the locked doors to my mind. I remember. My identity. Connor Westwend, son of Captain Eamon Westwend. Longbow lieutenant of Alder's first battalion. Confidant of the crown. Alder. My home.

How on earth did I end up on the other side of the continent?

I drift through hazy, jumbled memories of days long gone. Awareness filters in like a cold mist, uncoiling its tendrils until it fills the darkness. The onslaught of images turns the light throbbing in my temple into a painful hammering. Training with my father, late-night conversations with Ethan, my mother forcing me to dance with her at court, long summers at Aunt Jessamine's farm, Diago . . . I see my fifteen-year-old self brushing the black horse's mane—

Where *is* Diago?

I never traveled without him. Had he been with me when . . .

When what?

A fight. A muddle of shadows and flickers. I remember the weakness, my spent muscles, the pain . . .

The darkness.

The same black hole that holds me prisoner now. Understanding settles, confirming the commander and Felix's earlier suspicions. Who drugged me before? I can feel the answer lurking within the recesses of my mind, waiting to be found. But trying to force the memory worsens the hammering in my head. There's so much I still don't remember.

Years of my life are missing, like holes in a fabric, impossible to patch by sheer will alone.

Noxtail's effects start to wane an hour into my confinement. I realize it as soon as I can blink and direct my gaze without struggling. As the minutes pass, my fingers twitch to my own command. They must know the drug will wear off. Explains the shackles. I expect Felix will return at some point with another dose, but when the door finally opens, it's a servant who walks in. He approaches me, eyes on the ground and fidgety. I don't have the control to stop myself from drinking from the cup he tips to my lips. Once I've drained the vessel, he leaves a loaf of bread at my feet.

"Dinner," the servant mumbles, never meeting my eyes.

I stare at the empty chair where Vishal tortured me. How many poor bastards before me have sat there? How many of them have died in it? The table is gone, no longer needed.

I close my eyes to fight off a growing headache.

And I see *her*.

Not a vision—a memory. I watch her from a distance behind

the spectators. She climbs down a red carpet on a wide set of stairs, dressed in a blue-and-gold gown. I should be scanning her surroundings, but I have a hard time looking away. Her feet move tenuously down the steps, as though she might fall. She eyes the onlookers like a frightened mouse, unsure of herself, but when her gaze finds me, it's as if I've lent a steadying arm. Shoulders straight, she makes her way to the landing with newfound confidence, her eyes never leaving mine.

Meredith.

The stubborn, idealistic princess who doesn't know her own strength. The girl whose foolishness had me at my wits end. The girl who would put herself through hell to save a servant's life . . .

The girl I love.

My eyes fly open, hoping to see her ghost standing there, bleeding and staring, knowing she won't be, knowing I've been conjuring a fragment of her memory, because somehow, subconsciously, some part of me worried for her.

Far Water—

I sent her away that night on the outskirts of town. On Diago. Unconscious and wounded. I see it then, the moment he stabbed her. It hits me like a punch.

Elijah.

Fear and rage resurface, as though I am still there, in the forest. I feel my body tense in response, the remnants of the drug in my veins withering.

My strength leaves me by the minute, oozing through my

wounds, but my hands are an ironclad vise around Elijah's neck.

If I can clamp down long enough, this will all be over soon.

Elijah's eyes are wide, teeth bared and gritted. But his fury pales in comparison to the one roaring inside me. Like venom. He nearly killed her. If I hadn't jolted his aim—

I squeeze harder, the perforated puncture wound in my hand an afterthought.

The whites of Elijah's eyes grow wider. He thrashes under me, his arms searching for purchase. Desperate. I can feel his tenacity wavering, but then his arm swings down with a rock. I catch it a second too late. Pain explodes at the back of my head, and bright light floods my vision. I'm on the ground—he's pushed me off. I hear him wheezing, disturbing the underbrush as he rushes to his feet and takes off. When my vision returns, the forest is a dark, moving blur. I manage to stand, but I have no sense of direction. My legs threaten to give under me. He's fetching a blade to finish me off, *I think when I don't see him. My vision is too blurry to try to find a weapon, much less deflect an attack, so I listen for his approach. His footfalls are slow. Deliberate. Calculating. He knows the blow to the head cost me. He knows I'm vulnerable.*

But not for long.

The crash of leaves quickens. Elijah's shadow sharpens into view just as he tackles me back to the ground. My arms fly out defensively, expecting the cut of a sword that never comes.

The faint prick of the needle is undeniable.

Noxtail . . . it was *him*.

Why? Why didn't he kill me? And why am I here? Sunder is thousands of miles away from Far Water . . . neighboring . . .

He was taking me to Talos.

For what purpose? The frown on my forehead feels off, like I'm trying to move stiff, unwilling muscles. An echo of the drug, no doubt. For a brief, desperate moment, I consider breaking my hands and feet to slip free of the shackles.

Meredith.

I have to believe that she's alive, that she recovered and made it safely to Alder City. I can't think otherwise, or I'll never get myself out of this hellhole.

47

Meredith

Five days later, King Perceval and Queen Edith are laid to rest. A great procession of one thousand horsemen and hundreds of courtiers and city folk surround the seven-story hearse carved with effigies of the late rulers. It began over an hour ago, at the castle bailey, and moved through the markets and past the church, where the bells ring loud and somber. All throughout the cobbled streets, black-velvet-clad city folk prayed as we passed, or joined the cortege. Ethan and I lead the members of the council behind the horse-drawn hearse. The king's court follows at the council's heels. As we bend around a corner, my sideways glance catches Heloise's bright-red lips among the multitude of swishing black fabrics and veils. So much has happened since we last saw each other the night of the wedding. I try to catch her eye, but she looks straight ahead, not once glancing at the hearse, and I can't help but frown, feeling as though it's on purpose.

I turn my attention back to the hearse, to the coffins within it. My thoughts take me back to the last time I spoke with the queen. She left this world thinking me a traitor. I thought I would have time to prove her wrong. Now I'll never have the chance.

The transition of power has been abrupt, to say the least. Milus was appointed chief councilor only yesterday, signed and sealed by candlelight in Ethan's sitting room. In the days leading up to the funeral, Ethan and I remained cooped up in his rooms as is customary for mourning. Councilors seeking the royal seal came and went while he recovered from the poison. It was an organized chaos. Ethan's desk is still buried in stacks of paperwork: property rights disputes, crimes awaiting judgment, food shortages, and all manner of financial matters. I still can't get over the fact that I've been part of so many decisions. Ethan asked me to be at his side, not to comfort him as I'd assumed, but to assist him. He sought my opinion. More than that, he respected it. That alone gave me the spirit to remain awake late each night as we rifled through the endless duties.

I'm still reeling with all that's changed between us these last few days. We've spent more time together this past week than in all of the months we've known each other. And although we've been too busy to do anything but work, eat, and sleep, I am acutely aware of his nearness, of the way his hands graze my skin in the most subtle and fleeting of touches. I've come to love his warm, solid weight pressed against my back when I wake, and the feel of his arm around my waist. It comforts me, knowing my presence helps keep his pain at bay. Some days are harder for Ethan than others. His grief has manifested in all manner of ways: a heaviness in his steps, or a crack in his voice. But today of all days, his face is empty, a blank slate void of emotion. Four silver buckled straps fasten the front of his ebony leather surcoat, split down the middle to dark pants and boots that hike up to his knees. He hardly looks my way, and when he does, he stares right through me; better his subjects see him like this than the broken prince I know lies underneath his indifference.

By the time the funeral procession has circled back to its end at the castle gates, the cortege has thinned. Past the gates, the horsemen lead us across the bailey toward the castle abbey, a stone structure built like a church, framed by spires and buttresses and stained glass. The horsemen line up in half-moon formation, split at the abbey's arched porch. The coffins are unloaded from the hearse onto the shoulders of eight servants, whom we follow up a set of wide and shallow stairs into the abbey. The shuffle of feet echoes inside, where great stained-glass windows dominate like curtains throughout, meeting a ceiling of herringbone-decorated vaults and golden ribs. Stone sarcophagi cover the marble floor in pairs, carved with life-size effigies of those entombed within them. Though the sun burns bright through the abundant supply of windows, this day could not be darker. Ethan's glassy brown eyes affix to the coffins of his parents throughout the ceremony. I doubt he hears a word of the priest's sermon.

After it's over, when all those present have whispered their last prayers, Milus and I linger, waiting on Ethan like sympathetic shadows. He's still staring at the wooden coffins. Next to them, two sarcophagi lay open awaiting the bodies, their freshly carved stone effigies buttressed to the side and hidden from view. The servants that carried the coffins abide by the entrance wall, heads bowed and hands clasped at their backs, tasked with relocating the bodies and closing the tombs.

"I'd like a moment alone." Ethan doesn't look at us, his voice low and indifferent.

A quick glance passes between the councilor and me. I resist the urge to reach for Ethan, to search his face. Instead, Milus turns his palm to gesture me onward. "After you, my lady."

I hesitate with one last glance at Ethan's profile before turning away, our slow steps on the marble tiles loud in the silent abbey.

"Don't worry yourself too much, my lady. His Highness is strong," Milus assures me in his gravelly voice when we step outside.

"You'd think it would be harder to watch him fall apart, but somehow this is worse," I say, looking back through the open doors at Ethan's shadow; he hasn't moved.

"Saying good-bye isn't easy for him. Give him time, Your Highness. He will pull through."

I look at the councilor. He wears his chin-length white hair down today, brushed smooth and neatly parted down the middle, reminding me of a library scholar. "I'm glad he has you," I say.

The councilor smiles, flashing a set of not-quite-perfect teeth. "It's an honor to serve him. And you, of course, Your Highness. I look forward to the coronation."

Right, the coronation. Alder's new king and queen. Leave it to me to forget something that important. Now that I don't have years to prepare, the thought of wearing Alder's crown is suddenly daunting. But being crowned queen should be the least of my worries. I can't trust Chancellor Ulric's promise that Charles won't be harmed; every day that passes could be a day too late.

I worry more and more about Father, too.

Then you won't mind when we put his head on a pike.

Elijah's words gnaw at me. We've delayed too long as it is for the funeral, but Ethan's accession to the throne is as necessary a ceremony as the burial of his parents. "When's the coronation?"

"The prince has requested the coronation be postponed until his return from Stonefall, Your Highness."

"He has? Why?"

The councilor gives a bemused smile. "His Highness tells me you are anxious to come to the rescue of a cousin."

A hand over my heart, my gaze strays back to the abbey. Ethan's motionless silhouette twists my insides in a knot. I want to rush over there and put my grateful arms around him; it'll have to wait. Not taking my eyes off Ethan, I ask, "Who will be in charge in our absence?"

"His Highness and I will convene presently on the matter."

I nod. I meant to stay at Ethan's side after the ceremony, but now that I know he has plans with the councilor, I decide to look into a personal matter of my own. "You'll wait for him, then?" I ask, turning back to Milus. I would hate for Ethan to find himself alone when he walks through those doors.

"All day, if need be, my lady."

"How could you not tell me?"

It's the first thing out of Heloise's mouth when she receives me in her room, her glare as red as the pigment on her lips. I walk inside as understanding dawns on me. She points me to the set of couches near the gold carved hearth.

With the fifth battalion's arrival at the garrison, Heloise has learned about our plans to march to Stonefall the same way everyone else did: through gossip run amok. I'd meant to come sooner, but in the winding chaos that ensued after the wedding, I haven't had a chance to do anything but weather the storm at Ethan's side. During that time, reports of the fallen battalions began to arrive at the castle, the dispatches depicting outposts turned into mass open-air graveyards of infected bodies that no one has the courage to bury. As we had feared, all the other battalions succumbed to the plague. Only a small number of soldiers were lucky enough to avoid infection. As of yet, the towns and villages surrounding the outposts have not reported any symptoms. Sir Dormon attributes this to the plague's ability to destroy its host in a very short time, limiting its contagion to the outposts from which it spawned. But fear of the disease spreading across the kingdom remains.

"I'm sorry," I say to Heloise, and I mean it, but her mouth only tightens. "Please understand, I couldn't speak of it to anyone."

She looks at me, and her eyes flash with hurt. "I'm not just anyone." She crosses her arms, pensive, and stalks to the mantle, where two marble angels gesture with open arms at a sapphire vase with gold handles. "Did you really think I wouldn't have kept the secret to myself?"

"That's not—"

"I trusted you with my secrets, with truths that would ruin me, yet you couldn't trust me with yours."

My voice drops to a whisper. "It wasn't distrust that kept me silent . . . it was fear," I admit. She stares, her dark, piercing eyes tracing the air around me, and I wonder if she thinks me a coward. Without a word, she turns to the arched, paneled glass doors, arms still at her chest. Thick clouds cover the sun now and light snow falls outside, silently piling along the crevices of Heloise's balcony. "I worried someone would overhear."

As the fire warms my cheeks, I wait out her silence, listening to the subtle howl of the rising wind outside. I chew over my words, debating if I should say something else. But what else is there to say? Surely she grasps the gravity of the situation. It wasn't just my kingdom that was at stake. It was hers, too.

Her voice is an octave lower when she asks, "Did Lief know?"

I shake my head, but then I realize her eyes are still fixed to the frost-kissed glass. "No," I say. Lief hasn't broached the subject, either, though I haven't seen much of him despite the long hours he spends keeping watch outside Ethan's quarters. I can't even remember the last time we trained together.

"I heard you saved the prince from an assassin," Heloise says after a long pause, her back still to me, and I realize changing the subject is her way of telling me she's accepted my apology.

"Barely."

Heloise turns her head, smirking. "Do you ever not sell yourself short?"

I frown at her. "I'm not being modest. The assassin was a giant strap of muscle. Much as I would like to, I can't defy the laws of physics."

"My brothers would make good sparring partners if that's your concern," she says. "Perhaps you should train with them instead of Lief."

I scoff. "What is it with you two? Why can't you just get along?"

"We do get along." She smiles back at me through the reflection on the glass.

"I think Lief might disagree," I tease back.

Heloise turns from the windows and shrugs. "He's not one to brag."

Smiling up at her, I sigh and say, "I'm going to miss you."

"You won't have to, Your Highness. I'm marching south with you."

"You volunteered?" I can't say I'm surprised. A part of me knew she would. "But . . . what of your family?"

Heloise's hands clasp her arms as if to hug herself. "My father and brothers all volunteered. I want to fight alongside them. Die with them too, if it comes to that." Her words chill my bones, painting an image of death in my thoughts. I recoil from it.

"If we are lucky," I say, "there may not be a battle."

"Perhaps not at Stonefall. But sooner or later, we will have to fight. This is the beginning of war, Meredith. Marching to Stonefall is but the first step."

"And what happens when we return?" I ask her. "What reception will you come home to?" I can already see it. Heloise would be shunned from attending court, turned into a pariah, her family name ruined.

"That, I can't say for certain. But if we return victorious, I predict I'll become the second-most-respected female in all of Alder." She struts to the couch opposite of me and leans on its arm, smiling as though she's just beat me in a game of Justice Quicksand. Her smile broadens at my frown, teeth bright against her painted lips.

"Second-most?" I say. "Surely, you don't mean—"

"Of course I do," she quips. "Crowned or not, you are the queen of Alder now, the first one willing to wield a sword in battle and fight with our soldiers." She pushes off the arm and sinks beside me, eyes wide and glowing. "Meredith, the people will love you for it."

As hard as that is to believe, it's difficult not to smile. I've fantasized about that very thing—longed for it—for as long as I can remember. To be accepted. Not as others wish me to be, but as I am.

I cover Heloise's hand with my own and say, "For both our sakes, I hope you're right."

When I retire for the day, I find Ethan propped at the edge of our bed, still in his mourning clothes and deep in thought by the flame of one small candle, quiet as the night. His focus points at a suit of steel armor. Gone is the emptiness and the apathy from earlier, and it feels like a small victory to see the furrow between his brows disappear when he sees me enter the room. Judging by the strong flames under the mantle, I figure I just missed the steward. Ethan extends a hand to me, and I take it, feeling a trace of warmth in his palm despite his icy fingers. I kiss them without thought, trying to bring heat back to them, but then I look up from under my lashes, and his heavy-lidded gaze and half smile arrest me with self-awareness.

"Is that yours?" I ask through my discomfiture, eyes pointed to the shiny armor before us. The golden lion engraved on the whole of its breastplate stares back at me. Will there ever come a time when that crest doesn't remind me of him?

Ethan nods. "I sent the steward to fetch one for you from the blacksmith." His hand still in mine, he draws me to sit beside him. A dusting of stubble shadows his sculpted jawline, and his hair looks as though he's dragged a hand through it more than once. "We march in two days," he informs me. "Tomorrow, I will appoint Milus as regent."

"Thank you," I say after a pause.

"What for?"

"Delaying the coronation."

He smiles at me, creasing small wrinkles at the corners of his eyes. It's a tired, worn smile, but a smile just the same.

After a day like today, I'll take that as a good sign.

Ethan reaches to tuck away a stray lock of unruly hair behind my ear. "I should tell you how much it terrifies me to think of you in a battlefield . . . facing off against men who make a living out of bloodshed. If I lose you, too—"

"You will carry on and continue to fight until there is nothing left to fight for," I say with a strength I don't feel. "Promise me, Ethan." My throat closes up, but I push it open with a hard swallow. "Promise me you won't give up. And I will promise you the same in return." Whether he knows it or not, I ask for his sake as much as mine. No matter what happens, I don't want to lose myself again, nor do I want revenge to be my driving force any longer. I want purpose and honor. Holding on to this promise will give us that. It will give *me* that.

Ethan's sad gaze holds me for an eternity before he scoops an arm around my waist and pulls me close. He leans to rest his chin atop my head, his fingers caressing the small of my back. I feel the bob of his throat as he whispers, "I promise."

48

Connor

No one comes the next day. Not Felix, or the Commander. Not even Julius. Only the servant boy. He brings me bread and water, which I'm expecting to be tainted. But it's just water. Aside from that brief interaction, I'm left to my racing thoughts. My stomach grumbles, my hand throbs, and a headache hammers in my head. Why isn't the commander here now, demanding more information?

I don't sleep that night. I feel sick. My whole body is restless. The clammy sweat on my skin makes me shiver in the tepid twilight. It isn't hard to guess I'm experiencing withdrawal symptoms from that dastardly herb, but I'm still surprised at its potency. If this is how my body feels after one dose, I don't want to find out what it's like after weeks of it.

Hours later, the symptoms haven't subsided. I'm tossing and turning on the ground, unable to rid myself of the anxiety in my limbs, and though there is no pain, the constancy of it is agony; I think I prefer getting mangled by Vishal to this.

Felix makes an appearance in the morning.

I'm leaning against the wall, knees drawn close, head sagging at my chest. "How are you feeling?" he asks. I look up. He's alone. A wide leather belt supplied with a repertoire of remedies and tonics hangs at his waist. Judging by the way he studies me, I think he has his answer.

He crouches to touch my face, either careless or unconcerned that his proximity gives me the leeway to strangle him. Even in my debilitated state, I could overpower him. But he knows I won't. There are no keys on him. And I doubt I could use him as leverage.

"You have a mild fever."

He lifts a vial out of his belt and tilts its brown liquid past my chapped lips. The sourness isn't too unpleasant.

"Is the commander done with his interrogation?" I ask.

"No." Felix puts the empty vial back in his belt and moves on to my hand.

"He doesn't seem hard pressed to continue," I prod. "Are there other prisoners?"

"Just you," he says, erasing the rest of my doubts; the stunt I pulled at the inn worked then, gave Raven and Rhys the opening they needed to get away. Felix works on removing my bandages. "The commander feels it's important for you to understand what it's like to be deprived of noxtail."

So he *is* torturing me.

"Rat will bring some to you later," Felix reassures me. "You'll feel better then."

Better. That's an interesting word for poisoning me.

"Who's Rat?" I ask, steeling myself for the stinging salve on

Felix's fingers.

"The servant," Felix says simply. He rubs the salve on patches of exposed skin that haven't fully scabbed.

I draw a sharp breath, then let out a grunt. "What's his real name?" I ask after.

Disdain colors Felix's otherwise calm voice. "He's Rat to me."

"Why do you hate him? He's just a boy—like you."

"He's Sunderian," he explains while gently wrapping a clean cloth over my hand.

I doubt this conversation will lead to anything, but knowing the enemy is always an advantage, and peeling through Felix's willing layers will at least help me understand him better. "If you hate your enemies, then why are you kind to me?"

"I hate Sunderians because they're cowards."

"Not all are," I say, thinking of Flynn, and Tros and Amos, and all the other men who serve Uther.

"I've yet to meet one who isn't."

"I'm surprised at you knowing any, being secluded this long."

Felix is silent for a while, his face expressive with thought. He finishes bandaging my hand before he speaks again. "Years ago, when I first came here, I befriended a Sunderian boy. The commander's servant. He was older than me, a couple years older than I am now. He was the first Sunderian I'd ever met. The commander told me not to make friends with him, but I was a kid. And I was lonely. He played with me sometimes, when we were free of duties and the commander was too busy to notice. I didn't care that he was the enemy—to me he was just another boy."

"What happened to him?"

"He ran away," Felix says, unable to hide his disappointment. "And he used *me* to do it, tricked me into thinking we were playing games; I paid with blood for that."

"He escaped," I amend. You run away from homes, not prisons.

But Felix shrugs it off. "Does one escape if one never goes hungry or has a bed to sleep in? That's more than most children in Sunder could ask for." Bitterness darkens his tone.

"What bothers you more, that he left, or that he left without you?"

I know I've taken it too far when his face snaps in my direction.

"Are you mocking me?" the healer asks, defiant.

"I'm simply trying to understand why you would hold that boy's desire to be free against him."

Felix leaves without answering. He's still brooding when he returns that afternoon to continue the interrogation, and although the real me is pushed back by the drug, his questioning is clipped and icy, and I notice he writes in angry strokes. But he doesn't let his anger get in the way of his work. Soon enough, his questions lead him to my recently recovered memories. He isn't more shocked than I am to learn the person who first gave me the drug was none other than their crown prince. Knowing I failed to end the bastard stings like salt in a wound, but I channel my anger where it serves me best.

If I'm to find a way out of this, I'll first have to discover a pattern to exploit. But I have nothing. I can't break the shackles, and the servant carries no keys. The guard outside my cell does, but so far, he's only stepped inside at Julius's request when I was drugged. I'll have to bide my time.

A week passes before Felix warms up to me again.

I remain shackled during the day, sweating in solitary confinement. At dusk, the fidgeting servant comes by with bread and noxtail-laced water. My only source of it. In this heat, I'm dehydrated before noon. That's how they ensure I drink it. The servant was probably instructed not to speak to me, as he refuses to answer any of my questions. He never looks directly at me, an ambivalence I suspect stems from a great deal of suffering and torment.

Felix visits me every evening, once the drug has taken full control. I am fully under the influence by then, pliant as a reed. I divulge anything he asks. He inspects my hand before he begins his interrogation, checking for infection or improper healing. The pain has dulled, but it's ever present. Felix jots down every word in his journal, reporting back to the commander while Julius fetches me to clean up horse dung at the stables—a task he's been permanently assigned as penance for his failures in Fhalbo.

"This is your fault, so you're going to do it for me," Julius mutters the first night, staring at me with serpent eyes. He shoves a grimy bucket and a shovel into my chest and demands I pick up the droppings. "Get to work, Dog!"

Assured by my drug-induced obedience, he disappears, leaving me to finish his chores unsupervised. To my chagrin, the noxtail pulsing through my veins ensures I do as he asks. To a tee. But every system has a loophole, and while my arms haul dung into the bucket, my thoughts are hard at work, searching for it. The sentry shifts. The servant routes and tasks. Each day adds a piece of the puzzle. I drink less of the water, the bare minimum to thwart severe dehydration. It burns in my mouth like a sickly sweet poison. The compulsion to push it all down my throat is a battle of its own, but I let the rest drip down my chin when the servant turns his back. I assess my body's reaction, testing the limits of the herb in smaller quantities. Beside the headaches and muscle cramps caused by dehydration, I deduce the duration of noxtail's effects are directly related to the amount ingested, finding myself in full control of my body while still shoving horse droppings in the stables. I'm forced to pretend obedience on those nights, which is more challenging than I imagined, all while persuading myself every second not to impale Julius with the rake.

Reducing the amount of noxtail does have one disadvantage: by the time the servant comes with more the next day, I'm already suffering from symptoms of withdrawal. I endure the restlessness and the chills for hours at a time, craving like an addict. But the servant isn't Felix, and he doesn't know to look for those signs.

Today, Rat walks in as he always does. He scampers toward

me with the stoop of a coward, the cup of water shaking in his squirming grip. For a fleeting moment, I lament exploiting his weakness for my own gain. He'll likely be punished because of me. Or worse. But I don't have a choice. It would be smarter to wait another week and let my hand heal completely. Problem is, I doubt the commander has another week's worth of questions; leaving my fate to chance is too much of a risk.

When the servant offers the cup, I take it from his fretting fingers, as I have for the past eight days. I pretend to empty it. Watchful of his averted gaze, I hold the second gulp in my mouth. The boy exchanges the cup for the loaf of bread, and the second he turns his hunched back to me, I open my mouth. The water dribbles down the sides of my chin, and I wipe it with my sleeve. I distract my body's ache for more noxtail by stuffing my mouth with the loaf, forcing me to chew.

Arms limp at my sides, I'm staring at nothing when Felix walks in. He peels and replaces the bandages on my hand. "You're healing well despite the lack of proper nourishment. This is good." As usual, he positions his worn leather journal on his lap and opens it to the next blank page, but today he says, "This won't take very long." Felix holds out his pencil and asks me his first question of the day. "Meredith," he says, and for once, I'm glad of noxtail's poison running in my veins. "The Stonefall princess. How did you come to be her escort?"

"I volunteered."

He scribbles my answer. "Why?"

"It was an opportunity to determine her character."

Felix cocks his head in birdlike fashion. "To what end?"

"King Perceval sought to establish her suitability for the throne."

"And was she?" he asks. "Did you find the princess suitable?"

"Most people are too frightened to stand up for themselves," I hear myself say to her. I recognize my aunt's parlor even in the shroud of night.

"They might be willing if we give them the inspiration they need," she says, optimistic in spite of everything.

I kissed her that night. I hadn't realized the extent of my feelings until that moment. And it unnerved me. Love in itself can be a dangerous thing, but to love Meredith is insanity. Sweet insanity. It tested me in ways I never thought possible, made me question my loyalty to the crown, my honor as a soldier—codes I live by. If someone had told me before I journeyed to Stonefall that I would fall for Ethan's betrothed, I would have scoffed.

But I did.

"Yes," I say.

"I've never met a princess," Felix ponders. "I've always imagined them graceful and fragile . . . what was she like?"

Hoyden, stubbornly foolish, brave, kind . . . beautiful.

"Suitable," I say flatly.

Felix sighs disappointment as though I've crushed his imagination. Then, offhandedly, he remarks, "It is good then that she lives."

In the darkness, I inhale a sharp breath, my insides weak with relief, and though the jail is quiet, there is a whooshing in my ears as I turn his words in my head. *She's alive*. Is he certain? Or is this borne of gossip and conjecture? He's inches from me, close enough to touch without straining the chains. If I wasn't drugged, I'd foolishly reach for his collar and demand he tell me how he knows this and why.

Felix snaps his journal closed. "In case you're wondering, today's notes aren't for the commander—he has what he needs from you," he admits.

If the interrogation is done, it means patterns are about to change. Still oblivious, Felix shrugs, and his eyes flash with the inquisitiveness of a child. "I don't often hear stories such as yours anymore. I used to, when my master was still alive. He'd tell me all kinds of stories. Some of them too outlandish to be true, but I enjoyed them." He runs a thumb through the side of his journal, flipping the bound linen sheets like cards. "They're all here, along with everything he taught me."

Felix falls silent, his gaze faraway, a shadow of a smile on his face, lost in what can only be fond memories. I pity his good heart. It will rot in a place like this, serving men like Vishal and Julius. Perhaps—if things go according to plan—he might have a chance at a better life.

But things hardly go according to plan.

Perhaps I'll get him killed instead.

The sun is making its final descent when Felix takes his book and walks out, a pale-orange tint fading in the sky, taking little of its scorching heat with it. By the time Julius sends for me, it has sunk below the horizon, plunging the camp in indigo darkness. A tall redcloak with a soured sneer comes to fetch me tonight, and I obediently trail his shadow out the door and along the mud-beaten path. As we near the fort's mess hall, the sound of drunken banter spills out through its unlatched doors and into the quiet night. *Excellent*, I think as I walk on in an even, drug-induced stride.

At the stables, Julius is in a fouler mood than usual. I surmise it has something to do with the drinking in the mess hall, which he is clearly not a part of. "You're late," he snaps at the soldier when we cross the threshold of the tall double doors.

The soldier scoffs. "Oh, paggle off, you turd. Felix was questioning him."

"Why?" Julius asks, standing the shovel against one of the stalls. "The commander said he was done with him."

"Your job is to shovel dung, not to ask questions," the redcloak shoots back as he turns to leave, blind to Julius's seething scowl.

"That's Dog's job now. My job is to enjoy my free time and do as I please."

The redcloak stops dead in his tracks and whirls on Julius, towering over his spindly frame. I watch on, feeling the effects of the drug start to wane. "Having help doesn't free you of your punishment. You will clean the stables and groom the horses, and when you're finished, I want you to do it some more. Understood?"

"You expect me to sit out the Emperor's Day celebration?"

The redcloak sinks his bold eyes into him. "You think you're the only one on duty this evening?" he asks with curled lips.

"Duty isn't the same as punishment."

"Whelps like you don't get to celebrate." The soldier turns to leave, but stops short at the entrance to deliver a warning. "If I so much as see you near the mess hall, I will make a spectacle out of you."

With his back to me, Julius watches the man go, fists curling and uncurling amidst the buzz of flies. Once the retreating soldier's tread fades into the night, Julius predictably channels his tantrum towards me—the root of his rage. He turns, fist aiming for my face, certain I'll stand still and let him land a blow.

At the last second, I duck and turn back on him, clenching my good hand into a fist and slamming it into his soft belly.

Julius's face contorts with a gasp as he bends over, and I drive a knee to the bridge of his nose, feeling the solid crunch of bone. Julius swings backward, nose bleeding, the thump of his hard fall drowned by a spooked horse's neigh.

But the bastard's still conscious.

Clambering to one knee, he grasps for the pummel of his sheathed sword. He draws one-handed, the movement clumsy and slow, and the blade's path cuts too high. I crouch and intercept his wrist with my left hand, then bring my foot up into his chest, pushing him back to the hay-littered ground. The sword fumbles out of his grip, tumbling a couple of inches from his reaching hand. I kick it out of the way and step on his hand, his flesh soft under my boot. Feeling him squirm under my weight, I stretch an arm to the dung-covered shovel. Julius's free hand hooks around my ankle, and what feels like all his might pushes against me, his face growing red from exertion, frantic to throw me off him.

And he might have, had I not lifted the shovel and swung it at his head.

Raising the shovel one more time, I throw his arrogant words back at him.

"Third time's the charm."

49

Meredith

Under the pale morning light, Lorette works to pin my hair away from my face and neck in a crown of braids by the newly placed vanity in Ethan's bedroom. *It's your bedroom too now*, I remind myself. Ethan left before dawn to go over last-minute details with Councilor Milus, looking every bit a dashing soldier in his fur coat and shiny armor.

I'm frowning at my reflection in the mirror, unhappy with the bulky breastplate covering the bodice of my lapis lazuli linen dress, when the steward announces Heloise at the door. Lorette steps back from my hair and follows me into the sitting room. It takes me a second to register Heloise's appearance. Her top half is adorned in the usual jewel-studded brocade bodice over a silk chemise. But her legs—*Maker, she's wearing trousers!* I gape at her in shock and envy; Lorette has the good sense not to gasp in horror, though her mouth is probably as slack jawed as mine.

"I look that good, do I?" Heloise croons.

Two servants follow her in, carrying a large box tied with a red satin ribbon.

"What's this?" I ask when they set it on one of the tea tables.

Heloise teases me with a perfectly raised brow. "Open it."

I'm at the table in two strides, lifting the top off the leather-stitched box. I draw in a breath at the sight of its contents.

A neatly arranged plate armor.

The steel helmet is the first thing to catch my eye, its visor cut in the shape of a sleek *T*. Gingerly, I pick it up with both hands, admiring the etching on the front.

"Try it on," Heloise says when I glance at her in question.

Unable to hold back a smile, I lift the helmet over my braided hair and slip it on.

It fits like a glove.

"I may have blackmailed the seamstress for your measurements," Heloise quips, pleased with herself.

The visor's metal edges frame my field of vision, marginally restricting it. I wonder if I'll glimpse a battle through it. My fingers eagerly trace the golden scroll patterns embossed on the pauldrons and couters and over the breastplate and plackart. It matches perfectly with the painted gold trim outlining the edges of the many steel pieces that make up the armor. Feminine curves mold the chest and waist. I pick up an arm guard, marveling at how light it feels in my hands. But the most remarkable feature of all lies below the leather belt and the tasset: a pair of cuisses and greaves.

I'll be clad like a proper warrior, with no skirts to get in my way.

"Hel . . . did you make this?"

A hand at her waist, she tilts her hip up. "I'm offended you have to ask; blacksmiths have no sense of fashion."

"I . . . I don't know what to say."

"A thank you would suffice."

"Thank you," I say, feeling equal parts thrilled and spoiled.

Heloise and I smile at each other like a pair of giddy girls with new gowns for the ball.

"We'll be the most fashionable soldiers in the battlefield," she beams.

My elation deflates a little at that. I can't help it. What she said to me in her rooms, it hasn't left my thoughts. I'm torn. Part of me wants her to come, comforted beyond words, knowing that she will, but another part of me dreads what might happen.

Am I prepared to lose her, too?

"Are you sure you won't stay, Hel?"

Heloise looks at me like she can't believe I dared to ask such a question. "And let you have all the fun? Besides, I've never been to Stonefall. I'd love to see it." I manage a weak smile, and her obsidian eyes asses me. "Are you this smothering with all your friends back home?"

"You make it sound as though there's so many," I say with a laugh. "But yes, if you must know, so don't think yourself special."

Heloise steps close, her hands cupping my shoulders under her confident grip. "You are welcome to worry all you like, Your Highness. But if we are forced into battle, you best clear that royal head and focus your sword on the enemy. I don't want anyone else filling those queenly boots of yours."

I bite my lip and stare at my friend. Her esteem isn't unexpected, but I'm grateful nonetheless.

Heloise claps her hands through my stupor. "Are you going to remove that dreadful breastplate, or will I have to do it for you?"

Satisfied with the perfect fit of my armor, Heloise departs with her servants to put on her own steel, and I realize Lorette's scuttled back to the bedroom. I find her out in the balcony, hands on the thick stone railing, one of them still holding my blue dress, staring into the silvery horizon of clouds and snowy mountains. I join her, drawing a lungful of pine-scented air as a soft breeze caresses my face with its cold tendrils.

"It's been an honor to serve you, Your Highness," she says without looking at me, her voice void of the disapproval I've grown accustomed to. But the glistening of tears she stubbornly fights back makes me forget about myself for a moment. My future is uncertain and bleak at best, but so is hers. With me gone to Stonefall and Queen Edith dead, she'll have to find work elsewhere.

I clasp her hands at my chest, forcing her to face me. "I pray we meet again. Take care of yourself, Lorette."

"Maker's blessing, Your Highness."

I remain on the balcony and wait for her to leave before I say my own good-byes to this place. It had just started to feel like home. I can only hope I will live to see it again.

The freedom of walking through the halls without a bundle of swishing skirts is a joy of its own. I still can't believe I'm wearing trousers. Anabella would be ripping her hair out in horror if she were here; the thought brings a smile to my face.

As expected, I draw the stares of every person I cross paths with, servant and courtier alike. But for the first time in all my life, their gazes do not appear to judge me. I'm not sure what it is I see reflected in their eyes, but it fills me with an odd sense of reassurance—it emboldens me, instilling confidence in my stride. It's as if, for once, doing the right thing and following my heart are one and the same. Perhaps Heloise is right. Perhaps this is the turning point of an era, and I am but a witness to its roots taking hold.

And then there's the look on Ethan's face when he sees me.

Outside the stables, he is mounted on his horse, a white-spotted gray mare, mindlessly stroking its shiny black mane while muttering something to Lief, who sits on Daisy's saddle. Sunlight glints off Ethan's slicked-back hair as his eyes accidentally find me. His lips part in surprise, and I can't help but smile. The nobles who volunteered to march with us are here, too, their armors covered under fine fur and leather surcoats. I'm pleased at myself for recognizing them: the Earl of Campeon; Baron Apel and his son, Will; and Lord Whitefield, whom, I was told, is one of the wealthiest merchants in the city. Seven other horses are saddled. I recognize Heloise's black steed among them, so the others must belong to her family. It's not as large a group of volunteers as I expected from Alder's court, given its size, but I suppose war does have a way of filling normally courageous men with fear.

Treading through the snow-wet mud, my hands—so accustomed to dresses—seek to lift the ghost of a skirt; it's an odd sensation not to find any fabric to latch on to.

"Now there's something I've never seen," Ethan says, eyes roaming over me in a way that burns my cheeks. "The steel suits you."

"You can thank Heloise," I say, who arrives not a second later, accompanied by her father and band of armored brothers. She looks like a deadly masterpiece, outfitted head to toe in an onyx steel armor. If I didn't know any better, I'd think her their leader.

Humphrey's lips lift at the corners, appraising my armor. "See brothers, this is why you should always strive to be on Hel's good side. You never know what she'll craft with the hammer."

"Frankly, I'm a little hurt, Hel. You've never made armor for any of us," Marcus mutters, arms crossed at his chest.

Heloise walks to her horse and slips her foot in the stirrup, smearing it with the mud off her boot. She mounts in one smooth motion. I shouldn't be surprised that the steed's coat blends with her armor. Heloise adjusts herself in the saddle and flips her loose, silky hair over her shoulders. "I've made fine swords for the lot of you, which—I might add—you all seem to be carrying. So if I hear another complaint, I'll strip you of them," she tells her brothers, and snickers and chuckles rise all around.

I step over to Daisy, resting my temple at the base of her neck. I close my eyes for a moment, breathing her in. The scent brings me back home, to days where all I had to worry about was completing my lessons and pleasing Father . . . and to think I believed my cousin Charlotte was the worst of my troubles. Maker, was I naïve.

"Are you all right, my lady?" Lief asks.

I glance up at him, smiling wistfully. He sits straight in his saddle, wearing his blue-and-gold guard armor with pride. "As well as one can be at such a time, I suppose."

Lief nods, his lips a resolute line. "Whatever awaits us, we'll make the best of it."

"That's the spirit," Ethan chimes in, flashing us that charming, confident grin—I hadn't realized how much I'd missed that smile—but after I mount Diago, Ethan's expression sobers. He is walking his horse to the center of our gathering, drawing the group's attention. "Our army awaits us. If anyone is having second thoughts, now is the time to make your sentiments known." His austere gaze combs through all thirteen of us. "Should you choose to stay behind, we will hold no judgment. But should you choose to continue on this journey, Princess Meredith and I will be honored to have you by our side." The men's eyes shift to me for a brief moment. It's strange being called a princess when everyone looks at you as a queen. Perhaps after I'm crowned, I'll feel more like one.

If I'm crowned. There are no guarantees we'll return.

I try not to think about that, about what it will mean for our people—for the world—should we fail.

All eyes are on Ethan now, their gazes glinting with a solemn reverence that prickles my skin. Ethan nods, pleased at their silence. Then he turns to me and extends his hand, palm open and waiting for mine. I nudge Diago with my heels and guide us to Ethan's side. His dimpled smile returns when I reach for his outstretched hand. Shoulders squared and head held high, he declares, "We forge ahead, then. Onward, to Stonefall."

50

Connor

Julius is dead. The blow to his temple wasn't meant to kill him, but it's better this way.

I undo his leather belt and fasten it around my waist, sliding his sword in the scabbard. Not my weapon of choice, but it will do. I scoop hay in my arms and rustle it over Julius's body; that's as good a grave as he's gonna get. Beside the sentries perched up top in the rampart, there are no patrols tonight. I move to each of the stalls in the stables, pushing the latches open. *So long as the horses are free to run, they might survive.* Laughter echoes from the distant mess hall over inebriated shouts and the low murmur of conversation.

Then—amid the huffing breaths of the horses—footsteps.

A mouse skitters across the straw-scattered ground.

Treading. Scraping.

I spin around, and level the longsword at—

"Gods, you're a hard man t' find."

"Rhys?"

"Should've guessed you'd choose t' escape tonight." He scampers into the stables like a dirty, nondescript shadow. His face is a little scraped up, and his curly hair is frizzy and wild, but he looks well enough. Are those the jail servant's clothes he's wearing? The garb is identical, down to the frayed hem of the tunic. Smells like him, too.

I grab his shoulder and pin him to the rough wooden wall before he gets a chance to open his mouth. "What are you doing here?" I get in his face. "How the hell did you get inside the fort? And where's Raven?"

"Good t' see you, too," he wheezes, palms in the air, grimacing. At the press of my forearm against his chest, he hurries to say, "Oh, bugger off—we don't have time for this! You have t' come with me now!"

I release him but keep him cornered. "We're not going anywhere until you explain yourself."

He stammers, "Raven and I didn't know what t' do after you were captured—we barely escaped ourselves, thanks t' you—but then we heard about the upcoming celebration, figured it'd be our only chance at getting ya out."

"That doesn't explain how you got in."

"There's a secret tunnel under Vishal's rooms, built in case o' a siege. It leads north, t' the Willow Oak woods. Raven waits for us there."

My rigid shoulders loosen a tad. Good news at last—a welcome change after weeks of this miserable place.

But Rhys isn't off the hook just yet.

"And you knew of this tunnel how?"

Rhys's face flushes. He lowers his head, cowering from my

scrutiny, shrinking inwardly. I'm about to shake him back to his senses when he hisses, "If you tell Uther—if you tell anyone—I swear I'll kill ya." Though we both know I'd knock his teeth out if he tried, I nod. It takes him a second to spit it out. "I was . . . I used t' be Vishal's servant. I spent two years o' my life washing his linens and serving his food."

The words sink in . . . the Sunderian child that fled. Uther speculated about the fort's location while his right-hand man knew it all along. "That was *you*? You're the Sunderian boy who escaped." I think I understand Rhys's fear of redcloaks. It's attached to this place, to whatever nightmares he lived through before he escaped. It would explain his paranoia after we were first caught in Locke, how he knew we'd be sent here. Yet here he is, putting himself back in the last place in the world he probably wants to be. But why the shame and secrecy? He served Vishal against his will.

Rhys stares. "You knew?"

"Felix spoke of you."

"Peanut? He's still here?" he asks, but doesn't wait for an affirmation. "Never mind. We have t' go. I know Vishal's schedule. Once he returns t' his rooms, he won't leave them again till dawn, and he'll know something's amiss when breakfast isn't on the table."

"What did you do to his servant?"

He gives me a scathing look. "*Gods*, you think I killed the poor bastard?" he balks, offended like he's some kind of saint. "I only knocked his lights out, took his clothes, and tied him up; can't have him raising alarms when he wakes."

It probably escapes Rhys's mind that the servant will be punished for that. Or he simply doesn't care. "You said you know Vishal's schedule. Where is he now?" I ask.

"Why do you want t' know?"

"Because I can't leave this place until he's dead."

Rhys almost laughs, but the sound dies in his throat under my gaze.

"You can't be serious. You'll get caught!"

"Rhys, Vishal knows everything—he knows where the hideout is."

Rhys goes still. His eyebrows shoot up with disbelief. He looks at me very hard, and in a seething whisper, he says, "*You gave us up*? You bast—"

I intercept his fist before it connects with my jaw. "I was drugged, I had no control," I rush to say. "Someone else told Vishal about the Brotherhood."

He squints at me, face tight and skeptical, debating whether he still wants to punch me or not. "What did they give you?"

"Noxtail."

I search his face for signs of awareness, but it scrunches in ignorance. His fisted hand loosens in my grip.

"Noxtail?"

"I'll explain later. Just tell me what I need to know. I'll meet up with you at the tunnel."

"The commander should be at the treasury. He works on the ledger and reads reports well into the night."

"Even tonight?" I ask, just to be sure; high-ranking officers don't tend to consort with their soldiers.

"Vishal isn't a man who celebrates things."

"Good. Where's the treasury?"

"You can't simply stroll in there. Place is guarded."

"I'm not an idiot, Rhys."

"So what's your plan?"

"I'm setting this place on fire. You know the rest."

Rhys's eyes nearly pop out of their sockets.

"For the last time, Rhys, how do I get to the treasury?"

Rhys falls silent, searching the stables as if the answer he seeks is somewhere in the shadows. He's afraid, I see it in the gleam of his eyes.

But we've wasted enough time. And the hammering in my head is killing me.

"Rhys," I press.

He sweeps a hand across his forehead to wipe the sweat off his brow, and with a loud, uncertain breath he says, "I'm coming with you."

I stick to the walls like plaster to avoid the sentry eyes above. Their job is to watch for attacks coming from outside the fort, but I can't take any chances. I must make haste, though. A quick estimate in my head wagers I have no more than five minutes before

Rhys lights the barracks on fire. They should be empty. Any redcloak who is not on duty tonight is enjoying himself at the mess hall. Though, if anyone is inside those barracks, they're likely asleep; I'd hate to be that chum. A minute at most after that before the flames garner attention. I'm counting on the proximity of the buildings and the thatched roofs to spread the fire quickly.

As Rhys knows his way around the fort, I entrusted him the task. We split up at the stables and agreed to rendezvous outside the treasury. That he came back here for me is more than I ever would have given him credit for. Doubtless, Raven is behind it. But Rhys chose to stay and help me fight of his own will. I can almost forget what he did to Pip—almost. I wouldn't go as far as to say I like him, but the bastard is like a weed—he grows on you.

Hand on the hilt of Julius's sword, I listen for voices and footsteps in the windless night. Every noise seems to be coming from the mess hall, which makes it easy to track. I cross from one building's awning to another, bathed in moonlight for no more than a couple of seconds. I avoid the torches on the walls and posts, skirting around them in the shadows. I peer over a corner a couple dozen paces from the mess hall. The inside of the longhouse building is packed with redcloaks. Smoke holes overhead spew the smoke of the fire pits. No windows, only doors on either side of the hall. Is Felix in there? My gut says he's holed up in some servant's quarters. I should have asked Rhys. *I really hope you survive this, Felix.*

I glance up, checking for alert sentries. The one left of me is on the move, bow angled on his shoulder, headed west on the palisade rampart. I freeze, steps from cover, fully exposed in the moon's silver light. Dashing for the mess hall's awning might draw the sentry's attention. I hold my breath and wait for him to put enough distance—

He turns.

I lunge under the awning.

Maker's hell.

I cleave to the wattle wall, hard pressed for breath.

Did he see me? It's hard to listen with all the noise.

I lurk to the mess hall's door regardless; arrows can't hit me from under here. The creak in the wood goes unheard over the thrum of celebration. I push the latch into the lock. *One more to go*. They'll kick the doors down at some point, but I'm hoping the delay will lend me the time I need. I hurtle to the other side. The doors are closed but unlocked. In seconds, my task is complete.

The bulk of the fort's forces are locked inside.

Slowly, I risk a peek at the rampart. The sentry is back at his post, his back to me, preoccupied with the total darkness surrounding the fort. He won't be for long, though; I need to get to the treasury.

Head northeast from the mess hall, Rhys instructed. *You'll pass a storehouse and a freshwater well. Look for the dwelling with a chimney and a batten door*.

In a half crouch, I head east among the shadows, then north, seesawing around the torches. I see the well's stony lip ahead. No redcloaks in sight. But once Rhys lights the fire, the soldiers at the gate and the sentries up top will come running to fetch buckets of water, so I divert my path one block over.

I come up on the treasury through the back, its clay chimney pointing me to it. I ghost along its perimeter, sword unsheathed and gripped in my right hand. One look over the edge shows two silent guards out front. No sign of Rhys yet.

In less than a minute, the western perimeter is aflame. I smell the smoke before its silvery wisps curl around me. Urgent shouts spill from the rampart, followed by the boom of drums—the sentries are sounding off the alarm. Had I not locked the mess hall, the fort would be crawling with soldiers already. Back pressed to the wall, I listen as the treasury guards open the door to inform Vishal of the fire. Question is, will the commander try to leave with them or stay behind to guard the coin?

The smoke doubles by the minute. It's not long before it stings my eyes and forces me to crouch lower on the ground.

"It's coming from the barracks, my lord," a redcloak says.

"Where is everyone?" Vishal barks when he steps outside the treasury to see for himself.

"Most men were at the mess hall, my lord," the other redcloak reminds him.

"Symon, go check on the mess hall. Darian, you come with me."

Dammit.

Their boots pound into motion.

From the shadows, I spring forward.

My sword stabs into the back of the nearest redcloak with enough force to pierce the leather and mail—and his kidney. The other redcloak draws his sword and attacks. I thrust my still-embedded sword sideways, shielding myself with the wounded soldier just as the second redcloak jabs his sword. The blade cuts through his comrade and juts out from his back, its tip puncturing my groin. I stare into the shocked redcloak's face for a split second before Vishal takes a swing at me—I duck under it, yanking my sword out as I do. Vishal slices the shoulder of the dead soldier instead. I grit my teeth and rush Vishal, shoulder to sternum, knocking him down. His head hits the ground like whiplash. I aim for his throat, but the second soldier forces my strike into a block. The blow pushes me to the dirt. I'm on my feet the next second, blocking another swing. The soldier is heavier than me. I strain under his strength, shooting pain in my left hand as my fingers tighten around the hilt.

Blocking him isn't the way to go.

I spin and evade his blade. In my periphery, Vishal lumbers to stand, unbalanced. The redcloak recovers and comes at me again, arms above his head. I charge, drop to my knees, and slide under him, my sword slicing a half-moon above me, cutting across his wrists. He screams and releases the weapon, and I plunge my sword under the skirt of his armor, ripping clean into him. Blood splatters my tunic and the ground around me as I pull my blade free. The soldier falls unceremoniously, gurgling words. Heart pounding in my temple, I rise and turn to the commander.

Where the hell is Rhys?

Vishal sweeps his sword off the ground and points it at me. We face each other. Our blades cross, crashing and hissing between us in a spurt of parries. My hand is on fire. Vishal doesn't fight like his men. He deflects more than he charges, and when he does, it's calculated. As we circle for a chance to attack, his cold-blooded eyes gauge me. But this cannot go on forever. I let instinct guide me and wait for an opening between parries. Knowing he'll block me, I feint a thrust forward, expecting the turn of his heel to strike from behind. He does. I elbow him hard on the nose. Vishal reels with the blow, and I plunge my blade in his abdomen, but at the expense of a counter cut up the side of my leg.

"No!"

Felix runs toward us—toward the commander.

Ash stains his face and most of his tunic; he's come from the fire.

Vishal stumbles back several steps, holding blood-soaked fingers to his wound. Felix appears at his side, lending his small frame to help support him, glaring at me through watery eyes.

Trying to understand is pointless.

"I can't let him live, Felix," I rasp.

"You'll have to get through him first!" Felix's small chin points behind me.

Far down the path, from out of the smoke, comes a large figure. The blazing wall of fire that used to be the barracks burns behind him; it's starting to spread now to the adjacent buildings.

I know him; I never saw his face when he threw me in that pit of death, but a man that size is hard to forget.

And I'm in no shape to fight him.

He's on me like a bull, deflecting my sword and swatting me like a fly. Needles of pain explode at the back of my head. I blink, realizing I'm on the ground.

Gorgos's giant hand clutches my collar and lifts me in the air, bringing me eye to eye with the mammoth. His head is twice the size of mine. Spittle lands on my face as he growls, "Playtime's over."

51

Meredith

Like a dome on the snowy outskirts of Alder City, the cobble-work garrison stands guard under a cloud-streaked sky. Around it and beyond, a sea of unoccupied tents and blue-and-gold banners sprawl across the white landscape as a grim reminder of what's been lost. Marching south, a column formation of soldiers on foot stretches for miles behind us, where the leathers and furs and the blue-and-gold battle banners merge with the horizon. The higher-ranking soldiers wear steel under their furs and ride abreast on horseback, setting the pace for the rest of the men. Snow crunching underfoot, we lead the marching battalion, tailed by horses and donkeys that pull wagons upon wagons of barreled provisions and supplies. The soldier's kin—people who own no estates—have the freedom to volunteer and help feed and clean the troops. It's they who steer the wagons, riding inside or flanking them on foot. Peaks and mountain ranges border the land, painted across the sky in wide brush strokes. I could no sooner avoid smelling pine or feeling the cold. I hate that I can no longer look at those peaks without thinking of the Lucari boy and his lifeless eyes. Are there Lucari up there now, gazing down at us like we're a herd of cattle ripe for the picking? I shudder at the thought.

It's astonishing how much longer it takes to make progress when you travel with an army. Eventually, our path leads us to a mile-wide embankment of a sweeping and completely frozen lake. The thousands of soldiers in the battalion would almost fill its spanning length. Mountains circle around it in the distance like indomitable walls, creating an eerily beautiful view.

I glance behind me at Lief. "Did we cross this lake on our way to Alder City?" Winter had yet to arrive then, which means this lake can't have been frozen. As numb and detached as I was then, I think I would have remembered riding on a boat.

"We bypassed around the mountain through King's Ledge, my lady."

"Frozen Lake is a more direct path," Ethan explains to my left, slowing down his horse so that I catch up. "The only caveat is that we must cross slowly and not all at once; too much weight, and the ice could crack."

"Why not take King's Ledge then?" I ask.

Ethan dismounts. "The road's too narrow, and it would add leagues to our journey." He unties the waterskin off his saddle and steals a quick sip from it.

I squint up at the mountain range, spotting the snaking outline of a trail in the crags high above. The path seems to cut across the mountain ridge in the same direction of the lake; a direct path, albeit an impractical one, likely dangerous too, and not just from the terrain.

I point at the distant trail. "That's Lucari territory, isn't it?"

The name elicits sideways glances from our traveling party of nobles.

Ethan looks up. His nod is grim. "The Sunvale," he calls it.

"Has anyone ever set foot up there?" I ask.

I turn my head to the sound of Hel's snort. "Only those with a death wish."

While we cross the lake with our group of nobles, Lief, and several other soldiers, the field marshal remains at the bank and orders carefully timed groups of no more than twenty to cross after us, leaving the battalion at a standstill. Over the frozen lake, the hooves of our horses push the thin layer of snow aside, revealing ice so thick you can't see through it. Patches of dried weeds mark the bank at the other side, where we soon dismount and choose a place to camp. Four other groups and a provisions wagon make it across the lake before dusk, at which point the field marshal stops the flow of soldiers for the night, to be resumed at dawn. At both sides of the lake, fires are lighted, dinner is boiled, and double-belled wedge tents are set on poles. It's a ruckus of chattering and clattering. You could close your eyes and think you're in the middle of a market square.

Our group settles around the fire the Cresten brothers started, enjoying a bowl of boiled grains. I look at the faces around me and wonder if there is fear hidden beneath the armor and honor. I find only smiles and laughter. They share their favorite stories and sip their best wine with easy smiles and relaxed shoulders, as though there isn't a camped army in their midst. Perhaps it's the only thing one can do in times like these. I, too, should enjoy the night. I should forget about our uncertain future and appreciate the present before it's gone. So I sip the dry wine in my hand and smile when I ought to, and pretend my conflicted heart isn't rattled to its core.

But Heloise sees right through me.

"It's all right to be scared," she whispers as the men laugh at something I didn't hear.

"Is it?" I ask.

"You don't think *I'm* afraid?"

I glance at her, searching for traces of uncertainty in her confident features. "You don't look it."

"Because I'm a master in the art of deception . . . among many other things."

I chuckle at that. Then, in a quiet voice, I ask, "But isn't this your calling?"

She gazes up at the scrap of full moon peeking through the canopy of evergreens, her face glowing under the firelight. "Until a few weeks ago, it was but a dream."

"Fathom that, your dream is my nightmare," I mutter.

"It's not the bloodshed that draws me to it," she says, reading my thoughts. "To this day, I've wielded my sword without shedding a drop, and still, I get lost in the thrill of it, as though the sword and I are one and the same."

Different as we are, I understand exactly how she feels. Before I'd come to Alder, I would have named music as my calling.

I'd get lost in the thrill of the piano, the feeling of my fingers striking the keys. But its beauty no longer touches my soul the way it used to. Nothing does. Not anymore. "Then you have nothing to fear," I say.

She thinks about that for a moment, glancing at her brothers, who are having a turn at tasting Lord Whitefield's wine; the merchant claims his wine is better than the prized Far Water wine. "I fear failure."

A bitter smile tugs at my heart. "That sounds like something he would say."

My melancholy whisper isn't meant for Heloise's ears, but, catching the fleeting words, she asks anyway.

"Who?"

"Someone I used to know."

Not long after that, we retire to our tents. The fur blanket Ethan and I roll out does little to soften the bits of rock that poke my back, but as I know all too well, a day's worth of travel makes even the most unforgiving surfaces comfortable. Ethan helps me out of my armor, and without a word, he scoops me close on the blanket, his arms strong and warm, bringing more comfort than words ever could. It's strange how quickly I've grown accustomed to him, to the expectation of his touch and the feel of his lips. My glances strayed his way often during our journey here, surprised at my longing for his embrace. It scares me as much as it thrills me, but fighting against my own feelings is a battle I will never win; loving Connor taught me as much.

It takes three days for the entire battalion to make its way across Frozen Lake. By then, the tents have been dismantled and our supplies stashed away, ready to continue our journey. As we press on, the landscape starts changing. The bite of the cold lessens, and the never ending snow thins to a peppery sprinkle that clings to dead grass and leafless boughs. We move with the sun, stopping at creeks and rivers along the way to rinse off and restock our water supply. Heloise and I clean up in privacy with the other ladies before the swarm of men can flock to the cool water. We eat one bowl of oatmeal gruel at dinner, fending off hunger throughout the day by nibbling on walnuts and dried prunes. To my disappointment, the exhilaration of wearing armor erodes with each day; it becomes more and more cumbersome, giving me another reason to await sundown.

Since my conversation with Heloise, Connor has been ever present in my dark thoughts. As I ride abreast with Ethan and Lief, I fail to shut out his memory. It's not that I don't want to think of him, only I wish I could do it without that raw feeling sweeping over me, the feeling that sharpens the closer we get to Far Water. Inevitably, we tread the narrow path that cuts through the fated forest. This haunting place has invaded my nightmares many times, so much so that it leaves me blank to see it in the flesh, and under the full light of day, no less, its smell of damp earth and fallen leaves lacking the metallic tang of blood.

A few horses behind, I can hear Heloise poking fun at something, which draws a gripe from Marcus, but I don't hear what it is. My mind is haunted, reliving that night. Burning with hatred, my shaking hands grip Diago's reins tighter. It takes everything I have to stop seeing the flash of moonlight reflected on Elijah's dagger before it plunges into Holt's chest.

"This is where we met, my lady," Lief says, and the darkness in my head hisses like smoke as it vanishes. He trots up the small gap between our horses, wearing a proud smile.

"How could I forget?" I say, sporting a smile to match his, but Lief's knowing eyes spear me with sympathy, sensing the turmoil behind my smile. He was there, after all, an accidental witness to the shattering of my soul, along with all the other guards stationed at the outpost—who avoided me as though I was cursed. But not Lief. He looked after me, even when I didn't welcome it, and offered me food I had no stomach for, insistent that I eat. I tuck my eyes away from Lief's, grateful for his silence.

It's Ethan who lays my wound bare.

"These are the woods where Elijah took him?" he asks through a flexed jaw.

I'd exiled this from my mind since Elijah's arrival at Alder Castle, wishing never to think of it again. Knowing Connor lived beyond that night is in many ways more painful than his death. Would I have been able to find him, had I known? Would he be alive today if I had?

"Yes, Your Highness," Lief answers when I don't.

I dare a look at Ethan then and find a dark cloud whirring in his eyes, but that darkness brightens a little when he catches my gaze.

As it was in the handful of towns we crossed before, the people of Far Water line the paved streets of the quaint town to watch what's left of their army march by. The children bear grins and awe, at odds with the uneasy looks of the parents who hold them close. Their future is in our hands. Knowing this only adds to the burden. A burden that weighs like an anvil on my shoulders.

There is so much at stake, and so few choices.

After days of travel, the Borderlands are near at hand. The valley is starkly different from when I last saw it. Beneath the dull gray skies that hint of cold rain, where once stood a sea of stiff wheat bristles, there are far and wide stretches of muddy soil dotted with the green growth of dormant crops, blanketed by a vast, white haze that looms as far as the eye can see to the feet of the Tellinor Mountains. Two miles in, the haze thickens to a dense fog, making it hard to maintain direction.

"Your Highness," the field marshal says to Ethan. There's something in the fog.

I stare at the oak barks and the iron spikes buried in the mud, dumbfounded. An incomplete portcullis and a fraction of a barbican. Fortifications of a castle or keep. Anticipation furrows in my chest at the sight of it, building up and tensing my shoulders with each gentle stomp of Diago's hooves.

The building Jessamine spoke of . . . this must be it. A flash of shame comes to me as I realize I never bothered to ask after the troop of guards King Perceval sent here. I've been so consumed with revenge that it escaped my thoughts.

"That wasn't there before," I say to Ethan, who in turn narrows his eyes at the imposing structure, probably thinking the same as I. "Did your father's guards say anything about it?"

The mention of the king's scouting party brings an ominous gleam to Ethan's eyes. "They never returned," he answers.

"Sir," a voice calls out to the field marshal. The three of us turn to a soldier in armored leather, pointing a finger west of the half-built portcullis.

Up ahead, silhouettes break through the fog like ghosts, a party of six men on horseback, coming toward us on the road. Splinters of light that barely penetrate the mist glint off their spear points like beacons, and the entire battalion seems to wait silently, listening to the steady thump of hooves grow louder. That's when—straining to get a good look—I discern the marks on their faces.

A sharp breath leaves my parted lips.

Ethan's eyes cut to me. Reading my face, he asks, "Borderlords?"

I nod, fearing my voice will tremble if I dare speak. These are not the sickle and pitchfork men I envisioned. No, these are horse riders armed with spears, warriors perhaps, with hair as long as that of a lady, unbound and rippling at their backs. Though there are only six of them, it's more Borderlords than I ever care to see in my lifetime. The unbidden image of the one who attacked Jessamine's farm burns in my mind—the snake tattooed across his face, the panic I felt when I tried to escape, how consumed I was by it as he caught and dragged me away, stopped only by the grace of Connor's infallible aim.

If I were to face him again, I know I'd still be afraid, but I wouldn't run.

"Colorful lot, aren't they?" comes Heloise's sly remark amid the sudden tension. Everyone else remains silent.

"Stay here with the soldiers," Ethan says to me.

But I shake my head. "Together, remember?"

Ethan's mouth tightens, ready to deny me. He doesn't. "Together."

We ride out to greet the Borderlord horsemen, accompanied by Lief, the marshal, and two of his commanders. Despite myself, fear coils around my throat, choking me, even as a rational voice in my head says there is nothing to be afraid of, reminding me of the five thousand soldiers behind me, but even though the Borderlords are outnumbered, I'd be a fool to think they mean us no harm. Up close, I take them in, their thick beards and their belted tunics and leather arm guards. Nearly identical tattoos of the green snake paint their faces from ear to ear, dissimilar in as much as copied text ought to be, but the man in the middle, the one flanked by green snakes . . . he wears a different snake. The right side of his face is covered in black ink, a snake's tail painted down the side of his neck. Its menacing yellow eyes and bared fangs nearly cover his forehead.

"Is the king of Alder among you?" the black snake asks.

"King's dead," Ethan says evenly, as though those very words don't tear him up inside. "I'm in charge now."

The black snake looks at Ethan with hard, savage eyes. "And who might you be, *boy*?"

"The crown prince," the marshal answers in a booming voice, one fit for a man in charge of a battalion.

"Are you Zagar?" I blurt out, remembering the Borderlord leader's name Connor told me once.

The black snake's focus slithers to me, as though seeing me for the first time, and I bristle at his assaulting appraisal. He nudges his piebald horse forward, but stops when Ethan responds in kind. A canny smile pulls his lips back, and, with his eyes still pinned on me, he asks Ethan, "Is this your wench?"

Beside me, Lief's hand moves, poised to draw his sword.

I can hear the restraint in Ethan's voice. "She's my wife. You would do well to remember that."

The black snake chuckles, drawing amused grins from the green-snaked men herding him.

"Are you Zagar?" I ask again, interrupting their smiles.

This time the black snake does glance at Ethan. "Do all men in Alder let their women speak for them?"

Ethan's smile is hard. "Only the honorable ones."

The black snake's jaw clenches. When he speaks again, his wry lilt is replaced with vexation. "I am Karr, Zagar's fist."

"His *fist?*" Ethan asks, brow arched.

"Second-in-command," Karr clarifies. "I've come to fetch the ruler of Alder to dine with us." Looking down at me, he pauses and adds, "You may bring your *wife*, if you like."

"What does Zagar want?" I do my best not to sound defiant; I shouldn't goad him, no matter how much I wish it.

"You'll have to ask him that yourself," comes Karr's reply. The lilt in his voice is back.

Ethan looks over his shoulder at the throng of Alderian soldiers. They wait like effigies in the mist, ready to follow orders. "If your leader wishes an audience, it is he who must come, not I," he says. "I will not be lured away from my army."

"Then there will be no meeting," Karr snarls. "Zagar has information you seek, but he will not place himself in a position where it may be taken from him unwillingly."

Ethan's eyes narrow. He lifts his chin. "What information?"

"The location of your enemy's troops," Karr taunts.

"We already have that information," I say.

Karr's eyes brighten as though I've just given him what he wants. "Do you?" He nudges his horse, closing in. "You think your enemy is holed up in that crumbling kingdom of yours?" His chuckle mocks me. "You think you'll take Elijah by surprise with your mighty army?"

My eyes widen slightly. "How do you know all this?"

"Elijah said you'd come with five thousand men." Stretching his neck, Karr takes a gander behind us. "I'd say that looks about right."

I balk at the Borderlord.

For that to be true, it would mean the fifth battalion's evasion of the plague was no accident. Just how deep does Elijah's treachery run?

Ethan loses his poise. "*Where is Elijah?*"

This makes the black snake laugh. "You think Zagar would let me venture after you with that information in my head? He'd feed me to the wolves himself if I knew."

"Has he so little faith in his *fist*?" I bite my tongue the moment the words slip from my mouth. Out of the corner of my eye, Ethan's neck cranes with incredulity. My diplomatic skills, it appears, leave much to be desired. But I don't dare flick an apologetic glance in Ethan's direction, because the black snake is burning holes in my face with a murderous glare.

I grip the reins tight to steady my hands, waiting in feigned composure.

"I'd think twice before you speak again, Princess. A slip of the tongue like that in Zagar's presence will cost you dearly," he warns in a simmering voice.

I fight back the need to swallow my discomfort. The less he knows how frightening I find him, the better.

Ethan pushes his horse forward between Karr and me. "Precisely why we won't meet with him." Though he's regained his cool, his eyes are silent steel, the skin around them strained with anger.

Karr smirks contempt. "Have you no control of your woman?" Behind him, the rest of the snakes snicker. Lief hasn't moved an inch, his hand glued to his pommel, body rigid, ready to slash Borderlords at a moment's notice.

"I must insist," Ethan says over their mockery. "If Zagar wants to make a deal, it is *he* who will come. We'll wait for him. And should we fail to have an agreement, you have my word we will not use force against him or his men."

Karr wets his lips, the smirk not quite gone from his rugged face. "Your word?"

"On my honor as the crown prince."

"Your word means nothing to us," the black snake spits back. "All you jeweled folk have no spines. You prance around on your groomed horses in your shiny armor, and let your peasants kiss your hands as if you're the Maker's chosen, and yet you know nothing about war and conquest. Your enemy reaped the land while you hid behind your pretty castles and palaces, drinking your fine wines and dancing like fools. This"—he gestures at the foggy air around us with outstretched palms—"is your doing. Your father had the power to burn Talos to the ground, and he chose to do nothing. And look at you now, scurrying out of your nests with your tails between your legs."

Silence.

Repugnant as he is, the black snake's rebuke stings. I'm reminded of Krea, of her disdain of royalty, of our neglect of the Borderlands. It's not unlike Karr's scorn. Both sentiments justified. Only it's so much harder to agree with a savage who murders and steals.

It takes Ethan a moment to speak. "Our blind eyes have wronged the Eastern Kingdoms, this is true. But we are here to right to those wrongs. And we will lay down our lives for that purpose, if need be. So I ask again," Ethan says, growing fervent, "that you take me at my word."

Karr disregards Ethan's candor and refuses without a moment's thought. "If you wish to earn our trust, young prince, it is *you* who must take the leap of faith and take us at our word," comes his steadfast reply. "You either follow us and hear what Zagar has to say, or you leave and take your chances out there," he says, eyes pointed south to the fog-curtained horizon. To Stonefall. And whatever lies in store for us along the way. "Your choice."

Ethan turns to me, his gaze questioning, asking to be pushed in the right direction. But I am as stricken as he is. Trust the Borderlords? Making a deal with them is the last thing I want, but the black snake revealed just enough details to cast uncertainty in my heart. If what he says is true, we are playing into Elijah's game, and probably delivering what's left of Alder's army right into his clutches.

Seeing my indecision, Ethan turns to the black snake. "You seem awfully convinced I won't take you and your men as prisoners," he says, the words sharp and cold.

"We'd slice our own tongues off before we told you anything."

There is no mistaking the quiet viciousness of the man; he means what he says.

"We should leave someone in charge," I say to Ethan. "In case we don't come back."

Lief tries to object. "Your Highness—"

"You'll be in charge, Meredith," Ethan interjects. "There's no reason for the both of us to go."

My heart skips. The idea of him leaving with the Borderlords twists my insides with dread.

"Let me go in your stead," I offer.

Ethan's eyes narrow. His tone is low and scathing. "Absolutely not."

But I expected that. I've learned to expect it . . . this knee-jerk response from those I care about, their need to protect me. Seldom have I had the chance to be the protector.

It's time I changed that.

I lower my voice. "Ethan, you have been trained to rule—to lead. I was not," I remind him. "You are crucial to this war. Our army needs *you* at the helm. And if something were to happen to me, I know you'd fight for my people."

"As would you," he fires back, angry.

"I'd give it my best," I agree, ignoring his anger. "But we both know ruling a kingdom takes more than a well-intentioned heart."

He continues to stare at me, unblinking. "*No.*" His refusal carries all the weight of a king's command, but it does nothing to mute the desperate horror etched on his face, the same horror that courses through me. "No—you can't!" he says again to my defiant gaze. "What sort of man would let his wife be taken by Borderlords?"

"The sort of man who serves the people," I say softly, reminding him of Alder's creed, which he seems to have forgotten again, as he did back at the castle when Milus's life was at stake.

Ethan looks down at his hands, which seem to grip his reins as tightly as I grip mine. It takes him a moment to look up at me. "Are you sure you want to do this?" he whispers, eyes grim and dark and pleading.

I don't hesitate. "Yes," I answer, surprised at the steadiness of my voice. "I won't go alone. Lief will come with me," I add, determined to tip the balance in my favor, although saying it out loud makes my stomach queasy with dread. I don't want anyone to come along—Lief especially—despite the terrifying prospect of being surrounded by Borderlords, but I know Lief well enough to know nothing will persuade him to part from me. And to my shame, I can't help but be relieved.

At Ethan's reluctance to answer, I realize I've succeeded. The second he does, I know he will send me on my way, however unwillingly. But Karr mistakes Ethan's stalling for indecision and makes an impatient noise with his throat, prompting Ethan to act. "When should I expect you back?" he asks the black snake.

"At sundown." He holds a hand toward one of his men. "Seskel will stay behind as a token of our agreement."

"If you haven't returned by nightfall, I will track you down and kill every last one of you," Ethan snaps, to which Karr gives an off-putting smile.

Finally, Ethan looks at me, for what I can only hope isn't the last time. Defeat rounds his shoulders, stripping his eyes vacant, and it nearly breaks me. After a long, low sigh, he says in a toneless voice, "Go."

The invisible string that connects us spans the growing distance as Lief and I follow the Borderlords deep into the mist, and I can feel his eyes on me, shadowed with worry, begging me to look back. But I don't have the strength to convey what he needs to see, and one wrong look from me could undo everything. So I deny him, swallowing the lump in my throat, and force my uncertain gaze forward, praying I don't come to regret it.

52

Connor

Gorgos flings me with one flick of his arm, and I come crashing down on something that breaks. The adrenaline raging inside dulls the brunt of the pain. I lay on a bed of corn kernels and shattered wood, feeling sharp points at my back.

Gorgos has the upper hand and he knows it. He doesn't need a weapon; he can end me with his brute hands alone. Snap my neck. Break my spine. Crush my skull. Felix and Vishal are gone. It's hard to say if the wound I inflicted on the commander will send him to the Maker's gate. What I do know is that Felix will do everything he can to prevent that from happening.

Shouts burst from the western perimeter; the soldiers in the mess hall have broken free. I curse when I lay eyes on my sword, yards out of reach. I'll have to get past Gorgos to get it. That's not going to work. I grab the nearest object within reach: a shard of wood from the broken barrel. Gorgos strides toward me, looking like a demigod on a rampage, and I remind myself he's not invincible.

The mammoth's shadow looms over me in seconds. I drive the shard to the side of his neck. Gorgos roars, catches my arm as I try to retract the shard. He hauls me up above him and slams me down onto the ground. I feel the pain this time. It hurts just to breathe. *Maker, he's going to pulverize me*. When he lifts me up again, I pluck the shard from his neck and stab his shoulder. He drops me. I roll away, scrambling to get my legs under me and stand, but everything hurts. My aching limbs struggle to catch up with me, slowing me down.

Gorgos yanks on my arm so hard it pops out of its socket. My body jerks. The scream that claws from my throat is a beast of its own, loud and foreign. Gorgos swings me around to face him. My dangling body gives no resistance; I'm a puppet in his grip. His fist—easily the size of my head—hammers into my sternum, crushing my chest and emptying my lungs. I cave under his brute strength. Blood coats my tongue. I want to spit, but I can't get my mouth to cooperate. As I'm sprawled on the ground, Gorgos seizes me again, and when his beastly hands close around my neck, I know he's done toying with me. I paw with the one arm I can move. Useless. He squeezes my windpipe. My vision blurs.

I will fight for you.

Then I will hold on to hope.

Meredith's words drum in my ears. Our last moment together, before everything went wrong. I remember the fury, hell-bent on killing Elijah. But my wounds got the best of me. One moment I was fighting with my bare hands, the next I was tied up and gagged in a wagon.

And here I am now, staring death in the face.

Meredith . . . I tried . . . I'm sorry.

My vision is failing. My lungs burn. I'm slipping away. There's nothing beneath my feet. The darkness is a peaceful, timeless void in which I float. I embrace it and it embraces me, and I forget why I am here. I forget . . .

Something is wrong.

The stillness is disrupted, and something . . . something pulls me. I don't want to leave, but the pain—it's getting worse. I can't ignore it. A sharp ringing. Buzzing ripples through, humming in my ears. The darkness rejects me. It doesn't want me. I'm being carried away in a current of water. And I can't breathe.

I can't breathe.

"Breathe!"

Air fills my lungs in one raw, sharp intake of breath. I'm coughing. A blurred shadow watches me. It speaks to me in a slow, muffled voice. But then, all at once, my senses sharpen. I hear the flames, the distant yelling . . . someone's snarling.

"Raven," I try, but the sound is hoarse and unintelligible. What is she doing here? I swallow, and it hurts like all hells. I register Raven's frantic glances. Gorgos. The beast is pawing on a sword that sticks out from the back of his knee. Julius's sword.

That will slow him down, but it won't stop him.

Raven urges me to get up and run. But run where? Our escape route is compromised. If we make a run for the secret tunnel, Gorgos will chase us down, and in my current state, I won't get far. "We have to kill him," I wheeze.

"How?" she asks, helping me to my feet.

I watch Gorgos break the sword's blade in half with his bare hands and toss the pieces over his shoulder. He may have a limp, but we're still at a disadvantage.

"My shoulder." I point with my head. "It's dislocated."

Gorgos is set on finishing what he started, so Raven wastes no time. She pushes my torso to the ground and quickly gets a feel for the shoulder bone. Then she flops next to me, using her feet to hold me back while she clasps my wrist with both hands. She squeezes and tugs on my arm—

It's over in seconds, followed by a bursting bloom of hot, searing pain. Then, as I recover, a familiar sound slaps me to my senses. A distinctive *whizzing* in the air. I whip around at Gorgos's howl. He's cupping his right ear, glaring past us.

I jerk my head back. Atop the rampart, Rhys smiles down at us. In his hand is a sentry's bow.

"I told you I could shoot," he shouts. I'm too relieved to point out his target is the size of an elephant. Rhys leans back and flings the bow in the air. A second later, it scatters at my feet like a gift from the Maker himself, followed by the thump of its closed quiver. "Care to do the honors?"

Gorgos resumes his advance, moving impossibly fast, teeth bared and snarling like the wounded feral beast that he is. The trained archer in me takes over, moving by pure muscle memory. In those sparse seconds, the near-crippling pain in my chest is no longer a hindrance, my sore shoulder reduced to a nuisance. I grip the bow and knock an arrow over my index finger, pull the string taut at my cheek, and aim.

My arms are my temple, my target is my shrine, my arrow is my offering.

Gorgos is feet away, arms reaching, angling for my throat. At this distance, his armor is useless. But like a true warrior, Gorgos limps on, willing to risk his life on the off chance I will miss any vital organs.

I don't.

My fingers release the string, and the arrow shoots into Gorgos's chest, slightly to the left, right where I wanted it. But where Gorgos's life stops, his momentum doesn't. His body—already so close—comes crashing down in front of us, skidding to our feet and spraying dust on our faces.

Raven hesitantly nudges Gorgos with her boot until she's convinced he's dead. She stares at the inanimate body. "Gods, what a monster."

The haze provides plenty of cover, but it won't do us much good if a stray redcloak runs by, so I reach for Raven's elbow and walk us to a wall. I allow myself a brief moment of rest while Rhys climbs down the rampart unto a pile of crates. Tendrils of smoke scratch my parched throat. Dehydration and exhaustion are catching up with me, the feeling exacerbated by my wounds and bruises. I'm a mess of blood, grime, and sweat. But besides a few scrapes, my legs are unharmed, so I make do on my feet. With all the smoke, it's hard to see the redcloaks throwing water at the raging flames down the way.

"I knew you wouldn't stay in the woods," Rhys says to Raven when he joins us, a stolen sword in hand.

"I'm glad you didn't," I say.

Raven presses her lips into something of a smile. "I figured you could use an extra hand . . . and I needed t' make sure Rhys didn't run away."

Rhys scoffs at her. "I wasn't about t' let Connor get executed without saving his uptight rear first." He turns to me. "You saved my life before—I owed ya. And I may be an arse, but I'm an arse who pays his debts."

"Thanks," I say. "To both of you."

"Did you find Vishal?" Rhys asks.

"I wounded him, but he got away."

"We're the ones who need t' get away," Raven says, glancing between us. "Now's our chance."

Rhys's throat bobs. In a tight voice, he tells her, "The commander knows about the Brotherhood. He knows the location o' the camp. We have t' stop him."

Raven's eyes widen. Her chest rises and falls a few times before she speaks. "Where d'you think he ran off t'?"

"My guess is he's getting patched up in his quarters," I say.

We're silent, regarding each other with tired expressions until Raven says the obvious. "But that's our way out."

Rhys blows his cheeks out, then swallows the air back in to steel himself. "Let's go get the bastard."

53

Meredith

With Karr at the helm and his snakes at the rear, the single-file line of horses treads an unmarked path through the austere flatland. Lief rides close behind me. I don't have to turn around to see his anxiety, I can practically feel it, like a cloud of nerves floating around us, mingling with the fog. There isn't much to keep my eyes occupied, save for the parched vegetation crushed under Diago's hooves and the occasional bush that rattles as we pass. Everything else that might dot the landscape is swallowed by the cool, noiseless white mist that kisses my cheeks, and I can only marvel at how well acquainted Karr is with the territory. Navigating so effortlessly in such thick fog is impressive. I try to get a sense of the distance we travel as we lumber forward, except, without a point of reference, I quickly realize the feat is useless.

Even the passage of time seems illusory, as though the fog itself is an ageless realm. I curse its blinding presence. If only I could hear the scurry of a rodent, or the caw of a bird in flight, it would help dispel the etherealness of it all. But soon, the fog needles away to a thin, white layer, revealing the windswept remains of a farm at my left. At once, my thoughts turn to Jessamine. I trace the hazy field, searching for the place I once visited. There's a cottage held together by tenuous planks. It isn't Jessamine's. Ashamed once more at having forgotten all about her, I wonder what's become of her and her farm. I hope she's all right. And Krea . . . it's hard to imagine anything could happen to such a brash, headstrong girl. The memory of her bright scarlet hair . . . I can see it so clearly, like a red flicker out of the corner of my eye.

Lief's outraged cry rattles me back to the present.

We've stopped moving.

"The fog is lifting; I can't have you learn the way," Karr is saying, just as I feel someone from behind cover my eyes with a blindfold.

A pair of hands takes hold of mine before I can pull away. They yank me back into the saddle, tugging my arms sharply at my back and binding them with a coarse twine that scrapes my skin.

"Careful, Zohar," calls Karr. "Don't want the princess falling off her seat and breaking her pretty little neck." Behind me, I hear Lief struggle, fighting back in a series of grunts—then a loud thump.

"Lief!" I cry out, uselessly craning my head in his direction. The sliver of light below the blindfold reveals nothing. More grunts and yells follow, mingled with the snorts and neighs of the unsettled horses.

"You'll pay for that, kid," a snake growls. The whooshing scrape of a sword being drawn follows, and I feel the hair on my neck rise.

"Lief, don't resist!" I plead, and after a moment, the sound of sheathing metal signals his surrender.

I hate this, I think in despair, listening to Lief being tied up and blindfolded, seeing it in my head. I have no reason to trust Karr or any of the others, but it's not like I have a choice. If they mean to kill us, there's nothing Lief or I can do to stop them; resisting will only prolong the inevitable.

I brace for that moment to come, ears hot and hands numb, the tips of my fingers clamped around the back of my saddle to keep from falling off Diago, expecting it with every breath, thinking it might be my last. I focus on Diago's canter, listening for a change in pace. Listening for Lief, for any sign that something is amiss. My breath comes hard and strenuous, and the seconds feel like minutes, but despite the foreboding weight in my stomach, nothing happens. The horses trot the beaten path, trampling weeds as they go, and my muscles tire. I let myself unwind a little, and my frenzied heart lets up, allowing my breath to slow.

But then I flinch when Karr's voice echoes in my left ear.

"Don't relax just yet, Princess."

Diago halts, and I go very, *very* still.

Though I'm aware of the approaching hooves, I still shudder when I feel hands at my back. Freed from the rope, my hands spring to my face, and I tug at the blindfold, letting it fall to my neck as I take in the gathered snakes ahead, their camp sprawled behind them. My skin crawls with disgust. Human skulls. They're everywhere, strung up like curtains, dangling off the sides of tents and snaking around the supporting beams, skewered with strings through the gaping holes that once held eyes in them. Are these the remains of trespassers and pillagers? Is that what they do with them? Display them like trophies and decorations?

Or are these the skulls of victims?

Farmers like Jessamine, who refused to submit to their oppressive demands?

Towering over the men is another man with a black snake on his face. At first sight, I think it's Karr I'm staring at. But it can't be. Karr is at arm's length on his saddle. I squint at the stranger with the black snake, and upon closer inspection, I register the differences: the man is bald, with small gold hoop earrings, and his tattoo covers the left side of his face, not the right. A pair of ring swords is secured to the belt at his waist.

"I ask for a king and you bring me a girl," Zagar sneers at Karr.

I bite my lip. The menace in Zagar's rasping voice sends a quiver down my legs and to the tips of my numb toes. Lief appears at my side, Daisy abreast to Diago, nearly jamming our legs from the pressed weight of their flanks.

"The king is dead, my lord. This is the prince's wife, the Stonefall princess. She will speak for him."

Zagar's hard eyes narrow, piercing me with a look. "Only a coward would send a woman in his place."

I think about my response for a moment. Karr warned me to

watch my tongue, and whether he meant what he said or not, I'd rather not test my luck; Zagar looks like a man you don't want to say the wrong thing to.

"The prince agreed to meet with you, but I convinced him otherwise," I answer carefully. "He's indispensable to our cause."

Zagar cocks his head. "And you are not?"

Better that he think me insignificant. If this meeting is indeed a trap, the lie might keep me alive, so I don't contradict him. Instead, I say, "Should we come to an arrangement, the prince will honor my word."

Sensing my distrust, Zagar's cool features turn into a dangerous leer. "You think I'm going to kill you?" he muses.

"Are you?" I ask, heartbeat lurching. If that's his intention, I'd much rather face it head on than be surprised by a stab in the back.

"I haven't decided yet," he deliberates in a grave voice.

Gripping the reins with my left hand, I feel for the hilt of my sword with my right. This is what Borderlords do. They intimidate and take what they want, be it silver or food or lives. This is what they know. "If you kill me, none of us get what we want."

"I'm willing to live with the alternative," the Borderlord leader tells me, and from the look on his face, I know he means it.

"If you kill me," I say again in a fearless voice I don't recognize, "you won't live to choose the alternative."

Zagar smiles.

"I'm not afraid of death, girl. You, on the other hand . . ."

My blood runs cold. I stare, feeling helpless. Lief and I are at his mercy, as I suspected we would be. I didn't want to be right, but I'm glad I convinced Ethan to stay behind. Steeling myself, I proceed to dismount. Lief pulls Daisy over to give me room and then dismounts himself, joining me on the dead grass. I shoot him a quick, apologetic look. "I'm sorry for dragging you into this," I whisper.

"Where you go, I go, my lady."

He sounds more confident than I feel.

"Let's hope it isn't the Maker's gate, then," I say as he follows me toward the clan of snakes. With Karr and the others at our heel, we push through the congregation of Borderlords. The green-snaked men flanking Zagar point their axes at us, as though we might dare harm their fearsome leader.

I stop a few inches from Zagar's strapping form, close enough to converse but not so close as that he might stab me. Spatters of dried blood stain his weathered tunic, and I can't help but wonder if in the next moment, it will be stained anew. Zagar said he hasn't decided to kill me just yet, and if that's true, it means there's a chance he may not. But I get the feeling that decision hinges on my consent to his demands.

Determined, I turn my face up to meet his predatory eyes. Zagar looks down at me, unimpressed. "What is it you want?" I ask in feigned confidence.

"I want the Borderlands to be recognized as a sovereign kingdom," he says. "And I want to be proclaimed its ruler."

It doesn't come to me as a shock. I can't say it's an unreasonable request, either, not in and of itself. But if Jessamine were here, she would have denied Zagar in an instant. The Borderlord leader is an extortionist and a murderer, to say the least, and I doubt he'd be any different as the sovereign ruler of the Borderlands. Only he'd have complete control over the land and its people, and the wheat trade between our kingdoms would be his to command.

"Theros didn't offer this in exchange for your allegiance?" I ask, finding it hard to believe I'm the first to hear this request. If Theros were forcing the Borderlords to comply, he wouldn't be building them a fort, would he?

Irritation twists the leader's face. "Theros expects me to kneel."

"He wants everyone to kneel," I say, unsure of his point.

"I'm the leader of the Borderlords," Zagar says. "I don't kneel."

"Right," I mutter, losing a soft breath.

"I know what you folk think of us. I saw the look on your face. You think us savages because we string up the bones of our enemies. And we are. We have to be. There are no stone walls to protect us, no legion of soldiers at our command. Out here, it's us against the world."

I keep calm despite the bite in his words. He's right, though, I do think them savages. Months ago I thought Borderlords were the worst of them. Offhandedly, I wonder what someone like

Zagar might think of the Lucari, if he might still consider himself savage were he to encounter one of them. But shaken as I am to be surrounded by Borderlords—to be facing their leader—it pales in comparison to that day in the wintry woods.

"Is that what you want?" I ask. "A kingdom with a castle and a throne you can sit on? An army to do your bidding?"

"Let me worry about what I want. All you have to do is send word to the prince to proclaim me king of the Borderlands in writing, with Alder's royal seal. Once I have the decree in my possession, I will tell you what I know and you will be free to go."

I hold his contentious gaze, squeezing my hands into fists to keep from glaring. "You're keeping us hostage?"

"Just you," Zagar clarifies. Then he levels his gaze on Lief. "Karr will see that the little soldier delivers the message for you."

Not surprising. Extortion is the Borderlord way, after all.

"And if I refuse?"

"Then the prince of Alder will lose this war a widower."

Someone laughs. *Laughs*, at the Borderlord leader, amused as though it's the silliest thing anyone's ever said. A grating, mocking laugh that makes my toes curl inside my boots. A laugh I know all too well.

Seemingly out of nowhere, Elijah strolls into view. "If anyone's going to kill her, it's going to be me."

54

Connor

We dart in and out of the haze and grit, heads lowered and arms bent over our faces. The dragging weight of the bow on my shoulder steadies my stride. The way Rhys navigates the fort easily in poor visibility has me wondering how much time he spent here, serving the commander. I don't have to warn him not to take us anywhere near the well, either. The flames have grown significantly; their heat touches my back like a warning. It must feel like a furnace to the redcloaks fighting it, whose shouts carry over the smoke.

Just the kind of disaster we need to escape unnoticed.

Vishal's quarters aren't far. The small house is simple and plain, built of hardened clay and timber frames. A single window cuts into the front-facing wall. Soft candlelight illuminates the vague interior, its glow dispersing in the outside smoke. Hunkered outside the door, I fasten an arrow to the bowstring.

Rhys flashes a false smile when I look up from the bow, his face riddled with anxiety. "After you," he whispers.

Arrow drawn and aimed, I pull on the handle.

The door creaks open.

"I underestimated you," Vishal says in greeting. "Gorgos was one of my best soldiers." He sits on a bed in the high-ceilinged room, leaning against its headboard, bearing the pallid sheen of those not long for this world. Fresh blood stains the bandages layered around his midsection. The man's on his deathbed and he still exudes power.

To my immediate left, Felix looks up from a desk, fingers gripped on a quill feather over a piece of parchment. His brown eyes lift past me and widen, shifting his scowl to disbelief.

He pushes off his chair. "*Rhys*?"

"Hello, Peanut," Rhys mutters behind me.

"Rhys." It's Vishal who utters the name this time, turning our attention back to him. The commander curls a lip, the expression more unsettling than the man's remorseless eyes. "Is that really you?"

Raven pulls the door back in its frame as she steps inside behind us, cutting the stream of perpetual smoke.

"In the flesh." Rhys's tiny voice makes me cringe. The commander has left a lasting impression. Felix said he wasn't mistreated, but Rhys's reaction tells me otherwise.

I aim my arrow at the commander. No need to make this unpleasant encounter longer than it ought to be.

Felix stumbles forward, coming between my arrow and Vishal.

"Leave him be. He's dying," he hisses under his breath. "Thanks to you."

Though Felix's steadfast loyalty is disconcerting, I decide that

I don't care. Let him think what he wants, I'll end Vishal either way. I raise my aim, pointing the tip of my arrow to the exposed top of Vishal's head. It's a tight shot, but at worst, it might trim a few hairs off of the healer boy.

But Felix raises his arms above his head, blocking my shot. The fierce glare on his face dares me to shoot.

A wounded hand, then.

"I'd move if I were you," I warn him.

"Peanut," Rhys tries when Felix doesn't budge. "Do as he says."

"Don't call me that," Felix bites back.

I hear remorse in Rhys's voice. "I'm still your friend, Felix."

"We stopped being friends the day you ran away," Felix growls. "The commander was right about you."

"And after all these years, he's still a coward," Vishal remarks. "You always were disappointing, Rhys."

Rhys stalks around me, sword clenched in his hands, angled toward the commander. "Let's see how disappointed you are when I cut ya from navel to nose."

"Killing me won't change anything," Vishal says. "It won't change what you did."

"Shut up!" Rhys snaps. He steps forward, staring Vishal down. Though he's angry, fear is written all over his face.

I hold the arrow taut in the string and steady between my knuckles, watching for an opening. Holding the string isn't without its difficulties, though. Won't be long before my fingers cramp; we're wasting time. Rhys can overpower Felix, so why doesn't he? If he doesn't make a decision in the next moments, I'll have no choice but to hurt Felix.

"You haven't told anyone, have you?" Vishal continues, goading Rhys.

Rhys is shaking his head like he's about to lose it. "You made me do it!"

What he said at the fishing village, when he was drunk—it's creeping back to him now. A dark understanding fills me. Whatever Rhys has done, I sense it's much worse than I imagine.

"I gave you a choice," says Vishal.

Rhys is on the verge of angry tears, the white-knuckled grip on his sword shaking. "You call that a choice?"

"Perhaps we should ask your friends and settle the matter."'

Rhys falls uncharacteristically silent. His skin looks ashen, and not from the embers.

"Well? Are you going to tell them, or should I?" Vishal asks.

Rhys's brows pull in, his lips drawn in a slight grimace.

"Whatever it is, Rhys, it doesn't matter," Raven tells him. She's in my periphery, armed with her dagger. "We can end this right now."

We *should* end this. The commander means to torture Rhys—and it's working—but it might be a stalling tactic.

Vishal goes on, "Rhys wasn't so different when he was a boy. He was more skin and bones, but he was the same skittish wimp he is now. I thought I could make a man out of him, so I made him an offer he couldn't refuse—"

In a frenzy, Rhys cries out and makes a beeline for the bed, clashing with Felix just inches away from the commander. Rhys fights to push him aside as Felix's legs collide with the side of Vishal's bed, but Felix holds his ground, their hands locked in a tug of war on the sword's hilt. And though Felix's face is red with exertion, his limited strength only gets him so far. Once his burst of stamina wears off, Rhys gains on him quickly.

This will be over in a second. I'm ready to take my shot, angling for the commander.

Felix's body tilts sideways, giving me my window. I take it.

The arrow flies from my fingers at the same time I see a flash of metal. In a split second, the arrow strikes the side of Vishal's head, just as a longsword punctures clean through Felix's chest and into Rhys's stomach.

Vishal's body sags sideways, slumping off the bed. Felix sways, his eyes dropping to the sword embedded in his sternum. Rhys stumbles back and pulls himself free of the sword.

Raven shrieks Rhys's name, racing to him. She eases him to the earthen floor, then rips the hem of her ashy skirt with a tug of her arm, making a compress out of it.

Felix's frantic gaze is on Rhys. He sways again, losing his balance. I drop the bow and hurtle to catch him. My arms swoop around his back, breaking his fall. He tries to speak, but his words are lost to the gurgle of blood flooding his mouth.

And he's gone.

His eyes darken. They stare at the ceiling, unseeing. I close them gently and lay him down on his side.

You couldn't leave this world without taking others with you, you bastard.

Raven's coos wrench me from the bitter fog in my head. Her arm holds Rhys's head up, and she presses against his wound, muttering soft words in his ear. Rhys's frightened eyes seek me out. "The children," he hurries to tell us. "They send them to Talos for slave labor."

He's known all this time? I'm not surprised that Rhys had this information. I am surprised, though, that he kept it to himself. This revelation also means that Sunderian children have been going missing for years now. I take three steps toward Rhys and drop to one knee. "Is that why the commander wanted you dead?" Rhys struggles to nod. "What kind of slave labor?" I ask.

Rhys shakes his head slightly; he doesn't know. "I killed my parents—Vishal said he'd spare my life if I ended theirs." His breath comes in irregular gasps, quickening and slowing. "I didn't want t' die."

Is this why Rhys was so obsessive about Uther's attentions? Was he seeking some form of forgiveness by earning his love as a father?

"You were just a boy, Rhys."

"I should've died that day," he sputters.

"And your parents' deaths would have gone unpunished."

Rhys's lips quiver into a weak smile. "I was a coward for all o' my life."

"You showed true courage tonight."

He nods. A single tear falls down the side of his cheek. "Tell Uther I'm s-sorry." He might have been apologizing for his death, or his secret—or both. But as I watch him shudder one last breath, I realize it doesn't matter. Rhys did a terrible thing because he was scared, and he carried that burden as punishment for the rest of his life, a secret so terrible only death's door could persuade him to confess. But what he did tonight went beyond absolution: risking his neck for mine, choosing to stay and help when he could have run . . . tonight, though he paid the ultimate price, Rhys atoned for his sins.

Raven's tears leave streaks down her sullied cheeks. Her voice is a soft whisper. "I wish I could have done more for him."

"You did your best. That's all any of us can do."

She sniffles and wipes her face with the back of her hand, smearing some of Rhys's blood over the ash and soot on her cheekbone. "We can't leave him here. Do you think we can carry him t' the woods?"

"I'll carry him." Rhys's body isn't of a stout build, but his weight will slow me down regardless. I lean forward to take Rhys from Raven. I hoist him on my shoulder, then retrieve my bow and sling it on the other side over the quiver's leather strap.

"What's this?" Raven asks when she stands, her gaze drawn to the piece of parchment on the desk.

I follow her to it. The blotch of ink that dripped from the quill hides the last of Felix's words, but the whole paragraph that precedes it tells us everything we need to know.

"The location of the Brotherhood's camp," I say. Knowing he'd been mortally wounded, the commander was making Felix write it all down, including the person who revealed the existence of the Brotherhood. *A painter apprehended in the village of Locke under suspicion of association to a wanted felon*, the paper reads.

Walden.

The artisan's chattiness and whistling sound off in my head. Though Felix's words don't spell it out, I know he's dead.

"Rhys didn't die for nothing," Raven says as she lifts the paper and shreds it with her hands. She lets the pieces fall at her feet. Then she walks over to Felix's body and pulls the commander's sword free, wiping it across her dirty skirt. She hands the fine blade over, her face set in bleak lines. I slide it in the empty scabbard at my hip as Raven opens the hidden trapdoor to the tunnel. With a tired breath, she says, "Let's go home."

Home, I echo. The word invokes a reverie of frozen mountains and clear water lakes and evergreen seas . . . and those amber eyes, forever scored in my heart. Home.

55

Meredith

Elijah gloats, triumphant once again. I seethe at the sight of him. He's dressed in elegant steel, ready for battle as I am. His wavy hair is pulled to the back of his head, a few wind-tossed locks falling on his handsome face. My hand flies to Lief's arm before he draws his sword. "Not yet," I whisper.

"You forget where you are, Elijah," Zagar growls.

"I forget nothing, Black Snake," Elijah bites back with an angry smile.

"Seize him," Zagar orders, and the snakes answer his call. But surprisingly, Elijah isn't everyone's target. Some of the Borderlords rise against Zagar's order to defend Elijah. "Stand down!" Zagar orders them.

"They listen to me now," Karr answers, seeming to enjoy the confusion on his leader's face.

"You betrayed me?"

"You're the one who schemes, Zagar, plotting against Emperor Theros—who will soon rule the world. Instead of cementing our legacy at his side, you want to ally with these leeches," he says with a thumb pointed at me. "It's time the Borderlords had a new leader."

"And you think you'll do a better job?" Zagar is not amused.

"I know I will."

Zagar takes the ring swords from his belt and moves to a fighting stance. "Prove it!"

In a flash, the two black snakes charge at each other, and the Borderlord camp explodes into a fight between traitor and loyalist. Shouts and snarls fill the air, spooking the horses. Lief and I draw Diago and Daisy away. And as we do, two of the turncoats chase after us. Lief notices them before I do. By the time I stop to yank my sword out of its scabbard, he's armed and charging. And then Elijah is hurling toward Lief, too, aiming to strike him unawares while he fights the Borderlords.

Like hell you are.

I won't let him hurt anyone else I love.

I run to intercept him. Elijah veers to me when he sees me coming, eyes sharp and devilish, swinging fast and ferocious strokes. I parry backward, then sideways, then hunch at his vertical swing.

This is it, the moment I've been waiting for.

I clamp on my fear and anger. I forget about what Elijah's taken from me, all the pain and misery he's brought me, and let Lief's training guide me.

Be faster than your enemy. Evade until you have an opening.

"You've been busy, cousin," Elijah croons.

He comes at me again, sword slashing faster than I can blink. I pivot and sidestep, and then I lean sideways on his last downward swing, giving me the window to strike at his arm. My blade cuts him above the wrist, and as he hisses, his boot lands on my chest, kicking me to the yellowed grass. I lift my sword to block him, but Elijah isn't attacking.

Lief's cry jerks me to my feet.

He's hunched over from a wound, fighting off Elijah and a Borderlord one-handed, parrying their blows. Lief dances away from their blades, swinging low to slice at the snake's ankles. The Borderlord screams his way down, unable to get up. Elijah thrusts his blade like a spear, but Lief leaps out of the way.

I spiral with my sword, hitting Elijah's side, but only his armor takes the blow, leaving a mark that doesn't pierce through. Elijah blocks Lief and retaliates with a swing of his own. He ducks out of my next strike, and I manage to block his, but then I glimpse three more snakes gaining on Lief. "Behind you!" I scream, and Elijah hits me right between the brows with his pommel.

Lights flash.

The pain of a hundred headaches explodes in my head as my legs buckle under me. Elijah plops on top of me, stealing the breath from my lungs. My hand wipes the patches of grass around me, searching for my sword.

"Did you think I was going to let you become his new pet?" he asks in a bright, savage way as his cold hands wrap around my neck. The pressure is so intense that it's painful, making it impossible for me to inhale. "After all I that I do for him! After everything I've done. He thinks he can flick me aside and give everything to you instead? All because you share his blood and I *don't*?"

My lungs burn. My head feels like it's going to rupture. I try to move my legs under him, which makes Elijah laugh. I can't die here, and not by his hands. Not before I take him with me. His shadowed face takes my struggle with pleasure, his lips parted in expectation of victory. A black shroud narrows my vision, reminding me I'm running out of time. I'm still flailing my arms for my sword when I notice the dagger. Its hilt tucked into Elijah's hip. As my vision darkens, I pull it and stab Elijah's exposed side with it. His hands release me, and I roll away from him, gasping the longest breath I've ever taken.

I'm crawling on all fours when I hear him curse me, scrambling for me.

I flip around on my back. He's steps away, coming for me, sword in his grip. He smiles feverishly through his pain, knowing he's about to strike a deadly blow. I scan my surroundings for a weapon, and find only tufts of brittle grass and pieces of gravel. I scoot backward as fast as I can, which isn't fast enough. Elijah snarls as he brings his sword down on me. My arms come up instinctively, the vambraces stopping the blade. I'm surprised—and relieved—that he doesn't cut my arms clean off. Elijah's strength is waning; I see it in the brittleness of his sneer. It's me who smiles now, realizing he won't make it much longer than I will after he's done with me. His arms come up, higher this time, determined to make me bleed—

A horse plows into Elijah out of nowhere, sending him flying.

I gape at Krea. The windblown redhead jumps off the saddle and offers me a hand. "You all right?"

I nod as she pulls me to my feet.

"My lady!"

Lief calls from several yards away, running for me. His short curls are damp with sweat that trickles down his temples.

"Where are you wounded?" I ask.

"Just my shoulder—I'll be all right," he pants.

"Come," Krea says over her shoulder. "It's time we end this."

We find Elijah several yards away. His legs are broken and splayed at impossible angles. He spits blood at us, barely hanging on to his breath. Krea pulls out a knife and stabs his thigh, forcing a gasp of pain from Elijah's cut lips.

"*That*," she growls, stepping on the fresh wound, "is for Connor."

Krea hands me the bloody knife. I come down on my knees, watching Elijah's eyes go wild and furious. "Not smiling now, are you, *cousin*?" My voice is a raspy, hateful thing.

Elijah glares, refusing to be cowed. Though a part of me revels in his suffering, I mostly want this to be over. I bring up the knife and slice a clean line across his throat. As he drowns in his own blood, hating me until his very last breath, I say, "That's for Holt."

Krea isn't done with Elijah. Watching her cut away at his

throat with the knife, I think she's lost it.

I scrunch my face in a grimace. "What are you doing?"

"Alder's army is fighting Elijah's forces as we speak."

My stomach heaves, and I'm not sure if it's from revulsion or unease, because as shocked as I am by what she just said, I have to look away from her butchering hand. "But why are you cutting his head off?"

"You want to stop his army?" Krea barks. "Because if we don't, the Borderlands will be a graveyard."

Fighting nausea while trying to voice my frustration is harder than I thought. "You're not making any sense!" I'm too hoarse to raise my voice above a whisper, but I think my irked tone makes the point for me.

The horrible thud of Elijah's head on the grass fills my ears. I can't squeeze my eyes tight enough. The sound alone makes me heave.

"Guess I'll be carrying the head, then," Krea mutters, walking past me.

"Did she . . .?" I try to ask, daring a peek at Lief, who at the moment is struggling not to gag.

"Yes, my lady, she's got it."

I choke on a swallow. Pushing it down burns my raw throat. "Good. And what of the Borderlords?" I turn toward their camp. The battle is coming to an end. Bodies and gore surround those who haven't fallen. I can't tell which side won, though. They're all ruthless, snake-tattooed men. I'm not sure we want to stay, regardless of who wins, but I don't fancy being chased on horseback, either.

"Princess!"

I realize it's Zagar who's calling me when I spy the black snake tattoo crossing the field. I'm only slightly relieved it isn't Karr. Zagar gives Krea a once-over as she continues to her horse, curious at the thing dangling from her hands—which I refuse to look at. When Zagar walks up, the metallic smell of blood wafts up my nose, exacerbating my queasy stomach. He's splattered from head to toe. Even his beard is sprayed with it.

"Is that Elijah's head?" he asks, throwing another look at Krea.

"Yes," Lief says for me.

"What's she doing with it?"

I try to clear my throat. It feels like I'm scraping it from the inside. "Elijah's army attacked us," I say in my coarse voice, and Zagar's thick eyebrows arch inquisitively. "So, as you can see, your information is of no use to me anymore. If you'll excuse us—"

Zagar steps in, too close for comfort, and I hate the way my body flinches in fear. Lief reacts in kind, pointing his sword at Zagar.

"You're quick on your feet, kid." Zagar's lips curve in approval. But the brief amusement in his eyes fades when he turns his gaze to me. "I will pledge my snakes to your cause if you'll consider my request."

Is he . . . bargaining with me?

Oh, how the tables have turned.

"You hardly have any men left," I point out, itching to mount Diago. The longer we wait, the deeper dread burrows into me.

"I can recruit more."

I give him the best answer I can think of.

"Gather more men, and then we can talk," I offer.

He regards me with cold eyes for a moment, which I hope doesn't mean he's still thinking about killing me.

"Fair enough, princess," he agrees, stepping out of our way. "Until we meet again."

Elijah is dead, once and for all. It feels impossible, but it's true. But there's no time to savor this victory. Lief and I follow Krea at full gallop. The thick fog has cleared, and with a clear view of Krea's horse, I do my best to ignore the bouncing shape on her saddle. A few minutes in, Lief speeds up to Krea's side. "Thank you for protecting the princess, my lady," he shouts into the wind.

Krea all but glowers, her fiery hair flowing at her back. "I'm no lady!"

Lief throws a confused glance my way. Unable to shrug properly, I shake my head, but he's already moved on, asking Krea, "How did you find us?"

"I've been tracking Elijah for some time now," she shouts back. "I found him three weeks ago, was waiting for the right moment to strike when Alder's army showed up, and this one over here drew Elijah out of his rat hole." She means me, of course. If I wasn't so worried about Ethan and all the others, I probably would have smiled. Krea had been devising a plan to exact revenge, just like I had been, and destiny brought us together to that end. And my, did she come through. I know her saving my life doesn't necessarily mean she's forgiven me, but I take it as a good omen; I definitely want someone like her on my side. She's by far the scariest small person I've ever met.

Traveling at full speed, it takes significantly less time to make it back to Ethan. We hear the bone-chilling sound of battle before we're close enough to lay eyes on it. Upon arriving, we're met by a swarm of bodies and the blurry gleam of swords. Dust billows in the air. I push Diago as close as I can without putting him in harm's way. The chaos stretches so far in every direction that I'm not sure where it ends or begins. There's no way I'll find Ethan like this, but this close to it, I register the flashes of red on white that fight against Alder's blue and gold.

Stonefall soldiers.

Elijah brought them here to fight us. To fight me.

Maker, I have to stop this at once—before another life is lost.

"Krea!" I cry out as loud as my bruised throat allows. "Now!" Though my joke of a voice gets drowned out by the commotion, Krea gets the message, and moments later, I see her walk up toward the fighting soldiers, a spear in her hand—

I can't look at it. No amount of hate would make me.

Krea stands by her spear, drawing the attention of one, then three, then more and more soldiers, who call out the news among the ranks. Some, I notice now that the fighting is slowing down, are neither Stonefall nor Alder soldiers. They wear leather armor and hold scimitar swords. The real enemy.

"Elijah's dead!" they shout.

And then, "Princess Meredith!"

This, more than the grotesque thing on top of Krea's spear, halts the fighting on all fronts within minutes. The red and white soldiers kneel, their heads lowered in respect to me. I acknowledge those who can see me, hoping I wasn't too late. My eyebrows pinch together, searching for him. Where are you? Where are you? *Where are you?*

I wait on Diago for agonizing minutes, with no sign of Ethan or Heloise or any other familiar face. And I wait some more, growing weary in the haunting silence. If my voice wasn't such a mess, I'd be calling his name, asking the soldiers if they've seen him.

"My lady," Lief whispers.

His eyes point me to a man on his horse, galloping to bridge the distance between us.

Relief wells up in the back of my eyes.

Breathless, I dismount Diago and run to him, feeling like I'm floating. He jumps off his horse, running to close the distance between us. I practically slam into him, basking in the weight of his arms around me.

He's safe. We both are.

I pull back just enough to see his face. The sun paints his disheveled hair with its warmth, showing cuts that nick his brow, and there might be a bruise darkening his scraped cheek, but otherwise he looks unharmed. “Is Hel—”

“She’s fine,” he assures me with a smile that crinkles the corners of his eyes, pulling me back to him the next instant, as though he can’t bear the space between us.

I let him hold me, and I hold him, both of us relieved and grateful to be alive. To be together. I press my cheek against the beat of his heart and breathe him in. His soapy scent is now musk and sweat and dirt, but I don’t care. I never want to let go.

56

Connor

Long after the burning palisade disappears in the inky horizon, we lay Rhys's body in an underbrush of yellow wildflowers. I catch my breath, welcoming the scent of rotting wood and decomposing leaves. I would have carried him another five miles had my wounded and dehydrated and nearly crushed body not resisted. These far-reaching woods will be his final resting place.

I'm spent beyond measure, but the thirst is the worst of it. I had the last of Raven's water, which she'd left in the tunnel along with the rest of her and Rhys's provisions, and half of a dry grapefruit, but it wasn't enough. Still, it's hard to leave Rhys above ground. He deserves a proper burial. But even if we had a shovel to dig him a grave, and even in optimal soil, it would still take hours, and we need to put as much distance between us and the fort before morning comes and I start to feel sick.

The sparse oak canopy makes it easier to stay true north at night. Moonlight percolates through its foliage, bathing the dense underbrush in a spotted luminescence.

Raven mentions a creek she and Rhys came upon on their way to Vishal's fort, but in the midnight-blue shadows, she struggles to recall its direction. I use Vishal's sword to cut a path through dense underbrush and overgrown brambles; some snag my tunic. The hum of insects engulfs the silence, louder than the twigs crunching under our feet. Aside from the occasional spooked critter that runs away from our advance, it's all we hear for a while.

Raven hears the water before I do, which tells me I'm in worse shape than I thought.

She hurries ahead, stepping over roots and pushing branches out of her way. I come up behind her to a ravine. I can hear the trickle of a creek below. It doesn't sound too distant.

Raven leans forward into the dark. "This is it," she says through what sounds like a smile of relief.

"How far down is it?" I ask, unable to discern with my ears alone.

"About ten feet, I'd say."

We find a way down several paces away, where the walls of the ravine aren't as steep. I steady myself on the bark of a young tree, descending slowly over a slope of moss and fern. Though my eyes have long adjusted to the night, I can't make out much down here. I use my hands and follow the smooth, dry pebbles to the cold water. The stream is too shallow to cup in my hands, so I lower my cracked lips to it. By the time Raven climbs down, I've had several gulps . . . I'm still drinking long after she's had her fill. Then, fully hydrated, I rinse the layers of muck off my face and hair; it's too bad the creek isn't deep enough to dunk myself in it.

After refilling Raven's waterskin, we climb out of the ravine and resume north. Three hours and roughly nine miles later, pre-dawn light masks the woods in its violet shade. Morning dew sheens over the knee-high vegetation.

The sickness is coming, I can feel it.

When the sun nears the horizon, and dawn's light trickles between the trees, anxiety builds in my muscles, bringing that strange ache with it, weakening me. The sun is still rising when the cold sweats come. Soon, it becomes impossible to walk a straight line.

No longer treading through shadows, Raven becomes aware of my poor balance. "Gods, you look ill." She brings the back of her hand to my forehead. I'm not surprised when she says, "You're burning up." Instinctively, she drops her inquisitive eyes to the wound on my side.

"It's not an infection," I mumble.

She pulls open the slit on my tunic anyway. "Where else are you hurt?" I stave off a wave of nausea while her eyes dart voraciously about my bloodstained frame—not all of it mine—hands brushing all over me.

"Raven, it's not an infection."

Something in my tone makes her stop.

"Well, go on, then! What is it?"

"Withdrawal."

She isn't expecting that answer. Her eyes grow twice their size. "What did they get you hooked on?"

"Ever heard of noxtail?"

She frowns for a bit, but then shakes her head. "What does it do?"

"It makes you . . . obedient," I say, failing for a better way to explain it.

"That sounds dangerous." A pause. "Tell me your symptoms."

"Chills, nausea, restless limbs . . ." I hunt for a place to sit. "I need lie down a moment."

Raven's lips move, but I can't understand what she's saying. The trees blur together. I shake my head, trying to clear it. The last thing I remember is struggling to stay upright on my swaying feet.

I wake up to the smell of something burnt. My expression is frozen in a grimace. I feel . . . not good. The cold sweat, the aches—it's all there.

"I got your fever t' come down," Raven says before my sight sharpens. She sits next to me, her legs drawn under her skirt over a thicket of weeds. A wisp of smoke drifts from the burned stem in her hand. "But you're in no condition t' hike. We'll have t' camp out here until you're better. I suppose my feet could use a rest as well."

I make a sound in the back of my throat.

"How long?" I ask.

"It's hard t' say. All I know about noxtail is that it doesn't grow in Sunder. If it did, I'd know it."

I realize that even if she did know it, she would still need to know the dosage. Telling her I drank the bare minimum isn't much of an answer.

I ball my hands into fists and curl my toes in my boots to lessen the ache. It doesn't work.

Out of nowhere, Raven asks, "Who's Meredith?" I jerk my eyes to her. "You called her name while I was tending t' you," she explains. "Is she the girl in your visions?" she asks when I don't give an answer.

I close my eyes and nod, trying to see those golden tresses through my dizzy spell. "My memories came back," I say.

"Really?" I feel her lean forward. "So who is she?"

"Someone very dear to me."

Raven lapses into silence. Then, she says, "Explains why she never left you."

It's true, Meredith's been with me all this time. When I closed my eyes and there was nothing, she was there, entreating me to remember. But I abandoned her, gone without a trace.

"She must think I'm dead." The realization hardens my insides.

Raven's voice is bittersweet. "Then you must hurry home . . . wherever that may be."

"Alder," I murmur. Envisioning the leagues that separate me from Meredith is disheartening, but the thought of going home, of seeing her again—there's no distance I wouldn't travel. *One day at a time, soldier.* “We have to make it back to camp first.”

It takes two days for the symptoms to subside. By then, all of Raven’s provisions have been consumed, but her healer knowledge allows her to forage for edible berries and herbs, and once I’m able, I start hunting for meat with my bow. We continue our journey by moon and rest from sunup until midday to avoid lighting fires at night. After weeks of travel and too many blisters to count, Raven and I find our way back to the fishing village. Osberd, who’s still grateful for our coin donation, is happy to offer us a bath and serve us a meal of salted eel and ale at his table. We sleep in cots in the village hall, our first full night’s rest, and depart before dawn, supplied with clean clothes and a day’s worth of dried fish from the village fish flakes. As the next part of our journey will see us through other villages and cities, I request a specific item of clothing from the village weaver: a mantled hood. The brown cotton fabric does its job to cover my face—or my scar, rather—draping below my shoulders.

The redcloaks we encounter are too relaxed to have news of the fire. They will soon, though. Burning down the fort is too small a victory to celebrate—they’ll build a new one in time—but Vishal’s death, *that* is worth something. Though Theros will send another commander to replace him, undoing a monster like Vishal is a victory.

Giving the news to Uther one month later eases some of his pain at learning of Rhys’s passing. I explain the circumstances that led to his death without mention of his past. What he did to his parents, his servitude to Vishal—I don't repeat any of it. To do otherwise feels wrong. Uther's fatherly affection and approval meant everything to Rhys. I won't be the one to tarnish it. Better that his memory lives on as Rhys would have wanted.

"Dead?" Uther falters to his chair. The word floats in the air of the pavilion.

"His last words were of you," says Raven, offering an empathic smile, but Uther's too distraught to notice. She gives him a moment to process it all before asking about Asher. She had hoped to see her father when we arrived early this morning, but there was no sign of him at the tent, only a sleeping Pip occupied the space; Raven didn't want to wake him.

Uther looks up from his desk. He swallows, still grappling with the news. "He's been gone a time, looking for you." From his tone, it's clear he disapproves.

Raven's face falls. "Gone where?"

"He didn't give me specifics, and I didn't ask. I assume he's been searching the neighboring villages," he says numbly.

"I have t' find him." Raven turns to leave, but I catch her wrist.

"We just got back, Raven. Rest a few days, and if Asher hasn't turned up by then, I'll go with you to look for him."

Raven stares, incredulous. "I thought you were leaving for Alder?" she asks, unaware of her slip.

Uther clears his throat. He straightens his shoulders, looking straight at me. "Planning to desert us so soon?"

Raven attempts to rectify. "No—"

"Yes," I say over her.

Uther rises slowly, hands splayed on the table before him in a confrontational stance. Sadness and anger glaze his eyes. "Only death shall set you free, soldier," he says, repeating the Brotherhood's oath, as though I could forget.

"I'm aware, but I have a proposition for you."

Uther blinks. An impassive expression takes hold of his features. "An oath is an oath, soldier. You can't simply deal your way out of it."

"Not even for the help of the Alderian army?"

It's no doubt the last thing he'd thought he'd hear. His eyes widen at first, but then they narrow. "Do you think me that big a fool?"

"No, sir," I reply, staring calmly at his rigid face. "I recovered my memories."

He looks at me. "So who are you, really?"

"Connor Westwend, longbow lieutenant of Alder's first battalion; my father was captain of the guard and a close friend of King Perceval."

The look of dumb shock on Uther's face is a thing of beauty. His eyes roam over me in disbelief. Beside me, Raven smiles, knowing I speak the truth. "You're the answer t' our prayers," she blurts out.

"I can't guarantee anything," I say to both of them.

"What *can* you guarantee?" Uther asks, finding his voice.

"Any request I make to the king will be heard and considered by him and his council."

"You're asking me to let you break your oath on an outside chance that your king will agree?"

"It's the best chance you'll get," I say.

Uther regards me with a stroke of his stubbed chin, but before he can come to a decision, the tent flaps open.

It's Axel. "Sir, Asher's back," he reports.

Uther exhales loudly, forgoing a response. He waves his hands dismissively. I consider staying behind to finish our conversation, but I doubt he's decided, and his expression hints that he'd like a moment of solitude.

I understand the importance of the Brotherhood's oath. If Uther doesn't punish me for deserting, he risks losing the respect of his men. But what I offer matters more than any oath. I'm giving them a chance to free their people from tyranny. A chance to free themselves. But whether they make the right choice doesn't matter, because I know nothing will stop me from leaving. Still, I would prefer to leave without hurting anyone.

There is one thing I have to get off my chest, though.

Once Raven has gone, I stop at the pavilion's entrance on my way out. "I know Asher disapproves of Raven's involvement," I tell Uther. "But she saved my life during a fight at Vishal's fort, and fixed my dislocated shoulder so I could continue that fight; I would have died if it wasn't for her."

Uther accepts this with a solemn nod, and I slip through the flaps. Outside the tent, a small figure scuttles toward me, slamming into my legs.

"Pip!"

I drop to my knees, scooping his slight frame in my arms. He buries his head in my neck, his tiny arms clutching on to me. I let out a long breath. Holding him fills my chest with a weightlessness that brings light to my darkness, soothing my thoughts and reminding me that not all is lost in this bleak world.

Raven is just a few steps away, sharing in the joy of our reunion. She hadn't smiled since Rhys died, not a real smile like the one she grins with now. It takes me a second to realize I'm smiling, too.

"You came back!" Pip gushes when I set him down.

I rub his mop of black hair. "Of course I did."

"Raven!"

She whips around to the sound of her father's voice.

As do I.

And I see him.

Really see him.

Asher's appearance is like a gut punch that hurls my thoughts ten years back in a whoosh of memories.

I'm under the bed. A fire burns low somewhere in the room, lighting Mother's bare feet on the keystone floor. I don't see it, but I know she's holding a sword. In the quiet of the room, I can hear her breath bursting in and out. She's afraid. I'm afraid, too. I'm terrified. Someone kicks the door open, and a pair of muddy boots make their way inside. Eyes wide and sweating, I watch the aggressive dance of their feet as they charge and parry. The clash of steel is erratic, like a bard's song off key, and I flinch with each strike. I want to be strong and fearless like Father—I want to help Mother! But the fear never leaves me, not as Mother cries out and falls, not as I pull myself out of hiding and launch my small body at her assailant: a man with a black patch over his eye.

A younger version of the aged man I see before me now.

The man who's blade scarred my face.

My mother's killer.

"*It was you,*" I growl.

Asher's open arms fall at his sides when he looks at me. Understanding caves his face, and I know he knows. He *knows*. His interest in my scar, my memories—it makes sense now. All those times he asked, it wasn't out of curiosity. He wanted to know if it was me. If I remembered. And the coward never had the guts to tell me. I've lived under the same roof as my mother's murderer for months. I dined with him every night—shared bread with him. Hell, I fought his battles and aided his cause. It makes me sick to my stomach. It makes me want to snap his neck in two.

Grief sinks its claws into me as I relive my mother's death over and over, the moment her frightened eyes met mine and she drew her last breath.

A floodgate opens inside me, and my grief becomes wrath.

All I hear is the thrashing in my ears. All see I see is Asher.

I lunge.

My hands seize Asher's throat before he gets a word out.

Raven frantically tries to push me off him, demanding in shock that I stop. I squeeze harder, seeing my mother's blank stare, the blood soaking her hair. Asher doesn't fight back. His body struggles to cope without air, but his arms remain limp at his sides, making no attempt to pry me off, a haunted look in his eye. My bloodlust wavers for only a moment before it rages inside me again, blinding and unstoppable and all-consuming. Asher took my mother from me when I was just a child, and now I'm going to make him pay, make him wish he'd never set foot in my house all those years ago.

Asher is on the verge of unconsciousness when strong arms yank me off.

Axel and Jace restrain me on Uther's orders. I jerk my right arm free and elbow Axel's face, pivot left, and punch Jace in the stomach. They won't stop me.

"Have you gone mad?!" Axel wheezes.

Asher doesn't run or try to get away. He gasps for breath right where I left him. But he won't meet my gaze as I stride back to him. And that won't do. I want him to face me, to see what he's wrought manifested in me. Raven steps between us, arms wide at her sides and eyes glaring. "*Why are you doing this*?" she asks.

Asher's hoarse whisper answers for me.

"Because I killed his mother," he says, and the group of rebels falls into a dead silence. Confusion and shock splay across Raven's features. She swivels to face Asher.

"You knew who he was?" Her voice cracks with surprise.

Asher holds his throat in his hand. "I had my suspicions," he rasps, looking to me over Raven's shoulder. "Although deep down I think I always knew it was you . . . the little lad I marked with my sword so long ago." I want to rip him apart, but the thought of hurting Raven to get to him holds me back. After another bout of coughs, he continues. "I was a different lad then. For many years, I traveled with a small company of outlaw mercenaries, plundering and murdering everywhere we went, living off stolen goods, and I did so without remorse or mercy . . . I don't know how many innocent lives I took—hundreds. But your mother"—he looks at me, eyes pleading—"I swear she was my last. Watching you kneel at her side, crying . . . it broke me in ways my life of crime never could."

Listening to him recount the details of that night makes me twitch with rage, and I feel as if my skin is the only thing keeping me from bursting. I don't want to hear any more of this. I want to shut him up.

"Your remorse won't save you," I say through bared teeth.

"Do with me what you must. I won't ask for mercy," Asher says. "But I would ask for your forgiveness."

"Never," I hiss.

Raven turns to face me. "I won't let you hurt him," she warns me. "I am deeply sorry about your mother. Nothing in the world could make amends for it. But no matter what evils my father has committed, he's still my father. So if you want t' kill him, you'll have t' kill me first."

I stare at Raven, faced with a dilemma I overlooked in all my fury. Raven is an obstacle, though not as she's intending to be. I can easily shove her aside and kill Asher before she has a chance to retaliate. But killing Asher would destroy Raven. With a sinking feeling in my gut, I realize that—justifications aside—I would be doing to her what Asher did to me: taking the person she loves the most.

But how can I deny justice for my mother's cold-blooded murder? How can I walk away from something my mind and soul have hungered for these last ten years?

Within the tension-filled silence, the crackle of the fire is like a pin drop. The whole camp makes a ring around us, witness to my undoing.

Someone takes my hand.

The boy I used to be peers up at me with overly bright and frightened eyes that drip tears down his cheeks. The sobbing, tear-stricken boy who lost his mother at the hands of a murderous bastard. Only it's not me I'm looking at. It's Pip. And those tears aren't for my mother. They're for Asher.

And so it seems, the decision is made for me.

I swallow a painful, shuddering breath, fighting against my very fiber, against my unforgiving heart, and let the icy sting of bitterness and defeat cool the madness that courses inside me.

I fall on one knee. "I'm sorry," I say quietly. "You're not

afraid of me, are you?"

Pip shakes his head vigorously and wraps himself around me.

"I'm leaving for the North," I whisper as I hold him. "I'd like you to come with me." The journey will be long and arduous, but Pip will have a far better life in Alder than he ever could in this forsaken place. Even with Raven to look after him, his chances here are bleak. Still, it's his choice to make.

Not letting go, Pip's head brushes my cheek in agreement.

"Thank you for your mercy," Asher mutters, his voice cutting through my calm, scraping my insides.

Reining in my displeasure, I rise and turn to address him. "It wasn't for you," I say as evenly as I can, squashing the pity that twists my heart at the wretchedness on his face. I hate him, and I doubt I will ever forgive him. But I don't forget that he could have left me to die when he found me, as Elijah had intended. And I can't deny that the Asher I've come to know is not the same man I met when I was ten years old. But knowing the truth, knowing who he is and what he's done—what he's taken from me . . . I can't separate the two. The best I can do is walk away.

Raven presses a fist to her lips, wrestling with her own feelings. I hope my actions haven't pushed her away. I'd hate to lose her friendship. Regardless, I can't stay here a minute longer. Not if I want to keep my word to let Asher live. My body needs rest, but that will have to wait. I'd rather drag my legs through mud than wait another minute.

I find Uther's face among his men. "I'm leaving," I say.

"With or without your consent." I shouldn't push my luck, but I'm too angry to care. "Pip's coming with me."

All eyes cut to Uther. Silence falls around us.

Something crosses the leader's face, a gleam of unease that vanishes in seconds.

"Connor has made me an offer," he announces to the camp, looking around the gathered men. "To let him go in exchange for the help of his king, His Majesty King Perceval of the kingdom of Alder." More silence follows. I glance at the brothers, read their stern faces. Some don't care to hide their surprise, but most scrutinize me with skepticism. "So I leave the choice with you, his brothers. Do we let him go? Or do we cut his throat?"

Pip hugs my legs, tense.

Unexpectedly, Raven steps forward. "Let him go," she calls out. "Connor and Rhys defeated Commander Vishal and destroyed his fort—he's more than earned his freedom."

"Rhys was a coward and so is he!" someone yells from the crowd.

Several of the men hoot and holler in approval. "Rhys died fighting!" I shout them down, turning on my heel to look at them all. Axel, who must have left at some point, returns with Amos, Tros, and Zen at his heel. I go on, "He may have lived like a coward, but he died with honor, and he did it for all of you!"

Uther briefly hangs his head, hiding his face from the men.

"Connor can no longer stay in Sunder," Asher speaks out, voice still hoarse. He holds up one of Irven's posters for all to see.

I wager that's the reason he returned to camp. "The enemy knows his face, and they won't stop looking until they find him again." Asher addresses Uther. "As bad as things are, they're about to get worse. We need all the help we can get."

The camp lapses into silence again.

No one moves. Uneasy gazes flank me as doubt settles like a net over the men, trapping them in indecision. Tros is the first to step out from the circle. He stalks toward me and slaps a firm hand on my shoulder. "I'm gonna miss your stupid face." Then, with his back to me, he announces his vote. "I say we let him go."

Amos and Zen join Tros, their support a catalyst for the others, causing more to come forward in approval, including the camp's cook; I'm sure Raven's support has something do with that. The twins, Axel and Jace, are reluctant at first, understandably so; I don't think I broke Axel's nose, but I might as well have. Based off the looks they give me, I'm surprised they vote in my favor. But not all agree. Half of them, to be exact, many of whom I trained with the bow. After all is said and done, Uther's vote becomes the tie breaker.

He comes to me in a heavy stride, with a face that says he's made up his mind. "This is for Rhys," he says in my ear. Then, erasing all signs of emotion, he declares the verdict. "We let him go." None question Uther, proving he still has the respect of the Brotherhood. "I will hold you to your word," Uther says before retreating to his pavilion, likely to mourn Rhys in peace.

After I apologize to the twins and thank the keepers, Pip and I head straight to our tent to pack our things. It isn't much, and the Brotherhood doesn't have any supplies to spare, so we'll have to hunt and gather from the get-go.

I spy Asher hovering outside through the corner of my eye. I was hoping he'd keep his distance. "What do you want?" I ask without a glance his way.

"To make sure you didn't leave without this," he says. I look up. The ring of red around his neck reminds me of what I almost did. What I still want to do. Then I see what's in his hands: the pristine bow Flynn gave me, recovered from the armory no doubt.

I take it. "Here," I say, slinging the fort sentry's bow off my shoulder. At least they'll have a decent bow in stock to put their training to good use.

"I'd also like to say good-bye to the little lad," Asher adds.

"Fine with me."

As Pip leaves the tent, Raven walks in.

She engulfs me in an embrace from behind, her arms squeezing mine to my sides. She doesn't say anything. She doesn't have to. I sigh and wiggle in her grip to face her, my arms tightly around her now. We hold on to each other in raw silence, letting the seconds stretch our last moment together.

When she finally pulls away, her dark-brown eyes glisten with tears, but she smiles through her sadness and says, "Go get your girl."

57

Meredith

"Olivia?" Father calls, mistaking me for my mother. He lies in bed, his skin gaunt and ashen, eyes cloudy, looking more like a ghost than a king. I sit on the red upholstered chair next to his bed and take his clammy hand in mine. "I've missed you so, my darling."

Not once have I ever heard my father speak so gently, so adoringly.

"You really loved her, didn't you, Father?" I say, feeling something inside cave in, knowing that I will lose my father in the next hours, knowing there will never be a chance for us to make amends. For him to love me.

"Don't ever leave me again," he implores.

A lump squeezes my throat. "I won't. I'll be right here." Hearing of his condition when I arrived at the palace was hard to take in. I hadn't known what to expect, but it wasn't this. Father's been wasting away from a festering wound that never healed. A wound inflicted by Theros. What was left of my resentment dissolved into anguish the second I walked in his bedchamber.

Our reunion hasn't been all doom and gloom, of course. Reuniting with Beth and Anabella was a joy I can't describe. My heart felt like it could burst from happiness. They were well and safe, and I couldn't be more grateful. I have so many things to tell them. But we haven't yet had time to catch up. There is so much left to do. Soon after arriving, Ethan and I used our armies to regain control of the lost throne, removing all of Elijah's men—along with Chancellor Ulric—and sending them to the dungeon; I'm certain it was the first time my uncle was glad to see me. Although, the same couldn't be said about his wife. But that wasn't surprising. The duchess is beside herself, what with Charlotte gone to Talos. She'd left, voluntarily, with "Uncle Theros," her way of solidifying an alliance. If she truly is trying to help her family, I'll be the first to commend her efforts, but I find that hard to believe; Charlotte only thinks of herself.

Charles, on the other hand . . . He should be back in his rooms by now, receiving the first bath he's had in a long time. I would have gone with the guards myself to free him, but I know Charles wouldn't want me to see him in such a state. So I rushed to see Father instead. And now here I am, holding his hand as he offers the only smiles I will ever get from him, and though they're not meant for me, I treasure them all the same.

"Any day now, he will go," the physician said.

To think I almost didn't make it.

I kiss the back of Father's hand. "I love you," I whisper, feeling the words bring tears to my eyes. I don't try to understand how it is that I love him still, but I accept it. Or, I accept the part of me that does, however small it may be, and relish that my being here brings him comfort. "At least I can rest easy knowing you won't be around for the hard times ahead," I say meekly.

"I'm not going anywhere, my Olivia."

I pat his hand and fight to keep my voice even. "You'll be together again soon."

There's a soft knock at the door.

My father's ward comes in. He clears his throat. "My lady, Prince Ethan is asking for you in the front hall."

"Thank you, I'll be right there."

I sigh as I rise from the chair and press a soft kiss to Father's cold brow.

The hallways I've walked on for years feel strange to me now. Odder still is how I long for Alder Castle's stone walls and cold corridors, and not these marble columns or the tepid breeze that flows from the open windows. There is no telling when we'll return. Ethan and I must first devise a plan to inoculate our kingdoms against blue fever. Thankfully, Chancellor Ulric didn't have the stomach for torture, and quickly pointed us to Elijah's secret chest, where he stored vials of plague-infected fluids. Inoculation will come at a high price, however. The vials, dozens though there are, are not enough for even the palace inhabitants. If we are to vaccinate our people, we'll have to resort to infecting healthy hosts in order to procure more of the immunization. It is to our good fortune that the palace dungeon is overflowing with expendable traitors and Talosian soldiers who would have otherwise hung in the gallows. It will buy us some time, at least, and forestall the harrowing prospect of relying on volunteers. I remind myself over and over that the means will justify the ends. That once the populace is inoculated, we will have the leverage to convince other kingdoms to join our fight and amass the forces we need to take down Theros once and for all. But when the time comes, will I have the heart—or lack thereof—to stand by and witness the murder of innocents in the name of peace?

I push that dark thought away, and soon find myself pondering something else. Something that's been nagging at me since our journey from the Borderlands. I hadn't acknowledged Elijah's words then because he had his hands on my throat. But now that I've had time to ruminate, I'm more confused than ever. It's true, Theros extended a one-time offer for me to join him, one I vehemently refused. But Elijah clearly believed I was competition. So much so that he defied Theros and plotted an elaborate scheme just to get me out of the way; I can't make sense of it.

I'm almost to the landing by the front hall when I hear Ethan's voice. It's rather loud. He sounds . . . giddy.

I hurry to learn what must be good news—

And stop at the edge of the landing. At the bottom of the red-trained marble steps, Ethan beams pure and raw joy at a man whose back is to me, their hands at each other's shoulders.

I blink, heart in my throat, questioning my eyes.

No. It's not *him*. It can't be.

My step falters as I try to retreat from the polished railing. The stranger turns, and my heart stops. Those deep-blue eyes pierce through me as they always did, so surreal it hurts. There's a roaring in my ears. It's *not* him, I reason—I'm seeing things. He's dead. He's been dead for nearly a year now.

I want to scream at my own mind's cruelty for making me see this, for making me wish I could run down the stairs and touch him.

But he's . . . different.

His skin is darker than I remember. Kissed by the sun. His hair isn't quite the charcoal black of my memories, either. It's longer, too, just inches from his shoulders now. But most different of all is the way he gazes up at me, as though there is a chasm between us that I could never hope to cross.

I feel myself grow pale, afraid to believe my eyes, which glaze with tears at the sound of his voice.

"Hello, Meredith."

Meredith, Connor, & Ethan will return in the next installment of The Kingdom Within Series.

About The Author

Samantha Gillespie is a creative, helpless romantic who was born in Mexico, where she grew up with her family until they returned to the States at age eleven. An avid reader from a young age, Samantha finally gave into her passion for writing, making her debut with *The Kingdom Within.*

Samantha considered pursuing a degree in English Literature while in college but despite her family and friend's encouragement, she opted for a more practical career in Business. Now, with the publication of her first book under her belt, she occasionally hits herself on the head for it. Samantha resides in Houston, TX with her husband, David, and their pets, Foxi & Squeaky, where she lives the everyday life of a domestic princess.

Connect with The Kingdom Within

Website:	www.thekingdomwithinseries.com
Facebook:	www.facebook.com/tkwseries
Goodreads:	https://www.goodreads.com/book/show/25003086-the-lost-throne
Twitter:	@ S_gillespie_
Instagram:	@samantha_gillespie_

View the Book Trailer at:
https://youtu.be/6KQbEiVx19w

CPSIA information can be obtained
at www.ICGtesting.com
Printed in the USA
LVHW041549140120
643593LV00004B/738